A GAME OF BILLIARDS

Straightening, Miles quite casually removed his cravat to let
the neck of his shirt stand open. But he looked at her as he did
it, and she realized he was not deaf to the music at all.

"This is so unfair. . . ." She stared at his naked throat, wanting to lick the perspiration there.

"I've had years more practice at the game."

"You know that's not what I mean." Her eyes met his pleadingly, though she was not sure what she requested. "I can't
think. It's so hot."

He dropped his cravat on the floor. "Perhaps, then, we
shouldn't try to think." He walked around the table to her side.

Felicity took one step back. "What are you doing?"

He put his cue down on the baize. Then he plucked hers from
her hand and laid it side by side with his.

There seemed an absurd intimacy in those two neatly aligned
cues.

Then he pulled her into his arms.

"Miles!"

His lips silenced her.

The chord swelled but lost all menacing discord so Felicity
had no choice but to surrender to purest, sensual harmony.

JO BEVERLEY
DANGEROUS JOY

ZEBRA BOOKS
KENSINGTON PUBLISHING CORP.

ZEBRA BOOKS are published by

Kensington Publishing Corp.
850 Third Avenue
New York, NY 10022

First Printing: November, 1995

Printed in the United States of America

One

Ireland, January 1816

Miles Cavanagh frowned up from the legal documents in his hand. "Your father must have taken leave of his senses, Colum. *You* were supposed to be the girl's guardian."

His new stepfather put on a pious look. "When a man is about to take leave of these earthly shores, my boy, he can surely be excused if he abandons his senses first."

"Abandons them enough to be cajoled, perhaps?"

Colum Monahan, a middle-aged man still in his traveling clothes, waggled a plump finger. "Don't you try to blame me now, Miles. Father was dead and the deed done hours before I arrived at Foy."

Miles supposed that to be true, but it was typical of Colum that he had in some way dodged an onerous duty. He was a charming, indolent man who found humor in nearly everything and always expected the best in life. Amazingly, life seemed to grant it to him, including Miles's pretty mother.

And now the loss of a troublesome ward.

The man must have made a pact with the leprechauns.

"What the devil possessed him, then?" Miles demanded. "No one in his right mind would appoint a twenty-five-year-old man he hardly knew as guardian to a granddaughter."

"I have no idea . . ."

"His *twenty-year-old* granddaughter."

"My dear boy, there is no point in snarling at me! And Father is beyond your reach."

Miles ran a hand through his hair. "I'm sorry. But this is a damnable imposition."

"Tush, tush. You'll have a seizure yourself if you allow your choleric disposition to rule you."

"I do not have a choleric disposition."

Colum poured two glasses of brandy and passed one to Miles. "Every redhead is given to anger."

"My hair is not *red,* and I am the most easy-going of fellows." Miles unclenched his teeth in order to sip from his glass. "I simply do not want to be responsible for a young woman, especially one I remember you describing as 'that hellion Felicity.' "

Colum settled into his favorite chair. "The dear child is calming as she gets older. Nothing could have been more suitable than her behavior during the obsequies." He looked at Miles with a mischievous twinkle that made him resemble a portly leprechaun himself. "Sure and she's turned into a fine-looking girl, you know. Dark hair and eyes, and a very handsome figure."

"Devil take it, if I have to have a ward, I'd rather she be plain. I know the way young men behave."

"I'm sure you do, my boy. I'm sure you do. And just think," Colum added, smiling up at the fine plasterwork of the ceiling, "she's an heiress into the bargain."

Miles stared at him. "An heiress? Surely your father didn't leave her that much."

Colum lowered his bright eyes. "You forget her maternal grandfather, Miles."

Dammit, so he had. After all, he'd never thought his stepfather's niece's maternal relations were any affair of his.

This past summer, when Miles's mother had married Colum, Miles had accompanied the happy couple on a visit to his stepfather's family home of Foy Hall. But at that time Felicity Monahan had been off in England to visit her

mother's family and discuss an unexpected inheritance from
her maternal grandfather.

"You mean it amounted to something?"

A rich chuckle rolled through Colum. "When I think of
the dust Father kicked up about Patrick's match with 'that
miner's daughter from Cumberland . . .' And then the man
develops mines of his own and makes a fortune!" He raised
his glass in a toast. "Twenty thousand a year, my boy."

"Twenty thousand!"

"You might want to look at little Felicity with marriage in
view."

"Hellion," Miles reminded him, and downed a strengthen-
ing swig of brandy. Twenty thousand. That was more than his
own income. Hell and damnation. Every fortune hunter in
Europe would be after her!

Miles couldn't help thinking that if his mother hadn't taken
this unlikely notion of marrying again he'd never have known
the Monahans and would not be in this stew.

"Now, now, my boy. A man who likes horses should appreciate a bit of spirit in a filly."

"Devil take it, Colum, we're talking about a woman, not
a mare."

"It's all the same in the end." His stepfather emphasized
the comment with a merry wink.

Miles refilled his glass. He still wasn't comfortable with
the idea of having a stepfather at all, and one who clearly
enjoyed his mother in a very earthy way was enough to try
the patience of a saint.

The two of them were always touching, and a man would
have to be a nod-cock not to recognize the way they looked
at each other at times. In the middle of the day, too. Then
they'd make an excuse to go off alone.

It wasn't decent.

But since Miles's mother seemed happy, he was determined
not to make an issue of it. He'd be glad, however, to be leaving soon for England. Hopefully, by the time he returned,

Colum and his mother would have moved beyond newlywed fervor and be acting their age.

If he ever got to England, that was. He'd had the damnable luck to dislocate his shoulder in October, just as he was about to leave for the hunting season. And then the thing had not healed well. Resenting each missed day in the Shires, he'd given in to his mother's insistence that he stay home so she could be sure he wasn't risking his recovery by trying to manage one of his prime horses.

Then it had been Christmas, and since he'd not spent the season at his home for years, he'd decided to stay. Now he was ready to depart and *this* landed in his lap.

"It's a shame you're not married, my boy," Colum said. "If you had a wife, she'd look after the girl for you."

"But I don't have a wife, or any immediate intention of seeking one. I'm not ready to settle down."

Colum tut-tutted. "You are heir to Kilgoran and have your responsibilities."

Miles twitched his shoulders as if under a burden, though this was one he'd borne all his life, for his father had been cousin and heir to the Earl of Kilgoran. It was just that his father's death, and the increasing frailty of the old earl, meant the ax could fall at any time, putting an end to an almost idyllic life.

"If my revered uncle had accepted his responsibilities and taken a wife himself, I'd be in no need of marriage at all."

"True enough, but it makes the necessity of your marrying the more urgent. You're the last of the line, Miles. It would be sad indeed to see a revered old Irish title fall into abeyance."

"I have a brother."

"A naval officer. Now there's a nice, safe profession!"

Miles shot a thoughtful look at his stepfather. "It's not like you to be preaching the path of duty, Colum."

Colum's exaggerated expression of innocence confirmed Miles's suspicion that he was up to something. "Your mother would like you to take a wife, and whatever pleases Aideen pleases me."

"Good, because I doubt my mother wants me to be this girl's guardian. I'll have Leonard declared of unsound mind in his last hours. With the codicil overruled, you'll have charge of the girl."

Colum shook his head. "Alas, Miles, I doubt it would work. The codicil was witnessed by the doctor and Leonard's valet, and both are firm that he was of clear mind and determined on it."

"Damnation. There must be a way out of this."

"Not quickly." Colum looked, for once, completely serious. "I've had dealings with the Dublin courts, Miles, and my advice to any man would be to avoid them at all cost. In a little over six weeks, Felicity will be of age. A court case could easily grind on that long, and in the end all you'd have achieved would be to shovel money into the pockets of the legal vultures. No. It will be easier to just take up your yoke and bear it."

Miles took a restless turn around the cozy room. "I smell a conspiracy here, Colum. If you're so set on avoiding this task, there must be a catch to it."

"Not at all . . ."

"I've already missed two months of the hunting season, and this business will delay me even more!"

"Now, it wasn't my doing that you ripped your arm from its socket, Miles, and you can't claim it was! In fact, I told you to turn that horse into dog-meat months ago."

"Banshee has qualities I don't want to waste. But my horses are in Melton, and I'm stuck here. If I accept this duty, I'll have to at least go and meet the girl."

"Yes, I think you will. But it need be no more than that. She seems content to live at Foy, and my sister Annie is a suitable companion for her. Felicity has a Dublin lawyer and two other men as trustees for her fortune . . ."

Just then, Miles's mother, Lady Aideen Monahan, entered in her usual aura of crackling energy, eyes bright, smile wide.

Despite having been born into the august family of the Fitzgeralds, she had little use for pomp and elevation. She had, however, kept up the use of her title. After all, she said, there was something very *hausfrauish* about the designation "Mrs."

Plumply pretty in a blue wool gown, her sandy curls tucked into a lacy confection that hardly deserved the name 'cap,' she welcomed her husband home with a hearty kiss.

"Who has a fortune that needs managing?" she asked with interest. It was Aideen's willingness to manage Clonnagh that allowed Miles his unshackled way of life.

"Colum's niece, Felicity," Miles said.

"Oh yes! She inherited it from her maternal grandfather. Is there a problem?" If Aideen had the right kind of ears, they would have pricked. "Now I remember. You are her guardian, Colum."

"No," Miles said. *"I* am. Old Leonard Monahan changed his will on his deathbed."

She swung back, blue eyes sparkling. "How intriguing! Why?"

"Devil alone knows."

"As to reasons," Colum said slowly, "there was some talk of Felicity being in danger . . ."

"Danger?" Miles asked. "Of what kind?"

"He didn't say. Or wasn't understood. His speech was affected, I gather. Doubtless he worried about fortune hunters."

"Doubtless he did, but to talk of danger is proof his mind was affected."

Aideen looked at Miles carefully. "Are you very put out, my dear?"

"You can probably tell from the way my hair is standing on end." But he grinned.

She reached up to smooth it. "It should not be an onerous burden, and Colum and I will keep an eye on matters while you are away. A dying man's wishes must be respected, Miles."

From his mother, that was as good as an order. Miles sighed. "Very well. I'll ride over tomorrow to introduce myself to the girl. I'll even stay a few days. But then I'm going to Melton."

The next afternoon, Miles urged his horse into a gallop across a lush meadow, each fall of Argonaut's heavy hooves throwing mud onto his top boots and leather breeches. It was proving to be a wonderful ride, almost putting him in charity with the young woman who was the cause of it.

He headed the horse toward a long rise. Even after a thirty-mile journey, Argonaut took the slope as if it were flat, cruising up without slackening speed.

Laughing, Miles pulled up on the crest, patting the horse's lathered neck. "Ah, my beauty, you're all I expected and more. It'll break my heart to part with you."

The big bay sidled and preened, taking praise as his due.

"I'll see you go to one who'll appreciate you, though, my friend. Don't you worry."

Nudging the horse back down toward the road, Miles thanked the gods that he didn't breed horses for the money. All too many Irishmen did. They had to harden their hearts and sell to the highest bidder, even to a heavy-handed lout or a break-neck hunter who would kill his horses instead of himself.

Miles, however, could choose his customers. His normal practice was to take a string of hunters to Melton Mowbray for the hunting season. There, he either rode the horses himself or lent them to trusted friends, then negotiated sales privately. The Meltonians—the avid hunters—knew the reputation of Clonnagh hunters without having to see them run, but any man liked to see a horse in action before buying.

Once the hunting season was underway, Miles had more offers than the father of a grand heiress at Almack's.

Thoughts of heiresses recalled a certain grand heiress nearer to home. He prayed earnestly that he not be put in the position of judging contenders for Miss Monahan's fair and wealthy hand.

He kneed Argonaut onward, checking his direction against the setting sun. He was on course and couldn't be many miles from Foy, though he didn't yet recognize any landmarks.

Too bad the girl had not been at Foy during his visit so that he'd have some idea what to expect. He'd gained a clear impression from Colum's past comments that she was an ill-raised creature who rode astride and came and went as she pleased.

Her wildness was hardly surprising. Orphaned at ten when her parents drowned on their way to England, she'd been left in the care of her grandfather. Miles's assessment of old Leonard Monahan was that he had been as charming as his son Colum, but twice as indolent.

Leonard's land had been cared for haphazardly by a lacka-daisical agent, his house ruled by his equally indolent daughter, Annie, whose main interest in life was cats. She stirred herself for little else.

Yes, Felicity had doubtless been allowed to run wild, but Miles had no interest in trying to correct this neglect. He just prayed his unwelcome ward behaved herself for the next few weeks.

At a fork, a signpost told him he was two miles from Foy. As he turned Argonaut in that direction, another horseman cantered around the bend and drew up to exchange pleasant-ries.

"Rupert Dunsmore of Loughcarrick," the fine gentleman said, raising his silver-knobbed crop to touch the glossy bea-ver set with precise rakishness upon burnished pale-gold hair. Though his showy gray didn't impress Miles much, his elegant clothing—rather too elegant for riding—marked him as a gentleman. Miles had no choice but to respond.

"Miles Cavanagh of Clonnagh."

He wasn't sure why he was taking an instant dislike to Mr. Dunsmore. Perhaps it was the disdainful expression on his pale, narrow face, or the extreme Englishness of his accent. He was either English and determined to exaggerate it, or the sort of Irishman who tried to ape the invaders.

"You're a long way from home, Mr. Cavanagh." Dunsmore was eying him as if he suspected him of being up to no good. Horse thievery, perhaps?

Having been educated in England, Miles could be as English as the Regent if he'd a mind, but now he deliberately slipped into a brogue. "As far as I know, Mr. Dunsmore, the English have made no law against it. Yet."

They moved on at walking speed, side by side but not in harmony, Dunsmore having clearly decided that Miles was not worth the waste of breath. Miles could have ridden on and left the man behind, but Argonaut was due for a breather and the light was going.

"I'm for Foy, sir. And you?" he asked, hoping Dunsmore was headed elsewhere.

"Loughcarrick lies close to Foy."

Damn. "This is a fine part of the country."

"Indeed it is."

They might have continued this desultory conversation until they died of boredom if Dunsmore had not suddenly come to life. He turned sharply to look at Miles. "Cavanagh! You are not . . . ? You cannot be grandson to old Leonard Monahan of Foy?"

"Indeed I'm not." Then before the look of relief could settle on Dunsmore's face, Miles added, "I'm his step-grandson if such a relationship exists."

"But . . . but then you're heir to Kilgoran!" Dunsmore looked up and down Miles's serviceable buckskins and well-used brown jacket in disbelief.

"I don't dress fine for a long day's ride, Mr. Dunsmore." Miles cast a similar look over Dunsmore's too dandyfied clothes.

Dunsmore collected himself and summoned a social smile. "Then you'll be traveling to meet your ward, Miss Monahan."

Miles despised people who were only pleasant to those of higher rank, but there seemed no point in quarreling with this specimen. "Indeed I am. You are acquainted with her?"

"Very well acquainted. We are neighbors. She and my late wife were quite close."

A prickle down the back of the neck warned Miles that there was more to the words than first appeared. "I've never met the girl."

"She is a fine young woman. Forgive me for mentioning it, sir, but it must appear strange that such a young man be given charge of her, and she an heiress, too. Her friends must be concerned."

So you rank yourself as a friend, do you? Or something more? The man was apparently a widower. One looking for a second wife? A rich wife?

"Her friends have no cause for concern, Mr. Dunsmore," Miles said blandly. "As long as Miss Monahan doesn't try to wed a fortune hunter before March, we should rub along well enough."

Dunsmore's narrow face became even more pinched. "I mean no slight, Mr. Cavanagh, but it all looks—"

Before he could complete his sentence, he was pulled from his horse by a gigantic rooster. In fact, a company of animals had burst out of a copse. A goose. A ram. A horse. A bull. . . .

Miles gathered his wits and realized they were men wearing masks and cloaks. Then a pig was on his back, cursing fluently in Gaelic and trying to drag him out of the saddle.

Miles elbowed backward and kicked Argonaut into a rear that dislodged the man. He wheeled the horse to see four men on Dunsmore, pummelling him unmercifully. He charged over to scatter them.

But two assailants grabbed him, each clinging to a leg, and Argonaut wasn't trained to this. The wild-eyed horse began to spin and buck. Miles slashed at one creature with his crop, but the other managed to drag him off and wrestle him to the ground.

Two other men flung their weight on top of him, and he was quickly trussed. Argonaut was kicking at anything, and Miles saw a man strike him with a cudgel.

"God blast your eyes!" he yelled, struggling again, but a gag was shoved into his mouth and bound there ruthlessly. Argonaut made off down the road, a distinct break in his stride.

Writhing against the ropes binding his wrists and ankles, Miles vowed to flay every one of these rascals for hurting his horse!

But for now, he was out of the action, and the four men ran back to join the three who were beating Dunsmore. For what cause, Miles wondered, pulling against his bonds to no effect. Personal or political? These days in Ireland, it could be either.

Bruised and furious, he saw the goose thwack the cowering Dunsmore with a sturdy rod, blows designed to hurt but do no permanent damage. This affair was clearly a warning, but they must be mad to use an Englishman this way. By tomorrow, the area would be swarming with the military.

Then Dunsmore was hoisted back into his saddle, his battered beaver shoved cockeyed on his head. He slumped forward and clung to his horse's neck as the nervous gray was set to run on down the road.

Now Miles had leisure to wonder what his own fate would be. Most of the strange animals slipped off into the misty shadows, leaving the horse and goose behind.

The goose still held that rod.

"What the devil are we to do with him?" muttered the goose to the horse in Gaelic.

"Leave him here. Someone'll come by."

"It's starting to rain."

"Christ, he won't melt!"

"Connor's cottage is just over there."

"Jesus and Mary, do you want me to carry him? He's a big man. Why not just let him go if you're feeling so soft?"

"He's the sort who'll pick a fight. Look at the red hair on him. With time to cool down, he'll see reason."

Don't bet on it, thought Miles vengefully.

He was trying to note anything that might identify the men, but the light was fading fast. The horse was heavyset and perhaps a foot taller than the goose, but the goose was tall enough. Their nondescript clothes were largely hidden by their cloaks. The animal heads both hid their features and muffled their voices.

The horse came over. "I'm going to loose your feet so you can walk to shelter. Give me any trouble, boyo, and I'll knock you out and drag you."

Miles believed him. The horse helped him to his feet and steered him through a gate and over to a decrepit bothy just as the slight drizzle turned into steady rain. The cottage lacked glass or shutters on the windows and the door hung at a crazy angle to the opening, but it was dry inside. Miles was pushed down onto the ground and his feet were tied again.

"Someone'll come by later to let you free. If you're wise, you won't make trouble then or later."

At that moment, Miles would have tried to strangle anyone who loosed him, so he did see their point. Time probably would calm him a little, but he sent silent curses after them as they left him in the damp, musty dark.

He slumped back against the stone of the empty hearth, counting his bruises. There weren't too many. It was presumably just bad luck that he'd been with Dunsmore, and the rascals had been as gentle with him as they could.

He assumed they were the Farmyard Boys, who'd been operating around the eastern counties for the past few years, visiting sharp retribution on any landlord who oppressed his tenants or on any Irishman who sided with the English. True, the English yoke lay heavy on Ireland, with harsh laws and twenty-five-thousand soldiers to enforce them, but these vigilantes were not the way to improve anything.

All the same, if Argonaut were all right, he'd let the matter pass.

As darkness sank from dusky to deep, Miles's forbearance thinned. His bonds chafed his wrists. He was turning numb in some places and cramped in others. The gag stretched his lips and leached all the moisture from his mouth. He began to shiver, for it was a chilly January evening.

Damn their black hearts! Despite the pain, he began to work at the ropes around his wrists, hoping to loosen them enough to wriggle his hands free.

When he heard a sound outside, he stopped. About bloody time, too!

Then he wondered why he was so sure the person was coming to help. He was, after all, a witness of sorts . . .

The broken-hinged door creaked open, showing a dark shape backed by the lighter gray of a misty night. The shape crept forward, scarce making a sound other than the brush of a cloak against the dirt floor.

Something was put down with a clink.

A weapon?

Uselessly, Miles tensed for combat.

Two

It was a lantern, for a window was opened to spill golden candlelight into the shanty. The light haloed around the cloaked figure who had just placed the lantern on a wormy shelf on the wall.

Something in the cut of the cloak and the shape of the hands told him his reliever was a woman.

He let out his breath in relief. A clever move, for no matter how angry he was, he was unlikely to take it out on a woman. What were the odds that she was a pretty winsome piece, to boot?

She pushed back the hood of her cloak to prove him right—thick red curls, a heart-shaped face, and stunning dark eyes full of warmhearted concern.

"Oh, you poor creature!" she declared, hands clasped before an ample bosom like the more maudlin type of Madonna. Her voice marked her as a peasant, but it was a pleasant voice all the same.

He would have said something polite if he hadn't had a damn gag in his mouth. Was she simple? She continued to just stand there looking at him in melting sympathy.

He made some protesting noises, and she gasped. "Oh, your mouth, sir! Indeed, sir. I'll have you free in just a moment, sir. Don't concern yourself!"

She ran over to undo his gag. But instead of going behind him, as would be sensible, she stretched from the front, bringing her chest to within inches of his face. He was practically smothered by soft warm flesh and the sweet perfume of roses.

"Oh, they've tied this rag so tight, the monsters! How could they be so cruel?"

She leaned even closer.

Saints preserve them both but it was a very well-endowed chest, and she was wearing an old-fashioned laced bodice which confined only the lower part of her breasts while pushing them up. The generous upper part was covered only by a shift made fine by many washings.

Miles was not really in a situation to be thinking amorous thoughts, but his body reacted all on its own to this excess of magnificence.

For a peasant she smelled remarkably sweet, too, with a warm womanly scent and that delicate touch of rose. She was undoubtedly lacking some of her wits, though, for she was still struggling to free him by stretching her arms around him.

Why the devil didn't she just go around the back?

He tried to say something but only achieved a choking noise.

Still fumbling behind his head, she looked down at him, her beautiful eyes only inches away. She had long dark lashes so thick they seemed tangled with soot, but in this light there was no way to tell what color her irises were. They looked coal-black, which gave her an expression of unending concern.

He reminded himself that this was illusion, and that she didn't seem to have enough wit to come in from the rain.

He mumbled again, practically snarling at her.

"Oh, dear, oh dear. You poor man. Are you in *terrible* pain? Oh, I have an idea! Let me try to do this from the back."

She shifted around and sat him forward. Within moments, the gag was off.

Miles worked his aching jaw and tried to find saliva to moisten his mouth. "Drink?" he croaked.

"Oh, sir. Of course, sir!" She pulled a flask out of the

pocket of her old-style full skirts and uncapped it. "Sure, and this'll revive you in a wink, sir!" She held it to his lips and tipped.

Instinctively, he swallowed, but then he jerked back so most went down his front.

"What ails you, sir? 'Tis the finest Irish whisky! I swear it on my mother's grave!"

Miles coughed. "I'm sure it is, my dear. But it's not the thing for the thirst I have. Is there no water?"

She leapt to her feet, her hands—now around the flask—once more clasped to that bosom. "What a fool I am, to be sure! I'll not be a moment, sir."

She dashed to the door, then froze as if caught in a terrible dilemma. She frowned at the flask in her hand, then at Miles, then left—pouring the contents on the ground as she went.

Miles lay there, stunned. Definitely simple. It might be true that there was nothing else in which to carry water, but why the devil hadn't she just finished untying him so he could make his own way to the stream?

He sighed, recognizing another stroke of genius on someone's part. If he were unlikely to throttle a woman, he'd be even less likely to harm such a simple one. Some men, however, would not hesitate to take what that ample, exposed bosom offered.

Had they thought of that?

Perhaps it was part of the plan.

Again, his unruly body reacted.

She came back to hold the flask to his lips again. This time, cool, sweet water soothed his mouth.

"Thank you, my dear," he said, as calmly as he could, for he had no desire to alarm her. "Perhaps now you could untie my hands and feet."

She sat back on her heels and put a finger to her lips like a child. "Well, now, you see, sir, I was told to be very careful with you. That you might turn violent."

"Then perhaps one of those fine bullies should have accompanied you."

"It was thought on," she admitted, chewing her knuckle. "It was never intended that you be hurt, sir."

Miles's jaw was aching from the way his teeth were clenched, but he knew the slightest trace of anger could have this poor woman fleeing into the night. "I realize that," he soothed. "I promise I will not hurt you. Untie me, please. These ropes are very painful."

She gnawed on her knuckle a moment more, then stood and raised her skirt to reveal white stockings and sturdy shoes. They argued a slightly higher rank than he'd imagined. But what the devil was she doing?

The skirts rose a little farther, rose slowly so his gaze seemed guided by them—up shapely, cotton-covered calves; past a simple garter tied below the knee; and on to a creamy, naked thigh. He was bemusedly wondering just where this journey was to end when it halted at a leather strap holding a sheath. She pulled out a knife so long and businesslike that he instinctively shrank back.

Blade glinting in the candlelight, she grinned at him, then flung herself forward. Miles cursed and tried to wriggle away, but she seized the rope around his ankles to stop him.

"Just you stay still, now," she said cheerfully as he felt the knife bite at the ropes. The ease with which they parted told him he had not been mistaken about its sharpness.

She moved behind him. "Sure and I fear the ropes have burned your poor wrists, sir. Just a moment here, and you'll be free."

The ropes parted and he brought his wrists to the front to rub them, wincing at their tenderness. He tried to stand, but was so stiff he rolled to his knees. He staggered to his feet by holding onto the rough stones of the chimney. Muttering curses at all farmyard animals, he limped around the small room, trying to ease the stiffness, cramps, and pins-and-needles.

Then the girl snared his attention. She was still kneeling, and now it was the knife that nestled between her breasts, pointing up in a way that could only make a man think of a phallus.

The pain faded . . .

"Would you like me to rub your legs, sir?" She stretched a hand toward his thigh. But it was the hand holding the knife.

Miles leaped back with a yelp, and his left leg gave way, landing him bum-down on the hard ground. "For Christ's sake, girl, put that thing away!"

With a hurt look, she stood, raised her skirts again clear up to the top of her leg, and slowly, suggestively, sheathed the knife. She definitely had more in mind than just relieving him of his bonds. It was a prospect that appealed mightily to certain parts of his body, but he was hardly in a fit state to do her justice.

He pushed back to his feet, noting with relief that the worst of the stiffness and pain had gone. "Where's my horse, girl?"

"That lovely bay, sir? He's at the Shamrock. The inn in Foy village."

"And is he well?"

"Indeed he is, sir. As fine as fivepence!"

His main concern eased, Miles stretched and studied the wench with more leisure. Faith, and she was an interesting piece. She was tallish for a woman, with that interestingly generous bosom and a lovely full-cheeked face.

And lovely long, strong legs, too.

Not so strong in the head, though.

Damn those ruffians for sending such a simple lass to do their dirty work. He touched her cheek. "What's your connection with those strange animals, then?"

She lowered her lush lashes. "Now, you can't expect me to answer that, sir, can you?" But she rubbed against his hand like a kitten and glanced up at him—though he doubted she could actually see through the dense black fringe in such uncertain light. "You won't be making complaint to the magistrates, now will you, sir?"

Hell. She couldn't be plainer if she said it straight out. She was offering her body for his silence.

It was tempting, very tempting . . .

He teased her lower lip with his thumb, wanting to see her soft lips part a little for him. "So I'll not be making a complaint, will I not, sweetheart? For you, I might well hold my tongue, but Mr. Dunsmore will already have raised the military. Unless you've killed him."

She looked straight at him then, eyes wide with innocence. "Killed him, sir? By St. Patrick and St. Bridget, he's safe at home. A little the worse for wear, I'll grant you, but not near death at all, at all."

"In that case, he'll have the army out after your friends tomorrow. Do you have somewhere to hide?"

She lowered her head, but not before he saw her lips twitch. "Oh, I doubt that, sir. Even though he's a black-hearted Englishman, Mr. Dunsmore will not bring the soldiers down on these parts. So if *you* don't make trouble, no one will."

He raised her chin with a finger, seeking truth in those disarming eyes. "You seem remarkably sure of his silence. I wonder why? And I wonder what means you and your friends have in mind to make sure *I* don't lodge a complaint?"

"Sure, we'd never hurt a hair of your head, sir, you an Irishman, an' all. And I can see by your sweet face that you're no friend of the English tyrant!"

It was then Miles realized the girl was acting—overacting—a part. He moved back to study her. "I'm no friend of ruffians, girl, Irish or English."

She frowned slightly, then rested her hand on his chest. "You would see me transported, sir? I came to you unmasked."

He trapped her hand, part controlling, part to hold it against him, for he would miss it were it gone. "Perhaps that was foolish."

"Was it?" Her other hand slid up to his face and she kissed him quickly, temptingly open-lipped. Her hand on his chest turned to grasp his and move it to her breast. She rubbed it there, rubbed herself against it, speaking an invitation with her eyes.

Perhaps it was relief from danger, but he was abruptly ready for a woman, especially this one. His other hand slid around to hold her close. "You have an interesting way of buying safety, darling, but I'm willing. I prefer to have a name to put to a lover, though. What is yours?"

She stiffened slightly. "That would be foolish, wouldn't it, sir, to tell you my name?"

He brushed his lips against her turned cheek. "Come now, if I want to find you, it won't be hard."

After a moment, she moved to meet his lips and whispered, "Joy, then. My name is Joy."

He chuckled. "I doubt it, but it's appropriate. I'm sure you bring joy to many men."

Abruptly, she stiffened. "What? Why, you . . . !"

"Haven't you just come from buying off Dunsmore the same way?"

"I have not, you *spalpeen!*"

He resisted her token struggles. "I suppose he isn't in any state for this yet . . ."

He kissed her softly, tasting and testing with a keen sense of anticipation, exploring her generous body. She relaxed again and her lips welcomed him, but something—a lingering tension perhaps—told him this was no willing lover but a planned sacrifice.

He drew back with a sigh of regret. Though this baggage was not aware of it, as Felicity Monahan's guardian he had a position in this community. If Joy were unwilling, taking what she offered would cause nothing but trouble.

She doubtless thought he was passing through, that she could buy him off and never see him again. If he became her lover, however, he could end up having made enemies of a family, perhaps even the whole village. In Ireland, such matters could be dangerous indeed, as Dunsmore had found out.

He kissed Joy's hand—a gesture that appeased most women, especially those of the lower class. If he found out she was the local light-skirt after all, he might take her up on today's offer, for she was the most luscious piece he'd encountered in a long while. "I fear, like Dunsmore, I'm in no state to do you justice tonight, my dear. Perhaps another time."

She made no protest but held onto his hand. "And you'll not report the matter, sir?"

"If Dunsmore wants it kept quiet, I won't spill it."

She kissed his hand then with almost religious fervor. "Ah, thank you, thank you, sir! May Jesus and Mary guard you!"

She was overacting again. "Jesus, Mary, and Joseph guard you," he replied in the traditional way. "If you'll just lead me to my horse, sweet Joy, I'll be on my way."

"On your way? But it's late, sir. You should stay at the inn till morning. That's where your horse is, after all."

"I didn't think you'd want me lingering in the area."

The look she flashed him then was noticeably intelligent—aware of all the aspects to this situation. "The law around here doesn't take kindly to people who are abroad at night, sir."

Interesting. Perhaps they feared that if he fell in with the military he'd tell his story. His journey, of course, would take him only as far as Foy Hall, which sat in the old style close by the village, but they couldn't know that.

Impulsively, he decided to let this play out, to see if there were more to be learned.

"Very well, sweet Joy. Lead me to the Shamrock Inn."

She collected her lantern, but closed it before leading him down the track to the Foy road. Perhaps she did fear a military troop. With only a sliver of moon to give natural light, Miles had to watch his steps.

"So," he said when they were on the relative smoothness of the road, "what about Dunsmore makes him worthy of a beating?"

"What about him doesn't?"

"Since I don't know the man, I'd be hard pressed to say. He seemed courteous enough in a top-lofty manner."

"Top-lofty. Now there's a good word for him. And him a down-at-heels English captain before he married Kathleen Craig."

"Married money, did he? And English to boot. Now there's a series of wicked sins to be sure."

She flashed him an angry glance. "The man's gone through as much of his wife's money as he could get his greedy hands on. Now she's dead, he's stealing from his son's estate and squeezing every last penny out of his tenants without pity or mercy."

They were coming into the small village. " 'Tis not unusual for landlords to wring their people dry, my dear. But perhaps he deserved a trouncing for it. I'd be interested to know why you think he won't report it."

She stopped beneath the creaking inn-sign and he heard a fiddle scraping inside. The shutters were drawn, however, so only a glimmer of light spilled out into the road. "He has matters he'd rather keep quiet."

Miles noted with interest that she'd pulled up her hood again. Probably not the local light-skirt, alas.

He perched on an edge of a stone horse-trough. "If you can stop him from reporting an assault, I'd think you could stop his extortions altogether."

"He's growing desperate. He's a gamester, you see. Tonight was simply a reminder." She touched his sleeve. "Truly, he is a bad man, sir. Please don't betray us."

She really was an entrancing creature, and his body was recovering rapidly. He took her hand, and after a startled moment, she did not resist. "You offered payment for my silence before, sweet Joy."

He raised her hand and sucked gently on a finger.

She tugged tentatively. "It's late now, sir. I should be home."

He sucked the next finger. "Your parents don't know what you're up to? Or do you live with an employer? Tell me how to contact you—" he drew the finger suggestively deep into his mouth before sliding it free "—when I've regained my strength."

She tugged her hand harder, but he didn't let go. "Are you saying you won't be silent unless I sleep with you?"

The note of outrage told him she'd never meant to pay with her body. Perhaps she'd thought his roughing-up made him safe. A strangely naive view for such a bold piece. He decided to see just how far she would go and what he could learn from it.

He slipped his other arm around her and pulled her between his legs. "It wasn't sleeping I had in mind, *alannah*. I won't keep you out all night."

He could hear the unsteadiness of her breathing now, for her face was only inches from his. "I can't here, sir. Everyone would know."

"Do you still have your reputation, then?" He released her hand and cupped a breast as he'd wanted to do since first seeing her. Ah, but it was magnificent—full, warm, and firm. He bent to kiss the rising swell. "I won't ruin you. You have my word, Joy. Are you betrothed to one of those animals? Is he willing to have you pay this price, or will he be after me for revenge?" His thumb found her nipple, already hard, and brushed it gently.

She shivered, pulling back again. "I am betrothed to no man." After a moment, however, she ceased resisting. "But I will do what I must to save them all."

A true patriot-martyr, but such a tempting one. And the response of her flesh told him it wasn't all sacrifice. Or perhaps it was just the response of his own flesh, hoping it wasn't all sacrifice.

"Joyfully?" He teased her sensitive flesh again.

She grasped his hand. "Sir, please! Not here in public!"

He glanced around at the empty street. "Public? There's not a soul in sight and it's pitch dark. We could couple here with none the wiser, sweetheart. Let's kiss at least."

This time she was not pliant in his arms, but he tilted her chin and kissed her, using all his skill to overcome her scruples. To the devil with finding out her secrets. A night of Joy was becoming insistently attractive.

At last her lips did soften and part for him. Murmuring encouragement, he stroked her delightful curves. Easing her mouth further open, he kissed her fully, finding her every bit as sweet as he'd expected, and every bit as responsive.

He wasn't aware that his hand was inside her shift until she pulled away with an alarmed cry.

He quickly covered her mouth, abruptly remembering his resolve to be circumspect in this locality. "Alas, sweet Joy, this is not the time and place."

When he was sure she wouldn't scream, he freed her mouth. "Just direct me to my horse, my dear. When I've seen to him, I'll be happy to rest my bruises alone."

But she gripped his hand, bone-tight, preventing him from moving away. "You don't need to check on your horse, sir! Michael Flaherty has seen to him, and he's the best stable lad in five counties."

He twisted his hand free. "It's a practice of mine not to leave my horses to others, especially not a horse as valuable as Argonaut. The stables will be at the back, I suppose."

He set off toward the lane beside the low building, but she grabbed his jacket. "Sir, please. Don't leave me!" She towed him back and flung herself into his arms. "You cannot be so cruel! You've made me mad for you!"

She had him up against the horse-trough with enough weight and strength to bruise his back. "Darling, I've never left a lady desperate yet. Give me a moment to see to Argonaut and I'll ease your madness willingly."

"I can't wait! You can see to the horse in the morning."

He seized her hands and fought his way free. It was quite a struggle, for she was strong for her size. "Enough," he snapped. "Or—terrible waste though it'd be—I'll toss you into the trough to cool you down."

Her breathing was so rough it sounded like sobs. "Please . . ."

Her desperation was breaking his own control and he almost gave in, but Argonaut . . . He must check on Argonaut.

He put a comforting arm around her and led her down the lane. "Hush, *a muirnín.* Just a moment or two and I'll give you all you desire. Come on now. Open the lantern and let's find the fine fellow."

Her madness seemed to abate, for she managed to open the window in the lantern so he could check the loose-boxes. Two contained heavy horses, and then he found Argonaut.

The horse whinnied a greeting and pushed his head into Miles's chest. Miles stroked him fondly. "Taken care of you better than me from the looks of it, eh?" Then he saw the bandage on the hind hock. Not a bandage. A fomentation . . .

Lust dissipated. He was into the box in a second, feeling for damage. He moved the horse and took in the limp. "May hell wait for the lot of 'em!"

He erupted into the yard and seized the woman. "You and your louts have lamed my best horse!"

"We meant him no harm."

"Meant him no harm? I saw someone hit him with a cudgel. If Argonaut's damaged I'll see the lot of you in Botany Bay!"

Abruptly, she stood taller. "I see. People don't matter. Just horses, and then only for the price they'll bring in England." She wore a sneer fit for an ancient queen of Ireland.

He thrust her away. "Most horses are worth a deal more than most people. Especially whores."

"Whores! Damn your black heart, I'm no whore!"

"You'd have spread your legs to keep me from finding out

about this, wouldn't you? To stop me from reporting your
antics to the magistrates. That's whoring in my mind."

She laughed with scorn. "You weren't reluctant to take me
up on the offer, were you? Why is that more noble, my fine
gentleman?"

He turned back to the stall. "Just pray my horse is sound,
sweet Joy, or someone will suffer."

"Mick says it's nothing serious and he'll be easier in the
morning. If you'd only waited until then, you'd not have been
so distressed. Why the devil didn't you take me up on my
offer?"

Turning to face her, he was struck by her magnificence—
red hair touched to flame by the lantern, angry pride holding
her straight and tall. Damn, but he still desired her.

"Hurts, does it? Darling, you could be Helen of Troy, Deirdre of the White Breast, and the Gunning sisters rolled into
one, and you'd not have stopped me from checking on Argonaut. You're right. I do care for my horses more than most
people, particularly people who attack defenseless men on the
highway."

Before she could spit out her reaction to that, he stepped
by her, heading for Argonaut's stall. Just then the inn door
opened, spilling light and singing into the yard. "Who's out
there? Oh, it's you Miss Felicity. Where's the stranger?"

Miles froze, then moved back into the lantern-light. "He's
here." He turned to the young woman. "Felicity?"

She shrugged. "Another word for joy."

"I'm sure you're a joy to all who know you. Felicity Monahan, I assume."

Unease flickered in her dark eyes, but she said nothing.

"What an interesting young woman you are to be sure.
Allow me to present myself. I'm Miles Cavanagh, your legal
guardian."

Three

Not long after, Miles and his ward entered Foy Hall to be greeted by a dusty chill and the pervasive smell of cats.

Miles had to assume that Felicity Monahan felt some embarrassment at her situation, but the only emotion he'd seen cross her beautiful, stony face had been rage. She'd said not one word of explanation or apology.

Since Michael Flaherty—for it was he who'd interrupted them—seemed to know horses, there hadn't been much point in hovering over Argonaut. Miles, therefore, had escorted his ward to her home, gaining nothing from her but silence and a fine air of disdain. Miles intended to have an explanation of her behavior, though. By hades, he'd known she was wild, but not that she was a wanton and an Irish rebel!

A dying fire smoldered in the entrance hall's huge grate and he flung a log on it. "Are you regularly mixed up in these disorders?"

"You have no right to question me. Good night."

He caught her cloak before she could escape, and held her close. "Have I not? God knows, I wish I had no rights in this, but I have the misfortune to be your guardian, Miss Monahan. Clearly someone has to bring you to your senses, and it appears to be me. Do you have any idea of the seriousness of tonight's affair?"

With proud spirit, she snapped, "I am not a simpleton. Of course I have."

"Then what the devil were you doing mixed up in it?"

When she remained silent, he shook her. "Answer me, damn you. Are you part of that mad gang?"

Some notion of his seriousness must have struck her, for she grew wary. "No. They asked my help, that's all. They needed someone to release you. Someone you wouldn't attack. Someone who wouldn't be in serious trouble if you reported her."

He let her go. "Not in serious trouble? What the devil do you think would have happened if I'd gone to the military with this tale and pointed you out as the accomplice?"

She tossed her head. "You wouldn't have found me. You'd have been looking for a red-haired peasant, whereas I—" she unpinned a wig to reveal midnight-dark hair in a knot beneath "—am a dark-haired lady!"

He felt a strong desire to slap her. "I'd have found you. Beauty such as yours doesn't live in every cottage. And when we'd exhausted the cottages, we'd have started on the better houses."

"Even if you'd found me, what could the English do to Miss Felicity Monahan of Foy Hall?"

"My dear girl, you need a sharp dose of reality." He seized her by the shoulders and thumped her down in a hard, wooden chair. "Now," he said, hands braced on the arms so his face was only inches from her mutinous one, "what if the local military officials are of a ruthless inclination and very much want to round up the Farmyard Boys? I think Miss Felicity Monahan might suddenly disappear . . ."

"They couldn't!"

"Not permanently. But once in their hands, you would be offered a choice. Tell all or be raped."

She paled and pressed into the back of the chair. "They wouldn't dare!"

"Who's to stop them? Do the English in Ireland obey the rule of law? Even if it came out, you're a lawbreaker and they'd have a right to act against you. Legally, they could tie you to a tree and flay the flesh off your back, as has been done to other women they thought knew something."

"They wouldn't dare . . ." But it was a whisper now.

He moved away, disturbed himself by the picture he was painting.

A true one.

"Don't fool yourself, Felicity. If anyone did ask questions, the military would claim it was a mistake, particularly if they'd caught you dressed as a peasant girl. Their apologies would be profuse, but you'd still be scarred for life."

He saw her press her lips together to steady them. Dear Christ, what had her grandfather and aunt been about not to explain the realities of life in Ireland in these troubled times? Then he remembered the Monahans. They were all better at avoiding trouble than facing it.

"The same thing goes for rape," he said more moderately. "They'd say it was a mistake. Or that you'd wanted it. Wouldn't there be plenty to say you'd always been wild?"

"Not like that—"

"And would you even dare speak of it? What young lady would tell the world she's been the plaything of a barrack-room?"

She was looking sick. Good. He hated to do this, but he wanted her worried sick.

Then she sat straighter and rebellion flashed in her eyes. "This one. I'd rather be an outcast than let them get away with that. And true Irish folk would not hold such against me!"

"You're too trusting about that, *alannah*." But her renewed fierceness worried him. Reckless courage was admirable, but could land a person in grave trouble. Look at his own distant relative, Lord Edmund Fitzgerald, killed in the Irish cause.

"I'd take such a case to the courts," she declared. "To the highest court in the land."

"They'd claim you were willing, and your reputation would count against you."

"What reputation?"

"As a hellion. And as a wanton."

She flushed then and almost looked hurt. "My reputation is untarnished! And I would tell the soldiers nothing, even if they did rape me."

"Then they'd torture you. There are plenty of ways that leave little mark."

"You seem to know a great deal about such matters, Mr. Cavanagh. Done some torturing yourself?"

Miles sighed. What had he done to deserve this? He'd been roughed up, his best horse was possibly ruined, and he was landed with responsibility for this wayward creature whom he clearly could not let out of his sight for a moment.

And if that list of problems weren't enough, he still desired Felicity Monahan. He'd enjoyed kissing her, and he'd definitely been looking forward to the chance to take "Joy" to bed and enjoy every luscious inch of her.

He was, however, her guardian, dammit, and that meant she was the one woman in Ireland he absolutely could not seduce. In fact, it was his task to preserve her virtue for two long months. And that with just about any man who set eyes on her trying to get his hands under her skirts or into her well-filled bodice.

And her perhaps not putting up much resistance.

"Where's your aunt?" he demanded irritably. "Doesn't she care for you at all?"

It was a stupid question. Of course she didn't.

Looking at the frightened, rebellious girl left young in the charge of such useless people, he felt pity stir. It was how he felt about a fine horse ruined by cruel treatment. Sometimes he would take up the challenge of saving such a horse, but this was a person, and he doubted she felt she needed saving.

He ran his hand wearily through his hair. "Let's be practical. Can you be sure Dunsmore won't raise the alarm? Or was that wishful thinking?"

Panic flashed in her eyes, but then she looked down. "He's not a bad man. He'll not want to make trouble."

What new insanity was this? "Not a bad man? Not want to make trouble? If he's not a bad man, why was he trounced earlier? And if he'd not want to make trouble, why did you imply that you could force him to keep quiet?"

She leaped to her feet. "You misunderstood! I meant that he'll realize it's not worth bringing the military down on the area! Everyone would suffer."

Miles stared at her. This was the first time she'd really seemed flustered, and this was on behalf of Rupert Dunsmore whom he'd thought to be the villain of the piece.

He was suddenly exhausted. "Oh, to hell with it. If you think he'll not report it, the rest can wait until tomorrow. Is there any food in this house?"

It seemed a reasonable request, but it reignited her rebelliousness. "Certainly," she retorted. "But as the servants normally go to bed when Aunt Annie does, you'll have to fend for yourself."

"You aren't going to play hostess?"

"I most certainly am not. Now, may I go to bed, guardian dear?"

He wanted to shake her again, but fighting with Felicity was exhausting. He was beginning to have more sympathy for her relatives.

There was one more battle, though, that couldn't be avoided. He grasped her arm. "I'll have your word that you won't leave the house again tonight."

A resentful flicker told him she'd intended to go out.

Miles was tired, sore, hungry, and badly out of temper. "Your word, Felicity," he repeated, "or I'll chain you to me for the night. Oh, don't worry. I'm not threatening your chastity, if such a thing exists, but you're in my charge. One way or another, for the next six weeks you are going to live as quietly and virtuously as the best-raised girl in the kingdom."

Her magnificent dark eyes seemed to flash fire. "You have no right to govern me!"

He hauled her a bit closer. "I not only have the right, I have the responsibility and the will. Don't cross me. I am a dangerous man when roused. Give me your word."

"Why in God's name would you trust it?"

It was a good question. "You seem to have the cockeyed honor of a wild, patriot-boy. I'll trust your word."

He could almost feel the resentment coming off her like steam. "Very well," she snapped at last. "You have my word. I won't leave the house tonight."

As soon as he let her go, she turned and ran up the stairs, leaving him to fend for himself.

Miles supposed his valet must have arrived earlier as arranged, bringing his baggage, but it hardly seemed worth finding Hennigan, who could be no more familiar with this place than he was.

So he found the kitchen for himself. A young lad slept on a pallet by the fire, but Miles didn't rouse him. Three cats slid in to investigate, but as they didn't offer to serve him, he ignored them, too. The larder yielded a cold pie and a keg of beer. He drew some into a tankard, then sat at the table to enjoy his meager supper and contemplate the future.

This was going to play hell with the hunting season.

The next morning, Miles breakfasted with Annie Monahan, and therefore ate in the company of a half-dozen cats. Squat, grizzle-haired, and untidy, Annie was patently relieved to have him on the scene.

"Such a wild child," she said, ladling her plate with eggs and ham, and feeding morsels to the marmalade cat draped on her shoulder. "A dear, sweet girl in many ways, but wild at heart. I put it down to that Dunsmore."

Miles dislodged a young black cat that seemed intent on sitting on his lap. Black cats might bring good fortune, but he had no intention of stroking one at the table. "Dunsmore?" he queried, remembering the strange way Felicity had reacted to the subject last night.

"A neighbor of ours." Annie prevented a white cat from climbing on the table to eat off her plate. "Not when we have guests, Yffa."

Miles suppressed a shudder and dislodged the black cat again.

"A slick, slippery wretch of an Englishman," Annie continued with a touch of her niece's fire. "How Kathleen Craig could have been so foolish as to marry him, I'll never know. But she was always man-mad, you know, despite not having whatever it is that draws men to a woman . . ." She rambled off into stories of youthful rivalries. Since Annie and Miss Craig had clearly been contemporaries, the latter must have been considerably older than her husband.

A clear case of fortune hunting, but none of his affair.

The black cat was back, and when he tried to move it, it clung to his knitted breeches with needle claws.

Annie beamed. "Why, it's Gardeen and she likes you."

Miles simply pulled the animal free, walked around the table, and added it to the collection in Annie's lap. As he returned to his place, he heard her murmur, "There, there, little one. Men are temperamental creatures and he's out of sorts. He'll be kinder to you another time."

Don't bet money on it, Miles thought. He had nothing against cats—they were useful in a stable—but he had no interest in them at the dining table.

He could, however, bear to know why Felicity had grown flustered at the mention of Dunsmore's name. Was it possible she fancied herself in love with him? He could have sworn that "Joy" disliked the man intensely, but women seemed able to give their affections to men they knew to be scoundrels.

One thing was certain. Felicity Monahan would not give her beauty and fortune to Rupert Dunsmore as long as she was the ward of Miles Cavanagh.

Annie was still talking, meandering around topics like
smoke on a heavy day, and addressing herself randomly to
Miles, the cats, and even to absent people such as her dead
father. When she trailed to the indeterminate end of the saga
of a ball held twenty years ago, Miles interjected, "Dunsmore?"

"Dunsmore!" Annie seemed grateful for redirection.
"Dreadful man, and English to boot. Felicity fancied herself
in love with him as a green girl, and he already married to
Kathleen! Father chased the rascal off, of course, and sent the
girl away for a while. That put an end to it, but Felicity was
never the same. Wayward, wayward," she earnestly told a gray
cat, nose to nose. "And so *active.*"

The cat yawned, and Annie settled to a determined attack
on the cool, congealed food on her plate.

Miles sipped his coffee, oddly disappointed. For all her
faults, Felicity Monahan had seemed to have brains, courage,
and idealism. He'd not thought her the type to be taken in
by the facile attraction of a man like Dunsmore.

At that moment, his unwelcome ward tripped into the
breakfast parlor with a sunny, "Good morning!" and took a
seat at the table.

With difficulty, Miles suppressed a laugh.

In contrast to her appearance last night—in fact, in outright
denial of it—Felicity Monahan was acting the part of the
well-behaved young lady he had demanded.

She wore a demure and proper beige, merino gown with
just a moderate trim of ruched green ribbon. The neckline
was decently filled by a pleated chemisette edged with an
almost nun-like ruff at the neck. It was a shame, perhaps,
that not even that ensemble could disguise her magnificent
bosom, but she could hardly be held to blame for God's generosity.

Her hair, though its destiny was clearly to mass about her
head in rich, dark curls, had been drawn firmly back and

piled into a tidy knot bound with green ribbons to match those on her dress.

"I'm so pleased you are making yourself at home, Mr. Cavanagh," she said with social good humor. "I do hope you have everything you require."

And he had doubted her acting abilities! A minx, and a clever one. She must have been able to run rings around Annie and her grandfather.

"The hospitality of Foy Hall is as excellent as usual, Miss Monahan."

She glanced at him with a trace of suspicion, but then her carefree smile twitched back into place and she rang the bell. When a maid came, Felicity requested more coffee and fresh eggs. "May I order you anything, Mr. Cavanagh?"

"No, thank you."

While waiting, Felicity picked up a roll, broke it, and spread it with butter.

Nervousness? Perhaps merely a healthy appetite. As Annie had remarked, Felicity was a very *active* young lady, and she'd had a busy night.

"How long will we have the pleasure of your company, Mr. Cavanagh?" she asked sweetly. "I do hope you'll stay long enough to meet our neighbors. We could perhaps have a small evening entertainment in your honor."

"That would be delightful, Miss Monahan. However, I doubt I can stay for many days. I'm past due in the Shires for the hunting season."

Her smile became more genuine. "Indeed! We'll miss you, then, but also envy you. I hear the runs provided by the Shires are unequalled anywhere."

"True enough." Miles sipped from his coffee cup, watching her. "There's no need to be envious. You could accompany me."

It brought her up cold, almost seemed to throw her into a panic in fact, but the arrival of the coffee and eggs allowed her to hide it in action.

Felicity Monahan was an intriguing puzzle, and one Miles must solve if he were to handle his responsibilities for the next few months. He could hardly let his ward run wild and be taken up by the magistrates for sedition.

Miles was by nature a straightforward person, and he would much prefer to have a frank discussion with Felicity and come to an arrangement suitable for all. He had no faith that such a course would achieve anything here, however.

She cut into an egg so the yolk ran free, but made no attempt to eat. "I rather thought ladies were not allowed to ride with the Shire hunts."

"It is frowned upon. But ladies do visit the private houses in the area. I'll be staying with my friend Lord Arden, and I understand his wife is there this season. It would not be improper for you to accompany me."

She was now dissecting the bacon. "I fail to see the attraction of being in the Shires confined to the house."

Miles poured himself fresh coffee as he considered tactics. By accident, he'd hit upon the solution to his problems. If he could persuade Felicity to accompany him to Melton, he could hunt and show off his horses, while at the same time keeping her out of trouble. She would certainly not be running around with Dunsmore or the Farmyard Boys.

There were other advantages, too. From her years as a schoolteacher, Beth Arden had a deft hand with young women. She might be able to set Felicity on a more tranquil course. She could also introduce his ward to pleasant eligible men who would show up Dunsmore for the fribble he was.

The poor girl had probably never met any other candidates.

Yes, it was the perfect plan.

"It will not be dull," he assured her. "The marquess welcomes many houseguests, and there are other parties around the area. You can be sure of attending some events at Belvoir Castle, perhaps even with royalty in attendance."

Too late, he realized that this might not appeal to an Irish rebel—unless she had a weapon in hand.

"The mad one or the fat one?" she demanded scathingly. "If you could offer me a true monarch—a Stuart—I'd go with pleasure."

"The Stuart line is dead, Felicity. Do you not enjoy parties and dancing?"

She flashed him a withering glance. "Is that all you think fit for young ladies, Mr. Cavanagh? Parties and dancing? Is that what you do as you wait for your uncle the earl to cock up his toes? Dance and drink?"

"Now, Felicity," Annie interjected vaguely. "I've told you men aren't much for dancing. Except the fribblous type, of course. You'll only annoy them by making them be forever at balls and such."

Miles and Felicity ignored this, and as Annie appeared to be addressing the marmalade cat, it didn't seem to matter.

"I am not waiting for Kilgoran to die," Miles said, keeping his tone pleasant. "I sincerely hope he will live for decades. I keep myself well-occupied with horse-breeding."

"Well then, so do I!" Felicity retorted. "I've been managing the stables here for years and can hardly be expected to leave at a moment's notice."

"That's true." Annie now had three cats tangled contentedly in her lap. "Father hadn't been robust for years. Felicity has been a great help."

"And how do you sell them?" Miles asked her.

A sharp look from Felicity told him she was ahead of the game, already planning ways to thwart his next moves. By St. Bridget, but he hoped one day to match her at chess!

"Through a broker in London in the early autumn."

"Pre-season. You'd get better prices in Melton later."

She put down her knife and fork with the food reduced to tiny portions, but still on the plate. "There are plenty of gentlemen who know the quality of Foy horses and will buy on the name alone. They don't need to be tempted by the tricks of professional riders paid to make a poor horse look good over the sticks."

Miles put down his cup with care, lest he smash it. "I ride my own horses, Miss Monahan, or lend them to friends, and there is no trickery involved." Then he rose from the table before he lost his temper. "Speaking of horses, I must check on Argonaut. If he's damaged, there'll be hell to pay."

Annie looked up. "Have you injured a horse, Mr. Cavanagh? That is very sad. You must have Mick Flaherty see to it. He's a rare hand with anything equine."

"Thank you, Miss Monahan. He already has the handling of it."

"Oh, then it will be all right." She rose from her chair, sprinkled with cats, and wandered away. One small black cat stayed behind, however, staring at Miles as if fascinated.

Felicity rose, too, abandoning the pretense of decorous young lady. "I'm truly sorry about your horse, Mr. Cavanagh, but you shouldn't have tried to use him as defense."

"I had no way of knowing the attack wasn't murderous. I care for my horses, but not at the expense of my life."

She walked, brisk and fiery, toward the door, her demure gown transformed somehow into a provocative garment that swirled maddeningly around her shapely body. She turned at the door. "Let us speak plainly, sir. I am *not* leaving Ireland. In fact, I am not leaving this area. If you are intent upon it, you will have to truss me like a goose."

"If you act the goose, *cailín,* I will treat you like one."

She hissed, almost like a goose. "Don't try to govern me, Miles Cavanagh. I am *not* a 'little girl.' I am a dangerous woman."

And watching her swish out of the room, Miles believed her.

He'd go odds she'd been the goose among the Farmyard Boys.

Four

Miles was still pondering these matters as he strolled down to the Shamrock to check on Argonaut. The people he passed greeted him cheerfully with no hint that they had been part of the attack the night before. He knew only too well, however, the screen the Irish peasantry could put up before authority. They didn't know him yet, and he'd get nothing out of them until they did.

It could be that none of the men touching their forelocks and wishing him good day were members of the Farmyard Boys. Often these groups came from out of an area to deliver "justice" and then dispersed, making it less easy for the authorities to find them. It generally went hard on the local people, though, since the frustrated army would turn its soldiers loose on the population in revenge.

Miles could understand the anger that drove these "patriot" groups and sympathize with the way the peasantry supported them. Ireland had been cruelly mistreated for centuries. But improvement, when it came, would be through peaceful means—legal means—not through local acts of violence. He would have thought a woman as intelligent as Felicity could see that.

In the Shamrock stables he found Mick Flaherty rubbing down a draft horse.

"Ah, good mornin' to you, your honor!" said the sturdy, middle-aged man. "And a fine mornin' it is, to be sure."

"It'll be fine if my horse is fine, Mr. Flaherty."

"I think you'll see that he is, sir," the man declared, leading the way to the stall. "Still some swelling, of course, but nothing to last. Hey, my fine fellow! You're in prime trim, aren't you?"

The last was addressed to Argonaut, who was greeting the groom with deep devotion.

Miles drew the horse's attention to himself and received a rather more offhand response. He inspected the damage and led Argonaut into the yard to study his movement. A slight hesitation, but nothing to suggest a deeper hidden injury. The groom was right. Chances were that Argonaut would heal completely.

He slipped some guineas into Mick Flaherty's hand. "Thank you. A job well done."

"Oh, 'twas nothing anyone couldn't do, your honor." But the guineas disappeared into his pocket.

"Some people just have the gift. I hope you'll continue Argonaut's care while I'm here. And if you're ever looking for work, come to Clonnagh."

"God bless you, sir, and it's an honor to be asked, Clonnagh being famous the width and breadth of blessed Ireland! But I'm set to live my life in Foy Village, as my father did, and his father before him, if the Good Lord and the English devils permit. There's no place equal to the one where a man has lived all his days."

"True enough." Miles returned Argonaut to Flaherty's care, thinking that was one of many reasons he wished his uncle, the Earl of Kilgoran, a long life. He had no wish to leave Clonnagh and take over the earl's great estate near Kilkenny. He even wished the old man would take a wife and sire an heir, though since the earl was past sixty and bedridden, it seemed unlikely.

Miles's affection for Clonnagh was another reason he encouraged his mother and stepfather to live there—to keep the house alive for the good half-a-year he tended to spend in

England, first hunting, then enjoying London or house parties in the country.

It was the hunting which mainly drew him, however, and he was reminded that a willful Irish witch seemed likely to keep him away from it.

Miles left Mick putting a new dressing on Argonaut's leg and headed for the inn, hoping to enjoy some free talk which would help him handle his problem.

The rotund young innkeeper hurried forward. "Horse well, my lord?"

"I'm no lord," Miles said with a smile, taking in the man's genuine anxiety. He, along with many others, must be wondering whether Miles was going to bring trouble on them. He switched to the Gaelic. With his casual clothes, he hoped the people here would begin to think of him as one of their own.

"I'm Miles Cavanagh of Clonnagh, grandson-by-marriage to old Leonard Monahan of Foy Hall."

The innkeeper shook his hand warmly. "Brian Rourke, sir, and honored we are to have you here."

"Thank you, Mr. Rourke. Argonaut is healing. I've arranged for your stable boy to care for him during my stay. He seems skilled."

"Indeed, sir, Mick is a rare hand with horses. Old Mr. Leonard would have him up to the hall if ever a serious problem came up. It's a gift, you know. A fairy gift."

"I have no doubt of it."

"And can I get you something for your thirst, sir? I've good ale, or some smooth whiskey."

"Ale will be welcome."

When the foaming mug was set before him, Miles took a draught and complimented the innkeeper. Then he glanced around the low-ceilinged, smoke-darkened room. This early in the day, there was only one other person there, an ancient man hunched by the peat fire.

"My father," the innkeeper said. "Hardly ever budges from the spot."

"He's fortunate to have his spot, here in the place he's lived all his life." It was a guess, but a safe one.

"True enough, sir, and I'll feel blessed to be the same in time, if the Good Lord and the English devils permit it."

It seemed a common enough phrase in these parts, but the fact they used it in front of Miles showed they were willing to trust him.

"Have you had much trouble with the English here?" he asked.

"Not much, sir, not much. We've kept pretty quiet, Saint Patrick be praised."

"A quiet life is a blessing, that's for sure." Miles took another deep draught of the rich ale. "If I were you, though, I'd not want last night's trouble-making on the doorstep."

The innkeeper became very interested in polishing a pewter pot. "Sure an' no one wants that kind of thing, sir! Terrible, terrible. And not men of these parts."

Then how did Miss Felicity Monahan come to be embroiled? Miles wondered. "I'm sure not," he said out loud. "But they must have had a reason for singling out Mr. Dunsmore."

The innkeeper shook his head. "Truth to tell, sir, Mr. Dunsmore has been singling out himself by his wicked ways ever since he came back from Dublin."

"That was recently?"

"Indeed, sir. The earth had scarcely settled on Kathleen Craig's grave than her husband was off, with as much of her money as he could get his hands on. Now he's back trying to squeeze more out of his poor tenants."

"Hence the little reminder."

The pot received another thorough polish. "I suppose that could be it, sir, indeed it could."

It was reasonable that Mr. Rourke wouldn't reveal knowledge of the attack, but Miles thought the man's doubt about the reasons behind it might be genuine.

"He's very English," he mused.

Rourke replaced the pot on a shelf and turned to lean on the bar. "That's true, sir. English through and through. But I hope no Irishman would be so un-Christian as to attack a man merely for the misfortune of his land of birth. Why at times you could be taken for English yourself!"

The blue eyes were guileless, but the words could be either a warning or a threat.

Miles deflected them with a smile. "I had the misfortune to go to school in England, Mr. Rourke, and they whip the correct tone and manners into you there. But I have not one drop of English blood in my veins."

"Ah, blessed you are, then, sir. Blessed, indeed."

So, Dunsmore's unpopularity wasn't entirely for being a harsh landlord, or even for being an English twit. So what the devil was it?

"He seemed a pleasant enough man, for an Englishman," Miles ventured.

"He has a fine polish to him, true enough," said the innkeeper blandly. "Like the shine on still water in the summer sun."

Miles choked on his ale. Pond-scum, in other words.

When he had his breath back, he said, "I understand he made a fine marriage here."

The innkeeper turned to straighten a row of tankards. "Indeed he did, sir. He does seem to have a way with the ladies."

Interesting. So there's something in the matter of Dunsmore and women. That's what Miles feared.

He fished for a bit more enlightenment. "If Miss Craig used her estate to buy a handsome man's charm, perhaps she had a fair bargain . . ."

"A fine estate for a little charm?"

It wasn't the innkeeper, though. It was a female voice behind him, also speaking the Gaelic clear and true.

Miles turned to face his ward.

"You do hold women cheap, do you not?" she accused. She was dressed now in a severely-cut, blue wool walking dress and looking *active* again. What had she been up to? Was he going to have to watch her every moment of the day and night?

"I don't hold women cheap at all, Miss Monahan. In fact, I generally find them quite expensive." At the flash in her eyes, he hastily added, "But a fine estate and loneliness is no luxury."

"No one in these parts is lonely, Mr. Cavanagh. We care for one another."

"Some people need more than the kindness of neighbors. And if you are all so considerate, why did not some other man marry Miss Craig, since it was marriage she wanted?"

Miles thought that was the end of it, but the old man by the fire let out a paper-dry wheeze of a laugh. "Marry Kathleen Craig! Ugly as the church gargoyle and a tongue like a rusty blade. And proud besides. She wouldn't take any man not of her station, and none of the gentlemen here were desperate enough."

"Hold your tongue, Mr. Rourke!" Felicity snapped. "Kathleen might not have been a charmer, but she was kind underneath. She just needed loving, rather than the treatment she received because she was bone-thin and had a cast in one eye."

Miles hid his grimace in draining the last of his ale. He was as charitable as the next man, but it would have taken more than a moderate Irish estate to tempt him to a lifetime with Kathleen Craig. The interesting question, though, was whether Felicity was defending Miss Craig or the man who had married her.

"Then," he said, "if Mr. Dunsmore offered her love and kindness, perhaps it was a fair bargain."

"Perhaps it was," Felicity said with enough firmness to suggest doubt.

Old Mr. Rourke spat into the fire. "That Dunsmore doesn't have the kindness of a sharp rock on a cold day. Spoke ill of her behind her back—and to her face, too, I wouldn't be surprised."

Miles remembered something "Joy" had said. "And yet they had a son."

"True enough, sir, true enough. And a lovely lad is young Kieran."

Felicity suddenly paced toward the small window and back again. "For Kathleen, Kieran was worth any price. Any. She didn't want marriage so much as a child, and Rupert gave her one. The last three years of her life were the happiest she'd ever known. On her deathbed, she wept because she had to leave him. Kieran, I mean . . ." Her voice faded.

"You were there?" Miles asked gently.

She turned sharply to face him. "Of course I was there. She was my friend."

It seemed a most unlikely friendship.

"On her deathbed, she begged me to watch over the child. So you see, I cannot leave him to go to England."

Miles had no intention of discussing their personal plans in front of the village gossips. He rose. "The lad has his father and doubtless a nurse or two. But we can discuss this later. Now, if you would be so kind, I'd enjoy a tour of the village."

For a moment he thought she would refuse, but with a sigh of irritation, she led the way out into the village street, giving a terse commentary as they went.

Miles found it an interesting tour, not for the village, which offered nothing unusual, but for what he learned of Felicity Monahan.

Thus far he had encountered a wanton, a shrew, and the illusion of a proper miss, but it would seem that Felicity's repertoire might include a sweet-natured lady. She was clearly held in respect and affection by the people here. Everywhere, she was met with smiles and tidbits of personal information.

Children ran to greet her, sharing small animals, pretty stones, or a piece of carefully executed handwriting.

He gathered she had started a small dame school in the village and provided the necessary books and slates.

Though his wayward ward tried to maintain a chilly facade with Miles, it proved impossible. Her hair began to spring from its tight arrangement, and her cheeks flushed with color. She would frequently turn to him with the remnants of a glowing smile, and then her beauty knocked the breath right out of him.

Lord, but she was right. She was a dangerous woman.

They left the village and walked along the lane toward the Foy Hall stables. Miles tried to preserve the joyous glow, but almost immediately Felicity reverted to chilly antagonism.

"I wonder what it is you want me to believe of you, Felicity, and why."

She continued to stare ahead. "Why should I care what you think of me, Mr. Cavanagh?"

"Now, that is a remarkably foolish question. And you are not a foolish woman."

She flashed him a look. "Faith. What an admission! I'm sure I should be flattered."

"Only if it's untrue."

A light in her eye showed enjoyment of the verbal sparring-match, but they were interrupted by the sound of wheels in the lane. They both moved to the side to let the vehicle pass, but the one-horse gig stopped and a handsome blond lad of about four shouted, "Sissity!" It didn't take genius to guess that this was Dunsmore's son, for there was a marked resemblance.

It was as if someone had lit a lamp inside Felicity. "Kieran, my poppet! How lovely to see you all unexpected." She grabbed the lad at the waist and swung him around while the middle-aged woman driving the gig smiled.

"Now," Felicity said, returning him giggling to his place, "what adventure are you on today?"

"No 'venture. Just plums."

The older lady explained. "Cook wanted more of Mrs. Dooley's pickled plums, so I volunteered to drive over. To give the lad a break, you see."

This was said with meaning, but there was no need to guess the interpretation, for the boy pushed out his lower lip and said, "Papa's in a bad mood."

Miles supposed he was. But no wonder Kathleen Dunsmore had delighted in this late-born child. He seemed a fine specimen.

No wonder Felicity was fond of him, too.

She turned to Miles, once more thawed by interaction with others. "Mr. Cavanagh, let me make known to you two of our neighbors. This fine lad is Kieran Dunsmore of Lough-carrick, and the lady is Mrs. Edey, his companion. This is Mr. Miles Cavanagh of Clonnagh, who has the great misfortune to be my guardian for a little while."

Mrs. Edey said all the right things and Kieran shook hands in a well-brought-up way, saying, "Sissity's parents are dead, sir."

"I know," Miles said.

"And her grandfather is dead."

"True enough."

"So you will look after her?"

"I'll do my best." Miles could feel the silent objection from his side.

"My mother's dead," the lad confided.

"I know. You have my condolences."

The boy looked solemnly unsure of the word, but said, "I miss her."

Miles felt a strong urge to hug him. "I'm sure you do. My father died not long ago, and I miss him."

The boy said nothing, but something in the set of his mouth implied the thought, "I wouldn't mind if *my* father died." Miles hoped this poor lad wasn't being mistreated by Dunsmore. But if he were, there was nothing an outsider could do about it.

Felicity stepped forward. "Enough of this sad talk. We mustn't keep you, but if you have time, Mrs. Edey, you must stop at the Hall on the way home. I'm sure Kieran will be ready for a cake and some milk."

The boy brightened. "Currant cake?"

She kissed his cheek. "I don't know what we have, poppet, and it's too short notice to make currant cake, even for you." She poked him gently in the tummy so he giggled. "And I don't think there's a cake made you don't like, young man!"

Mrs. Edey clicked the horse on, and the gig disappeared around a bend, the small lad twisting to wave goodbye to "Sissity." She stood waving, even after the gig had gone, a strangely bereft look upon her face.

"A fine lad," Miles said, wanting to warn her not to grow so attached to someone else's child.

"Yes, he is." Then she turned and led the way briskly into the Foy stable yard. "You wanted to see the stallions. We have two. This is Finn."

Finn was a handsome bay who appeared perfectly made and of a proud but amiable disposition. Miles wouldn't mind using him to cover some of his mares.

"And this is Brian."

Brian was a white-stockinged chestnut of equal quality but more highly strung. He moved restlessly when approached and had to be wooed into good humor. Miles liked spirit in a horse, though, as long as it was within control.

He patted the neck of the now-polite Brian. "Are they Foy horses?"

"Finn is. He's by Angus Og, who was my grandfather's pride and joy. Angus Og was just a little long in the back, though. Grandfather's attempts to correct that are scattered around Europe, and all are fine horses but short of perfect. Finn was his great success. He's out of Fionuala." She led him over to the paddock gate so they could see the mares at pasture.

Felicity gave a boyish whistle, and a solid older bay mare raised her head then trotted over with a swish of her tail. The other mares, some twenty of them, followed. Miles had the distinct impression that they wanted to race ahead to greet Felicity, but if Fionuala was trotting with dignity, they had to hold back. There was no doubt who was lead mare in this herd.

While Felicity greeted the bay, Miles made friends with some of the others, but it was clear that he was just a stopgap for yet more creatures who adored Felicity Monahan.

"They're a fine bunch. How many do you sell in a year?

Felicity began to move down the line of horses. "We generally have ten five-year-olds. Geldings and a few mares."

"The ones you don't fancy for breeding stock."

"That's right." She rubbed the ears of a white-blazed chestnut. "Eileen here has slipped two foals. We won't try to breed her again, so she'll go to England next year. I hope she goes for a hack rather than a hunter, though. I worry sometimes about the way you men ride the creatures."

She had turned to face him, and Eileen leant her head on her shoulder so he was facing two accusing females.

"I've only killed two horses in my day, and those with broken legs that could happen anywhere if a horse is ridden at more than a trot."

"It's foolishness, though, to be risking horses just to hunt down a fox that is of no use to anyone."

"Charlie's of great use to the huntsmen, since he provides the run. I confess I'm surprised, Felicity. I'd not have thought you squeamish."

She tossed her head and moved away from the fence, leading the way up to the house. "I'm not at all squeamish. But when I've seen a foal born and worked with it for years, to hear it was killed by a clumsy rider, doubtless the worse for drink, forcing it over a fence that should never have been attempted . . ."

"I feel the same way," he said quietly. "That's why I sell my animals myself. So I know the purchasers. Come to Melton with me and see how it's done."

She swung suddenly to face him. "Oh, so that's what all this is about! It will do you no good, Mr. Cavanagh. You are *not* dragging me off to Melton Mowbray, not even for a lesson in horse-trading!"

She marched up the path and Miles followed, wondering whether his guardianship did give him the right to truss her like a Michaelmas goose and carry her off to England.

"Are we in a hurry?" he asked mildly.

"Yes," she threw back. "Kieran might be waiting."

It touched his heart the way she cared about the lad, but worried him, too. He lengthened his stride to come up beside her. "If you're so keen on children, perhaps you should marry."

To his surprise, she stopped and answered quite moderately. "Perhaps I should, at that."

"What better place to go husband-hunting than Melton? It's crammed with eligible young men."

Her eyes widened in mock astonishment. "What? Try to catch the eye of a man who's surrounded by prime horseflesh? You're mad, sir! And besides, how would I find an Irish husband there? I will not marry out of Ireland."

She had him on both points. "There are some Irishmen in England now and then."

"But there are assuredly more in Ireland, aren't there? So I'll do my husband-hunting here."

She turned and swept toward the house. As they entered through a conservatory in which the only healthy plant was catnip, Miles had the distinct feeling he'd lost that round.

To Felicity's disappointment, Kieran wasn't at Foy yet, but she used his imminent arrival as an excuse to go to her room and change out of her dusty gown. In truth, she wanted to escape Miles Cavanagh.

Damn the man. He seemed to have her constantly teetering on the edge of disaster. And damn her grandfather for changing his will at the last moment. She could have handled Uncle Colum as easily as she had always handled her father's family.

She wasn't at all sure she could handle Miles Cavanagh.

She gave the bell-rope a sharp tug. A clever, strong-willed guardian could ruin everything, and the consequences didn't bear thinking of.

She caught sight of wind-wild hair in the mirror and pulled out pins and combs, admitting she could have liked Miles if they'd met in other circumstances. He was a fine figure of a man—not that fancy handsomeness that Dunsmore was so proud of, but with robust, practical looks that appealed greatly to her. Clear blue eyes ready to laugh, red-gold hair with a crisp curl to it, and a square jaw that spoke of firmness.

Of course, the last thing she wanted in a guardian was firmness.

She began to drag a brush through her tangled curls, telling herself that Miles had a bit too much of the English about him. But her heart told her he was as Irish as soft mist on green grass, and just as pleasant.

After all, he could have made a great deal of trouble about what had happened last night. He could have been even more unpleasant about her own part in it. He'd harangued her finely, but today he'd not mentioned it at all.

Of course that could mean that, man-arrogant, he assumed a few sharp warnings would scare her off.

She attacked her hair sharply enough to bring tears to her eyes, muttering to herself about yet another disastrous turn of fate. Dunsmore, Kathleen, Kieran, Miles . . .

Why?

Why?

She wouldn't say she'd always been a saint, but she'd never

done anything to warrant the pain she'd suffered and the terrible problems that plagued her now.

She sighed and put down her brush. There was no purpose in going over the past. It was the future that mattered. The future and her plans. Miles Cavanagh could not be allowed to ruin them.

Where the devil was Peggy? She tugged the bell-rope again, then paced the room, trying to think of ways to bend her guardian to her will. One way came to mind, and she assessed her charms in the mirror with an objective eye. She knew her lush figure attracted men—seemed to turn them into cock-driven idiots, in fact—but she'd never deliberately used it against them.

Until last night, of course.

She turned red at the thought and covered her cheeks with her hands. Jesus and Mary, what must he think of her, acting the strumpet like that? She'd virtually thrust her half-naked breasts in his face. She'd let him . . .

The memory of his hand on her breast started a tingle there all over again.

She spun away from the mirror. She wasn't a wanton. She wasn't! She'd been playing a part to help her friends because they had been trying to help her.

And she hadn't liked a single moment of it.

She hadn't.

She'd only played that game because an innocent man had been caught in the net she'd laid for Dunsmore and she'd felt she must set him free without endangering her friends. It had seemed a good idea at the time to befuddle him with lust, and Denzil and some others had been close by in case of trouble . . .

She gave up on Peggy and twisted to undo the buttons down the back of her gown.

She'd been confident last night that her status made her safe from English tyranny, but she had to admit that Miles's warning made sense.

Why, not many years before, when some Irish had tried to side with the French in the war, hadn't the English flogged and tortured innocent people—including women—just to squeeze out fragments of information that might lead to the capture of the insurrectionists?

She stopped struggling to reach the middle buttons, wondering what it would be like to be tied to a tree, stripped to the waist, and flogged.

It was beyond her, and she prayed it always would be.

Then Peggy hurried in and set down a jug of warm water. Ignoring Felicity's scold for taking so long, she quickly unfastened the rest of the buttons and stripped off the blue gown. "Master Kieran's just arrived, miss, as fine as ever."

Felicity forgot servant discipline and hurriedly washed, reminded of why she must persuade her unwelcome guardian to leave her here in peace. By heaven, she wished her life were as simple as it had been two months ago. Before Kathleen died. Before Dunsmore returned to make everyone miserable. Before her grandfather changed his will.

She couldn't leave Ireland when it meant leaving Kieran to his father's uncertain mercies. She simply couldn't!

For Kieran Dunsmore was her own son.

She heard his voice in the hall and let Peggy toss her beige gown over her head and tighten the laces. Then she tied her hair back with a ribbon and ran down the stairs.

Five

In the spacious entrance hall, Miles tossed a soft ball back to young Kieran, surprised to find himself enjoying the lad's company. At the sound of light footsteps, he looked up to see Felicity flying down the stairs, face aglow with joy. Her beauty staggered him, but such radiance should not be summoned by another woman's child. It was a path to sorrow.

A few days ago he had not known Felicity. Now her welfare was a pressing concern. Did all guardians come into their responsibilities so forcefully?

As they took tea and enjoyed crisp ginger fairlings, he observed Felicity with the child and strengthened his resolve. He must get her away from Ireland and Kieran Dunsmore.

Even if Felicity had promised to watch over the child, she shouldn't devote the best years of her life to him. After all, she could do nothing practical for Kieran. If Dunsmore mistreated his son, she was powerless.

Then he thought of the attack the night before. Had that been Felicity's response to some cruelty of Dunsmore's? A shiver went down his spine. If so, she wasn't entirely powerless, but what risks she ran!

He studied the lad, who was happily building with some blocks of wood. He was rosy-cheeked and ready with a laugh and chatter. Clearly he was coming to no great harm.

Gardeen had taken advantage of Miles's thinking to curl in his lap. Miles removed her, resolving to take Felicity away from Foy, away from the Dunsmores, and away from danger. Forcibly if necessary.

Before resorting to force, however, he would try reason and charm, even though it would mean staying at Foy longer than he'd intended.

So, over the next few days, Miles said no more of his plans to take Felicity to England. Instead, he played the amiable houseguest, but in a way that meant they spent time together.

When Felicity rode out on business, Miles accompanied her to see more of the area. When she walked to the village, he carried her basket. He tried not to give the impression that he was guarding her, though that, too, was part of his plan.

As he hoped, it proved impossible for Felicity to maintain her artificial coldness.

They shared a passion for horses, after all, and spent much of their time in the stables supervising the management and taking part in the training. As he'd heard, when working with horses, Felicity wore breeches and rode astride.

"There's devil a bit of use in training these beasts to be lady's mounts," she said when he mentioned it. "It's not what Foy is known for."

In breeches, Miles discovered, Felicity behaved more like a man. She strode about briskly and rarely watched her tongue. He rather welcomed it, for it made it easier to ignore the shape of her in tight-fitting leather. She did not have a shape one would call boyish.

Most evenings, they sat together after dinner. He discovered, as expected, that she was skilled at chess. Her style was clever attack, his more careful strategy, but they were evenly matched.

They also shared tastes in reading, both the modern philosophers and humorous novels. Sometimes they would read to one another, taking parts. They also enjoyed music. She was skilled on the harpsichord. He could hold his own with a flute.

It was dangerous, though, this casual closeness, for Annie was not a scrupulous chaperone. She either nodded off by the fire or took herself off to bed entirely. Generally a cat or two would remain behind, and little Gardeen hardly left Miles's side; but despite the fact that Gardeen meant little guardian, the cats could hardly be depended upon to protect Felicity's virtue.

Of course, a young lady's guardian could be expected to do that, but when the guardian was only a few years older than the ward, and when he was potently aware of said ward's charms, it was not at all proper.

Miles liked and enjoyed women in all their aspects, but he couldn't remember ever responding to one as he did to Felicity. He enjoyed her company, and if she were absent, he missed her. When she was around, however, her physical presence disturbed him.

He couldn't help but be aware that she didn't favor strong corsets. In the evenings, when she leaned forward to move a chess piece, her decently covered breasts swayed slightly, begging to be touched. Memories immediately arose of those breasts only half-concealed by threadbare linen, of the weight and warm softness of them in his hands.

He wished to Hades she'd confine temptation beneath a few sturdy layers of linen and buckram.

When she stood close against the paddock fence discussing a horse's paces, he was aware of her body next to his as if they were naked. When she turned to him with a smiling comment, he was often hard-pressed not to drop a kiss on her full red lips.

He began to avoid touching her because he could not be sure one touch would not lead to more.

Miles's initial impulse to reject the guardianship had been selfish, but now he lay awake at nights thinking that an honorable man would back out of this situation before he behaved improperly. He couldn't help thinking, too, that having done so, an honorable man would be free to pay proper court to his one-time ward. He could kiss those tempting lips, if she'd permit it, touch that sensuous body . . .

But the same arguments held. By the time the legalities were sorted out, Felicity would have come of age anyway. And he couldn't leave her affairs in limbo now he knew the dangers surrounding her.

No wonder Leonard had changed the guardianship at the last moment. Colum would be no hand at this.

In his saner moments, Miles told himself he'd no desire to court Felicity Monahan anyway. True, she had the power of Deirdre and Grania, Irish beauties who had driven men mad. She also had the added attraction of intelligence and humor often missing in those ancient heroines. But she was so damnably willful and inclined to plunge into danger.

And, after their first encounter, he very much doubted she was as pure and innocent as she should be. The future Countess of Kilgoran should be above reproach.

Add to these problems Felicity's possible involvement in Irish sedition, and a wise man would flee to the Antipodes before becoming involved with the wench.

Tossing and turning in the night, Miles convinced himself that his best course was to get Felicity to England and hope a firm-handed but fair Englishman would marry her and keep her there, well out of trouble's way.

So, walking on eggshells, Miles spent two weeks teaching Felicity to trust and like him, while watching her carefully to be sure she wasn't plotting with the Farmyard Boys or any other unruly elements.

Kieran visited most days, inevitably causing Felicity to melt into almost motherly delight. At least there was no evidence of any brutality by his father, though Miles heard rumors in the village that Dunsmore was back at his old tricks, threatening rent-raises and refusing to pay tradesmen's bills.

Miles shrugged such matters off. Let the Farmyard Boys

handle it if they wanted, just as long as they didn't involve him or Felicity again.

Once it became known that Miles was in the area, the local gentry paid calls and left cards. Soon there were invitations, too, and evenings spent at local houses. These bucolic affairs were not precisely to Miles's taste, especially as there always seemed to be a large number of bright-eyed misses waiting to be introduced to the heir to Kilgoran.

Driving home in the carriage one night, Miles said to Felicity, "There do seem to be a remarkable number of pretty young ladies in this locality. Is it something in the water?"

Annie snored contentedly in the corner, her bonnet skewed one way, her frilled cap the other.

Felicity chuckled. "Sure, it's something in Foy Hall, not the water! Hasn't every family in Ireland with a connection in the area sent their prettiest contender to visit? One day soon, you'll be finding a lost slipper on the steps, Prince Charming, and be expected to go around searching for a foot to fit in it."

"Lord save me! Just as long as they don't start chopping off their toes in the cause."

"And here I was thinking you men enjoy seeing women torture themselves for your sake."

It was the first time she'd expressed her supposed antipathy to men. "Now why would you think that?"

She looked away, out at the dark countryside. "Isn't it true?"

"Not in your case. You're a grand heiress. Men will chop off their toes to win you."

She looked back then. "Would you?"

He couldn't read the meaning of the challenging question. "You forget. I'm your guardian."

"I don't forget." It was the merest whisper. After a moment, she added, "I wish I were not so rich."

"Wealth is not a burden if used well. It can be used to benefit others."

It was as if she shook herself out of melancholy. "Yes, of course. That's how I intend to use my fortune. And very soon."

"You don't have free use of it until you're thirty," he reminded her.

"Or until my marriage."

"But it will still be under the terms of the trust your grandfather set up, with your husband as trustee. What is it you are so keen to do? I'm sure money could be released now—"

"It will wait."

Miles had the distinct feeling that he would not approve of these good works. What did she have planned? The financing of an armed rebellion?

"I'm not an unreasonable man, Felicity. Why not tell me what you want to do? Don't marry just to get access to your money. A man you think would make a malleable husband and trustee could surprise you."

She looked at him across the shadowy carriage. "Nothing men do could surprise me."

It hardly seemed an appropriate comment for a proper young lady.

Eventually Felicity had to carry through on her offer to hold an entertainment at Foy Hall in Miles's honor. "We might as well make it a grand one," she muttered rather ungraciously one evening, "and hold a ball. You are, after all, the heir to Kilgoran."

"And it's a true albatross around my neck, I assure you. Why not just have a small dinner?"

It was one of the dangerous occasions. Annie had retired to her room straight after dinner, and Felicity was curled up in a big chair, her hair entirely loose around her shoulders, a big black cat in her lap. There was only the light of two candles and the fire to break the intimacy of darkness. Miles wanted, with alarming power, to take her on his lap and ravish her.

He rather hoped the cat was there to oppose such an act.

She appeared unaffected by their situation. "A small dinner?" she echoed with a grin. "But that would deprive all those imported hopefuls of the opportunity to dance with you! No, Prince Charming, we'll clear out the hall for dancing and turn the whole house upside down in your honor. The cats will hate it." She lifted the one in her lap to face her. "Won't you, Neill?"

It miaowed, eerily as if in answer.

Miles found the Foy Hall cats rather disturbing. "Then don't try to pretend it was my idea. Since the felines rule this place, I'd doubtless be found delicately shredded one morning."

"I wouldn't say they rule it exactly, but it's true they have their say. You should get Gardeen on your side. She'll protect you."

Miles looked down at the small black cat curled by his boots. After the first day, Gardeen had made no attempt to climb on him, but like the most patient courtier, merely followed him everywhere, occasionally offering gifts—a feather, a scrap of silk, and once a half-scone which had been left under the sofa.

At least she had more taste than to bring him dead birds.

"The others would eat her," he said.

"Oh, I doubt that. Gardeen is special. For one thing, Annie doesn't seem clear where she came from. She does generally know all the cats, and who their mothers are."

Miles looked down. "A stray, eh?" On impulse—perhaps a protective one—Miles picked up the cat.

Immediately, the silver eyes opened and a quite ferocious purr began. How did a small body make such a loud noise? Gardeen so radiated triumph that Miles hadn't the heart to put the animal back on the floor. After a moment, he placed her on his lap.

Felicity chuckled. "She's won you over at last, has she? A persistent female will always win, you know."

For the first time, Miles wondered whether Felicity was stalking him just as Gardeen had. Perhaps these disingenuously intimate evenings were no accident at all.

"Don't bet your all on it," he said, enjoying the warm silkiness of Gardeen's fur. "I merely took your advice and recruited a feline ally."

Felicity smiled in a strangely cat-like way. Miles reminded himself that she claimed to be a dangerous woman, and he believed her. It would be a serious mistake to forget that fact.

The next day, Felicity was not at breakfast. Miles was alarmed until he heard she had eaten earlier and was now in the library. After taking his own meal, he went to find her, trailed by a smug little cat who pranced along, jaunty tail announcing to the household that she'd caught a particularly fine prey.

Females!

In the library he found Felicity at the desk looking unusually flustered. Her long hair was escaping in coiling tendrils around her flushed cheeks and her fingers were inky.

He picked up Gardeen and strolled over. "You look like a schoolgirl slaving over a primer, *cailín.*"

She scowled up at him. "This is all your fault, Miles Cavanagh!"

"Now how do you come to that conclusion?" He picked up a paper and saw it was a letter of invitation, carefully written in reasonably neat handwriting. The problem, he assumed, was the number of discarded efforts scattering the floor.

"Faith, did you never go to school?"

She threw down her chewed pen. "I had a governess."

"Whom you bullied, as you've bullied everyone else in your life, so she never taught you anything useful."

She surged to her feet. *"Bullied?* Why, you wretched man, if there's a bully here, it's you. If you don't care for my penmanship, why don't you write the things yourself?"

He nudged her out of the way and took her seat, placing Gardeen on the desk, safely away from the ink. "Very well. But don't think you've been as clever as this little puss. You aren't escaping scot-free. Play to me while I scribe for you."

She swept a curtsy. "My pleasure, sir. You see, Miss Herries did teach me something useful. She just didn't place great weight on calligraphy." She sat at the harpsichord and began a sparkling performance. Three cats ran in, as some always did when she played, to leap onto the instrument and enjoy the music, tails almost seeming to sway in rhythm.

Gardeen stayed on the desk, but her tail swayed as well.

With the fire crackling merrily and music filling the air, this was one of the dangerous moments when Miles began to think fondly of living this way for the rest of his life.

He shook his muddled head, trimmed the battered pen, and began to write out the letters of invitation.

All was well until he came to one name. "You're inviting Dunsmore?"

Her clever fingers missed only one note. "It would be impolite not to."

Miles supposed that was true, but he wondered if she *wanted* to invite the man. He realized he'd been avoiding the subject altogether, hoping it would go away.

"How is Dunsmore regarded by the other gentry hereabouts?" he asked, writing the invitation. "I haven't encountered him in anyone's house."

"You know how it is. No one has a choice in neighbors, so everyone rubs along. Which doesn't mean one has to arrange to meet them all the time." The music flowed smoothly from her fingers.

"And was Kathleen more acceptable?"

"Kathleen lived here all her life."

"So, as her husband, Dunsmore was accepted everywhere?"
It was like pulling nails out of oak.

"He spent most of his time in Dublin or England."

Miles gave up and moved on to the next invitation.

He doubted he'd get much out of his ward by direct questions, but it would be interesting to see how Dunsmore behaved, and how everyone acted toward him. Miles had the feeling that Kieran's father might be an inconvenience in his life.

It would be surprising if Dunsmore were completely accepted, being a foreigner. But unless he was an outright proven scoundrel people would be civil.

Of course, Dunsmore might not attend. He must realize he was unpopular, and that the whole area would be enjoying the tale of his trouncing by the Farmyard Boys.

On the full-moon night of the ball, however, Rupert Dunsmore turned up, coolly arrogant toward his more hearty neighbors. Miles noted that he was practically ignored by the local people but treated more warmly by some of the imported hopefuls. Perhaps they were hedging their matrimonial bets.

Miles didn't at all like the look in Dunsmore's eyes when he greeted Felicity, though. It was almost proprietal. *Oh no you don't. You are not getting your hands on another heiress!*

Not that Miles could blame any man for being attracted by Felicity Monahan tonight. She normally favored serviceable garments, but she clearly had finer clothes in her wardrobe. He had been staggered by the first sight of her this evening, adorned as she was by a cream sarsenet creation, the bodice of which did not truly cover her endowments.

As if unaware of its effect, the minx had cheerfully said, "I know grandfather's death was rather recent, but he hated mourning. I stripped some trimming from this to make it plainer."

"So I see." The trimming, he suspected, had filled the low neckline.

"And I *am* wearing mother's jet beads."

Indeed she was, and wearing them in what was called the "Greek manner," which meant that the long row of square beads was clipped to the edges of her short sleeves and to the jet brooch which nestled intimately between her breasts. It gave the alarming impression of being solely responsible for keeping the dress from falling off her.

And of being inadequate for the task.

Annie had exclaimed at how fine Felicity looked and, indeed, with her hair elaborately dressed, and a black-and-silver silk shawl draped elegantly over her elbows, she was fine enough for Dublin. Miles, however, felt a powerful urge to order her to her room to change into something more suitable.

She's twenty years old, he reminded himself. *Many women are married by then.* Besides which, his brief tenure as guardian hardly required him to manage her wardrobe. The issue was settled, anyway, by the arrival of the first guests. Miles couldn't help wondering whether Felicity had timed her late entrance with that in mind.

Just what was she up to?

Seeking to attract Dunsmore?

Surely not.

Seeking to melt the resolve of her guardian?

Probably.

She'd love to be able to twist him around her lovely fingers. He still didn't know what her master plan was, but he did know that his intent to take her to England threatened it.

And he was determined to take her to England, no matter how beautiful and seductive she was.

Stepping carefully around the cats which continued to attend Annie, Miles went to greet Dunsmore and draw him away from Felicity toward the punch bowl. A soft brush near his ankles told him he had his own small, black attendant.

Damnation, he'd locked Gardeen in his bedroom.

"Cavanagh," Dunsmore acknowledged, with a smiling nod, though the smile didn't reach his eyes and looked more like a sneer. Either he did despise his present company or he had a most unfortunate facial tic.

Miles kept a cheerful smile in place and picked up Gardeen before she was trodden on. "I've had the good fortune to meet your son, Dunsmore. A fine lad."

At the sight of the cat, Dunsmore stepped back. "Kathleen and I were very fortunate to have such a son." Miles noted then that he was warily tracking the various cats as if he expected them to attack him.

One of the men by the punch bowl passed Dunsmore a glass. "The Lord smiled on you indeed, sir. Without the child, Loughcarrick would have gone to Kathleen's cousin, Michael."

"True," Dunsmore agreed, though his jaw twitched.

That could be because of the cats, however, rather than the comment. Gardeen had established herself on Miles's shoulder, from where she was eying Dunsmore as if he were an intruding but juicy mouse.

The smiling men had similar expressions. Doubtless they did resent an outsider and an Englishman having at least temporary possession of one of the area's finest estates.

Miles made sure everyone's glasses were full. "I don't think I've met a Michael Craig. Does he live in this area?"

"No. In Liverpool." Dunsmore's gaze swept the hostile group. "So, no matter what happens, Loughcarrick will be in English hands."

"Ah, now, it's blood that counts," someone remarked.

"Indeed, it is," Dunsmore replied. "And I am proud to be of English blood."

Miles—quite sure Gardeen had just hissed—gave the man credit for courage and none for discretion. "Kieran actually holds the estate, though, and he's half-Irish, born and bred here. So all will come right in the end. Now, I hear the music starting up for dancing. I hope some of you gentlemen will

come to partner the ladies, or we have card tables set up in
the library."

That brought about a satisfactory dispersal of the group.
Miles saw Dunsmore look longingly at the card room, but
then turn toward the hall where the dancing was to take place.
He must be a desperate gamester, indeed, to be drawn to
penny-point whist with people who disliked him.

When Miles saw Dunsmore capture the first dance with
Felicity, however, he wished the man had settled for cards.

Foy Hall was not a large house, but it boasted a spacious,
open entrance hall and this had been prepared for dancing.
It could hold two sets with comfort and three if necessary.
It even had a kind of minstrels' gallery on the upper floor,
and two fiddlers and a flute player were doing their part there.

Unfortunately, there were more ladies than gentlemen interested in dancing. Miles wondered if Felicity realized she
should ensure they all had their chance. It was really Annie's
job, of course, but she was in the drawing room with friends
and cats, talking about friends and cats.

Miles plucked a small black feline off his shoulder and
held her nose to nose. "I can hardly dance with you up there,
little one. Nor can you run around the floor with all this
twirling and hopping going on. I think you should go back
to the bedroom."

This time the hiss was unmistakable.

"I suppose it's the music that appeals to you. If I put you
in the gallery, will you stay there and behave yourself?"

Taking the twitch of a tail and the lack of a hiss as assent,
Miles carried the cat up to the little balcony and placed it
by the flute-player, who grinned understandingly.

"There. You can even guard me from here and leap down
if necessary to rescue me from the toils of some other determined female."

The cat immediately leapt onto the balcony ledge and took
up what looked like a guarding pose.

Kitten *couchant*.

Miles returned below, convinced Foy Hall was finally driving him mad. Not mad enough to haunt his seductive ward, however. Instead, he did his duty by asking the plainest wallflower to dance.

Six

Nuala Yeates was a sturdy girl and rather dull in conversation, but she danced with vigor and enjoyment, so Miles was not displeased. When the dance ended, he made sure to stand and chat with another couple so that when he asked that lady to dance, her partner had little choice other than to ask Nuala to honor him with the set. Beyond that, she would have to take her chances.

He worked in this conscientious manner until supper was served and felt he had earned his refreshment.

A glance showed him Gardeen still patiently on watch, which Miles assumed to mean that he hadn't done anything too foolish yet. Then he shook his head at his nonsense and went off to enjoy duck, roll-mops, shrimp, and delicious cakes.

After supper, his willpower failed and he snared Felicity for a dance. She let herself be captured, but then said, "Do you know, I am far too stuffed with pickled herring and cake to romp for a while. Why don't we sit and talk?"

There were no seats in the hall and so he moved toward the drawing room, but she grasped his sleeve. "Not in there." She led the way to the wide stairs curving up from the hall, and he saw a number of couples sitting there. Felicity found a space and subsided in a swirl of cream sarsenet and rose perfume, one he remembered all too well.

"You don't have parties like this at your home?" she asked.

"My parents held dinners. A ball was rare. Why do you ask?"

Her eyes twinkled with mischief. "You're working too hard."

"I beg your pardon?"

"You seem to think people need organizing. I don't know what it's like around Clonnagh, but here people just need food, drink, and music and they'll make their own enjoyment. You, dear guardian, are being extremely *Sasanach* tonight."

Miles didn't appreciate the rebuke. "Is it English to be kind? If I hadn't asked Miss Yeates to dance, she'd doubtless have been standing by the wall all night."

"Nuala? Nonsense. Everyone likes Nuala. She was just waiting her turn. Now, if you're feeling noble, you could befriend Miss Hill and Miss Manning."

To his irritation, Miles realized that the two prettiest girls— two of the imported beauties—had been sitting out most of the evening.

He looked a question at Felicity and she said, "They're strangers, and they think a great deal of themselves. I've coerced some men into doing the pretty, but enough is enough."

"Very well, I'll dance with the pretty wallflowers, but only if you dance with me first."

Felicity flicked open her jet fan and peeped over it coquettishly. "But sir, is it proper?"

"Assuredly. I'll be protecting you from baser men."

"Baser? But they've been friends since I was a child."

"Believe me, Felicity, that gown could turn your closest friend into the basest villain known."

"Really?" She swept the fan down and aside, looking at the revealed flesh as if surprised—thus drawing his eyes to follow the same path until he realized it and looked up again.

To see laughter in her eyes.

"Damnation," he said without heat. "What are you up to now?"

"Amusing myself."

At that moment, Gardeen arrived and leaped into Miles's lap.

On guard? But guarding whom?

Felicity raised the fan again so only her eyes peeped over the top. "Perhaps I'm husband-hunting, guardian dear. If I want control of my money before thirty, I must have a husband."

Miles stroked Gardeen, hoping she was a talisman against rampant lust. "Let me take you to England, then. There's more selection there."

The dark eyes turned watchful. "I wish to marry a local man."

He looked down at the dancers. "If this is the best the area has to offer, *cailín*, your choice is limited. There's few enough who are single, and it's clear why they are languishing on the vine."

She closed the fan with a snap, playfulness done with. "Better the devil I know."

"Better no devil at all. Felicity, let me guide your choice."

"I don't think so." Then she spread her fan again and peeped over the lacy edge. "Are you sure you don't want to marry me yourself, Miles Cavanagh?"

In a deliberate imitation, Miles raised the cat and peered between silky ears. "Yes."

She flushed and lowered the fan. "Why not?"

"Are your feelings hurt? Perhaps I want a better housekeeper."

"Then you should hire one!"

Her eyes were bright with anger. It would be interesting to see those eyes flashing with warmer emotions. . . .

Miles lowered the protective cat and stroked her. "Ah, but I'm a niggardly fellow, my dear, and would prefer to get one free through marriage."

"In that case, I'd think an heiress would be of great interest."

Miles turned Gardeen and addressed her. "Faith, but I think

the woman is after me in truth! First, she flaunts that creamy bosom. Now, she flaunts her wealth." He looked back at his red-faced ward. "Try me again when you're of age, my dear, and I'll consider the offer."

She closed the fan and rapped it hard across his knuckles. "Oaf!"

But she immediately controlled herself, which was both interesting and alarming. He wasn't sure he knew the real Felicity, or what game she was playing.

The music paused and she rose. "You requested a dance, sir, I believe." Without looking back, she headed down to the hall in a swish of silk. Miles returned his feline protector to the music gallery and then followed at his leisure.

Felicity awaited him, her foot tapping with impatience.

The music started for a line dance, and they joined in. Perhaps because of the trace of anger still in Felicity's eyes, Miles was struck again by her beauty. She was certainly no milk-and-water miss. She was strong, brave, clever, kind. . . .

Desirable.

Perhaps he should have kept the cat to hand.

If Felicity had planned to stir his lustful attentions this evening, she was being completely successful.

The dance involved a lot of swinging, and he soon found himself touching Felicity more than he had since that first night. Then he realized she was using the dance to press and rub against him. With another type of woman, he'd think he was being primed for a night of pleasure, but Felicity wasn't that type.

Or was she?

He remembered Joy.

Angered by her behavior, he crushed her tight against him and nipped sharply at her earlobe. Spinning her free, he said, "Don't play with the animals, *cailín*. They have sharp teeth."

She was angry, but she was also shocked. That convinced him of her fundamental innocence. Devil take it, she had to be stopped from playing these games before some man took advantage.

The dance over, he saw her safely partnered with a middle-aged man and asked the beautiful Miss Hill to be his partner. Despite physical perfection and a determined effort to please—and the fact that she was doubtless highly trained in domestic management—Miss Hill did not stir his interest at all.

Miles stole a look up at Gardeen's ledge to see the cat cleaning herself. Obviously, Miles was safe. . . .

Faith, if he kept up this fancy, he'd be believing it!

But when the set ended, Miles realized Felicity was no longer in the hall.

At first, he was not concerned, for there were doubtless many tasks requiring her attention. Even so, he needed to know where she was.

She wasn't in the drawing room with the older ladies and cats, or in the card room. She wasn't in the refreshment room or on the stairs. She wasn't dealing with some domestic emergency.

There was a sharp frost, so she would hardly be in the garden.

There were few remaining possibilities, and one alarmed him.

He went to her bedroom door.

Miles had never been in Felicity's bedroom and hesitated to intrude. As he debated it, however, Gardeen appeared and wove around his ankles, miaowing. Taking that as a sign, Miles knocked. When there was no answer, he turned the knob and walked in.

Felicity was there, standing far too close to Rupert Dunsmore. They turned, both wearing insolently disdainful expressions.

"What the devil are you doing here, Dunsmore?" Miles asked.

"Miss Monahan invited me," the man replied, taking out a gold snuffbox and inhaling a pinch of the powder.

"Felicity?"

She tossed her head. "Heavens above, Miles, are you going to play the grim guardian? I wanted to talk to Mr. Dunsmore about Kieran, that's all."

"In your bedroom?" There was no evidence, but Miles would bet Argonaut that these two had kissed in this room. Felicity had invited Dunsmore here and let him kiss her?

His hands became fists.

She sighed with impatience. "The house is full of people and we wanted privacy."

"I'm sure your discussion could have waited until tomorrow." Miles stepped back from the door. "I believe you wish to leave, Dunsmore."

Dunsmore eyed him with considerable hostility. "But that would leave Felicity here alone with you, sir."

"I am her guardian."

"A laughable conceit."

"Not at all. It is both full and legal. And as her guardian, I might rethink my tolerance of your improper behavior and make this a matter for pistols."

"Well, really!" Felicity exclaimed.

"Be quiet," Miles snapped.

"I might welcome that," said Dunsmore icily.

"I certainly would."

Felicity stepped forward. "I *won't* be quiet. I forbid you to fight over me!"

Miles ignored her, keeping his eyes on Dunsmore. He wanted the man absolutely certain that if he took one more irregular step with Felicity, he'd die.

Perhaps Dunsmore understood the message, for he wet his finely shaped lips. "Since Miss Monahan does not wish any fuss, I will avoid it. This time."

"Very wise."

As Dunsmore walked toward the door, Gardeen leaped onto the back of a nearby chair and hissed. The man jumped with alarm, then snarled back at the cat before hurrying on his way.

Miles closed the door and faced his ward.

"This is most improper," Felicity said, color high. "To be in here with the door shut . . ."

"It was even more improper to be in here with Dunsmore."

"I'd trust him rather more than you!"

"And what have I done to deserve that?"

"You *bit* me!"

"That was a warning, not a seduction."

She looked at him with troubled eyes. "You want me."

"No—"

"Don't deny it! I can sense it." She ran her fan nervously through her hand. "It . . . it unnerves me."

She was right, damn it. "Dunsmore wants you, too."

"Not in the same way."

Had she been in here with Dunsmore because she felt *safe* with him? She needed some wits shaken into her.

"Felicity, you're a very attractive, very rich woman, and many men will want you. Yes, in a sense I want you, but I won't attack you. I won't even try to seduce you. I wouldn't say as much for Dunsmore."

"He won't attack me either."

"Damn-it-all, are you blind?"

"He won't attack me because he won't need to." She raised her chin. "I will kiss him willingly. Anywhere, anytime."

Miles sucked in air, feeling as if he'd been punched. "As you were doing before I intruded?"

"Exactly." But she turned away to look into the dancing flames in her fireplace.

"Felicity, Dunsmore's no catch."

She spun back. "Don't try to make these decisions for me. I know what I want."

"You know nothing! What's the appeal of the man? He's handsome enough, but cold as a fish and has scarce a penny to bless himself with other than his son's money." Miles stopped dead. "That's it, isn't it? Kieran."

"That's what?" But she wouldn't look at him.

"You're trying to marry Dunsmore so as to look after Kieran."

Her color betrayed her. "And what is wrong with that?"

"Everything! Hell and the devil, Felicity, even if you marry the man, you can't protect the child. If Dunsmore decides to thrash Kieran every day, or send him away to the cruelest school in the land, you won't be able to stop him. If you were to try to take the matter to court, your position would be impossible. You'd only be his stepmother. And in the meantime, you'd be Dunsmore's wife. Think what that means!"

Though her deepening color spoke of her agitation, she kept her eyes wide and steady on his. "You mean the marriage bed? I'm sure Rupert is an excellent lover."

"I doubt that. He's not a man to be kind once the courting's over. Think of his behavior to his first wife."

"Kathleen said he was a lusty lover."

"Doubtless trying to get her with child so as to have a claim to her estate."

"Whatever the cause, she had no complaint except that he ceased his attentions after . . . after Kieran."

"Dammit, Felicity, she had no business speaking of such matters to a young girl."

"Oh, for heaven's sake, why should she be mealymouthed? I've held the mares for covering. I'm no swooning innocent. I would have thought that after our first encounter you'd know that. In full knowledge, I plan to marry Rupert Dunsmore. So, can we have an end to this matter of dragging me off to England? It will do no good and I would prefer to marry Rupert immediately."

"Good or not, you are coming to England with me, Felicity. You need to meet some real men."

She slapped the fan into the palm of her hand. "I don't need to meet *real men*. I am sure you think of yourself as a *real man.* I've met you, and it hasn't changed my mind at all!"

She would have swept out of the room, but he seized her arm and dragged her close. "Perhaps you need more than a mere meeting, then, to see Rupert Dunsmore for what he is."

She twisted angrily. "Are *you* going to show him up? But, no. You're my guardian, and you take your role so *seriously.*" Her tone was scathing, and her eyes shot magnificent rage.

"Since you won't be guarded by me, it's a lost cause." He spun her onto the bed and crushed her beneath him. She fought with every inch of her strong body, but he pinned her down ruthlessly. She tried to scratch, so he captured her hands.

"Get off me, you foul, pox-ridden—"

He silenced her with his lips. She bit him, and he jerked back with a hiss. She twisted again and almost won free, but he regained his hold.

A burning pain shocked him back to his senses.

He saw a row of deep scratches on his hand, already beading blood, and a small cat hissing inches from his nose. Horrified by his actions, Miles loosed his bruising grip and eased off Felicity, half-expecting to be clawed by her, too.

She slithered off the far side of the bed, rubbing her bruised wrists, hair and eyes wildly disordered. "Try something like that again, Miles Cavanagh, and I'll put a pistol ball where it'll do the most good. On the Cross of St. Patrick, I swear it!"

She scrambled to her feet and ran from the room. Miles collapsed into a chair, staring at an agitated black cat.

"And by the Cross of St. Patrick, Gardeen, I'd deserve it. Thank you, little guardian."

Felicity watched from nearby until she saw Miles leave. Then she ran back into her room, slammed the door, and locked it.

She collapsed onto the bench before her mirror and tried to pin her hair back into order. Her shaking hands were useless, however, and she sank her head onto them, fighting tears.

She would not cry over any man, particularly not one like Miles Cavanagh.

It had been as much her fault as his, though. She shouldn't have played with him as she had earlier, but it had been as if a wildness had seized her, commanding that she prove she could stir him as a man.

A sob escaped as she thought of what might have been. Imagine if they had met more casually, he the stepson of her uncle, paying a visit to Foy Hall; she a simple, well-bred young lady. Then, their teasing conversations, their intertwining music, their moments of understanding could have been so precious.

If she'd flirted with him, then, and he'd reacted with that hot, intent look, they could have kissed. They could have touched. . . .

Imagine if she'd been worthy of an honest man.

Imagine if she'd never met Rupert Dunsmore.

She pushed violently to her feet and paced the room.

Damn Rupert Dunsmore to hell.

He was desperate, though, and turning the screws. A week ago, he'd stopped Kieran's visits. Tonight, he'd told her he'd spanked the boy for insolence before leaving the house.

The thought of her beloved son crying under that treatment broke her heart, particularly as the cause had been nothing the child had done, but her own actions.

She stopped her pacing and tried for perhaps the millionth time to see some way out of the morass other than marriage to a man she despised. But for the millionth time, she failed.

A mere child of fifteen, ill-guarded and not advised at all, she had let Rupert Dunsmore seduce her. She'd believed his tale of a miserable marriage. She'd believed his promise that she'd never become pregnant by him. When she'd found her-

self with child, she'd believed his protestations of guilt and
repentance and let him and her grandfather save her from the
consequences.

She'd actually been *grateful* at the time!

They'd arranged for her to visit "relatives in England" accompanied by Miss Herries. At the same time, Rupert had
taken his "pregnant" wife to Cheltenham. In due course, the
Dunsmores had returned in triumph to Loughcarrick with a
healthy son.

Some time later, Felicity had returned with a fine new
wardrobe and tales of the pleasures of England to support
her long absence. Some people, she remembered, had remarked that England did not seem to have agreed with her.

Losing her child had not agreed with her, but life had improved. Once sure Felicity did not intend to snatch the boy
back, Kathleen had welcomed her at Loughcarrick and Felicity had come to know her son. Poor Kathleen had been so
utterly devoted to Kieran, and so deeply grateful for "the gift
of him" as she put it, that Felicity's pain had been soothed.

Since Rupert was generally absent, enjoying life in Dublin
or London, and Kathleen was always pleased to have Felicity
visit, life had settled into a tolerable pattern. Over the years,
as Kieran's honorary aunt, Felicity had felt blessed to have
such a happy outcome to her folly.

If only Kathleen had not died.

Felicity had been genuinely grieved simply because she had
come to like the brusque woman. She had not realized at
first how Kathleen's death would ruin her own life.

Would Rupert have sought her in marriage without her
newfound fortune? She'd never know the answer to that. She
only knew that once Rupert discovered she was an heiress,
he had been relentless.

Oh, at first he tried to sugar it with protestations of devotion, claiming he had always loved her and only been restrained by his marriage vows. Felicity was no longer a naive
fifteen, however, and she had long since realized that he had

deliberately set out to gain the child he needed if he were to have a life-interest in Kathleen's estate.

He had stalked Felicity because she was wild enough to be accessible, but well-born enough for her family to be desperate to avoid scandal.

His plan had been completely successful, but she had no mind to add to it by giving him control over herself and her inheritance.

That was when he had pointed out the consequences of refusal.

"My dear Felicity, I am a lusty man. If you do not marry me, I shall have to marry elsewhere."

"Then do so, with my blessing." She had agreed to meet him in a coppice between their estates and now turned to remount her horse.

"That will make some other woman Kieran's mother."

That did cause a pang. "Kathleen was Kieran's mother as far as the world knew."

"But my new wife would not know the truth, and would not welcome your haunting of Loughcarrick." He smiled thinly. "I'd make sure of it. In fact, I'd probably move my family away."

It was a blow to the heart. "You . . . you *weasel!* Have you no thought of your son's happiness?"

He seized her arm in a cruel grip. "No thought at all. In fact, my dear, Kieran could die tomorrow without my shedding a tear. My life-interest in the estate would not be affected, you know."

It was a threat, like a knife set cold against the throat. "What do you want?"

"You in my bed. Your fortune in my hands. I know it's tied up in a neat trust, but once you marry, you will have control of it with only your husband as trustee." He relaxed his hold to stroke her neck. "Ideal, don't you think?"

She twisted free. "And what will you do when you've run through it?" She rubbed her bruised arm, sickened at the thought of marriage to this swine. "I'd be astonished if it lasted a decade!"

"Perhaps I'll let you be frugal for us, Felicity. If you please me, in bed and out." It was an invitation to slavery, with the constant threat to Kieran to keep her in line. "My creditors are somewhat pressing," he continued. "We must marry now. I'm sure Leonard will agree if handled right. . . ."

But her grandfather, bless him and curse him, had not agreed. For once, he'd turned unmovably stubborn and her pestering had, perhaps, contributed to the seizure that had led to his death.

A death which had left her in the power of Miles Cavanagh, who seemed determined to prevent her marriage to Rupert at all cost.

She paced the room again. She knew as well as Miles that her powers as Rupert's wife would be limited and her duties unpleasant, but she had to believe Kieran's life would be better than if she refused.

Angered, Rupert was capable of whipping Kieran daily until the blood ran. He could even kill him if he thought he'd get away with it.

Once in funds again, however, he'd be off to Dublin or London, to his drinking, whoring, and gaming. As long as the funds lasted, she and Kieran would be left in peace, and to be Kieran's mother in the eyes of the world was worth any sacrifice.

And perhaps, if matters became truly impossible, she would find the courage to kill the weasel.

She'd taken a loaded pistol to one of their meetings, planning to put a ball into his heart. She'd even drawn the pistol when he'd turned his back. When she'd cocked it, he'd spun to face her, turning pallid with fear.

But, damn her paltry spirit, she'd not been able to squeeze the trigger and deprive a man of his life.

She'd cursed her weakness then, and cursed it now, but it seemed she did not have the nerve for cold-blooded murder.

Which left only marriage.

Taking a deep, steadying breath, she sat at her mirror again and rearranged her hair. Then she wiped her face with a cool cloth and went downstairs to attend the closing hour of a truly disastrous evening's entertainment.

Seven

By the next morning, an observer might have assumed that Miles Cavanagh and Felicity Monahan had overindulged in inebriating liquids. In Miles's case, the truth was that he'd hardly slept. Perhaps the shadows under Felicity's eyes were from the same cause.

Normally she had a hearty appetite, and he hated to see her push ham and eggs around her plate, then make do with a piece of toast. He wanted to reassure her that she need not fear him, but Annie was at the table working her way through a plate-load of food.

Annie suddenly looked up. "You're very quiet, you two. Usually, it's chatter, chatter. It's all that dancing. Worn you out."

"You could be right, Aunt," said Felicity, wilting slightly. "I think I should rest." She drifted wearily from the room, but Miles quickly followed.

"Felicity." She froze, one foot raised to climb the stairs. "We need to talk."

"We do not."

It was a choice between grovel and command, and Miles chose command. "Indeed we do. In the library. Now."

She swung around. "How *dare* you give me orders!"

"I'm your guardian, remember?"

"After last night, you have the effrontery—"

"In the library. You can berate me there."

After a moment ringing with rebellion, she marched into

the dusty room. Miles let Gardeen slip in before he closed
the door. The cat's intervention might be needed again.

Felicity faced him mutinously. "I doubt I'm safe with you."

"You'll be safe as long as you don't try my patience too
far."

"And why shouldn't I try your patience? You have mine
stretched as thin as silk!"

He prayed for control. "Felicity, I was wrong to attack you.
I apologize. It will not happen again."

"Indeed it won't, for I'll shoot you in the ballocks if it
does."

"Felicity . . ."

"Oh, stop this!" she snapped. "You thought to charm me
into doing as you wish and you failed, so, man-like, you
turned to bullying instead. Now, listen to me. I have intended
to marry Rupert Dunsmore ever since his wife's death. I am
not suffering any illusions about him. I know that is what I
want to do. It is what I *will* do as soon as I am of age. You
are just making difficulties for nothing."

He leaned back against the desk to steady himself. "Why
the hurry. Are you pregnant?"

She flushed, then said, "Yes."

"You're lying."

"No, I'm not. I'm pregnant, and I want to marry Rupert
before it becomes a scandal in the area."

"If you marry Dunsmore, it'll be a scandal in the area,
babe or not. Very well. We'll have the doctor in. If he con-
firms that you're with child, I'll authorize the wedding."

She hissed with annoyance and tossed her head. "Oh, all
right. I lied. But it's an excellent notion. It shouldn't take too
much effort to make the lie true."

He gripped the edge of the desk until his fingers hurt. "It
will take magical powers. You're confined to the house unless
accompanied by me."

She paced the room like a caged animal. "You have no
right to do this, no right! You know nothing of me, nothing

of my life or what I want." Then she stopped suddenly and seemed to collect herself. She looked at him with what appeared to be honest intensity. "With my eyes open and my wits about me, Miles, I want to marry Rupert Dunsmore."

Her control helped him to calm. "Because of Kieran. I do understand. But I won't let you do that to yourself."

Tears welled in her eyes, and it was the first time he'd seen her cry. "Please," she whispered.

He would have given her almost anything to ease that misery, but this one thing he could not give. "No."

"Then damn you to hell," she said flatly and walked out of the room.

Gardeen gave a snarling miaow, but Miles was not sure whom she was berating.

Probably both of them.

He rubbed his hands over his face, feeling as bruised as if he'd gone a round with Jackson. He could believe Felicity's desperation, but he could not let her throw her life away in such a cause. Dunsmore was doubtless threatening the child, but Miles still could not let Felicity sacrifice herself. It would be like letting someone run back into a burning building to rescue a child already beyond hope.

There was nothing for it. He had to get her away from here.

He gave her a day, keeping a wary eye on her from a distance. Then, as a first stage toward detaching her from Dunsmore, he suggested a visit to his home in Clonnagh.

It was dinner time, and her appetite had revived, even if her good humor hadn't. "And why should we do that?"

"Just to be sociable. My stepfather is your uncle. My mother is now your aunt."

"It's a pleasant idea," said Annie, "but I really don't care to travel. I miss my poor kitties so."

"And I can't travel without a chaperone," Felicity declared with something close to a smirk. "What a shame."

"Nonsense," said Miles. "We can travel in an open carriage. It's less than a day's journey."

He was waiting for her next objection, but was surprised.

"Very well," she said. "But we ride."

"It's a long ride for a woman."

She shot him a scathing look. "I'm no delicate blossom and I prefer to be independent."

He decided not to fight that. "Very well. Argonaut is fit and could do with a long run. What mount will you use?"

"Cresta, I think. We spoke of breeding her to your Midas in the spring, so it would be a way of getting her there."

She was so cordial Miles was suspicious. "And how would *you* get back?"

"Perhaps I'll be so worn out you'll have to send me in the carriage." Now she was almost teasing. Warning bells began to clang. "But no," she said lightly. "You must have a good mare you'd like to breed here in exchange. I'll ride it back with a groom in attendance."

Ah, now he saw the reason for her good spirits. "You mistake matters, Felicity. If you ride back, it will be with me in attendance. For the next few weeks we are inseparable."

She turned pale. "You're going to *live* here?"

"No. *You* are going to see more of the world."

She opened her mouth, then shut it with a snap. "You'll see," was all she said.

He could as well have said the same words himself. When it came to a battle of wills, he had all the weapons. Why couldn't the infuriating woman accept that?

Since war—or at least, rebellion—had been declared, Miles tried not to let Felicity out of his sight. He could not, however, watch her every second, and while he was using the privy, she gave him the slip.

But surely, he thought, as he searched for her, she could not have gone far in an indoor gown and no bonnet.

After checking the rambling house and interrogating blank-faced servants, Miles slammed a rebellious groom against the stable-wall to force him to tell all. The dratted woman had apparently ridden away bareback in her gown, showing her legs up to her garters.

Hell and the devil!

He grabbed Argonaut and set off at a gallop, reckoning he knew where Felicity had gone. But she'd outfoxed him. When he arrived at Loughcarrick he discovered she had never been there. The worst thing was that Dunsmore wasn't there, either. He'd ridden out about an hour before.

The thought that his ward might actually be with Dunsmore trying to get herself pregnant was like acid. He resolved that even if she did get with child he would not permit the marriage.

Mrs. Edey was perplexed by the whole thing. "Miss Monahan hasn't visited here since Mrs. Dunsmore died, Mr. Cavanagh. I can't imagine why you thought she might be here today."

"I must have been mistaken." He turned to take his leave, but Kieran came running.

"Is Sissity here?"

"No, pet," said Mrs. Edey, taking his hand to control him. "It's Mr. Cavanagh. You remember him."

The boy gave a rather sulky bow. "I want to see Sissity."

"Another day, dear."

It occurred to Miles then that after the early flurry of visits, Kieran hadn't been to Foy Hall in a week. "Why don't you drive over this afternoon? Felicity and I are going away for a few days, and I know she'd like to see you before we leave."

Mrs. Edey was already shaking her head in a silent signal to him. Now, she said, "I'm afraid we can't, sir. Kieran's father has forbidden him to leave the estate just now."

"It's not fair, and I hate him," the boy stated fiercely.

"Hush!" Mrs. Edey said. " 'Tis wicked to speak so, Kieran."

The lad just scowled and kicked at the polished hall floor with the toe of his sturdy leather boots.

Miles told himself he had enough to worry over without being sorry for the child caught in this sordid conflict. Presumably once it became clear to Dunsmore that he wouldn't be allowed to marry Felicity before her majority—in fact, once Felicity was safely out of his orbit—there would be no more petty tormenting of the child.

He tousled the lad's curls. "By the time Felicity is back, I'm sure your father will have lifted the restriction." No point in troubling the boy with how long that might be. A month would seem forever at his age.

As he left the house, Miles decided Kieran's welfare was yet another reason for taking Felicity to England. It would be healthier on both sides if the bond were weakened. In time, Dunsmore was going to give up and find some other woman to marry and Kieran would learn to love his new stepmother.

Miles realized then that he had no intention of ever letting Felicity marry Rupert Dunsmore. He just wished he knew how the devil he was to stop her once she was of age.

The first step was to prevent her getting pregnant.

He took Argonaut's reins from the groom and scanned the surrounding countryside. Was there any point in searching far and wide? He really couldn't imagine Felicity setting out brashly to fornicate with Dunsmore, but made himself consider where such a pair might meet.

Not in the open on a frosty day in January.

Barns and hovels, then. He spent a frustrating hour checking all the barns and abandoned cottages between Foy and Loughcarrick and found no trace of the truant lovers.

By the time he arrived in the Foy stables, he was exhausted, angry, and worried half to death. There he was met by two females. Gardeen sat stiffly on a wall, exuding all the disdain of an abandoned cat. Felicity leaned nearby, looking smug, and as fresh as if she'd not so much as mounted a horse that day.

As a substitute for laying his crop about her shoulders,

Miles said, "I saw Kieran. He very much wants to see you. Shall we ride over there, since he seems to be confined to quarters?"

She caught her breath as if he had hit her, but then masked it with a shrug. "There seems no point. I'll see him when I return. And of course, soon, we will be one family."

She turned and left the stables. Miles dismounted and tossed Argonaut's reins to a groom, wondering if she could have carried through on her threat to try to get with child. Scooping up the still-haughty cat, Miles followed his ward's path to the hall, recalling and analyzing the look of her just now.

"Not at all," he told Gardeen, "like a woman who had recently engaged in carnal intimacy in a barn."

Gardeen decided to be wooed and began to purr.

"But then," said Miles with a grimace, "she didn't look like a woman who'd been riding about the countryside in her morning dress, either. Damn the tricksy jade. She's capable of anything."

And that, of course, was what made her so fascinating.

Miles did his best to watch Felicity for the rest of the day, both guarding her and looking for signs of recent debauchery.

All he saw was a proper young lady preparing for a visit. She organized the packing of a trunk which would be driven over to Clonnagh by coach at first light, along with Miles's bags and his valet. She attended to some estate business and made sure the Foy servants had instructions. She sent out a few messages to inform people of her absence.

Miles resisted the urge to check her correspondence. The only person he cared about was Dunsmore, and any message for him had presumably been delivered in person.

With relief, he decided that her rash ride had been just that—a means of communicating with her illicit admirer. It was impossible that any woman surrender her virginity and appear so unperturbed by it.

If, of course, she was a virgin.

She must be.

Of course she must. Her boldness was just playacting.

He'd be devilish glad to have her away from here and under his mother's eye, however.

The next morning, he found her already at the breakfast table, dressed in one of her sensible habits. She showed no trace of resentment, but breakfasted heartily. Soon they rode out, hoar frost crunching beneath the horses' hooves, ostensibly in perfect accord.

Miles found this rather more wearing than sulks would be, but in the face of her good humor, it was impossible to be cool. Soon they were as relaxed as old friends again.

Somewhere inside, he knew "old friends" wasn't what he wanted at all. He smothered the notion. He cared for the girl. Nothing more.

They'd covered a mile or so, warming the horses slowly, when a *miaow!* made him look back. A black shape was racing along behind.

"Hell and the devil, it's that imp of Satan!"

Felicity reined in to look back, then laughed. "But of course! Now Gardeen's adopted you, she's not about to be left behind."

"I left her locked up in my room."

"Perhaps you have something to learn about trying to keep females captive."

Before he could respond to that, the cat arrived at the horses and leapt. She couldn't quite make his lap, but she hooked her claws into his breeches and clambered up from there.

Miles picked the cat up. "Don't you know the meaning of the word *no?*"

Gardeen gave her snarling commentary on that, on him, and on the world in general.

Felicity broke into laughter. "My, but she's a tongue on her like a fishwife. No supper for you tonight, sir!"

Miles fell into laughter, too, and putting the irate feline on his leg, smoothed her fur and her feelings. Gardeen kneaded his thigh, and he had the distinct impression she thought she was digging her claws into him. Since he was wearing leather breeches, however, he was safe enough.

He tickled her chin. "Pax, little one. I won't try to leave you behind again. How was I to know you truly wanted to leave your home? But how are you to travel?"

"Fifty years ago," said Felicity, "you would be wearing a sensible skirted coat with enormous pockets."

"Whereas, now, my only pockets are in my breeches and completely inadequate to the task. Ah, the follies of this modern age."

"I, however, choosing practicality over fashion, have very large pockets in my habit and could carry her if she'd allow it."

Though her tail twitched with suspicion, Gardeen did allow herself to be handed across and put into Felicity's pocket. Once there, however, she arranged herself nose out and fixed Miles with a watchful stare.

"Faith, what mischief does she expect me to get into on a simple day's ride?"

"What indeed?" Felicity asked, flicking her horse into motion again.

They stopped for lunch at an inn. Gardeen accepted milk and some morsels of chicken. Felicity, however, disdained Miles's offer of a dainty meal and tucked into the men's fare of rabbit pie and a jug of porter. She was showing absolutely no tiredness from the ride. Sometimes, Miles wished she were a more proper young lady, but at others, like this, he thought what a comfortable companion she was.

As they ate, they chatted about Irish history, but ancient history which did not include as many traps for the unwary as more recent times.

"Your mother is a Fitzgerald?" she asked at one point.

"Yes, and very proud of it."

"So she should be when there's fairy blood in that line."

"When speaking of fey matters, it's Foy that comes to mind."

"Merely from the sound of the word?"

"No. There's something about the place."

"It's just the cats. Cats are magical."

As if summoned, Gardeen appeared from behind a settle and jumped up onto Miles's lap. "Certainly this one is," he said. "Who named her 'little guardian'?"

"Aunt Annie names them all, though she claims they tell her their names. It's rare for one to choose to leave Foy."

"I can't imagine why I was so favored."

"There's no profit at all in trying to understand Irish cats."

"Or anything else Irish, I think at times."

Chewing an apple down to the core, Felicity looked out of a window across some rolling hills. "Ireland changes so little. Sometimes, I think Finn mac Cool himself could come to save us."

"Then he'd have to fight Arthur. The English have their mythic heroes, too, you know."

Her eyes flashed at him. "Arthur was a Celt. He'd never side with those Saxons and their German king against a true Celtic race!" But it was in fun, and it was sweet to be here like this, enjoying light matters. Too sweet, perhaps, for guardian and ward. . . .

"Arthur's myth has run through Normans, Welsh, and Scots," he said, careful to keep his tone academic. "He's attached to the land, I think, not a monarch."

"Sure and the Irish have no designs on English land," she said. "We just want our own."

"Have you forgotten, perhaps, that I'm Irish, *cailín?*"

"You act like a damned Englishman at times."

"And I suppose Dunsmore doesn't." Shockingly, pure rage surged in him, rage that she might prefer that man to himself.

Rage such as he'd felt that night in her bedroom. . . .

Perhaps she sensed it. Tossing her apple core on the floor, she jumped to her feet. "Better an honest Englishman than an English-Irishman who doesn't know which he is!" Then she was off in search of the privy.

Or in search of escape.

Gardeen leapt off Miles's knee to pounce on the core as if it were a fleeing mouse. Miles drained his ale.

He'd persuaded himself that attack had been a momentary madness, but it hadn't been momentary. He itched to get his hands round Dunsmore's scrawny neck—not in righteous anger at his sins, but out of plain, bitter jealousy.

Madness, and it had to be controlled. He was Felicity's guardian, nothing more. And her only interest in him was to twist him around her fingers.

He used the privy, too, then they set off for the last stage of their ride to Clonnagh. It hadn't been an arduous day for the horses, so now they gave them their heads and raced cross-country.

Miles kept an eye on his companion. Though Felicity was an excellent horsewoman, he wasn't sure she was up to a whole day in the saddle, especially a sidesaddle. She didn't seem at all weary, however.

She'd be completely wasted on Dunsmore, this wild Irish warrior-queen with milk-white skin and jet-black hair and a heart as fierce as a storm. . . .

They made a last stop five miles from Clonnagh to water the horses at a stream by a small wayside inn. Felicity took Gardeen out of her pocket, and the little cat romped off in hot pursuit of some tufts of sheep's wool.

When they led the horses to the water, Miles thought his companion might be a little stiff. "It's not far from here," he said. "We could rent a gig if you wish."

The slight limp he'd noticed disappeared. "Not at all!" After a moment, she grimaced and added, "If you must know, I'm suffering for vanity."

"What?"

"She raised her skirts to show smart, glossy boots. "They're new, and I wanted to look my best. But they pinch, damn the boot-makers for shoddy work. It's not too bad riding, but walking is somewhat painful."

"There's a bench there to sit on," he said. "Shall I carry you?"

"Heaven help us, but you'd crumple under my weight. I'm no feather . . . *Miles!*"

He swung her up and carried her to the seat in question, then stood there with her in his arms.

"All right, all right!" she declared, deliciously flushed by laughter, her hat askew. "I'm suitably impressed by your Atlas-like strength. Now put me down before you kill yourself." Her voice trailed away, and her color deepened.

He knew his breathing had changed. Yes, he was showing off like a village boy flexing muscles for his chosen wench, but surely that look in her eyes wasn't artifice? Where was Gardeen when he needed her?

"Oh, Miles, I wish—"

"Oh, Miles, I wish you weren't my guardian?" he asked softly.

But the moment passed. She looked away. "I certainly do. You are making my life very difficult. Do put me down."

He lowered her slowly, wishing for that moment back, at least to savor, perhaps to analyze, perhaps to exploit. Well, they'd have a few days at his home without Dunsmore or Kieran to complicate matters. Perhaps then he would be able to think straight.

She stepped away from him and fussed with her habit. "I think I could use some tea before we go on. It's turning clammy."

He glanced at the darkening sky. "It's getting late, but we can afford a half-hour."

It would mean the light would be going as they neared Clonnagh, but he knew the country here so well he could

ride it blindfolded, and Argonaut could find his stable without
guidance. The truth was that they seemed to have fallen into
a fairy journey, where reality faded to mist and the impossible
seemed likely. The look in her eye, the response in his heart,
could not be real or practical, but it was precious.

The small inn had no private accommodations, but was
empty at this hour. The old woman there was happy to provide tea and buttered scones as well as a saucer of milk for
Gardeen. The small, low-ceilinged room lit only by a blazing
fire was the stuff of fairytales, too. Weren't there stories of
people who took fairy meals and were trapped forever?

"Tell me about your home," she said.

Miles shook his head and pushed away his mad musings.
He obliged with a monologue about Clonnagh and his childhood there, with frequent reference to his two sisters and one
brother.

"But none live at home anymore?"

"No. Ellen and Moira are both married, and Declan is a
naval captain. Bold with lace and growing fat on prizes."

"What about your mother? What sort of woman is she?"

"A fine woman, a strong woman. She trained us all in the
highest standards and never had any time for idleness."

Felicity, feet tucked under her on a big settle, wrinkled her
brow. "I don't wish to offend, but she doesn't sound the ideal
wife for Uncle Colum."

Miles laughed. "You'd think not, wouldn't you? But she's
blooming. With her children grown and her first husband
dead, she needed someone to manage."

"Poor Colum!"

"Devil a bit. He worships the ground she walks on and
revels in her managing ways, though I notice he still only
does what he wishes to. They also clearly enjoy the intimacies
of marriage." Then he wished the words unsaid. He'd relaxed
too far to blurt out such a matter like a raw youth.

Felicity stared at him. "But they're as old as Annie!"

He almost laughed at her astonishment, and in pleasure at

her naivete. "Such matters aren't just for the young, you know."

"Such matters shouldn't be for the young at all," she said sharply, then looked as if she, too, regretted her words. He came alert. What was behind this?

"How would you define young?" he asked.

She looked away, color high, but not just with embarrassment. "Children. Younger than I."

"You're twenty. Many girls are married at that age. But I agree that marriage is not for children."

Still seeking a reason for her distress—for it was not too strong a word—he wondered whether Dunsmore had sunk so low as to threaten to harm his son in a sexual way. "It's illegal for children to marry," he pointed out, choosing his words with care. "And those who mistreat children in an intimate way are subject to the law, too."

She stared soberly into the tea in her cup. "If any complaint is ever laid. Everyone is so concerned about reputation. Even an innocent child is smirched by such matters." She put down the cup and uncurled to her feet. "We should be on our way. The light's going."

He rose more slowly, though it was true. They had lingered longer than intended. They would have to return to this discussion later, however. If Dunsmore were using such a threat, it was even less reason for marriage and it could be handled in other ways.

Miles was beginning to develop a strong desire to handle Dunsmore with his fists and make sure the man never threatened child or woman again.

It was dusk and misty-chill, and as they set out, Miles felt strangely as if they were riding out of enchantment. The winding lane ahead of them faded into a uniform gray, melted by sea-mist from the nearby coast. The tang of salt was in the air, and curlews cried not far away.

They could go no faster than a walk, but the leisurely pace gave Miles time to think about Kieran and Dunsmore.

He could understand Felicity's dilemma. For her to refuse to sacrifice herself for the child would seem selfish indeed. It would be a problem even if the child were a stranger. Her willingness to sacrifice herself was one of her many virtues.

Miles tried to imagine what he would do if called upon to choose between his own life and that of a small child. How could anyone not choose to save the child? It might be the act of a friend, however, to stop such a sacrifice.

The problem was that in less than a month Felicity would be able to give herself and her fortune to Dunsmore without hindrance, and she would do it unless she could be persuaded it was folly.

The best eye-opener would be for her to fall in love. She certainly didn't love Dunsmore. Miles ran through the friends they might encounter in Melton, seeking one able to attract Felicity.

Stephen Ball, perhaps. No. Stephen's interests were political—and urban, not rural. Miles could not see Felicity as a political wife.

Con Somerford. Now, he was more likely. A sound man with a pleasant nature and wide estates. But Felicity said she wished to marry an Irishman.

Which led, as he'd known all along, to himself . . .

"Halt!"

Miles snapped out of his musings to see two cloaked horsemen training pistols on them.

"What the devil—" He'd never heard of highwaymen in these parts before.

"Come along, Felicity."

Then Miles recognized Dunsmore's voice. He turned to stare at his ward.

"I'm eloping." Her straight back and raised chin spoke defiance, but she couldn't quite meet his eyes.

"Oh no you're not."

"You can't stop me."

He kicked her horse in the gut so it reared, unsettling her, then grabbed her around the waist, hauling her off Cresta and in front of him.

"Damn you!" She writhed and flailed with an earnestness that infuriated him. No unwilling bride, this. He thumped her on the back hard enough to knock the breath out of her and set Argonaut to circling so the men couldn't be sure of a shot. It wasn't easy to reach down for his right pistol while managing the horse and a squirming woman, but he got his hand to the butt, then felt something press against his groin.

"Be very still," she said.

Miles calmed Argonaut and went very still indeed.

She'd drawn the left pistol from its saddle-holster and was pressing it damn close to his balls. He didn't know if she'd cocked it, or even knew how, but he wasn't willing to gamble on it.

"Felicity—"

"Enough of that. This is where your tyranny ends. *Denzil!*"

Dunsmore was holding back, but the groom came forward, leading Cresta. Soon his pistol was close enough to Miles that it was impossible that he miss.

"You can get down now, Miss."

Miles heard the safety cock back down. He should never have doubted that Felicity knew pistols. Damn her for a canny, ruthless, headstrong, dangerous jade.

She slithered off, landing unsteadily, but gathering herself. Then she looked up at him. "Get off."

"Go to the devil."

"Get off, or Denzil will shoot Argonaut."

He had a great desire to kick her in the teeth.

He obeyed, however, and swung off his horse. Felicity led Argonaut over to a tree and tethered him. "We wouldn't want him running back to his stable and raising the alarm, now, would we?"

She walked back to her horse and looked at Miles. "Help me mount."

He wanted to tell her again to go to the devil, but Denzil

still had his pistol angled toward Argonaut. He'd wondered what he'd do for a child. It appeared he would do a lot for a horse. But Felicity wouldn't get away with this.

He walked over to her, looking for uneasiness or remorse and finding none. He linked his hands.

"Don't do anything foolish," she said before putting her booted foot into his hands. It certainly was tempting to hurl her right over the horse's back, but he tossed her efficiently into the saddle.

She nodded.

He thought it was with approval, but then he knew no more.

Eight

God, but his head hurt.

When Miles tried to put his hands to the pain, he realized they were bound behind his back.

He muttered a stream of curses into muddy grass and promised that Felicity Monahan would pay with interest for every ache and cramp.

He was lying face down beneath the hedgerow and found it impossible to roll over. The struggle to do so, however, showed that the rope around his wrists had been hastily tied. There was give to it. It took longer, almost, than he could bear, especially with every movement causing his head to pound as if freshly hit, but he managed to work first one hand free, then the other.

He pushed stiffly to his knees, and then to his feet, which caused his head to pound like a bass drum and his vision to cloud. But he saw the bulk of Argonaut nearby and staggered over to rest against his solid warmth.

"Thank God they didn't hurt you."

The horse whiffled in what might have been equine concern.

After a few moments, Miles decided he wasn't going to throw up, which he supposed was a blessing. And if he stayed very still, the pain in his head was merely a solid ache. Gingerly, he felt the back of his skull and found a large lump and the stickiness of blood. Since he was alive and moderately alert, however, he supposed he'd avoided serious damage.

No thanks to Felicity Monahan.

He'd never have thought she had that degree of brass-faced ruthlessness. It all went to show how little he really knew the slippery jade. Perhaps she and Dunsmore deserved each other.

But they wouldn't have their way.

Gradually, the world was steadying to a sick roll. Miles studied the surrounding misty gloom. There was no one nearby, of course, but he knew exactly where he was. Tyfahan Cross, about two miles from Clonnagh. It was strange that Felicity and her swain had waited until here for the attack. There had been any number of more isolated spots on the way.

So why had they?

Elopement, she'd said. So they must be intending a flight to Scotland. Miles moved suddenly and cursed as the pain made him nauseated again.

His mind remained clear, however, and he could follow their plan. Tyfahan Cross was only half-a-mile from the small port of Barragan. Dunsmore doubtless had a vessel tied up there, ready for a speedy cast off.

By waiting until late, the pair also had the advantage of darkness and the fact that most honest people were home enjoying their supper.

Miles looked quickly at the sky, trying to estimate the passage of time since the attack. Not long. Twilight had just been settling when Dunsmore made his move, and it was scarce true dark yet. With luck, they'd expected his bonds to hold him longer.

He checked and found his pistols were in their holsters. Since no shot had been fired, he assumed they were ready for use.

He untied Argonaut and hauled himself into the saddle, kicking the horse to speed even before his head settled. He was clearheaded enough to steer into the westerly branch of the fork and by then could settle to making best speed, trusting to heaven alone that there were no potholes to bring them down.

His head screeched with every jolt, but that only made him more determined to stop Felicity from boarding ship.

He needed to throttle her.

After he'd beaten her.

After he'd expressed every scrap of fury and betrayal in his soul.

In the hamlet of Kilgloch, a few people peered out warily at the horseman galloping by; and then he had Barragan in sight. It was little more than a string of fishermen's cottages along the shore, with boats bobbing at anchor not far off. But—by God—one fishing boat was tied up at the wharf.

They had not sailed yet!

A small clump of people were talking, and the horses still stood nearby.

When they heard him, heads turned and the group wavered with alarm. A struggle started.

Miles pulled a pistol from its holster, cocked it, and fired as close to the group as he dared. The cluster of people fragmented, one running for the horses, scooping trailing skirts up high.

Felicity.

What the devil was she up to now?

She scrambled into the saddle and headed off along the shore.

Miles checked for a moment, unsure which target to follow.

Then Dunsmore ran toward his horse. Kicking Argonaut forward, Miles put himself between Dunsmore and Felicity, his unfired pistol in hand.

The four other men—Denzil, a servant of some kind, and two fishermen—seemed inclined to stay out of trouble.

Dunsmore charged after Felicity as if he would ride straight through Miles.

Miles raised the pistol, completely willing to shoot.

Perhaps Dunsmore realized it, for he pulled his horse to a rearing stop only feet away. "Such a conscientious guardian." But it was close to a snarl.

"Note that fact."

"You can't guard her day and night."

"I won't have to when you're out of Ireland."

Dunsmore calmed his horse and regained his superior manner. "I have no intention of leaving Ireland without my promised bride."

Miles raised the pistol. "I despise you and your actions, Dunsmore. My head feels cracked, and I am entirely out of patience. Board the boat or I'll shoot you."

"My men would kill you!" Dunsmore blustered.

"I doubt it, but at the moment it seems worth the risk."

Dunsmore stared at him, looking like nothing so much as a thwarted child. "You can't do this!"

Miles didn't dignify that with an answer. He nudged Argonaut forward a step or two. In lieu of shooting Dunsmore, beating him to a pulp was extremely attractive.

Perhaps Dunsmore read the intent, for he suddenly wheeled his horse and rode back to the wharf to dismount and shout, "I'll come straight back!" He sounded even more like a spoiled child.

Miles followed slowly. "Not to Barragan, you won't. You're on Clonnagh land; and once I put the word around, you'll not be welcome here. Ned Tooley, is that you?"

The stocky young fisherman rubbed his face uneasily. "It is, your honor, it is."

"I assume the gentleman hired you to take him to Scotland."

"Aye, your honor, he did. I saw no harm in it, God be my witness!"

"Nor was there. Take him to his destination. But," Miles added, "do not bring him back."

The man's eyes brightened, and he winked. "Right you are, sir, and a pleasure it will be."

Miles studied Dunsmore, wondering how Felicity could contemplate tying herself for life to such a specimen. "You won't marry Felicity before her majority, Dunsmore. That, at least, I can promise."

Despite his defeat, the man smirked. "I wouldn't lay odds on that, Cavanagh. Desperate women are capable of a great deal, as you have seen. And she is. Desperate."

Miles fired a pistol ball into the ground inches from the man's foot then, leaving Dunsmore still dancing and expostulating, headed off down the sand after Felicity.

His head still ached like the devil, but it appeared fury could overwhelm even pain.

His traitorous ward was nowhere in sight, but her horse had left hoofprints in the sand. Slowly, because of the uncertain moonlight, he tracked her up Hickey's Gully and back to the road to Kilgloch.

There he banged on a cottage door. "Open up, Molan! It's Cavanagh."

The door opened, and a gray-haired man peered out. "Is it truly you, your honor? Sure and there's devils out tonight!"

"Devils indeed. Has someone ridden past in the last few minutes?"

"Indeed they have, your honor. A lady pretty as Sinead, thrown up by the water and asking the way to Clonnagh."

Devil take it, was she going to ride on to his home as if nothing had happened?

"Thank you, Molan. Good night to you."

"And to you, your honor! But take care, for the Danaan are out tonight!"

Miles cantered off, knowing that, already, new myths were weaving. Did all magical tales have such sordid origins?

It was a risk to go at speed, for it was too dark now to see clearly, but he did it anyway. He hoped Felicity, on strange

territory, would not be as rash. He was proved correct when
he saw her ahead, riding at a slow walk.

She twisted to look back, but then turned forward again
and resumed her steady pace.

His head throbbing and his jaw tight, Miles eased his pace
until he came up with her. "Get off the horse."

"Why? So you can beat me?"

"Don't you deserve it?"

"I don't acknowledge your authority over me." Tears glinted
on her face, though. Tears from losing Dunsmore, dammit?

He seized her reins and, when she didn't let go, rapped
her knuckles sharply with the handle of his crop. With a hiss,
she released her grip.

"This has little to do with authority," he said. "You attacked me, and I will retaliate."

"I never touched you!"

"And I'm not going to touch you. Get off."

She glared at him for a moment, then slid off the horse.
"Now, what?"

"Now, you walk. It's only a bit over two miles."

"Oh, I'm quaking. Is this your punishment?"

"It'll do. I seem to remember your boots pinch."

"You bastard!"

"Being lied to, tricked, and knocked over the head brings
out the worst in me."

With that, he set both horses in motion again and ignored
her. He supposed if she absolutely refused to walk, he'd have
to make some arrangement to get her to Clonnagh. She wasn't
riding there, though, and one way or another she was going
to hurt as much as he did.

Perhaps she realized that, for he heard footsteps behind.

A two-mile walk gave plenty of time to think. Too much
time. Miles couldn't reconcile his admiration for Felicity's intelligence and courage with his disgust at her behavior today.
The child was no excuse. She was intelligent enough to realize that the world was full of children and that, all in all,

Kieran Dunsmore did not have the roughest track under his well-shod feet.

There was some piece of the puzzle missing.

He realized then that he was nursing a pain greater than the throb in his head. It was the pain of knowing that Felicity didn't trust him enough to tell him the whole truth.

He thought he heard an irregularity in her step and stopped to look back. She immediately froze, standing straight, as if unconcerned.

Damn the stubborn, pride-ridden jade.

He headed forward again. Yes, she was limping and there was at least half-a-mile to go.

Was that the key to it all—pride? Was she the type who'd ride to destruction rather than admit a foolishness?

He found it hard to believe.

After another furlong, he stopped again.

Again she froze.

Damnation. He turned in the saddle. "Get back on the horse."

"No."

"Hades, Felicity. For once, just do as I say!"

"No. I deserve to walk."

He dismounted, intending to throw her on if necessary, but moonlight glinted on fresh tears and showed a haunting sorrow in her eyes.

"Why, Felicity?" he asked gently. "Tell me all about this."

"It would do no good. I'm going to marry Rupert Dunsmore."

"No, you are not!"

"Once I'm twenty-one, you cannot stop me."

"Don't lay odds on it."

"How?" she asked, truly distressed.

Unable to help himself, he brushed a tear from her cheek with his thumb.

"Like this," he said, and kissed her cold lips.

They surrendered to him, but it was the surrender of exhaustion and helplessness, with no desire in it at all. He kissed her anyway, trying to give her some awareness of her true worth.

"Felicity," he murmured against her chilled and dampened cheek. "You are a treasure. Many men will want you. Choose wisely."

"The choice is made," she whispered. "It was made long since and cannot be changed. Don't do this, Miles. It only makes it worse."

He kissed the dampness from her eyelashes. "I care for you. I cannot see you hurt."

She laughed unsteadily. "Then why am I walking on blistered feet?"

He laughed, too, in the same bittersweet way. "Because you're an infuriatingly willful creature and my head still aches like the devil."

She reached up and ran her fingers over the back of his head to the bump. "Oh dear."

"That's what happens when you bash someone on the head with a pistol butt."

"If only Denzil had tied you tighter. . . ."

He pushed back and looked at her, to see that she was completely serious. Her regret was that he'd escaped and stopped her elopement. Without a word, he remounted and led the way to his home.

By the time they arrived at the Clonnagh stables, Felicity was limping badly, but Miles had heard no sound from her. When they stopped this time, however, she eased from foot to foot, clearly trying to find a comfortable spot and failing.

Miles did his best to ignore it.

A couple of grooms came out to welcome him home and take the horses, then Miles led the way up to the house, resisting the temptation to carry her.

He remembered their stop, when he'd swung her into his

arms. For a fleeting moment magic had danced between them, magic that—as in most of the ancient tales—had only led to sorrow.

God, it made no sense to his poor aching head.

They entered by a side door which passed near to the aromatic kitchens. "We're late for dinner," he remarked. "I suppose you want to change."

"Yes, I suppose I do." But she said it numbly, as if she'd agree to walk off a cliff if invited.

He guided her into the spacious hall and toward the curving staircase, but at that moment, a door opened and his mother appeared.

"Miles! At last. We were concerned. And Felicity. Welcome to Clonnagh, my dear." Felicity accepted the embrace with good grace, but Lady Aideen did not miss her distress.

"Why, whatever has happened? You look exhausted. And Miles, you look none too clever yourself."

She'd been followed out by five dogs, two of them belonging to Miles. He returned their greetings as he said, "We had a little run-in with some ne'er-do-wells, Mother. They tried to kidnap Felicity. I think she'd be happy to eat in her room tonight and have a good rest."

"Kidnap! My gracious! Yes, of course you must rest, you poor child. Come along."

Felicity resisted the gentle urging, however, and turned back to Miles.

"I'm sorry," she whispered. He thought it was a general repentance, but then she drew something out of her capacious pocket.

One of the dogs whined.

Of course. He'd forgotten Gardeen.

She placed the small cat in Miles's hands, and only then did he realize it was a limp, cold form.

"He killed her," she said.

As a deadweight, the young cat weighed scarcely anything.

Miles looked at Felicity. "Why?" It encompassed more than the death, but that was all she answered.

"She scratched him."

Then she turned and limped up the stairs.

Likely as not, he thought, all the tears she'd shed had been for this little life snuffed out. He stroked the black fur, hardly able to believe that the cat wouldn't stir back to life again.

Poor Gardeen. And poor Dunsmore, for there would be vengeance for this senseless act.

Then his stepfather was there.

"A cat? Poor thing. What happened to it?"

"Like many guardians, she fell with honor in her task."

"A guardian of the guardian, eh? Plato would not have approved. Where did she come from?"

"She's one of Annie's brood."

Colum's eyes widened. "St. Bridget defend us, then, for she'll not be happy at this. And nor will the one who caused the death." He flapped the fine linen serviette in his hand and draped it over the corpse, then rang the silver bell on the table. When a footman appeared, he said, "I think your master would like the small creature buried."

Miles felt strangely reluctant to surrender the body, but he could hardly wander the house carrying her. He folded the serviette around the cat and handed her over. "See her laid softly, Gerald. By the sundial, I think. In the herb garden."

"Yes, sir." Gerald O'Farrell carried the corpse away with the respectful majesty only an Irishman could offer a dead cat. Miles let his stepfather steer him into the dining room.

"Kidnapping, did you say? In this area?"

"I think they were from elsewhere. Don't forget she— Felicity—is a considerable heiress."

"Even so. Terrible thing, terrible. And how did the little cat come to be involved?"

"She adopted me."

"And one of Annie's, you say? Oh dear, oh dear." And for once, Colum did seem struck to somberness by an event.

"She will be in a state over it. And it's rare indeed that one of her little ones takes to a stranger. Oh dear, oh dear."

"I suppose I should write and tell her."

"Only if you want her ire directed upon the malefactor."

"I'd like nothing better." Unfortunately, Miles could not imagine Annie Monahan's ire amounting to much. His own could, however. He now had a personal grudge against Dunsmore, and began to contemplate a number of ways he could make the man's life thoroughly unpleasant. He'd start by checking out his creditors.

"But come and eat," said Colum. "Come and eat. Oh, don't worry about your dirt. Your mother won't mind."

Miles thought his mother would mind a great deal anyone's sitting on the new satin seats when covered in mud, and eating with foully dirty hands. He wondered at what point the glow would wear off and his mother and stepfather would come to blows.

"I'd rather clean up a bit, Colum. I'll be down again shortly."

When he left the dining room, however, he was drawn outside again, needing to be sure his little guardian was being suitably treated. Accompanied by Donn and Dubh, he went to the herb garden where he found Gerald had already dug the small grave, despite the frosted ground, and was laying the cat in it. Donn and Dubh sat on either side of the grave, strangely as if on honor guard, and stayed there while Miles and Gerald filled the hole and built a cairn of white stones over it.

Miles sent the man back to his proper duties and stood for a moment in the winter-bleak garden to mourn an unlikely friend and protector. And to vow vengeance.

Then Miles went to his rooms and found Hennigan waiting for him. The valet clucked with distress over the considerable amount of Irish earth adhering to his master's garments and began to strip layers off him, placing them carefully on the wooden floor beyond the edge of the Axminster.

Miles was down to his drawers and shirt before he thought of something. Telling his valet to prepare a bath, he washed his hands, pulled on a clean pair of pantaloons, and went quickly down the corridor to knock on the door of the best guest room.

There was no answer.

Alarmed, he threw the door open—to find Felicity sitting despondently on the bed in her knee-length shift. She immediately straightened, pulling a corner of the coverlet over her bare legs. "Get out!"

Miles continued in and shut the door. "If you'd answered my knock, even to telling me to go away, I wouldn't have intruded."

"Go away, then."

"Too late now. I'll leave as soon as I have your word that you'll not leave the estate without my clear permission."

She closed her eyes. "Oh, when will you stop bullying me?"

"When you're of age."

She opened her eyes, but only to stare at him miserably.

He went closer to lean on one of the bulbous posts of the bed. "Believe me, Felicity, I'm even more determined now to prevent your marriage to that villain. If necessary, I'll tell the whole household what's going on and keep you under lock and key."

"Oh, damn you." But it was more of a hopeless whisper than a cry of defiance.

"And, in case you have hopes, Dunsmore won't be riding up to the door like Lochinvar to carry you to freedom. He's on his way to Scotland."

"What? He's gone without me?" It rang with shock and outrage.

Miles thumped the post so the bed rocked. "Damnation, Felicity! How can you still want to marry a man who would kill a defenseless cat?"

"Perhaps *because* he could kill a defenseless cat."

He understood a little, then.

"You weren't able to stop him," he pointed out ruthlessly, "and Dunsmore's wife or not, you won't be able to stop him from harming Kieran."

She closed her eyes for a revealing moment, but made no response.

Miles sighed and sat on the corner of the bed, well away from her. "Dunsmore will be gone for near a week, Felicity. It'll be a day and a half before he gets to Scotland, and longer before he's back. I've told Tooley not to bring him back himself."

"A week." It was whispered, but as one might say, "Fairy gold."

It told him so much about her situation that it nearly broke his heart.

"We both need this time. Give me your word that you won't leave Clonnagh without my permission for a week."

She appeared so exhausted he wasn't even sure she was capable of a coherent response, but then she said, "You have my word, Miles. But just a week. No longer."

"At the moment, *cailín,* a week seems like heaven."

His anger had drained away and he wanted to hold her, but she'd doubtless reject all comfort.

She'd keep her given word, though, so Miles felt safe in leaving her there alone.

When Lady Aideen came to tell her niece that her bath was ready, she found Felicity asleep, collapsed on the bed like a rag doll dropped by a child. She smoothed tangled black hair from the girl's forehead, aware that more was in hand here than a simple attack on the road.

In another case, she'd think a man to blame, but there were few men on earth less likely to distress a woman than Miles.

Did he have a romantic interest in Felicity? There was something between them, she'd swear it. For one thing, Miles wasn't in Melton. Anything that could overwhelm hunting in his mind was significant.

And if Miles had a romantic interest in Felicity, how did Felicity feel about it?

Aideen knew the girl wasn't a conventional miss, and she rather thought she wasn't much interested in men. That was what Colum said, anyway. But Colum hadn't told all. Aideen respected her husband's right to keep his counsel about his family's affairs, but if it were becoming an issue in *her* family it was a different matter entirely.

And what of that cat? She'd never known Miles to be fond of cats—he was a horse-and-dog man—and yet he'd looked at the sad creature as if it were a dead child.

"He killed her," Felicity had said. *"Because she scratched him."*

Who was this unpleasant "he?"

Aideen summoned a maid to help her tuck Felicity in bed, looking forward to a juicy tangle to sort out.

Nine

As Hennigan shaved him the next morning, Miles reflected upon the changes since he'd last been shaved in this way in his home.

His peaceful life was now in turmoil.

He was heading for a confrontation with Rupert Dunsmore which might well result in bloodshed.

His head still felt cracked.

And so did his heart.

The last thing on Miles's mind a few weeks ago had been marriage. If he'd given the matter any thought at all, it was that in a few year's time he'd look for a sensible, well-bred young woman whom he found congenial, someone suitable to be Countess of Kilgoran.

He had not intended to become overly fond of a dark-haired, poorly-raised jade who racketed from one headstrong disaster to another.

And who was devoting her considerable will to marrying another.

It seemed Felicity had managed to crash her way into his heart, however, and was lodged there quite firmly. He found hope in some of their encounters, but then remembered her stating clearly that she wished to be on the boat to Scotland.

"Sir! My apologies!"

Miles's sudden movement had caused the valet to nick him. As they stanched the trickle of blood, Miles marked down another wound to Felicity Monahan's tally.

She'd claimed to be a dangerous woman and was proving her words true.

A wise man would flee someone like that. Miles, however, was legally bound to her for four more weeks.

As he buttoned his shirt, Miles reflected that at least he'd have one week of peace. He could trust Felicity's given word. Surely in a week he could convince her that marriage to Dunsmore was simply impossible.

He laughed out loud, causing his valet to flash him a startled look. But the thought of convincing Felicity Monahan of anything was ludicrous, particularly now Dunsmore had succeeded in putting the idea in her head that he would break Kieran's neck as easily as he'd broken Gardeen's.

He might, too. That was the rub. Though at heart a coward, Dunsmore had all the mean ruthlessness of the true bully.

Miles decided he needed his mother's help.

He completed his dressing, then went to knock on the door to Aideen's sitting room. He waited cautiously for permission to enter, for these days one never knew what one would find. His mother was alone, however, sitting at a small table by a window, attending to correspondence.

"Come in, my dear! I am just writing to Ellen. You must add a few words. Such a fretful mother as she is becoming. It's so droll! Here she is lamenting little Hugh's addiction to climbing trees when *she* once attempted the rose trellis on the west wall!"

He grinned as he kissed her cheek. "You needn't convince a horse-breeder that qualities pass down the line."

"Felicity seems to have avoided the amiable indolence of the Monahans."

Trust his mother to bring matters straight to the point. "Since she arrived here in a state of exhaustion, I can't see how you know whether she's indolent or not."

"Don't be foolish, dear. The way she gritted her teeth was far from indolent. Or amiable, for that matter. What have you been doing to the poor child?"

"Has she been blackening my name?" he demanded. "I've been trying to save her from disaster, that's all."

"She said nothing, my dear. It is all my own interpretation. So, what disaster looms?"

"It's complicated."

"A man," Aideen stated. "Is there a girl born who does not at some point fix her heart on a scoundrel? But you must have handled it badly."

Miles threw himself into a chair. "Don't be thinking this is some simple infatuation, Mother." And he told her the story.

His mother nodded thoughtfully. "One can see how heavily the welfare of a child would weigh on a warmhearted girl. It's a shame those farmyard creatures didn't kill this Dunsmore."

"What a bloodthirsty woman you are. Anyway, it would have been disastrous. Warts and all, he's an Englishman. The military would have been down on the place like a blight."

"Unfortunately true. Dunsmore will be back soon, though, and up to his old tricks. Short of a dungeon, it will be impossible to keep Felicity here against her will. And how can we be sure the vile man will not harm the child if thwarted?"

"We can't. That's the most damnable part of this." Miles rose from the chair to pace. "I'd like to think Dunsmore would hesitate to hurt his own son, but that's stretching my faith to breaking point. I do think, however, that he'll hold his hand if there's no point to it."

"You mean if Felicity were out of reach, he might leave the boy alone?"

"I think so."

His mother tapped a finger thoughtfully on the glossy burled walnut. "It would be even better if the boy were under a watchful eye."

"Wonderfully better. But how could we arrange that?"

She winked at him. "Leave that to me. You attend to your

willful ward. Try to convince her to abandon her plans. If not, you'll have to take her to Melton by force."

"Good Lord, I was joking when I said that!"

"What alternative is there? If she remains determined, she'll soon be off again. You presumably wish to be in Melton, not here trying to prevent the inevitable. Take her with you, and Dunsmore will have much more trouble contacting her. Involve those Rogues of yours and it will be close to impossible. Since it's obvious that the man is deep in debt and has run to the limit of the money he can squeeze out of his son's estate, there's always hope he'll come to a dreadful end without your intervention."

Miles shook his head. "Whatever became of the notion of the weaker sex?"

"It has only ever been a convenient fable, my dear."

Felicity awoke, aware almost instantly of being in a strange bed. Since it seemed an effort to open her eyes, she lazily analyzed the strange aromas—lavender and rose, and a wood rather than a peat fire. She noted a lack of the dusty, musty smell which was normal to her, the smell of Foy.

Then she remembered everything and raised heavy lids to see the gracious elegance of Clonnagh.

Miles's home was not large—only a little larger than Foy, in fact—but it was of more modern construction and greater elegance. Long windows and light interiors gave the impression of greater space, and excellent housekeeping was apparent. Felicity was sure she'd find no dust in even the most awkward corners of this room, no mildew near the windows, no worm in the wood.

She sighed, knowing her mind was dancing over trivialities, trying to avoid deeper matters.

Such as the sound a pistol butt made when it knocked a man insensible.

Or the sight of Miles sprawled unconscious in the mud.

Or the look on Rupert's face when he broke Gardeen's neck.

She flung an arm over her eyes.

It had all seemed so *easy* in the planning. Since clear reason said she had no choice but to marry Rupert Dunsmore, and since his threats against Kieran had intensified, she had decided to get it done. With Miles watching her so closely and the local people disapproving, she'd not wanted to try eloping from Foy. Once Miles proposed a journey, however, she saw her way. Somewhere along the road they could immobilize him, and once at sea, no one could catch them.

She hadn't counted on the sweet intimacy of a lazy journey, or on the reality of what it would take to stop her unwelcome guardian from guarding her.

Both her unwelcome guardians.

She pushed herself up in the bed to study the raw spots on each heel. Damn that Dublin boot-maker. That was the last time he'd have her custom. And yet, in a way, she was glad of the punishment. Without it, she wouldn't be able to face Miles today.

Even with wounds to soothe her conscience, she still wasn't looking forward to their next encounter. He'd surely be angry at the trick she'd played and the injury she'd caused him.

If he'd put all that aside, he'd blame her for Gardeen's death. With reason. She should have remembered the cat and left her safe with him.

If he could forgive her for all that, he'd still be after answers to questions. Answers she didn't want to give.

And, if he didn't press her for answers, he'd be acting the friend again, making the passing hours sweet with understanding and laughter.

Weakening her resolve.

She sank her head in her hands. Each day made it harder to turn her back upon the warm sun of Miles's friendship and give herself to the cold wind and frost of Rupert Dunsmore.

What's more, Miles tempted her to foolishness.

Foolishness like telling him all.

She launched herself from the bed, as if movement could shake off such thoughts. Seeing the appalling state of her hair, she began to attack it with the brush.

What good would the truth do, when Miles was powerless to change the way things were? She was no damsel waiting for the gallant knight to rescue her. If a way out existed, she'd have found it for herself.

Tears sprang to her eyes, but she assured herself they were from the pain of her knotted hair.

The simple fact was that Kieran was Rupert's son. Nothing could change that.

She could, if she wished, prove the boy was her child, not Kathleen Craig's, but that would achieve nothing other than to lose him Kathleen's fortune. Kieran would still be Rupert's son, and Rupert would still have all the legal power over him.

There was always the option of killing Rupert, but she'd found there was a place in her that balked at taking human life. She held the idea to her, however. If her sacrifice did not keep her son safe, then somehow she would find the strength to take that final, dreadful step.

Killing Rupert before the marriage was pointless, though, for Kieran would pass into the care of Kathleen's cousin.

Would it improve matters to explain everything to Miles, including that she contemplated murder?

She laughed bitterly. He'd have her clapped in a madhouse.

She rang for a maid and, to please Miles, had herself arrayed in the illusion of a well-bred young lady. She discovered with relief that her soft slippers did not rub the blisters on her heels, so she didn't have to limp down to the breakfast room.

She was somewhat late, and the butler informed her that both Lady Aideen and her husband had eaten earlier. The man made sure she had everything she required, however. Felicity thought sadly of her discourteous welcome of Miles to her own ramshackle home.

Then her guardian strolled in, a smile on his lips but, for the first time, a rather distant expression in his blue eyes. "Good morning, Felicity. I hope you have everything you want."

"Oh, yes," she said, through an ache in her throat. "And Hillsmore is having fresh eggs cooked for me." In the face of his cool civility, she attempted social chatter. "I'm absolutely ravenous. Lunch yesterday was completely inadequate for someone who would have no dinner."

Then she bit her lip, remembering why she'd had no dinner.

Miles said nothing, however, apart from directing her attention to the kippers.

She gave an artificial shudder. "I abhor fish at breakfast."

He took one himself and began to work the smoked flesh off the bones, giving the business all his attention.

After a few minutes, the silence became unbearable to her. "I like your home. It's so light and airy."

He looked up politely. "You could achieve a similar effect at Foy by painting the rooms white."

"You forget, it's Aunt Annie's house, not mine. Grandfather left it to her, and she prefers it as it is."

"I suppose I had forgotten. What little is done to care for the place seems to be done by you."

"I do what is necessary for my comfort, that's all. I have no domestic skills." Felicity sighed. Despite her good intentions, she was back to bickering with the man.

The alarming thing was that he did not react. "I hope you find no shortcomings in the comfort here."

"Everything is perfect, as well you know." To prove it, her eggs arrived, cooked to perfection. She slid two onto her plate. "I shudder to think what you must have suffered at Foy."

"It was hardly suffering, for the company was—on the whole—pleasant."

Felicity decided silence was welcome after all and settled to eating. She stole a glance at Miles every now and then, wishing he were the lighthearted friend again.

Hardly surprising that he was not.

But why, when he was so cool, did she feel so stimulated by him? So aware. She'd breakfasted with him most days these past two weeks without any effect on her appetite, but now it was quite a challenge to eat the food her body needed.

When she'd cleaned her plate, she was at a loss as to what to do next. What to do next that would be safe, that is. Music, she suddenly thought. For many years, music had been her refuge and her solace, and now she needed it.

"Do you have an instrument here?" she asked. "A harpsichord?"

He took a last drink of coffee. "We can do better. We have a pianoforte."

"I've never played one."

"Never?" A spark of surprise lightened his expression.

"We did not have one, as you know."

"But other houses in your area have. I've seen, and heard, them. I wondered why you didn't play, since you have more skill than most of the performers."

She could feel awkward color invading her cheeks. "I was too embarrassed to try in public. Too afraid I'd not play well."

"Have you never simply visited a house that had a pianoforte? They are a recent development, but not so rare as that."

"Until I went to Whitehaven to see my mother's family about my inheritance, I had never visited anywhere at all."

Too late, Felicity realized that wasn't true.

"Colum said you visited England a few years ago."

"Oh, that!" She laughed, and even to her ears it sounded shrill. "I just stayed quietly in the country pressing wildflowers."

What, in heaven's name, had Colum told him?

After a frowning moment, Miles rose. "Come then, and I'll show you the instrument."

He led her to a music room containing the piano and an Irish harp. She trailed her fingers across the harp strings, summoning a ripple of music. "I've never played one of these, either."

"You're welcome to do so, though I'm not sure your keyboard skills will help you much there."

"I fear that's true, and the wires are hard on the fingers."

Felicity sat on the silk-covered bench, surveying the handsome mahogany instrument. How she had wished to explore one. And, she knew well, her kind neighbors would not have minded any fumbles. Pride had held her back, pride and a fear of revealing any weakness or want.

She touched a key cautiously. As she'd been told, a quite gentle touch summoned a note, a softer more resonant note than the harp-like twang of the harpsichord.

Miles leant over beside her and stroked out a chord. "Piano—" Then he thundered one. "—forte. I don't think you can hurt it. Explore."

She started to play a familiar piece but stopped, dissatisfied by the difference in touch. "It's difficult to break a lifetime habit of hitting every key sharply." She turned to look at him. "Go away, please. I wish to make a fool of myself in private."

For the first time since she'd betrayed him to Rupert, he smiled. "I'm sure you'll make beautiful music, but I will go away for a little while."

His leaving created a hollow space.

Felicity filled it with music.

Miles was sitting in the library with a book open but unread, listening to Bach, when his mother came to speak to him.

"She plays beautifully," she said.

"It's her only accomplishment."

Aideen laughed. "I doubt that. She strikes me as a young woman who excels at everything she puts her hand to."

He closed the book and placed it on a table. "Then she never chooses to put her hand to suitable skills—such as handwriting and domestic management. I sincerely doubt she even knows how to thread a needle!"

"How very sad. After all, she might fall on hard times and have to take in mending."

At the caustic tone, Miles realized he'd never seen his mother with a needle in her hand either. He grinned, knowing he was probably as transparent as the glass in the long window.

"So," said Aideen. "Tell me what she has put her hand to apart from music. You will not convince me she's indolent."

He laughed at the thought. "She's cunning at chess, rides like a trooper—and swears like one, too, sometimes—knows nearly as much about horses as I do, and can handle a pistol."

"A useful list of accomplishments."

"For the Countess of Kilgoran?" Then he wished the words unsaid.

"I don't see why not, Ireland being Ireland. Now, I came to tell you that I have arranged the safe stowage of Master Kieran and his governess."

"So soon? How did you manage that?"

"I've written to his governess to say that the boy's father has been called away and wishes him to visit some cousins."

"Cousins?"

She waved a hand. "The gentry of Ireland are all interrelated."

"Don't I remember being whipped a time or two for stretching the truth?"

She twinkled at him. "And there were many times you weren't. It is all a matter of knowing how far one can stretch truth before it breaks. Now, should we tell Felicity?"

"The less we speak of the boy the better."

"Not speaking of him will not wipe him from her mind."

"It might let him slide from the forefront of it."

Then Miles detected what his mother had heard—a certain desperation in the flood of music coming from the pianoforte.

He sighed. "Once we have news of where he is, I suppose we should let her know. It can hardly make matters worse at this stage. But sooner or later, she'll have to let go of the child."

"I'm sure something will work out." Aideen smiled blithely and hurried away.

Devil take it, she was even beginning to *sound* like Colum.

Miles decided Felicity should be over her musical nerves and went to listen from closer by. She was so caught up in the music that he could study her at leisure.

She played, it seemed, with her entire body, swaying in search of finer harmonies. Her eyes, however, stayed focused on some distant, darker vision. Could Dunsford and his son really cast such a shadow on her life? Miles wanted, desperately, to bring back joy, in both senses of the word.

He did the only thing he could and interrupted her with an invitation to tour the house. She did not seem unhappy to leave the music. Perhaps if he filled her days with commonplace matters, ones that would arouse no unpleasant thoughts, she would learn to smile again.

Dangerous though that would be. . . .

He should have known that avoiding unpleasantness was not Felicity's way. The first thing she wanted to see was Gardeen's grave. When he hesitated, she challenged him. "You have buried her properly, haven't you?"

"Of course."

Reflecting that bringing joy to this woman's guarded heart was likely to be an heroic task, he borrowed a servant's woolen shawl for her and took her outside. Accompanied by the dogs, they walked to the sundial in the middle of the herb garden.

It wasn't the best of days—they were being whipped by the tail-end of a storm—but the sweet tang of the herbs was in the air, rising powerfully when they stepped on the chamomile and thyme running between the cracks in the paved path. He directed her to the small mound. Donn and Dubh once more took up sentinel positions.

"She'll be happy there," Felicity said, holding the shawl close about her head.

"I think so." *But how can I make you happy, Felicity? And why is it becoming so crucial to my own content?*

He watched as she broke off a spray of early forsythia and crouched to tuck it among the white stones. Her next words were so soft the wind almost snatched them away. "I would have gone with him and we'd have been under sail before you could have reached us, had it not been for her. We argued about whether to take her."

"He not wanting a cat along."

She rose to face him. "On the contrary. Lacking Kieran, he wanted her as hostage."

"Felicity . . ." He reached to pull her into his arms, but she evaded him, facing him from a couple of yards away.

"And I was determined that she stay safe with you. I took her out to let her go."

"What happened, then?"

"He tried to grab her. She scratched him." He thought she would say no more, but then tears glossed her eyes and she added, "He broke her neck. It was so quick. . . ."

Again, he wanted to gather her into his arms, but it was as if a wall stood between them. "A quick death is a blessing. And it sent you running from him."

A slight toss of her head seemed to throw off weakness. "I regretted it immediately."

"But it was done. It wouldn't surprise me, you know, to learn that Gardeen knew what would happen and made her own death in the cause."

She frowned at him then, tiny drops of the blowing drizzle on her curly hair and even on her lashes. "That's nonsense."

"Is it? Or don't you want to admit that no one, no creature on earth, thinks you should marry Rupert Dunsmore."

She turned sharply away. "I do what I have to do. And to be thinking there's a conspiracy of cats out to stop my marriage is to be moon-mad, Miles Cavanagh!"

She swept back to the house and he followed, dogs at his heels.

His words had largely been whimsical, but now he wondered. There'd been times in his life when he'd felt, like Hamlet, that there were more things in heaven and earth than are dreamt of in logical philosophy. In Ireland, belief in magic and mysteries ran deep.

He glanced back at the tiny grave, remembering the way the dogs had seemed to honor it, unsure what was reasonable anymore.

And what of Felicity? Was Irish magic at work there, too? His feelings were shifting, growing, without any hope of conscious control, so that her care, her happiness, were central to his life.

And it had nothing to do with guardianship.

But she, of course, was still dead set on marrying Rupert Dunsmore.

The best he could do for Felicity's happiness was to keep her distracted, so he insisted on giving her the tour of the house. By hard work, he soon reestablished superficial good manners between them, and even a degree of humor and teasing.

He wanted that moment back, that moment on the journey when he'd carried her in his arms and a chord had hummed between them. He'd settle for some ease, however, and a smile now and then.

As he showed her the family portraits, she began to relax. Admiring the skilled plasterwork of the dining-room ceiling, she made a joke about the half-naked deities. As they handled his father's porcelain, his hand brushed hers. The way she flinched away gave him hope.

Hers was not the manner of a fearful or disgusted woman.

It was the manner of a woman disturbed by a touch, aware of the vibration of the air between them.

"Have you more delights to show me?" she asked rather breathily, clearly hoping he would say no.

"One last thing." Without further explanation, he led her toward the west wing.

"What?" she asked, being careful not to touch him as they walked.

He opened the door on the billiard room specially constructed by his father, who had loved the game.

"Oh," she said, moving forward. "I've always wanted to try. It's generally considered a man's game."

He'd guessed right. A man's game was exactly the thing to enthrall Felicity Monahan. "I'd be happy to teach you."

With luck, this would take her mind off her troubles all afternoon and keep her nearby, where he needed her to be. That need bothered him, but he was losing the will to fight it.

She hesitated, poised for flight, but then walked in to inspect the rack of cues.

With a sigh of relief, and perhaps of surrender, Miles explained the rules of the game. He soon found, however, that the intimacy of their situation intensified the nerve-tingling atmosphere. It took immense control, as he guided her hand and aligned her body, not to turn each touch into a caress.

And his control was weakening . . .

When Colum came to join them, Miles could have hugged him, for he brought sanity with him. He was disconcerted, however, when his mother arrived and picked up a cue. During his father's life, she had shown no interest in the game at all.

"Colum has been teaching me," Aideen said. "I find it a game of considerable skill and challenge."

Much to Miles's astonishment, she beat him.

Colum beamed and applauded. "Sure, and isn't she the

finest woman in the world? But I don't need to tell you that, my boy."

He didn't, but to Miles it seemed against the rules for a mother to change so dramatically mid-course, so to speak. Now he came to think of it, the caps she wore these days were more flighty, and he suspected she'd had her dresses altered to be more formfitting.

When the happy couple wandered off, Felicity chuckled. "You look dumbfounded. I think I'll practice so I can beat you, too."

That wasn't what had knocked him for a loop, but he didn't say so. He was just delighted to hear her laugh. "By all means. You have the eye for it. You'll master the game in no time at all."

The glow of laughter dimmed. She turned back to the table and lined up a shot. "That's as well since I only have a week."

Ten

Felicity sent a red ball slamming into a corner pocket, wishing . . .

She didn't know what she wished for anymore. Yes, she did. She *had* to wish for Rupert's return and their marriage. She had to wish to evade Miles, to escape his care, his concerned eyes, his gentle humor.

His touch.

She knew he was working hard to ease her day and both loved and resented him for it.

No. Not love. Never that.

Her thoughts warred with each other until she was tempted to scream, or to run and hide like a child fleeing a thunderstorm. For it was a storm, a wild energy thrumming in the air around them all day, like a deep, disturbing chord.

A chord that could shatter the guard on her heart.

There was nowhere to run to, though, so she steadied her nerves and settled to mastering the game of billiards.

Surely a safe enough way to pass the time.

Or was it?

The lesson involved Miles touching her—to adjust her grip on the cue, to align her body for a shot. There was nothing untoward in his manner, and yet she felt each touch as a shiver on her skin, even through layers of winter clothing.

It was worse when he leaned around her, encompassing her, as he helped her master the more difficult techniques.

Could he really be oblivious to the atmosphere, deaf to that nerve-jangling chord?

She glanced at him, and he smiled quite calmly.

Then his eyes darkened and seemed to shift, to linger on her lips.

She realized she was licking them.

Hastily, she concentrated on the white ball at the end of her cue, though her hand shook and a tendril of hair fell over her right eye.

If only it weren't so hot!

It was just the fire . . .

It must be the fire, for Miles was stripping off his woolen jacket. Her own long-sleeved, high-necked gown of sturdy Circassian cloth was stifling, and yet she had no layers she could shed. Her careful shot ricocheted pointlessly from cushion to cushion.

She stepped back to let him play, brushing the damp curl back and relieved to be able to move as far as possible from that distressing fire.

It did not reduce the heat at all, for it gave her a clear view of him. How could fine linen shirt and brocade waistcoat seem so wantonly underdressed?

He bent and stretched to take his shot. Without his jacket, the strong line of his body—wide shoulders to firm buttocks, then down long, muscular horseman's legs—forced itself on her senses like a crescendo from a massed orchestra, supported by a hundred drums.

The red ball fell neatly into a corner pocket.

Damn him. He felt nothing at all!

Straightening, he quite casually removed his cravat to let the neck of his shirt stand open. But he looked at her as he did it, and she realized he was not deaf to the music at all.

"This is so unfair. . . ." She stared at his naked throat, wanting to lick the perspiration there.

"I've had years more practice at the game."

"You know that's not what I mean." Her eyes met his

pleadingly, though she was not sure what she requested. "I can't think. It's so hot."

He dropped his cravat on the floor. "Perhaps, then, we shouldn't try to think." He walked around the table to her side.

Felicity took one step back. "What are you doing?"

He put his cue down on the baize. Then he plucked hers from her hand and laid it side by side with his.

There seemed an absurd intimacy in those two neatly aligned cues.

Then he pulled her into his arms.

"Miles!"

His lips silenced her.

The chord swelled but lost all menacing discord so Felicity had no choice but to surrender to purest, sensual harmony.

With a master's skill, he kissed her deep, he kissed her light, he brought her to join with him in kissing so she had no idea who was giving, who was taking. He raised the heat a great many degrees, but somehow, she didn't care.

Perhaps because by now her gown was unfastened down the back.

"Miles!"

His lazy eyes were heavy with passion, but not lazy anymore. He slid her dress off her shoulders and nipped at her skin.

She clutched the dress at her breasts. "It's the middle of the day!"

"No one will come here."

"Your mother . . ."

"Is off being similarly treated by Colum, I suspect, damn his wicked heart." But there was no anger in him.

"Miles," she whispered faintly, "you're my guardian . . ."

"I see no profit in it at all, at all," he murmured, sliding into a brogue that stole the strength from her hands so her dress pooled on the floor.

His hands stilled as he looked at her, absorbing her as she

wanted to absorb him. "You have the beauty of the Danaan, *a muirnín, mo chroí.* This is our destiny."

Then the pins came out of her hair and he spread it around her, every delicate touch of his fingers a sweet chord along her nerves.

He cradled her breasts, cupped by her white linen corset but largely vulnerable to his touch, shielded only by her silken shift. "It's not fair that a woman be so well-armored," he murmured as his thumbs softly teased her nipples.

"A corset is armor?"

He laughed and loosened the ribbon at the neck so her shift fell loose over the upper swell of her breasts. "Your armor, my fair swan, is what lies beneath it. . . ." And he brushed his lips, breath hot, over her.

Felicity swallowed, murmuring a disjointed prayer. Though what god would have any part of this, she didn't know.

He loosened the corset-laces and slid it off, but all the time his mouth teased at her ear, her neck, her chest. . . .

She clutched his hair, holding him close, though somewhere in the heated maelstrom of her mind, she realized this did not fit in with her plans at all.

But they had a week.

Didn't they deserve a week?

A ripple of maddening pleasure flowed through her. Her knees gave way and she would have collapsed to the floor, but he swept her into his arms and carried her to the sofa. Placing her there gently, he knelt to slide her shift up, gazing at her legs as she gazed at him.

He had never looked more beautiful. With his red-gold hair disordered and his features in intent repose, he stole her breath and took the remnants of her sanity with it.

His shirt was loose at the waist. Perhaps she'd loosened it. She wiggled her toes under and pressed her foot against his ribs, trying to work the shirt up and expose more of his body.

He grinned and moved to sit on the edge of the sofa, leaving her shift as it was, hanging loose in the top exposing her breasts, and rucked up at the bottom almost to the top of her thighs.

Laughing with him, she began to tug at his shirt, using her very useful ability to grip things with her toes. As the front came free of his breeches, he asked, "Can you do buttons?"

"No, but I can tickle."

He captured her feet and tickled back, so they tangled and tussled on the damask sofa until the shreds of her decency were entirely lost.

Then he kissed her between her legs and in her navel and on her breasts and around her neck until he reached her lips and she could kiss him back. And if her toes could not undo buttons, her fingers could, and could do other interesting things, things she had never done to Rupert. . . .

But no. She would not think of Rupert Dunsmore now.

She curled her hand around Miles's erection, determined to take this moment and find the fullness of it.

Fullness.

"You're very big," she murmured.

He'd been licking her breasts in a leisurely, thorough way, but now he stilled. "I was thinking perhaps I should ask if you were a virgin."

She stilled, too. How had she ever imagined they could do this and keep her secret? "I wish I were."

He turned her face toward him. "It doesn't matter, *a stor.* And," he added with a grin, "I'm exceedingly pleased that I'm bigger."

She fell into laughter, then, though there were tears in it. He drank the laughter from her lips and the tears from her eyes and slid into her so smoothly she scarce felt the change from two to one until they were in complete harmony of the flesh.

She cried out from the perfection of it, and from the sensual sweetness sent running flamelike through her body from crotch to dizzy, whirling head. She kissed him then, holding tight into his curls so he could not resist, wrapping her strong legs about him so he could not retreat, contracting her inner muscles in raptured seizure.

Mine, said a primitive part of her, and would not let cold logic intervene.

Mine.

He murmured to her as he moved, in English and in Gaelic, and his message was the same as hers—a raw possession like a wild Irish raider seizing a maiden on the shore. Like Diarmuid stealing Grania from the High King and holding her against man and magic, against heaven and hell for the sake of this roiling madness, this golden rapture of the soul.

But even in myth, the rapture ends and lovers must fall back to the chill earth.

Cool again, melded, welded, changed.

Sane.

Had Grania felt like this when she came to her senses and realized what she had done? Felicity turned her head into his hot damp neck and, against her strong will, tears escaped.

He moved her into his arms, onto his lap, to hold her, rock her, soothe her, tease her. "No need to cry, my wild, dark-plumed swan. We can do it again."

"But only for a week."

She felt his sigh. "Felicity . . ."

She pushed back. "Did you think this would change anything?" At the look on his face, she cried, "You did! Is that why you did it? Just to change my mind?"

She would have torn free of his hold, but he strengthened it brutally. "That is not why I did it, why *we* did it. Do you really think this was planned? I've wanted you now for weeks. God help us both, I *love* you. But if you'd shown any reluctance, *mo chroí,* I would have stopped."

She slumped back against his chest. "Oh, Miles, I was not reluctant. But how could you think it would change anything? It just makes it harder."

"I want it to be hard. So hard it is impossible."

"That can never be."

"Then I will simply have to stop you."

"Once I am of age, you cannot."

She hated this talk, this bickering, and drowned it in the senses, exploring him again with mouth and hands, tasting the sweat that dewed his smooth skin. "We have a week, Miles. Let's drain the joy of it."

He sank back in surrender, his hand speaking need and sorrow to her skin. "Ah, but it's a dangerous joy, *a taibhreamh, a chroí,* like the wild loving of legends, leading only to tears."

How frightening that he shared her thought. "Better perilous joy than no joy at all."

And they found the joy again—all the searing heat and bitter sweetness of it—even as they knew the pounding hooves of the High King of reality would soon steal all magic away.

Eventually, reluctantly, they had to acknowledge his presence. They had to resume their clothes and the cares of the fast-expiring day. The room was nearly dark and the long-untended fire was merely a starving glimmer.

He buttoned her gown; she buttoned his waistcoat. She straightened his hair as best she could without a comb, and he assembled some sort of knot for hers and fixed it with the pins.

Then they looked at one another and laughed.

"Not exactly pattern-cards of perfection, are we?" he said.

"Ah, but it's a fine wild game, the game of billiards."

"A fine, wild game indeed. Can I come to your room tonight?"

The sweet thought of it made a pain near her heart that was like tears held there. "We shouldn't. . . ."

"There'll be no scandal. I'll make sure of that."

With sanity came a new fear. "And what of a child?" She pressed her hands to her head. "Dear God! How could I have been so mad?"

He reached out to soothe her hands down. "Ah, *muirnín.* I can think of nothing I'd like more."

Felicity stepped back sharply. "No! How could I—"

"How could you marry Dunsmore with my child in your womb? You couldn't."

She saw the glint in his eyes and the pain was now like a sword in her heart. *"That's* why you did this! *Diabhal!* What of our truce?"

All humor left his face. "I never made a pact with you, Felicity. I intend to stop you from marrying Dunsmore, and I will do anything—"

She put the billiard table between them. "Then I take back my word. Now! My promise is as mist on the wind. It is nothing. I will leave here when I will."

"Then I will guard you night and day, or set others to guard you. My will is unbreakable on this."

"As is mine."

They faced one another, enemies who had so recently been lovers of the closest kind, their enmity too deep, too strong for outrage or for snarling mouths.

Felicity broke the silence. "Since my future husband is surely not back in Ireland yet, I will regive my promise, if that is the price of peace from you."

"You will not leave Clonnagh without my permission?"

"I will not, for six days now. But on condition," she said fiercely. "On condition that you do not seek again to get me with child."

He regarded her, as a warrior might regard a naked sword. "It is in the hand of fate, then. I accept your terms."

"And if I prove to be with child, that will not stop my marrying Rupert."

"I will stop you from marrying Dunsmore, child or not."

The dinner bell rang, a startling reminder of everyday things.

He shook his head, becoming once more a civilized gentleman of 1816. "Hell, and we need to change."

With exactly the manner of one who has been playing billiards and has lost track of time, he ushered her out of the rapidly cooling, darkening room.

Felicity would have loved to avoid meeting Miles over the superficial normality of the dinner table. She disdained to plead sickness, however, and there was no other reason to give except the truth—that she wasn't sure she could sit through a meal opposite Miles and not reveal something of the afternoon, of the ecstasy or the misery.

She dressed for the meal, acknowledging that it was even possible that her uncle and aunt would guess they had been lovers. Such things often showed. If her grandfather and aunt had been more observant people five years ago, they would surely have noticed her turning into a lovesick fool.

Perhaps they might have forestalled the whole tragedy, a tragedy still being played out today, undermining what could have been a fine and magic love.

Love.

It was a bitter herb that love had come too late, and quite impossibly. It was sharp-edged terror that she might have conceived Miles's child today, horribly complicating her already wretched situation.

Felicity draped a large Norwich shawl of green and gold around her shoulders. A last check assured her that she was the very image of a proper young lady, one who would never dream of an afternoon of wanton sensuality in the billiard room.

Armored in that belief, she swept downstairs to dine with her lover and his parents.

There she discovered, if she hadn't already known it, that both she and Miles were clever actors. They bantered as if mere genial acquaintances, easily taking part in discussions of books, poetry, and even politics.

At times she wondered if the afternoon had been a mad dream.

Had this lighthearted gentleman, with his ready smile, his pleasant manners, and the witty stories of hounds and hunting, lain naked between her naked thighs stroking her to delirium?

She had to slip the shawl from her shoulders, for the room was becoming exceedingly hot.

Neither Colum nor Miles's mother showed any awareness of impropriety. Colum matched Miles story for story, his mainly about the administration in Dublin. Lady Aideen contributed stories of Society.

Felicity noted that Miles often made mention of a particular group. "Now, who are these Rogues?" she asked at one point, mostly to break her silence before it became obvious. Anyone who knew her would find a long silence remarkable.

It was Lady Aideen who answered. "Oh, the Rogues. As big a bunch of rascally ne'er-do-wells as the world has ever seen!" But she was laughing. "I'm sure as individuals they are all fine young gentlemen, but when they are together, heaven protect us all! Why, we had some of them here once, and they were nearly shot by Lord Whitmore's gamekeeper."

"He had man-traps out," Miles said, "and we decided to spring 'em."

Miles's mother lost her smile. "I still shiver to think of it. Even though you managed to outwit the keeper, you could have sprung one with a leg, you foolish boy."

"We were only sixteen."

"You were fortunate your father decided you were too old to flog."

"I think we'd rather have had the flogging than to be confined to house for two perfect days and set to learn whole chunks of Tacitus."

"But," said Felicity, "this still doesn't tell me who these people are, and why you—for I see you are one of them—call yourselves Rogues. I'm surprised you want to advertise the fact."

"Proud of it," said Miles with a warm smile that must have been the best acting of the evening. "You see, my Uncle Kilgoran insisted I be educated in England. That wasn't to my taste at all. Having seen some of the cruelty of the English soldiers here, I hated everything English with a passion. But he insisted, probably for that very reason."

"Exactly for that very reason, Miles," said his mother. "We were no happier about it than you, but we could see Kilgoran's point. In time, you will be a force in Ireland, and you must be able to deal with the English on equal terms."

Miles grimaced. "So, as fervently rebellious as Fitzgerald and Grattan combined, I was dispatched to Harrow School where I found myself surrounded by the cream of English manhood and stood ready to challenge them all."

"And you lived to tell the tale?" Felicity remarked, intrigued despite herself.

Miles laughed. "Only because of the Rogues. A certain Nicholas Delaney decided to gather twelve boys under a vow to stand together against cruelty and oppression. A blow against one was a blow against all. It deterred bullies very well indeed."

Then the goose was brought in, and he stood to carve.

Felicity wondered how someone carving neat slices of meat from a bird's breast could be so appallingly sensual. She made herself look at his face instead. "And what did you do, you Rogues, when not standing against oppressors or sabotaging man-traps?"

He smiled at her. "Believe it or not, we helped each other with studies now and then. And in holidays, we spent time together, or at least smaller groups did. Twelve of us in one house was more than even the most tolerant parent would permit."

He flashed an amused look at his mother and gestured for the footman to pass around the meat.

"Besides, we didn't always agree on a perfect holiday. Nicholas picked a very varied group. Not all of us were horse-mad, for example. Lucien, Stephen, Hal, and I were generally off finding the best riding we could persuade our fathers to allow us. Nicholas, Francis, and Roger were more interested in antiquities."

"It all sounds like fun," Felicity said wistfully.

"It was. Still is, for the bonds still hold. It's a shame you didn't go to school and make friends."

Felicity fought back tears. At sixteen, when Miles had been hunting or sneaking into his neighbor's coverts to spring man-traps, she'd been in exile, enduring a long pregnancy which would end with her giving up her child.

"So you all still meet to enjoy your adventures?"

Miles resumed his seat as vegetable removes were passed around. "Not all of us, alas. Three have died in the war."

"I'm sorry for that."

He smiled. "I suspect that when the rest of us are toothless and gouty, we'll envy them their eternal youth in the Land of the Happy Dead."

"Hey, hey!" interrupted Colum. "No morbid talk! But these Rogues do all sound like fine, brothy boys, and I hope to meet them one day."

"I'm intending to leave shortly for the Shires, and some of them will be there. You'd be welcome to come along, Colum."

There was a moment of wistfulness, but then Colum said, "No, my boy, no. I could not leave behind the pleasures I have here." He toasted his wife. "Some other year, perhaps."

"When the pleasures are fading?" queried Aideen with a wicked twinkle.

Colum reddened. "Oh-ho, my love! You have caught me on a lazy thought. True it is, that I am likely never to move from your side."

"Silly man. I'm sure that, in a year or two, we'll be able to part for a while, and the absence will give greater spice to our happiness."

Colum toasted her again. "What a wise woman you are, my precious one."

Miles raised his glass as well. "And pleasant memories ease the lonely traveler." But his eyes were upon Felicity and she understood his message. He was trying to seduce her into more lovemaking before their week ended.

She should have extended her conditions. It was not enough that he not try to get her with child. She wanted him to cease attempts at intimacy altogether.

After dinner, Felicity played the piano, for a while managing to lose herself in music. Then Colum and Miles's mother sang a duet, their voices blending perfectly.

Felicity glanced at Miles, and he grinned. "Don't even think of it. I have no singing voice. But I can play."

To her surprise, he picked up the harp, sitting it on his knee and leaning it snugly against his shoulder. "Don't look so surprised. It's Ireland's ancient instrument."

"I've never actually seen it played before."

Aideen laughed. "I think Miles decided to learn it out of sheer perversity when told he was to be educated in England."

"Probably," he agreed, plucking a delicate waterfall of sound. "Then I delighted in the surprise everyone showed. There's nothing a youngster enjoys as much as surprising his elders."

He proceeded to play with considerable skill upon the instrument, his strong fingers summoning lively music to dance through the receptive room.

As those strong fingers had summoned music to dance through her receptive body . . .

Felicity rested her head against the back of her chair and closed her eyes, seeking pleasant thoughts.

Those that came, however, were disturbing.

Rupert had no musical instruments in his house. She had suggested to Kathleen that Kieran should be taught music, but Rupert, apparently, thought such skills unmanly.

When her son visited Foy, she encouraged him to play on

the harpsichord, and he showed an aptitude. But he was already being affected by his father's views and thought music for milksops.

It was frightening to think of the effect Rupert could have on the boy in the future if unchecked. Thus far, he had largely ignored Kieran, but if he chose not to . . .

She must marry the man, and soon.

Then she realized her hands were resting low on her abdomen and her troubled mind settled on her major fear.

How could she have been so stupid, so mad?

She opened her eyes to look at Miles and knew exactly why. It was as if he'd cast a spell over her.

She could be carrying his child.

Deep inside, a primitive part of her rejoiced, but it was a tragedy in the making, especially if it were a son, his legal heir if they were married.

With the possibility that she carried his child, he would never let her go.

Then she realized the music had stopped.

She flushed. "I'm sorry." She meant for more than her abstraction.

"You look exhausted," Miles said. "Do you want to go to bed?"

The mere word "bed" had her protesting. "No. no, I'm not tired at all."

Miles raised a skeptical brow but said, "Then perhaps we could have a few hands of whist."

The older couple agreed and the table was arranged, with Felicity and Miles as partners.

There was nothing Felicity wanted less than to spend an hour or more opposite Miles.

Opposite the man she loved.

Opposite the man she had loved in a manner, she was sure, few humans ever did.

Opposite the man she might have to betray by stealing his child.

Oh, how had she let herself slide even deeper into the morass?

And she had given her word not to try to escape for a week.

At ten o'clock, Lady Aideen announced that she was too tired to continue. Soon the older couple headed up the stairs, not looking particularly weary at all.

Felicity hastily picked up the candle awaiting her, but Miles halted her escape with a gentle touch on her arm.

"There was very little calculation in what happened this afternoon, Felicity. I was driven by desire. And love. I do love you."

"Don't . . ."

"I doubt I can change it now. I can choose not to speak of it, but why should I? How else am I to win you?"

"You cannot win me, Miles. Accept it."

"I am not a man who easily accepts defeat, *mo chroí.*"

She twitched out of his hold. "I *warned* you. I warned you from the first that I was dangerous. And see what has happened! Let me be, Miles. Let me be, and be you safe."

He just shook his head. "It is beyond that."

She turned toward the stairs, but at the first step, his voice halted her.

"Felicity, if we have nothing else in this life, we have one week. My door will be open to you tonight."

"Then you'll have a chilly room." With that, she climbed the stairs without looking back.

Felicity's room was not chilly. In well-run Clonnagh, a fire burned cheerfully in the grate, hot water awaited, and the handle of a warming pan stuck promisingly out of the covers of her bed.

Still, she shivered and rubbed her arms as if in drafty Foy.

At a tug on the bell-rope, a maid hurried in to help her out of her gown. Felicity couldn't help thinking of the way Miles had unfastened her buttons without her even noticing.

Oh, but he was a cunning rascal.

Which had her thinking of what had come after—a loving as different to her memories of Rupert as silver is to tin.

It would be sweet indeed to gather more of that to her heart before . . .

But she wasn't about to court disaster twice!

Once down to her shift, Felicity sent the maid to bed. Then she stripped naked and washed, scrubbing away any reminder of her afternoon's insanity. When she glanced toward the mirror, however, she saw a mark on her shoulder.

She ran over to check. It was! It was what they called a love-bite. Rupert had marked her that way, too, careful to place it where she could hide it.

At fifteen that hadn't been hard, for she'd not needed a maid's assistance out of her gowns.

He'd relished the mark on her, though.

She'd relished it, too, infatuated as she had been. She remembered how desperately she'd wanted to tell someone of the wonderful things that were happening, of the fact that a handsome, mature man loved *her*.

Dear God, what fools young girls could be!

And what wicked wretches the men who took advantage of their sweet willingness.

Miles's mark was not as careful, though. If she wore a low-necked gown, it would show. She was sure that was deliberate. He intended to claim her.

Shivering, she touched the mark, which neither roughened the skin nor hurt. A magical thing, really.

She wished she'd marked Miles. At the thought, she smiled, a wicked womanly smile that made the naked creature in the mirror something quite different to Felicity Monahan—sometimes hoyden, sometimes proper young lady of Foy Hall.

Here, in a strange house, she was truly becoming a woman, realizing her woman's magical powers for good or ill.

Becoming Grania.

Grania, who was chosen by the High King, Finn mac Cool himself, to be his bride, saw Diarmuid—Dermot as he was called now—and fell in love. Grania, who used her woman's magic to seduce the hero from his lord and his friends.

Diarmuid had tried to resist, but Grania's spell had proved too strong. They had fled together with the High King in pursuit; but by strength and cleverness, Diarmuid always triumphed so that they found peace together.

But only for a time. In the end, Finn had gained his revenge and Diarmuid had paid with his life for Grania's love.

Most Irish love stories ended in blood.

Felicity shivered. Was there a warning there? Though she tried to be modern, there was too much magic in Ireland for it to be dismissed entirely.

Was Miles her Diarmuid?

But then she grimaced. That would make Rupert the great hero, Finn, and that she could not believe.

No, if anything, she was Diarmuid, trying to hold to her allegiance not to Rupert but to her son, while Miles Cavanagh cast his sensual spells. And as in the myth, surrender could cause nothing but suffering in the end.

Felicity turned from the mirror to cover her disturbing nakedness with her sensible cotton nightgown and her wild hair with a cotton cap. Then, blocking her mind to the insistent temptation of a certain open door, she climbed into her warm bed and insisted that her tired body sleep.

And after an hour or two, it succumbed.

Eleven

Felicity awoke from dreams of magical caves and blood-stained swords, with always a small black cat at her side. Miles had not been in her dreams at all—unless he'd been the helmeted warrior roaring defiance, or the dark presence reaching for her, calling for her, tempting her to destruction. For a modern house, Clonnagh was strangely fertile ground for such matters.

She breakfasted in her room, plotting activities which would keep her out of her guardian's way. When she could delay her exit no longer, she took desperate measures and asked Miles's mother to teach her something of domestic management.

It seemed to Felicity that Lady Aideen's eyes turned sharp and shrewd, but she agreed cordially enough. "A young lady contemplating marriage should certainly take interest in such matters."

Felicity's mind immediately went to Miles, and she almost protested that she was contemplating no such thing. Then she recalled that she was, in fact, contemplating marriage—to Rupert Dunsmore. With a suppressed shudder, she mumbled something vague.

"Not that I am the best adviser, my dear, if you want to know how to pickle beetroot or smoke a ham," declared Miles's mother. "I never had patience with such matters myself."

"But Clonnagh is so well run."

"The secret is to hire good servants." Lady Aideen led the way briskly to the small drawing room. "Then reward excellence and punish laziness. It is very like raising children and at times can seem more trouble than it is worth. But if done well, there are rewards. Now, since I normally spend the morning taking care of such matters, why don't you observe?"

Accordingly, Felicity sat beside her hostess as Lady Aideen checked the housekeeper's and the cook's accounts and endorsed their plans for the day. She went with her to the lower regions and stood by as storage cupboards were unlocked for the distribution of necessary supplies of tea and wine.

"You may think such precautions mean-spirited," Lady Aideen said as they returned upstairs to investigate a matter of worn hangings, "but it is simpler for all. If the valuable items are not safeguarded by the mistress, then a member of the staff must be the guard. Then they are always worried they will be blamed if there is a theft. In a grander house like Kilgoran, of course, the steward or groom of the chambers can be entrusted with such tasks."

"I suppose you would have liked to have had charge of Kilgoran."

"Faith, no," Lady Aideen declared. "It's a monstrosity, and even with the best servants, a terrible amount of work. And, of course, the Earl of Kilgoran must keep open house for friends and connections, so there's little peace and privacy."

"It sounds horrible."

"Indeed." Lady Aideen paused to run a finger along the top of a chair and frowned at the trace of dust. "Miles's father had to work hard to persuade me to marry him with such a threat hanging over his head, poor man."

"And poor Miles."

"Oh, I'm sure he'll find a woman willing to share his burden. He offers many compensations. He's a good man, strong but gentle."

It was the strength that sent a shiver down Felicity's spine.

Lady Aideen led the way into a spare bedchamber and inspected the hangings, which an observant maid had discovered to be frayed in places. "Moth," she declared, checking all the cloth in the room. "There's more here, see."

Felicity dutifully studied the frayed holes, though in truth, she was very familiar with moth-eaten fabrics and these did not seem badly damaged.

Lady Aideen, however, took it seriously, ringing for the housekeeper and ordering the hangings taken down to be cleaned, treated with camphor, and repaired. At the same time, the whole room was to be scoured in an attempt to get rid of any remaining eggs.

"There, you see," she said with a grin, leading Felicity down to the drawing room. "All I have to do is order a great deal of work for others. It will be the same for you if you organize things well."

Felicity immediately thought of herself organizing Clonnagh, picking up the reins of this organized household. But then she gave herself a shake.

It was Loughcarrick she would be managing, which had always been well run under Kathleen's eye. What she had learned here today would help her to keep up the standards and be a good wife to Rupert Dunsmore.

She shuddered again, even though in well-run Clonnagh the drawing room was warm and free of draughts.

Miles noted that Felicity was avoiding him. It was hardly surprising, but in a twisted way it gave him hope. If she'd seemed comfortable spending the morning with him, he would have been more concerned.

Faith, after yesterday, there was surely no question of indifference. He could distinguish between casual sex of even the most passionate kind and that joining of heart, mind, and soul. Surely to God, it must have meant the same to her and make impossible the idea of marrying another.

Perhaps she just needed a little time to grow accustomed to the change.

So he settled to handling a number of administrative matters, hoping against hope that at some point his exasperating ward would seek him out.

Instead, he was interrupted by the sound of carriage wheels on the gravel drive.

He left his study to greet whoever was arriving. When he opened the door, however, he was stunned to see Mrs. Edey descend from the coach, then turn to help Kieran down.

Was this some devious plot by Dunsmore? He could imagine nothing more injurious to his plans.

Bags were being taken out of the boot as if the two anticipated a long stay. Mrs. Edey led the excited lad up to the steps, clearly admonishing him to mind his manners. But then Kieran looked up.

"Hello, sir!" he cried. "Is Sissity here?"

"Yes. Come in and I'll have her found for you." What else could he say?

Miles was attempting to be courteous, but perhaps some trace of his feelings showed, for Mrs. Edey said, "Did you not expect us so soon, Mr. Cavanagh? Lady Aideen's letter implied that we were to come here immediately."

His mother? His mother had done this?

He forced a smile. "I'm merely surprised at your speed, Mrs. Edey. You must have started at the crack of dawn. But you're very welcome. Come in and we'll have tea."

Even as he led the way to the small drawing room, Felicity emerged from it. Her eyes fixed immediately upon the boy and lit with joy. "Kieran, my poppet. What a lovely surprise!"

He ran straight into her open arms and was hoisted up on her hip. "Is it? I hope it is. We came ever so fast. And we changed horses twice. I saw a big, big magpie. . . ."

The lad chattered away as Felicity carried him into the drawing room, sat him on a chair, and took off his coat and hat. "It all sounds like a wonderful adventure, dearest. But I'm sure you must be hungry. What would you like to eat?"

"Now, now," Mrs. Edey said, hovering, "you mustn't spoil him, Miss Monahan. Master Kieran will eat what he is given. And he must wash his hands first, too."

Miles saw the brief flash of resentment on Felicity's shining face before she accepted the other woman's rights. "Of course, he must. I'll take him to the dressing room down here, for there is water there for washing."

Aideen stepped forward to welcome Mrs. Edey, which let Felicity escape with her treasure.

Miles looked after her, deeply disturbed. Kieran Dunsmore could well be an opponent no mortal man could defeat.

When Colum arrived to bear part of the duties of hospitality, Miles drew his mother apart. "What the devil possessed you to bring the lad *here?*"

"You wanted him safe." She was so blandly innocent that he knew there was a plot in this.

"If I'd wanted him here, I could have arranged it myself, don't you think?"

"There are any number of things you could do for yourself that you seem to like my arranging for you, even to ordering your shirts. I have no idea why you're glaring at me. The child hardly seems a monster."

Since the child was just returning with Felicity, charmingly regaling her with some long, complex story, Miles couldn't deny it. "He's an acceptable urchin, but Felicity is far too fond of him."

"No bad thing, surely, when she intends to marry his father."

"She is not going to marry Kieran's father, but that's not made easier by this turn of events."

"If you want my assistance, dear boy, you have only to ask."

"There'll be drought in Kilkenny before I ask your help again."

Luncheon was announced, and his mother flashed him a very knowing look before bustling off to arrange matters.

Mrs. Edey tried to protest that Kieran did not eat with adults yet, but was overruled by everyone except Miles, so the child sat at the table on two thick books to raise him up. Miles found nothing to object to in the lad's table manners, but he could not like the way Felicity was focused on the boy.

It was as if the child was the center of her world.

Which was a position he wanted for himself.

How the devil could he block her marriage to Dunsmore when it would steal from her the center of her world?

But then he remembered Gardeen. How could he let Felicity put herself in the power of such a vicious wretch?

His mind swam out of confused anger and into logic. Clearly, if he wanted to save Felicity, he would have to find a way to safeguard Kieran as well.

But how could anyone permanently separate father and son?

Short of murder.

It was an appealing notion, but he didn't take human life as lightly as that.

Perhaps the Rogues could come up with a cunning plot.

After lunch, when Felicity took Kieran into the garden, Miles accompanied them even though it was painful to witness her absorption in the child. It was even more painful to be apart from her.

He showed Kieran his favorite climbing tree and boosted him onto the lowest branch. He introduced the lad to the dogs and encouraged him to play with them. He sagely discussed the points of the horses in the closest pasture.

Virtue was rewarded as Felicity gradually grew less wary. It was doubtless mostly for the boy's sake, but he would take what crumbs he could.

"I like that white," said Kieran, sitting between them on the top rail of the fence. "I want a white horse."

"You wouldn't like that one, my lad. He's a devil incarnate."

Kieran clearly didn't understand the words, but said firmly, "He's white."

"Gray," Miles corrected. "Horses like that are called gray."

"I think he's white."

Felicity grinned over the boy's head, then asked, "Why keep the horse if he's so wicked? And I'd hardly say he was well conformed, either."

"Ugly as sin," Miles agreed, "despite excellent bloodlines. But the stamina of him. If he could be ridden, he'd be an impressive steeplechaser. The wretched beast can't bear to be behind."

"Is he not even broken, then?"

"Oh, he's broken, and I have the scars to tell the tale. He'll behave himself well enough under a firm rider, but his gait is not one I'd want to endure for ten miles or more."

She shook her head. "Feed him to the dogs. No man will ever buy him."

"You think not?"

Her old spirit flashed in her eyes. "I'm sure of it."

Delighted by her relaxed high spirits, he asked, "What will you wager, then?"

She turned wary. "What do you propose?"

"After seeing your new devotion to domestic matters, I think you'll owe me a cake baked by your own fair hands."

"A cake?" she laughed. "Do you want to die of the gripe?"

"I've more faith in you than that. So, do we have a wager? If I sell Banshee, you'll bake me a cake?"

She eyed him suspiciously. "To speak of setting one impossibility against another . . . and what will you do if you fail?"

"What would you want?"

He saw revealing emotion flicker across her face but could not read it. "I think the stakes should be equal. If you lose, *you* bake the cake."

He laughed. "I probably know as much about it as you. Which is nothing. Very well. You're on."

"Ah, but wait, you tricksy rascal. I know you. You'll sell him for a penny to the first kennel you pass."

Kieran looked up at that. "Are you going to sell the white horse for a penny, sir? I have a penny."

Miles ruffled his hair. "No, lad, I'm afraid not. I'm going to sell him to a fine gentleman for fifty guineas."

Felicity broke into genuine laughter, and it was the sweetest sound Miles had heard that day. "Fifty guineas! Miles Cavanagh, you're mad! I'm going to enjoy that cake you bake for me."

With Kieran restored to his governess and settled for a nap, Felicity looked as if she would escape again, but since Miles's mother and Colum had gone out to visit friends, her wings were clipped.

"Felicity," Miles said, "you can trust me, even without a four-year-old chaperone. Let me show you my stables."

Genuine interest warred with caution, but interest won. "Very well. I'll change into my habit, for I'd dearly love a ride."

"Ask my mother's maid for a pair of boots."

She flashed him a grimace, but there was a smile hiding behind it. Just perhaps, they were friends again. Soon they were strolling through the gardens toward the extensive stables.

"Did you develop this all yourself?" she asked.

"My father started it. I've introduced some ideas of my own, though."

She wandered around, giving the bustling place an expert scrutiny and asking shrewd questions.

"It's wonderful," she said at last. "I'm surprised you can tear yourself away from here to waste time in England."

"You have a low opinion of the country."

She flashed him a grin to warm his heart. "Sure, and I've nothing against the land and trees. I just have a very low opinion of the inhabitants."

"Yet your mother was English."

"Now there you're wrong." She moved on to the next stall with a jaunty step. "My mother's father was a Scot who moved down to Whitehaven, and my mother's mother was from Antrim."

"Ah. That doubtless explains a great deal."

She flashed him a look. "It clears me of the taint of English blood, at least."

"It also shows you know scarcely enough of the English to pass judgment." He stepped next to her. "I'll agree that as a nation they've not done well by Ireland, but as individuals, they can be tolerable. You need to meet more of them, Felicity."

She immediately moved away, on to the next stall to consider Miles's prize stallion, Horatio. "You could at least give your horses good Irish names."

"My mother has the naming of them."

She turned to him with a skeptical look. "And why would a daughter of the Fitzgeralds have such a classical turn of mind?"

"Perhaps she, too, thinks we Irish need to look beyond our shores to find the key to our own identity. Of course, neither she nor I would carry it far so to marry English blood."

She stiffened as the dart found its mark. "Ireland has tamed invaders before. The Fitzgeralds themselves are descended from Norman stock."

"And do the Monahans claim purer blood?"

"Grandfather claimed to be able to trace us back to Miled."

"To the first true Irishman, hero of myth and legend? After whom I'm named myself, after a fashion. But then the Fitzgeralds claim to have the blood of fairy in them, through the third earl's wedding with Ainé of the Danaan."

"Sure, and are we into genealogical rivalry here?"

"Why not? As horse breeders, we understand such matters." He patted the neck of the fine stallion. "Horatio here has the blood of the Darley Arabian and the Godolphin Barb in him. I would think it a shame to mate him with common stock."

She scowled, then marched on to feed her mare some carrots. "You can mate him to Cresta without concern. Her bloodlines are excellent."

"I'm sure they are. You understand these matters."

She turned to face him. "It seems to me you are obsessed. Look at Kieran. He's the son of Rupert Dunsmore and Kathleen Craig, but a finer lad would be hard to imagine."

"Doubtless the mother had many excellent qualities."

"She was ugly."

"Then the lad is fortunate, though ugliness is not a crippling problem."

"It was for her. Men looked no further than her appearance."

"Was she such a sweet-natured being, then?"

She bit her lip. "No. But I'm sure she could have been if shown more kindness."

"Perhaps, though it seems to me that kindness draws forth kindness. It's true, however, that even a sweet-natured horse can be ruined by cruel treatment." He deliberately moved the discussion closer to the true heart of the matter. "Just as a fine child can be so ruined."

She looked at him sharply. "Then why do you persist in trying to interfere in my plans."

"Because I care. If I can find another way, will you let me?"

She turned from him. "Oh Miles, there is no other way. But I do want to thank you for bringing Kieran here. It means so much to me to know he is safe, for now."

"Then I'm content, for now. Come, let me have Achilles saddled for you. I think you'll enjoy his gait."

And for the rest of the afternoon, he would permit no troubling matters to come between them.

Hours later, Miles and Felicity cantered back into the Clonnagh stables in relatively good spirits. Miles nodded for a groom to help Felicity down, not wanting to disrupt the harmony in any way.

"So," he said as they strolled back up the lane to the house, happy dogs at their heels. "What do you think of Achilles?"

"He's wonderful, as well you know. You do seem to have a knack of hitting gold more often than dross."

"Skill, *cailín*. Skill."

She flashed him a wicked look. "But then, there's Banshee. And it's occurred to me that he's the only horse here lacking a classical name."

"True," Miles laughed. "Mother looked at him newborn and refused to name dogs' meat."

"Why did you keep him?"

"Perhaps I was just fattening him up?"

"Or thinking he was a changeling, and the fairy-folk would give you back your own beautiful colt?"

"Now, there's a thought! That would explain a great deal." He rubbed the side of his nose with the pearl handle of his crop. "In truth, I felt sorry for him, poor ungainly little thing. If I'd known his nature, I might have hardened my heart. By the time it became clear he'd be hard to handle, I'd made such a matter of finding the good in him that I couldn't give up."

"Male pride," she said innocently. "I understand perfectly."

"As if you were lacking in pride."

They were smiling as they turned the corner where the stable lane joined the carriage path around the house. Smiling as they came face to face with Annie Monahan, glowering massively in a heavy mud-colored woolen cloak. Miles thought for a moment that she had a brindled cat in her arms, but then realized it was an enormous fur muff.

"Laughing," she accused, "and the poor dear creature in such distress!"

It took Miles a moment to realize what she meant. "I'm sorry about Gardeen."

"So I should think! You should have taken better care of her."

"True enough. But none of us came through unscathed."

Felicity chimed in, "It was my fault, Aunt."

"I have no doubt of it. You've always been a careless girl." She fished in the enormous fur muff, pulled out a smaller one, and gave it to Miles.

Then he realized it was warm, alive, black. . . .

"Gardeen?" he asked. Then felt idiotic.

"And who else would it be?" Annie demanded acidly. "The poor creature staggered home yesterday bedraggled and exhausted. You should have known she would try to follow you."

"But . . ." Miles looked at Felicity, and she put out a wondering hand to stroke the warm fur.

She answered his unspoken question. "I don't know."

"Take care of her this time," Annie barked. "You won't get another chance."

"I thought cats had *nine* lives," Miles said.

Annie's eyes narrowed. "And what makes you think any human is given more than one of them?" She turned and tramped off up the drive toward the house.

"Oh, dear, she is in a state," Felicity said.

"So am I. What the devil . . ." Miles raised the small cat to look into its silvery eyes. Unblinking cat's eyes stared back, but whether the message was *Why did you abandon me?* or *Why did you let me get killed?* he could not tell.

In silent accord, Miles and Felicity went to the herb garden, to the little mound marked by white stones. He noted that the dogs paid no homage, but snuffled around after intriguing smells.

"I buried a cat here," Miles said, aware of the black cat warm in his hands. He looked at Felicity.

"Oh, no!" she protested. "If you think I had time or inclination to be finding an identical little black cat . . . and why, for Erin's sake, would I want to?"

"I don't know. But I hardly studied the corpse. Perhaps it wasn't very like Gardeen at all."

Her face stilled with anger. "Miles Cavanagh, I'll tell you this once and once only. The cat in my pocket was the one that was killed, and the one whose body I gave to you. Perhaps we picked up a stray cat on the way and just assumed it was Gardeen."

"Perhaps." But Miles didn't believe it. He looked at the cat again, but Gardeen—or Gardeen II—just purred contentedly.

They returned to the house to find that Annie was staying for a few nights, though grumbling about missing her cats.

Aideen looked at the small black cat in Miles's arm and raised a brow. "I've never known you to be fond of the creatures before."

"I'm not sure if I'm fond of them now." But Miles's finger touched the silky fur of its own volition. "This one seems to have adopted me."

"It's very like that dead one, surely."

Miles shrugged. "This is Ireland. Perhaps we shouldn't ask too many questions." He went up to change for dinner, taking the cat with him.

Once in his room, Gardeen became active, roaming her new quarters, exploring all the corners.

"You won't find any mice here, little hunter." Miles rang for Hennigan, then started to strip off his clothes. "I wonder what you'd have done yesterday. Would you have stepped in to protect me? Or to protect Felicity. Just whose guardian are you?" He stopped in the middle of unbuttoning his shirt to frown at the cat, wondering if he were running completely mad.

He was very tempted to dig up the corpse, but it would be pointless. That cat had definitely been dead. And that cat had been the one they'd brought from Foy, for when Felicity spoke like that she was always truthful.

He thought back to when they'd been leaving Foy, to the black cat which had chased after them. Perhaps it hadn't been Gardeen. Perhaps there had been two identical kittens in the litter.

Or perhaps this one wasn't Gardeen.

It shouldn't matter. But Miles suspected he was going to need a little guardian in the coming days.

Hennigan arrived with fresh hot water and looked down his thin nose at the black creature leaping and rolling on the silk damask bedcover.

"Yes, she's back," Miles said. "And around to stay. I hope."

When Miles went down to dinner, he left the cat in his room with a dish of milk and some morsels of fish and chicken. He thought he'd closed the door, but after dinner when the music began, Gardeen appeared, tail twitching in rhythm.

Miles picked her up and placed her on the top of the piano, but she immediately leaped, paws sliding on the glossy mahogany, off and onto his shoulder.

"My, but she does seem to be attached to you, Miles," his mother said.

"Scared to let the thatch-gallows out of her sight!" Annie declared, still simmering.

"Miss Monahan, I promise to take the greatest care of her from now on."

"You'd better," said Colum with apparent seriousness. "Things happen to people who are unkind to Annie's cats. I remember a lad tied a burning rag to the tail of one. Within weeks, he broke his leg."

"Indeed?" Miles met Annie's threatening eyes. "Do your worst." He knew it could be taken as referring to himself, but he meant it to refer to Dunsmore.

Annie's eyes narrowed. "Oh, I intend to, young man. All in my own good time."

"You know," said Colum, "it's a rare privilege to get one of Annie's cats. I never had one adopt me. Nor has Felicity."

"They go where they're needed," mumbled Annie round a mouthful of cake.

Miles squinted sideways at his guardian cat, who stared back complacently. But it curled its tail around his neck in a surprisingly sensuous, possessive gesture.

Miles looked over to where Felicity was playing the piano and wished the caress on his neck were from her. It wouldn't be, though. He'd caught her unawares once, but she wouldn't let it happen again.

What if, instead of waiting with his door ajar, he went to her room? He felt sure he could seduce, or tease, or coerce her into sex again. The more often they made love, the deeper the bond would be. And the more likely that she would get with child.

But that was what held her back.

Miles looked at the cat again. What would Gardeen do if he tried to coerce Felicity? The line of scabs on his hand gave him his answer.

His gaze was drawn back irresistibly to his tormenting ward. He longed to curl his hand around her elegant neck veiled softly by tendrils of dark hair escaping from her knot. He could almost feel her clever fingers dancing over his body instead of over the smooth hardness of ivory and ebony. . . .

But at the moment, such matters were obviously far from her mind. She was lost in music and at ease, and he would not steal that from her. She so often lacked ease.

Annie had called her active and wayward.

The word, however, was troubled, even anguished, and in a very deep sense.

So what troubled Felicity Monahan, down deep, far deeper than the matter of caring for a neighbor's motherless child?

She looked up as if suddenly aware of his questions. Her fingers completed the piece too soon and she rose. "I think I'll see if Kieran is asleep yet. I'd like to read to him."

She was gone before anyone could comment, though no one but Miles seemed at all disturbed. He knew, however, that Kieran had progressed from just being a barrier between himself and Felicity to being a shield she could deliberately raise when needed.

Miles moved away from the company to look out the window, stroking Gardeen. It was shameful to be jealous of a child, but he was. Kieran was his main rival here, not Dunsmore. Without Kieran, Felicity would melt into his arms tomorrow.

But how could anyone fight the allure of a charming four-year-old boy who needed love and protection?

Twelve

The next day—the third of Miles's week-of-grace—progressed much like the day before. Miles and Felicity spent the morning with Kieran. Miles had borrowed a small gray pony, and Kieran was thrilled to ride around the paddock on it. He was ambitious, though, and continually demanded to be allowed to ride Banshee.

Miles, leaning against the fence chewing a blade of grass, muttered a curse. "If I thought he'd survive, I'd put him up there just to teach him a lesson. Has he no sense?"

"Shush. He's stubborn sometimes."

"Like someone else I know." He took the grass out of his mouth and tickled her nose with it.

She swatted it away, but smiled.

"You haven't come to my room the last two nights."

"I never will." But extra color touched her cheeks.

"Never? That's a long time."

"True enough. On both counts."

He teased the pale skin under her chin with the grass. "If I promised you'd be in no danger of getting with child, would you come?"

"I would not." But her blush intensified and she didn't brush the grass away.

"We only have a few more days of truce, *a muirnín*. 'Tis a great shame to waste them."

Her lips parted slightly. "I'm not wasting them."

He drew the frond of the grass over her red cheek to brush

those tempting lips. "Do you not lie awake at night, thinking?"

She turned to him, swatting the grass away. "Thinking of what?"

"Of balls and rods . . . of billiards."

She choked on a laugh. After a moment she said, "I don't believe you lie awake over me."

"Don't you?" He brushed the grass across his own lips and saw her dark eyes follow it. "Then why not test me out? Come to my room this night. If you find me asleep, you'll know you're right. If you find me awake . . ."

"Yes?"

"Then you'll have to stay awhile."

She licked her lips, and it was almost more than he could do not to kiss her. "Maybe," she whispered before running off to lift Kieran from the pony.

The evening, too, went much as the night before, with Felicity going off to read to Kieran and not returning to the company. Miles, desperately anxious for the real part of the night to begin, was forced by courtesy to spend two long hours playing whist with his mother, his stepfather, and Annie Monahan.

He rather feared Annie was staying to keep an eye on him and Gardeen and hoped she wasn't taking up permanent residence. Gardeen was watcher enough. She lay curled in front of the fire, but whenever Miles looked over, the cat's silver eyes were upon him as if she didn't trust him not to disappear.

He still hadn't worked out a rational explanation for the cat's existence, never mind deciding whether it had a part to play in his affairs. He fervently hoped Gardeen wasn't going to interfere in whatever happened tonight, though.

He thought the game might drag on until midnight, but eventually Annie announced that she was going to bed since she must return to Foy the next day. She pushed away from the table. "The poor cats will already be distressed."

"I'm sure they will," said Aideen as everyone rose politely. Miles tried hard not to show his relief.

"I must say," added Aideen, "that having Gardeen around almost inclines me to having a house cat."

"An excellent idea." Then Annie fixed Miles with a look. "But *you* had better not be careless with yours again or I will not be accountable."

He raised his hand in a fencing gesture. "I promise."

She nodded and trundled out.

Aideen gathered the cards. "She certainly grows quite ferocious on the subject."

"A truer word was never spoken," declared Colum, sinking back into his chair. "Miles, my boy, if you value your skin, don't let harm come to that little creature."

Miles sat, too, studying his stepfather with a frown. "Very well, Colum, let's hear your opinion about Gardeen and the cat that was buried."

"Opinion?" Colum's eyes widened. "Faith, you want an opinion on such matters? I suppose I would have to say that cats have nine lives."

Miles knew there was more to it than that. "But according to Annie, a person only gets to share one of them."

"Sure and that could be true. After all, there do always seem to be those cats that just appear. But cats are just cats."

"That isn't what you said a moment ago."

"I was saying that cats are not just cats to Annie."

For once, though, Colum seemed almost agitated. Interesting. Very interesting.

Miles snapped his fingers. He wasn't at all sure the cat would respond, but after just enough hesitation to preserve her dignity, Gardeen pranced over and leapt elegantly onto his lap.

"So, little guardian, I wonder how many lives you have exhausted."

Gardeen said nothing to the point, however, and since Miles's mother was looking at him strangely, he carried the mysterious feline up to bed.

"And now," he said to Gardeen as they entered the room, "begins the interesting part."

The cat showed no excitement, however, but curled into a neat circle in front of the fire and appeared to go to sleep.

"Is that a good omen or a poor one?" Miles was saying as Hennigan came in.

"I beg your pardon, sir?"

"Nothing," said Miles hastily. Faith, but he'd end up in Bedlam before this was done. As soon as he was ready for bed, he sent Hennigan away, set his door slightly ajar, chose a book, and settled to staying awake.

Staying awake shouldn't be a problem, for he'd been truthful about two restless nights. But now, with the contrariness typical of such times, weariness crept over him.

Midnight chimed, and he yawned. When would she come if she came? Could he risk stealing a nap?

No.

Would he be too exhausted if she came in the middle of the night?

No.

Could he fall asleep at such a cost?

Quite possibly.

He nudged the cat with his slippered toe. "Ho there, Gardeen. Can't you think of a way to keep me awake?"

The cat stirred for a moment and opened its eyes. Then it settled back to sleep, its stomach rising and falling with mesmeric tranquility.

Miles settled to reading Oedipus in the Greek, hoping the challenge would keep him awake.

Felicity read to Kieran, then stayed with Mrs. Edey in her room for a while, chatting of this and that. She knew she was putting off the time when she must return to her own room and temptation.

Eventually, however, she had to leave this sanctuary. As she went to her room, she heard voices below and knew the others must still be up. That was good. Perhaps she could fall asleep before the question even arose.

She prepared for bed and settled into it, feeling for some reason that she should prove to the maid that she had no intention of going anywhere else.

She wished she could prove it to herself.

Good sense left no room for doubt. A virtuous young woman, a sensible young woman, would stay safe in her bed tonight.

In fact, she'd lock the door!

So why was the desire to leave this bed, to slip down the corridor just two doors, as powerful as the fiercest itch?

Felicity turned over and arranged her pillow, willing sleep to come and take all choice away.

It didn't.

She must have turned a score of times before she heard Annie thump up the stairs to her room. Not long after, she heard other footsteps. Soon, lying flat on her back, open eyes staring at the shadowy ceiling, she knew the house was settled for the night and the decision time had arrived.

She had no moral qualms at all. That time in the billiard room did not lie on her conscience, and no awareness of sin kept her from Miles's bed. She was a sorry case; but having had her virtue stolen from her so young, she could not feel fervently on the subject.

Her only hesitation was because she would not again risk becoming pregnant. She placed her hands over her abdomen, wondering if already a disastrous child grew there. Because Rupert had been so convincing in his assurances that she could not become pregnant by him, it had taken her months last time to realize she was carrying a child. If there'd been signs in the early days, she'd missed them entirely.

Miles had promised that if she went to him tonight there would be no additional risk, but Rupert had promised no risk, too. Men would say anything to get their way. Why should she trust Miles Cavanagh?

But she did, deeply and absolutely. She trusted his given word.

Her hands moved over her body, over belly, breasts, and down between her thighs, summoning in mild form the pleasure he could bring her. But in truth, it wasn't that wild pleasure she longed for. It was the closeness of two bodies together, skin to skin, breath to breath, of soft words whispered in the dark, all barriers down.

If they could just lie together in the warmth of his bed and talk, she could imagine nothing sweeter, even though they could not talk of the most important thing. . . .

She was out of the bed without thought, pacing her room, uncertain of the next step.

But sure she would go.

She pulled on her loose nightrobe of soft cream wool, then, impulsively, dropped it to strip off her nightgown. She looked in the mirror, startled by her own pale shapeliness in the firelight. Studying herself, she unplaited her hair. When it was a dark cloud around her shoulders, she pulled on the wrap again and warily opened the door into the corridor.

The house was silent except for the ticking of clocks. A small lamp burned on the wall, but it scarcely raised the darkness to gloom. Taking a deep breath, Felicity slipped barefooted along the carpet runner to Miles's door.

For a moment, a devastating moment, she thought it was closed. But then she saw that it was the tiniest bit ajar.

She hesitated, prudence urging her to turn back, to return to her own bed where her purpose could not be weakened.

But her heart urged her onward, arguing that she deserved this brief joy.

With a gentle touch, she eased the door silently open.

And what was she going to do if the wretch were fast asleep and snoring?

He was not. But he was staring into the fire, a finger between the pages of a book, and did not hear her quiet entry. It was Gardeen who raised her head and miaowed.

He looked around sharply, and then a smile of such sweetness lit his face that tears came to her eyes. He held out a hand and she went to him.

"This is not a good idea, Miles Cavanagh."

"It seems a grand idea to me, *a muirnín.*"

How could a woman respond so powerfully to the touch of a man's hand? It was the one area where men and women were allowed to touch. Though usually gloved.

His thumb rubbed against hers. "Why did you come?"

"I'm bewitched."

He glanced down and nudged the black cat with his slipper. "Is this your doing then, Gardeen?" The cat stirred to her feet and stretched, but then ran across the room to leap onto the windowsill. "At least she's not going to fight me off you this time."

A jolt of alarmed desire went straight through Felicity. "You said . . ."

"I said I'd put you in no risk of becoming pregnant. There are many things for a man and woman to do that carry no risk at all." He tugged her gently into his lap. "You are quite an innocent, aren't you?"

To be cuddled on his lap, warm fire toasting her back, was as close to heaven as Felicity could imagine, but she had to disturb it. "You know I'm not."

He stroked her hair. "You're not ignorant or untouched. But innocence, yes, you still have some of that. As have I, thank God."

She shifted enough to look up at him. "Innocence?"

"Freedom from the darker side of sex. I have a friend who explored that land, and he still bears the scars."

Felicity wasn't sure what he was talking about; but she had

to admit that, though she felt scarred by betrayal and loss, the physical activities she had shared with Rupert Dunsmore had not been such as to scar her, body or soul.

Perhaps she should be grateful for that.

It was late and she was more comfortable than she could ever remember being. She let her eyes drift shut.

He nipped her ear. "Did you really come here to sleep?"

Felicity stirred almost resentfully. "Yes. This is so pleasant, and there isn't much else we can do, is there?"

A smile twitched his lips. "We can kiss before we sleep."

"I suppose we can do that."

She met his lips willingly, sweetened by the knowledge that this wasn't a prelude to seduction, but a dish taken for its own delights. Once or twice, she supposed, Rupert had kissed her like this before he'd persuaded her into other matters. Once they'd become lovers, he'd hardly bothered.

Since Rupert, she had allowed no man the privilege of deep kissing until Miles had burst through her resistance.

Astonished by the intensity coming just from a kiss, Felicity moved her hands to Miles's shoulders and explored the shape of him as she tasted him, breathed with him, became one with him.

She was only distracted when he rose with her in his arms. It almost hurt to separate her lips from his. "What are you doing?"

"We'll be more comfortable in the bed."

She stiffened. "But we can't . . ."

"We can do as much or as little in the bed as in the chair. Just in more comfort. Trust me."

She relaxed enough to allow him to slide her between the covers, still in her wrap. He joined her there. His body brushed her hand, and she realized he was naked.

She sidled away. "You wouldn't . . ."

He captured her hand and kissed each finger. "I wouldn't what?"

"Trick me? Seduce me?"

"I should beat you for suggesting it. Don't you have my word?" He wasn't angry, but he appeared serious.

"Give it to me again."

"Felicity, I promise I will do nothing here tonight that might cause you to conceive a child."

She relaxed, and he drew her back close to him. He loosed the tie of her wrap so it spread open to his hand. Concealed by the covers, he explored her belly, her thighs, her breasts. It was the same journey her own hand had taken not so long ago, but different, so different. Her eyes drifted shut to savor the delicate pleasure.

She was so relaxed that he had only to nudge her thighs for them to spread, allowing his fingers into her.

Her eyes shot open and her thighs tried to close.

"Easy, my white swan," he murmured. "My fingers cannot impregnate you. But they can do almost anything else." And he set about proving it.

"Oh my," she gasped.

When he lowered his head to suck on her breast, she clutched his hair and surrendered to the wonderful building passion, trying to stifle her noises for fear of discovery.

For fear of interruption.

If anything interrupted . . .

Nothing did, but as if he sensed her imminent release, he slowed his hand, holding her on the trembling edge until she begged, until she pleaded, half-laughing, half-crying.

Then, only then, did he give her ecstasy.

Limp, sticky, and sated, Felicity curled against him. "It's amazing to me that people risk babies at all."

He laughed. "Perhaps there are not so many men as noble as I." His clever hand began to roam again, but she seized it.

"We wouldn't want you to get too full of your own nobility now, would we?" Pushing back nervous uncertainty, she slid her hand down to encircle his hot, hard flesh.

A spasm rippled through him.

"Does that hurt?"

"I wouldn't exactly call it pain."

Feeling amazingly more wicked than she had even the first time she had let Rupert enter her body, Felicity moved to straddle his thighs, putting both hands around him. Watching his face, she slid his skin up, then down.

His lips parted and perhaps an almost-silent groan escaped. "Is this all right?" she asked, repeating the movement.

"I'll scream when it's not."

She giggled and, as an experiment, lowered her lips to his small, flat nipples to tease them with her teeth.

"Struth!"

She looked up. "Was that a scream?"

He grinned at her, eyes dark and heavy-lidded with passion. "You'll know when I scream. But you might want to think about what to do when I erupt."

For a moment she was confused, then she said, "Oh. I shouldn't be doing this?"

"I didn't say that."

She moved her hand almost absent-mindedly. Then stopped. "It would make a mess of the bed, I suppose."

"The servants would just assume I'd been doing this to myself, terrible sin though it is and sure to turn a man blind."

"Oh, is *this* what men are not supposed to do?"

He stifled laughter. "You are an innocent. Do you mean you've never touched yourself that way?"

Felicity knew she was blushing. "A little. I never knew, though, that I could . . . could do it all."

"I wouldn't say you can do it *all*. Now, are you going to leave me here between heaven and hell?"

The feel of his thighs between her legs made her squirm, which distinctly made his hips tense.

This was fascinating.

She moved her hand a little and saw his breathing change. "But what am I to do?"

"You're a resourceful woman. I leave it, literally, in your hands."

As a response to that bad joke, she leaned to set her teeth in the flesh around his nipple, to bite sharply enough to make him jerk. All over.

"You'd better make up your mind," he said unsteadily.

She didn't want to leave him, but she ran over to the washstand and returned with a towel. Then, watching his face, she used her hand again.

He kept his eyes on her as long as he could, speaking mysteries she couldn't understand except at the deepest levels of her soul, where such things are real. His grip on her legs would leave bruises, but she didn't mind the pain.

She almost reveled in it.

He arched, raising her as if she were riding.

She forced him down again, fighting him, sensing how that excited him.

Knowing it excited her.

She ached, almost losing control and going with him on his journey.

When she saw his skin flush and dew with sweat, heat rushed along her own nerves, setting her skin atingle with a similar heat, her breathing as desperate as his.

It would be so easy to move a little, to take him into her ache. . . .

But no. She had strength enough to resist that.

Remembering his touch on her, she slowed. He groaned, teeth gritted, gripping tighter at her thighs. "Now, now . . ."

She gave in to his pleas, but almost forgot the cloth. Then, she watched his slow return to self and sanity.

When his sated eyes opened, she teased, "Sure and I still can't see why people risk unwanted babies, for that was very interesting indeed."

"Interesting, was it?" He flipped her on her back and covered her. "You've forgotten all too soon what it's like to share that, *mo chroí*. And, for my sins, I'm honor-bound not to remind you."

But his kiss reminded her, and her body began to tell her, rather insistently, that fingers were not the real thing.

She pushed him away. "No!"

He froze. "What's the matter?"

"My body wants more."

He relaxed and kissed her again. "So does mine. But bodies can be ruled. Or appeased. Let me destroy a little more of your innocence. . . ." And he slid his mouth down over her breasts and over her belly to between her legs.

"Oh no . . ."

He stopped. "No?"

She breathed deeply. "I don't know."

"Scream if you want me to stop," he said, laughter in his voice. The rub of his tongue over her most sensitive spot made her cry out aloud.

"Was that a scream?"

"Yes. No. No!"

"Two out of three wins."

Afterward, she coiled around him, wishing she could grow into him like ivy on oak. "I never knew . . ."

"Never knew what?" he asked, hand wandering over every curve.

"This. All of this." Then suddenly she was ashamed. "Miles," she whispered, "I don't think I can do that to you."

He pulled her closer. *"A muirnín,* you don't have to do anything you don't want to. And besides, I heard a clock strike two. Don't you think it's time for sleep?"

"I can't sleep here."

"Ah, but it's so sweet to lie in one another's arms. Stay a little while, love. I won't let you sleep too long."

So, wrung to limpness, Felicity let her heavy eyes close and slept warm in her lover's arms.

* * *

Miles stroked his beloved's lovely hair, feasting on her sleeping, trusting features, resolving to cherish her forever.

Despite herself.

How many days could he count on, though, before Dunsmore returned like a serpent to Eden to destroy everything?

At the thought of Dunsmore, Miles's hold tightened slightly on Felicity. At one time his concern had been to protect her from her own generosity. Now care was drowned by a possessive need to keep her for himself.

Perhaps his earlier motivations had been noble, but this wasn't noble at all. It was entirely selfish. He needed Felicity as he needed breath itself.

He waited as long as he dared, but when a clock struck four, he eased away from Felicity and put on his banjan. He took the damp towel and threw it on the fire, watching to see that it burned up. Then he gathered his beloved into his arms and carried her to her own room and her now-chilly bed.

Which meant he had to lie with her for a little while to help her warm it.

Where unfortunately, he fell asleep.

He was woken, thank heavens, not by a maid coming to rouse Felicity with chocolate, but by his mother.

It was no great mercy.

Aideen's eyes snapped anger. With a crook of her finger she drew him out of the bedroom and down the corridor to his, which by its disorder told a tale. "Think what would have happened if anyone else had caught you!"

"I fell asleep."

"That is not the issue, and you know it! How *could* you?"

He went to place some wood on the lingering glow. "I'm doing what I must to prevent her marrying Dunsmore."

"By getting her with child?"

"Not in last night's games."

"Miles, you must stop this. I'm the girl's chaperon."

"I've probably done as much as I can anyway."

She frowned even more. "Is that all it is? A cold-blooded attempt to turn her from Dunsmore?"

He felt the color rise in his cheeks. "No."

"Good," she said more moderately. "For if it were, I would not help you."

"Help me?"

"To get Felicity out of Ireland. While you've been playing your illicit games, I've been keeping an eye on matters. Ned Tooley returned from Scotland safe enough, but says Dunsmore found a boat to take him to Larne. This morning, my watcher at Loughcarrick reported his return home. We can expect him here today, I think."

"Damnation. I'd hoped to delay him longer."

"You failed. Now we have to act. Colum and I are going to visit Kilgoran Castle and take Kieran and Mrs. Edey with us. Dunsmore may follow us there, but he'll have little success snatching his son away from your uncle without offending him."

"You hate visiting the Castle."

His mother's reply was tart. "In the midst of all this dramatic romance, I can afford to make a small sacrifice or two. It's likely Dunsmore will keep his eye on the main game—Felicity. Take her to Melton and he'll follow. What you and your Rogues do there is up to you, but you need to find a true solution to this problem, not just a patch. I'll keep the boy safe for a week or two."

Unready for this after a stormy, sleepless night, Miles ran his hands through his hair. "She'll never consent to going."

"That's hardly news. How did you ever intend to take her? Don't tell me, you hoped to seduce her into compliance. Miles, when will you learn? When resolved upon something, women have wills of iron, resistant to even the most devastating manly charms. Drug her and carry her off by force."

Miles stared at his mother in shock. "I can't do that."

"Then wait for her to run off with Dunsmore again."

At that moment, Gardeen uncurled on the bed and leapt down to twine around Miles's ankles, miaowing.

"And what's that supposed to mean?" Miles asked irritably.

Aideen swooped down and grabbed the cat to hold it up in front of him. "Miles, this is a *cat*. She cannot be your guide. I, however, am your mother and can. I'm going to give Felicity a cup of chocolate that should keep her sleeping into the afternoon. What you do with the opportunity is up to you." She dumped Gardeen into his hands and left in an irritated swish of silk.

Miles stroked Gardeen until he realized he was waiting for some mystical sign from the cat. With a shake of his head he placed her back on the bed and rang for Hennigan.

When the man arrived, he told him to prepare for immediate departure for England.

Thirteen

Felicity awoke from vague tangled dreams of intimacy, a smile teasing at her lips. It was hardly surprising that the world seemed remarkably unsteady. Nor was it strange that after such a night her lids felt almost too heavy to raise.

She stretched, reveling in the sensation of her own body.

Then she realized that she had a headache.

Now that *was* strange.

In fact, though the memories were sweet, she did not feel particularly well. More as she had after experimenting once with her grandfather's port. Heavy, dull, and slightly sick.

Then she realized that the smell in the air was not the smell of her room.

Tar.

Salt.

Sea?

She forced her eyes open and found herself on a narrow bed in a tiny cabin on board a rolling ship.

Miles was standing, looking out a porthole. He turned, his expression wary.

Felicity squinted against the light digging into her eyes. "Where are we?" It came out as a croak, for her throat was horridly dry. "Why . . ."

"We're at sea," he said levelly, "heading for England. Would you like some water?" He moved toward a carafe held safely within a brass rail on the small round table.

"No!" But then Felicity stopped her instinctive rejection.

She needed water, she needed clarity, and she needed time to think.

England?

He poured water into a glass, then raised her gently and helped her drink. Strength returned a little, though the headache was made worse by movement.

Or perhaps it was the sharp edges of the thoughts jangling within her skull.

When he would have settled her back onto the pillow, she fought free and sat up. "Take me back!"

"No."

"Miles, you can't do this. The week's not even up."

"Perhaps your parole still holds then."

"My *parole?* You must be demented! What of yours?"

He moved away to lean by the porthole again. "I never gave you any promises at all."

A moment's thought told her it was true. "Miles . . ."

He turned with a sigh. "Don't beg or threaten, Felicity. I'm taking you to Melton Mowbray where I intend to do my damndest to ensure that Rupert Dunsmore gets nowhere near you. If you want to extend your parole, you can travel in comfort. Otherwise, you'll go in whatever manner gets you there."

She lurched off the bed, then stopped with a hiss to clutch her pounding head. "Damn your black heart! What did you give me?"

"Nothing. It was my mother, and I don't know what she used."

Despite willpower, tears were leaking onto Felicity's cheeks. "Oh, God. Oh, God. What of Kieran?"

"He's as safe as can be," he said, with the first gentleness she'd heard from him this day. "My mother has taken him to Kilgoran Castle. She'll do her best to keep him safe, and my mother's best is formidable."

Felicity stared at him, trying to make him appear the monster he was. "She can't refuse him to his father!"

"Is Dunsmore going to claim that she and Kilgoran have kidnapped him? Anyway, I believe he'll follow you." A glimmer of humor touched his bleak face. "Tooley says he suffers from seasickness."

That did give a spurt of satisfaction, but Felicity refused to be mellowed. "So Rupert's back already. And before you expected him. When did you find out, I wonder."

"This morning."

But something in his manner—perhaps an embarrassment—made Felicity distrust him. "I think not. I think you knew at least yesterday when you teased me into weakening. You needed another chance to charm me out of all reason so you could pull this foul trick upon me. It was all planned—"

"No. On my word—"

She spoke over him. "I will never let down my guard with you again, Miles Cavanagh. I swear it. It is war between us now." With satisfaction, she saw him wince. "I take back my parole. You will have no cooperation from me. None."

"Felicity . . ."

She stared into his gentle-seeming eyes. "None. Now I would like my privacy."

She thought he might argue on, but he nodded and left the room. As she sank back down onto the hard bed, she heard the key turn in the lock.

Grief hit her like a crashing wave, rolling her onto her back, arm over brimming eyes. Regardless of the letter of their agreement, he had betrayed her trust. He had used her just as Rupert had used her. He had betrayed her just as her grandfather had betrayed her.

She'd learned years ago that no man could be trusted. Why had she forgotten that hard-won lesson? They lied; they cheated; they took as God-given that they should run a woman's life.

Felicity was terrified for Kieran but, more than that, she was devastated by the way Miles had stolen her freedom and rendered her powerless before his will.

But Kieran must be her first concern.

She sat up and drank some more water, forcing herself to analyze the situation. Honesty made her admit that Miles's plan might work, for a while at least. Rupert would hesitate to take on the Earl of Kilgoran.

Yes, unless Miles had lied, Kieran was safe for the moment. So what would Rupert do?

He'd fall into one of his livid rages, for a start. Warned off squeezing his tenants dry, hounded by duns, thwarted in his elopement, carried against his will to Scotland, then returning—seasick—only to find both Felicity and his son snatched out of reach.

It summoned a laugh, though it wasn't funny. He'd be in the kind of frigid rage when he was capable of anything as long as it did not require physical courage on his part. She wished she could send a warning to the whole of County Meath. Petty cruelties would happen unless he was in direct pursuit of her.

She hoped he was. At least she and Miles were on their guard. With a shudder, she remembered the way Rupert had killed Gardeen. Casually, but delighting in the pain and terror it caused Felicity.

She had recognized the warning. If she married him and were docile, she could expect him to behave in a reasonably conventional way. If she thwarted him, he would terrorize something or someone just to spite her.

She shuddered at the memory of those weeks between Rupert's proposal and her grandfather's death, when her grandfather had refused to allow the marriage.

Kieran had fallen down some steps and scraped himself quite badly.

Mrs. Edey had been definite that the boy's father had been trying to stop him from falling, but Felicity had known the truth. She'd thrown herself desperately into convincing her grandfather that she was madly in love and had to marry Rupert immediately.

But then her grandfather had died, leaving her fate in the hands of Miles Cavanagh. She hadn't known then what that would mean. What little she'd known of the man had indicated he was as feckless as her Uncle Colum. She'd felt sure she could bring him around.

"Hah!" she said, looking at her prison.

Of course, it might have gone better if she'd met Miles, as planned, as a demure Irish miss instead of wanton Joy. Even now, she winced at her performance that evening.

Miles had warned her then that he was a dangerous man, not to be crossed.

The next day, she'd thrown his words back at him, referring to herself in the same terms.

They had both spoken the truth, and the danger terrified her. They could end up dragging each other to destruction when all either of them wanted was the sweet tenderness they had shared last night. . . .

A sudden warm movement made Felicity flinch out of her thoughts, thinking Miles had returned. But it was Gardeen that had touched her arm.

She pulled the warm cat into her arms and nuzzled its fur. "Oh, Gardeen. Are you the same come back? Can I read hope into you?"

The little cat just purred.

"Or are you just another black cat of Annie's? Either way, little one, you don't seem to bring me much luck."

Felicity eased out of bed with Gardeen in her arms. Her head seemed a little less obstreperous, and she moved the few steps to the porthole to look out. All she could see from here were rolling gray waves, but there were gulls in the rigging, so they could not be so very far from shore.

Which shore, though?

Such matters were irrelevant. She couldn't prevent Miles from carrying her to England, but when they docked, she would escape and get back to Rupert before he had a chance to do real harm.

How?

She put the cat down and searched the small cabin. In drawers under the bed she found some of her clothes and she slipped out of her nightgown.

Nightgown.

She'd gone to Miles without it. Had *he* dressed her in it? The thought was disturbing but strangely arousing.

"Feeble woman!" she muttered to herself as she stuffed the nightgown into the drawer in place of the clothing she had taken. She pulled on her shift and the light, front-lacing corset.

The gown, thank heavens, was one of her sensible wool walking dresses, designed to be easily put on alone, to allow her complete freedom of movement, and to be comfortable in nearly all circumstances. When it came time to escape, she'd have as good a chance as possible.

Her hairbrush was there, and so she tidied her tangled curls into a plait, then rolled it into a knot at the back of her head. She pushed in the hairpins, thinking they might be of some use. She couldn't think how, but the bent wires were the closest thing to a weapon she possessed.

Having armored herself as best she could, Felicity searched the cabin thoroughly, looking for weapons, money, or anything that could be turned into money.

She found nothing but a few other items of clothing, a couple of books, and a chamber pot.

As she used it she berated herself for not having a silver-backed hairbrush rather than a wood one. Such extravagances had seemed frivolous, but now such a hairbrush could be useful. Silver was a saleable commodity.

She covered the pot and checked the room again, hoping against hope for a dropped coin in a forgotten corner.

Nothing.

So, what should she do when someone came? She could run through the door . . . and do what? Jump over the side?

She was desperate for action but, in fact, it made no sense to do anything until they reached port.

She tried to settle to read one of the books, but it was something dull about tribes in America. The other was a history of England under the Tudors. As if she cared.

She prowled the small space, wishing someone would come—even Miles—just to break the monotony.

It was dark, however, by the time she heard footsteps and Miles entered carrying a lamp and a tray. "I'm sure you're hungry."

Felicity resented his distant courtesy. He should be embarrassed, guilty, or pleading his case.

He did not oblige, so she sat on the bed and inspected the meal. Chicken, ham, potatoes, brussels sprouts, and a pudding.

She began to eat.

"I'm glad you're not going to starve yourself."

"I'm going to need my strength."

"Felicity, you will not escape me. Why not just accept it?"

She gave him a scathing look and continued to build up her strength.

He said no more, and she found it gradually harder and harder to swallow. His presence in the tiny space began to overwhelm her.

She looked up and found him staring at her as if he were equally disturbed.

"I love you, Felicity."

It was like a blade in the heart. She took the time necessary to gather the moisture in her mouth, then spat at him. He flung up his hand to block it, but his face paled with shock.

Felicity looked down at the food and made herself continue to eat despite the tears blocking her throat. She was aware that he turned to look out at the rolling sea.

Why was he was even staying here? Probably to guard the knife and fork. She looked at the silver knife and wondered if she were capable of using it on him. But if she'd not been able to shoot Rupert Dunsmore, she surely could not stab Miles.

The mere thought was making her feel sick. Or perhaps it was just the meal on her unsteady stomach. She eyed the jam pudding and decided it was not essential to nutrition and could, therefore, be left.

"I'm finished," she said.

He turned back, once more impassive, and came to take the tray. But instead of reaching for it, he flipped her onto her face, put his knee in her back, and snared her hands.

Felicity struggled but could not move. She tried to scream, but her face was pressed so far into the pillow she could hardly breathe. Something cinched her wrists in moments, then a gag was tied into her mouth. Her legs were bound—not at her ankles, but just below her knees, beneath her skirts.

Pointlessly, she screamed her opinion of the treacherous snake into the lump of cloth in her mouth.

"I'm sorry, Felicity," he said rather unsteadily. "I'd much rather we travel in comfort. I can see you intend to fight me, though, and I don't underestimate your intelligence or your courage, so it has to be this way. We're already into the Mersey, and we'll be in Runcorn in a couple of hours. I'll carry you to the carriage as if you're seasick. Once there, however, I'll try to make you more comfortable."

He turned her gently so she was on her side, but arranged her facing the glossy planks of the wall. She didn't even have the satisfaction of glaring at him as he left.

Since it was the middle of the night, there were few people around to see Miles carry a cloak-shrouded figure off the *Ellen Jane* and into the waiting carriage, for which he could only be grateful.

She kicked and groaned as he had expected, and he covered it by responding, "Ah, but you'll soon feel better, my dear, now we are on dry land. . . . No, I assure you you do not want to go home, for that would mean another sea journey. . . . Well now, I fear you will have to go home one day, but perhaps by then you'll have grown sea legs. . . ."

He'd brought his own carriage over on the boat, with his own men to manage it. He hired horses here to draw them to Nantwich where he could join up with his more usual route from Holyhead. From there, the inns knew him well and would dispense with the postilions.

He definitely didn't want strangers as witnesses to this kidnapping.

Felicity tried her best to resist being put into the carriage, doing it so well that he eventually allowed her to knock her head against the door. That stunned her enough to let him get her inside and dump her onto the seat. Hot, disheveled, and disgusted by what he was forced to do, he called for Hennigan to hurry, and soon they were on their way.

The valet had reluctantly carried Gardeen, who now leapt onto Felicity's lap and glared at Miles just as fiercely as she was doing. Hennigan tucked himself into a corner, back to the horses, dissociating himself from these scandalous goings-on.

Swaying with the movement of the speeding carriage, Miles leaned to unfasten the gag. She jerked away from his touch.

"Dammit, Felicity, stop fighting me or I'll be pulling your hair here."

She froze, glowering.

As soon as he'd plucked the soggy cloth from her mouth, she started swearing at him, using terms he'd hesitate to use himself.

"Enough," he said sharply. "Or I'll gag you again."

When she subsided into dark silence, he asked, "Do you want some water? I seem to remember from my recent experience of being bound and gagged that it is required."

He could see how much she wanted to reject the offer, but she nodded. He held the flask of water to her lips and let her drink. He hoped she remembered their first meeting in similar circumstances. What was sauce for the gander could indeed be sauce for the goose.

After a few sips, she shook her head to indicate that she was finished. He recapped the flask. "If you give me your parole, I'll untie you."

Again she shook her head.

"Unless you plan to throw yourself from the carriage, you'll have no chance to escape for a while. I'll re-tie you when we come to a change, if you want."

This time she made no response at all.

Damn the stubborn jade.

Miles was sure this was the hardest thing he had ever done in his life. Only the thought of Dunsmore, of her married to Dunsmore, kept him to the task.

"I'll tie your hands in front, at least." She resisted, but he turned her, unbuckled the strap, then before she had the chance to get the strength back into her stiffened arms, pulled them forward and recinched them in front of her, nudging a fretful Gardeen out of the way.

Both cat and woman hissed, and he feared Felicity's hiss was from pain in her stiffened arms. When two tears escaped, he was sure of it. Miles took out his handkerchief to dry her cheeks.

From between clenched teeth, she said, "Don't touch me."

He had to allow her that right, so he put the handkerchief into her hands and settled back into his corner of the seat. She raised the cloth awkwardly to her eyes, then sniffed.

He shot a glance at her. She was furious as much as miserable, and he doubted that pathetic little sniff. What would the cunning woman do next? Absolutely anything to gain her freedom.

Gardeen circled restlessly for a moment, then settled on Felicity's lap under her bound hands and stared at Miles.

What that said about the rightness of his actions he didn't know.

The road was fairly smooth, and the swaying of the carriage soporific. Miles had not slept more than an hour or so the night before, and it would be dangerously easy to fall asleep now. But he mustn't . . .

He was jerked out of a doze by the abrupt turn the coach took into the inn in Nantwich. He lurched over and slapped his hand over Felicity's mouth just before she screamed. He dragged her down onto his lap and flung the hood of her cloak over her head so it would look, he hoped, as if she were sleeping.

She kicked out, landing a solid blow on the carriage door, but fortunately she was only wearing soft slippers. He trapped her legs between his own and kept her head pressed hard against his thighs.

Christ, but it was taking nearly all his strength to hold her.

"Really, sir . . ." Hennigan protested, white-faced.

"Shut up."

Then, after a thankfully speedy change, they were off again and he could release her. He pushed her up straight, expecting more blistering language.

She seemed more dazed than anything else, however, and just sat there, red-faced and panting, staring at him.

"I'm sorry Felicity. I'll make sure you're gagged before the next change so there'll be no need of that sort of thing."

She started to cry. The effort she made to hold back the tears was as painful as cudgels, and he reached for her.

She shrank back. "I hate you!"

"And I love you."

With a wail of bitter laughter, she turned her head into the satin squabs of the corner and sobbed. Miles had never heard such pain before. He looked at Hennigan, but the valet was staring fixedly out the window, tight-lipped. He looked at Gardeen, who stared back balefully from Felicity's lap.

With a muttered curse, Miles reached over and unbound Felicity's hands despite her resistance. "Don't forget, I'll stop your escape by any means."

She pressed the handkerchief to her face, fighting her tears. After a moment she gained composure and undid the strap around her legs. Then she tossed the piece of leather into his lap and turned to stare out of the window.

Miles wanted to talk to her, to try to make her see that he had no choice in this, but he didn't know if he had the words. And anyway, he couldn't imagine attempting such a conversation with his embarrassed valet as audience.

Hell and damnation, how had he ever ended up in this predicament?

When they drew close to the next change, he said, "I must rebind you now unless you want to give me your parole."

She turned, stony-faced, and held out her wrists. He fastened them, then replaced the gag. He pulled her hood well over her face and placed his arm around her waist, holding her close, wondering if any chance of happiness between them could survive this journey.

She held herself as stiff as a board, and he knew she would take any opportunity to escape. A twisted smile tugged at his lips because he knew this was three-quarters pride. Felicity Monahan would bend her will to no man.

How, then, did she intend to survive life married to Rupert Dunsmore?

For the first time he wondered if she had murder on her mind. He wouldn't put it past her, but it was terrifying. When a man died mysteriously, suspicion turned first to the wife, especially if there were a hint of marital discord. Did she know it was still possible for a woman to be burned for the murder of her husband?

Petty treason, they called it. Little treason. Rebellion against the domestic lord and master.

Fourteen

As they gathered speed with the new horses, Miles unbound his beloved.

The first thing she said was, "I need to relieve myself."

Miles hadn't thought of that problem. With a full moon, he'd intended to drive straight through if the weather held. The coachman and his assistant could take turns driving.

Of course, he'd planned on occasional stops for ease and refreshment, but then he'd expected Felicity to give in gracefully.

How foolish.

"Give me your parole and we'll stop at the next inn."

"No."

He stared at her. "Damnation, Felicity . . ."

"No parole, ever. I'd rather soil my gown."

She would, too. That was why he loved the woman to madness even while wanting to wring her neck. He tried to persuade her to see reason, but it was like talking to a marble effigy. In the end, on a deserted stretch of road in Northern Shropshire, he opened the trap and called for the coach to stop.

Felicity watched him warily, and he saw hope and plans flickering through her mind.

"Don't even think about it. We're miles from anywhere. But just to be safe, I'll have your shoes."

She tucked her feet under her skirt. "Be damned if you will!"

"By force if necessary."

"You won't find it easy to overpower me, Miles Cavanagh, without surprise or cooperation."

"But I can do it if I'm ruthless enough. You're not the only one with a will of iron."

She frowned, and he thought he saw the same realization that had struck him—that the very strengths that drew them together were the ones making this battle so fierce.

"Or you can just soil your gown," he added. He was bluffing, but it worked.

With a resentful sigh, she unlaced her slippers and tossed them to him. At him, in fact. Then she pulled her skirts up above her knees, untied her garters and slowly rolled off her cotton stockings. "No point in ruining them," she said, positively flaunting her lovely legs, naked up to the thigh.

Oh, she had a fine understanding of her arsenal, did Felicity Monahan.

Hennigan was wisely staring in the opposite direction, but his neck was red.

Holding onto both temper and lust, Miles opened the door and let down the steps. "You can go behind that hedge."

As soon as he was on the ground, however, he realized the road was sharp with frost. He held up his arms. "I'll carry you to the grass."

She stayed in the doorway. "I never want you to touch me again." She waited until he lowered his arms and moved out of her way. Then she stepped down and walked gingerly over to the almost-leafless hedge.

Miles checked that his coachman and groom were looking away. He, however, had to keep an eye on his ward, his lover, his torment and delight.

A moment's carelessness and she'd be gone.

The dense tangle of hedge-branches and the dim moonlight gave some privacy, but didn't hide Felicity entirely. He could see that she hadn't taken off barefoot across the rough sheep run.

Unless she'd taken off her dress and hung it there . . .

A closer look assured him she was still in the gown. He wouldn't put any trick past her, though, and he suspected nothing was beyond her courage, not even running off in her shift.

Ah, but she was a queen among women, was Felicity Monahan, and worthy to wear a crown in Tara. It was a bitter fate that had them enemies in this.

Gardeen appeared in the doorway, whiskers twitching, and leaped down on the same business. But the cat was back before Felicity. He suspected the delay was mostly to annoy him, especially as her feet must be freezing.

Eventually, she emerged to return to the coach. Miles took time to relieve himself, too, then indicated that his men should do the same. When Hennigan returned to the coach, he asked, frozen-faced, whether he could ride in the uncomfortable trundle seat at the back. Miles agreed, though he felt he should probably tie Felicity up and make her travel there. It was her stubbornness that was causing all the trouble.

When all was settled, Miles climbed into the coach, taking the backward seat now there were only two of them inside. He'd give her as much relief from his presence as he could. She'd put her shoes and stocking back on, he noticed, and didn't appear to have suffered frostbite.

This was such a damned ridiculous affair.

After a while, he decided they'd have to stop for food. His coachmen, at least, needed to eat for strength.

Who'd ever have thought kidnapping to be so tricky?

He looked at Felicity. "Are you hungry?"

"Not hungry enough." Though she'd deigned to reply, she was back to her representation of a marble effigy.

"Faith, and have you thought of making your living striking attitudes, Miss Monahan? You could do resentment remarkably well, indeed you could."

Her lips tightened, but she made no response. He dearly missed the time when she would at least have returned fire.

"Felicity, I am not the enemy. You are going to have to learn to trust—"

She came to life at that. "Trust you! I fell asleep in your arms, Miles Cavanagh, and awoke a prisoner! Is it surprising that I don't *trust* you?"

He winced. "It wasn't planned—"

"Planned or not, I am here where I have no wish to be, threatened with violence if I object."

There was no reasoning with her, and the devil of it was that in her position, he'd feel much the same way. "I'm going to stop at the next inn to give the men a chance to eat. You can spend the time sitting by the fire eating your dinner, or trussed up in here."

She turned to stare out of the window. "Trussed."

He ran his hands through his hair in exasperation. "Felicity, it is not a sin to bend before *force majeur.*"

She looked at him then, a direct and honest look. "You're too tricksy for me, Miles Cavanagh. I'll give you no rope at all."

He understood then, a little, for he felt exactly the same way. It would be so easy for either of them to use their attraction as a weapon.

It was dark in the coach, for they'd lit no lamp. A darkness which brought out secrets and soul-talk.

"No tricks, Felicity," Miles said gently. "I meant what I said and no more. I intend to get you to Melton and hold you there. Nothing beyond that."

"It doesn't matter what you intend, or even what you do. The trickery comes just from your being you."

"You mean you love me."

She turned away again. "I can't love the man who betrayed my trust."

"Then let's say that you are moved by me."

She gave a short, bitter laugh. "To exasperation. To fury."

"To emotions other than that, Felicity. Can we not be honest, at least?"

He thought perhaps she sighed. Softly, she said, "I could love you if it were possible."

He wanted quite desperately to take her in his arms. "Is love under such control?"

"I think so. Would you let yourself love a friend's wife, for example?"

"No. I would let myself love no man's wife."

"Then," she said with shocking crispness, "think of me as Rupert Dunsmore's wife."

"Never."

A stray moonbeam turned her gaze cat-like. "It was to him I gave my virginity, you know."

He'd guessed, but he didn't like it any the better when spoken. "He stole it, you mean."

"He did not. I was embarrassingly eager."

Miles felt his teeth grind together. "He had no right to take what you offered."

"Faith, are you a believer in chastity for men as well as women?"

Miles hastily steered back to the main path before she tied him in knots entirely. "If Dunsmore was your first lover, he wasn't much of one."

She turned away, as if uninterested. "He seemed exciting enough at the time."

"And have there been others?"

She stiffened. "I don't have to answer that."

"True enough." He studied her averted face. "But I don't think there have been others. Even were you inclined to promiscuity, there aren't many suitable men around Foy, and even fewer who'd risk fooling around with the likes of you. And you've not led a wandering life."

"I never even found a private piano until you provided it." She tilted her head slyly toward him. "A piano and some wondrous loving. I should be your slave, shouldn't I?"

"None of that was calculated. None of it."

"You didn't deny the hope of getting me with child."

"After the fact. Believe me."

"I'm not sure I can. You've broken faith with me, Miles, and perhaps it can't be mended."

Miles cursed his mother and her plan, even though he couldn't see an alternative. He could have woken Felicity and explained the situation, then made a straight-out fight of getting her on board ship.

Despite the resulting bloodshed, it might have been a more honest way. But he knew it was the night of pleasure before the trick that really wounded her, and he would not have missed that.

They rode in silence until the coach began to slow to enter the town of Leek. "Trussed or not?" he asked wearily.

She laughed, though it cut the air like a sword. "Faith, Miles Cavanagh, but you're as blind stubborn as I am!"

"Well matched, are we?"

"Oh, very. Have you ever seen two equal fighting cocks duel to the death?"

Then she held out her hands to be bound.

Though he hated every moment of it, Miles bound and gagged her, then opened the hatch to speak to his coachman. "You, O'Grady, and Hennigan can go into the inn and eat. We'll stay here. Bring a basket of food when you leave." Then he rolled down the blinds and gathered Felicity into his arms, prepared for anything.

It was a long half-hour, but Felicity made no move to resist or escape. Miles didn't feel free to speak, for when she could neither block his words nor reply, that would be unfair.

Miles wondered if she was finding the same bitter comfort at being in his arms as he felt at having her there. Or the same frustration. He was strongly tempted to shift his hands, to make the confining hold a different kind of embrace.

He restrained himself, thank God. That, too, would be a gross abuse of the situation.

He had two separate roles here—guardian and lover—and must never confuse them. This bondage was to keep Felicity safe, to protect her against herself. He would be as base as Dunsmore if he took advantage of it.

At last the door opened and, head averted, Hennigan gingerly placed a basket of food and a bottle of wine on the floor. Miles wondered if the valet would tender his resignation at the end of this journey.

He kept a firm hold of Felicity until they were out of town and picking up speed. Only then did he let her go, untie her, and light the lamps so they could investigate the basket.

Gardeen miaowed, and so he fed the cat some pieces of salmon. Then he simply invited Felicity to help herself as he opened the wine. He was sure she'd enjoy the grand gesture of refusing to eat but, as on board ship, she was strictly practical and took enough food to preserve her strength.

He poured the burgundy into the two glasses and passed her one, watchful that she didn't throw it in his face. She sipped appreciatively, though. "An excellent vintage. You get good service."

"I'm well known on this road. I generally bring over my own curricle and drive myself, but however I travel, they know me."

"So if I were to escape and accuse you of kidnapping, they'd likely not believe me."

"Likely not," he said levelly. "Especially as I have the papers with me that appoint me your guardian. I would explain that I'm preventing your marriage to an unsuitable man. Which has the virtue of being true."

She tossed the crust of her bread back into the basket. "Do you have any idea how galling this is?"

"I have a clear memory of being bound and gagged."

Color touched her cheeks. "We only kept you tied until we could release you with as little danger as possible. Would you rather have been beaten like Dunsmore?"

"You don't have to remind me what an angel of mercy

you were, sweet Joy. Especially when you flaunted your lovely legs a short while ago."

Her lips tightened, but she didn't lose track of her main point. "We took you prisoner to keep you safe. This abduction is an attempt to totally overrule my will."

"You overruled my will, and I have taken you prisoner to keep you safe."

"You have no right! Even if what I plan *were* disastrous, I would have the right to choose."

"Not as long as I'm your guardian. Surely that is what guardianship is all about—protecting the young and innocent from their own follies and the wickedness of others."

A noise escaped her, and though it could have been fury, he rather thought it was a strangled laugh. But her anger did not abate. "This has *nothing* to do with guardianship. This is all to do with your lust!"

"No," said Miles firmly. "If I were as uninterested in you as I am in . . . in Nuala Yeates, I would still do my damndest to stop your marriage to Dunsmore. What is between us is a very unfortunate complication."

She tossed her head. "Unfortunate, is it?"

"Damnation, Felicity, don't bring those games into this. You've given me more pleasure and more pain in the last few weeks than I ever expected to have in a lifetime."

"We share the pain, at least."

"And the pleasure. You came to my room, remember?"

She gasped as if hit. "Damn you. Do you have to throw my weakness in my face?"

"If it's weakness, then I'm as weak as you. I'm aching for you now."

"The flesh is weak," she said, but not as firmly as she perhaps wished. Then her voice firmed. "If you are slave to your flesh, though, I'm willing enough to use it against you."

"You'll make passionate love to me here if I'll let you go?"

She bit her lip, then said, "I will."

"Well, then. I'll make passionate love to you if you'll promise to stay."

She flared deep red. "Damn you!"

"Felicity, if we duel with those weapons, we'll kill each other for sure, for we are equally matched. That's why our love—"

"Not love!"

"Yes, love," he said firmly. "That's why our love is unfortunate. It can destroy us. We have to be very careful until we find the solution to your problem with Dunsmore."

"Solution! Miles, you must believe in fairy gold! Why can't you accept that there is no solution. I will not seek my safety at Kieran's expense."

"Then I'll have to find a permanent solution to the problem of Kieran."

"There isn't one . . ."

". . . short of Dunsmore's death. I know. But that can be arranged."

Abruptly, she turned pale. "But, Miles, that solves nothing unless I marry him first. On Rupert's death, Kieran would be in the care of Kathleen's cousin, Michael."

"He'd be safe there, surely."

"He would, but . . ."

They were back to her unhealthy obsession with the child. "Felicity, you will have children of your own in time. Save your devotion for them."

She looked away in strange confusion. "How can I know they'll be kind to him? Orphans in a strange family are often neglected. And they won't raise him in Ireland. Poor Kieran will be taken from all he knows and sent to strangers. And what's more," she said, turning back, "he's the only thing standing between Michael Craig and Loughcarrick. There must be a better way. Promise me you won't kill Dunsmore out of hand. *Promise me!*"

Her desperation dragged the promise from him before he had time to think. He immediately regretted it.

"And you mustn't set your friends to kill him, either," she begged, leaning forward to grasp his hands.

He turned his hands to hold hers. "Felicity, the man deserves death a dozen times over."

"No one deserves death."

"That's nonsense."

"Promise me, Miles. *Please!* Promise you won't do anything to bring about his death."

And weak man that he was, he gave her that promise, too.

The weather held and the moon stayed clear, enabling them to travel through the night. Once more they stopped by the road for Felicity's convenience. Miles did not take her shoes. When they halted in Derby for another food basket, however, he bound and gagged her as before.

Most of the time, Felicity appeared to sleep. Miles, despite aching weariness, didn't dare. When they finally rolled up to Vauxhall, the Duke of Belcraven's Melton hunting box, he felt as if he'd reached heaven.

It was noon on a fine, crisp day, and the sun hurt his gritty eyes. It was Friday so the Quorn would be out. On such a fine day, no Rogues would be at home. Beth Arden should be here, however. He hoped so. He wasn't sure how to handle his rebellious ward without help.

Felicity sat still and watchful. He made sure there was no uncertainty in his manner as he asked, "Trussed or untrussed?"

Her lips parted in surprise, then her eyes narrowed. "You're bluffing."

"Try me."

Hennigan opened the door and let down the steps. The door to Vauxhall spilled servants hurrying to attend to the arrivals.

"Well?" he asked, trying not to let a scrap of his leaden exhaustion show.

Fifteen

Felicity stared at Miles, feeling as if she were transported into a dream-state where nothing was real. This large, modern house with long gleaming windows and carefully tended grounds was the height of respectability. How could Miles be threatening to take her in there bound and gagged?

There were even servants. Respectable-looking servants who could not—like Hennigan and the rest—owe their allegiance to Clonnagh.

She looked at Miles again, seeking a trace of uncertainty or hesitation, but saw none. His resolution astonished her and even summoned a degree of admiration. Truly he was turning out to be a foe worthy of her mettle. If the matter were not so serious, she could almost enjoy the battle.

The coach door swung open. Felicity hesitated, tempted to make Miles bind and gag her simply because she knew he'd hate it. . . .

Suddenly, though, she was weary of it all. She'd rest and reconnoiter the land before continuing the war.

"I give you no parole," she said, "but I'll walk into the house peacefully enough."

The breath he exhaled told her he'd been less sure of himself than she'd thought, but it didn't change matters. He'd succeeded in bringing her here. First skirmish to him. She doubted he could hold her, though, unless they had a dungeon to lock her in.

She picked up Gardeen, let a footman hand her down, and

walked toward the house. All the time, she studied the area like a general preparing for battle. The house lay close to the road, and the estate was unwalled. Not that a wall would keep her in, but the open effect of rolling meadows on all sides made this place a very unlikely prison.

A lady appeared in the doorway, a handsome brunette in a comfortable blue wool gown and capacious but costly Indian shawl. "Miles! How wonderful. We'd almost given you up. Lucien's riding one of your horses today. He said you'd written asking him to."

"Indeed I did, or they'd have been fat as slugs by now. Beth, may I present to you Miss Felicity Monahan of Foy Hall in Meath. She has the great misfortune to be my ward. Felicity, this is Beth, Marchioness of Arden, our hostess here."

Felicity felt she should be surly, but Lady Arden appeared so pleasant, so ordinary, that she simply couldn't. She curtsied. "Good day, Lady Arden. I'm sorry to arrive uninvited and unannounced."

"Think nothing of it," her hostess said cheerfully, ushering her into a well-lit beech-paneled hall. "The Rogues all come and go as they please."

The hall was decorated with a great many fox masks interspersed with hunting prints and a couple of fine oils of magnificent horses. No doubt as to the purpose of this establishment.

"It must be a great convenience to them," Felicity said, "to have a residence so close to good hunting."

Lady Arden grinned. "One might almost think Nicholas had that in mind when he chose Lucien to be one of the Rogues. Nicholas," she added with a smile, "is King Rogue. Oh, but you don't want to hear me chatter. You look exhausted. Let me show you to a room."

"Thank you." But as Beth led her up the wide, wooden stairs, Felicity heard Miles coming behind.

"Who's here?" he asked.

"Just Lucien and I, and Hal and Blanche," Beth said over her shoulder. "Stephen and Con were here until yesterday. Con's visiting his estate. Stephen is discussing some political matter at Belvoir. He'll be back tomorrow."

"Good, because I have a problem."

They had reached the upper landing, and Lady Arden turned. "A problem?"

"Felicity."

The marchioness looked between them, mildly surprised. "She doesn't look like a problem to me."

"Hah! She's a hellion."

"Miles!" Lady Arden objected.

Felicity could feel her cheeks redden with mortification and annoyance.

"There's no point glowering at me, Felicity," he said. "You've refused to give your parole, so I have to take other measures." He turned to Lady Arden. "She's hell-bent on marrying the basest scoundrel ever to crawl about Ireland on his belly, and I'm determined to stop her. But she'll run if she sees a chance. I have to get some sleep. Is there somewhere to put her where she'll be safe?"

Lady Arden studied them shrewdly. Felicity thought of making some plea, but what Miles said was the truth. Anyway she, too, needed sleep.

"I have rooms with doors that will lock," Lady Arden said, "and if we put a man to watch the window, she should be completely safe."

"Thank you," Miles said, visibly relaxing.

"Won't the man think it very strange?" Felicity asked as she was led down a carpeted corridor.

"They're well paid not to think too much about some things," Lady Arden replied, as if imprisonment were commonplace. "And anyway, since the end of the war, the duchy has taken on a great many extra servants just to give them employment. It's often quite a business to find things for them to do." She flashed Felicity a mild smile. "You are doing an act of charity, you see."

"I'll take comfort from that fact."

Felicity's room bore no resemblance to a dungeon. It was a normal bedroom with russet draperies of jacquard weave and a square carpet over polished boards. The sight of a proper bed made Felicity ache to collapse onto it.

"Your bags will be brought up in a moment," Lady Arden said, "and a maid will come to assist you. I'll have a fire made in here, too, within moments."

"Better not," Miles said.

"Good heavens, do you expect her to freeze? It's January!"

"No fire unless she promises not to burn the place down." Lady Arden stared, which infuriated Felicity.

"Do you think me mad?" she demanded of Miles.

"I think you capable of anything."

In a strange way, it was flattering. Burning the house down had never occurred to Felicity, but she could see it might enable her to get free—if she avoided being turned into a cinder. She could never endanger others that way, however.

"You have my word," she said frostily, which was easy when her breath made little puffs as she spoke. "I'll not use the fire in any way in our struggle."

He nodded. "That should be all right, then." To Lady Arden he added, "You can trust her word. But never trust her smiles."

"Miles Cavanagh, that is most unfair!"

"Felicity Monahan, I'm too tired to be fair. I'm hoping you are, too, but I don't forget a pleasant journey we enjoyed not long ago and what happened when I let down my guard."

"I do what I must."

"Quite."

A footman entered with her trunk, and another arrived with coals to make a fire. In moments, a maid bustled in with a warming pan and hot bricks for the bed, accompanied by

another bearing a jug of hot water. This servant stayed to
unpack the trunk.

Miles prowled and tried a door in a side wall. It opened
into another bedroom. "Is this room vacant, Beth?"

"Yes. But it's not your usual one."

"It'll do." With that, he went through and locked the door
on the far side.

Lady Arden shrugged at Felicity. "I'm sure we can sort all
this out. Your clothes will be chilled. I'll send a warm nightgown." With that, she, too, left.

Felicity still had Gardeen in her arms and was a little surprised that the cat hadn't insisted on going with Miles. But
then Gardeen II had never shown the same devotion to Miles
as her previous incarnation—or dead sister—had.

Sighing, she shrugged off her cloak, bunched it on a chair,
and put the cat in the still-warm folds. Gardeen curled into
a sleepy ball. Felicity knew just how she felt. She'd dozed a
little on the journey, but most of the time she'd been faking
sleep to avoid talk. Now she, too, wanted nothing so much
as to curl into a ball and forget the world.

The maid helped her out of her dress so she could wash.
The fire was already warming the room, but Felicity shuddered with the chill of exhaustion. She hurried into Beth's
nightgown. Then the maid gave the bed a final sweep with
the warming pan before leaving. When Felicity slid between
the sheets, she was able, like Gardeen, to curl up in comfort
and fall instantly asleep.

Miles woke when shaken. "Up you get, Miles! You've had
six hours, which must be enough to tide you over."

Miles rolled over groggily to see Lucien de Vaux's aristocratic features and blond hair made macabre by a single wavering candle.

"Hell. All right. I'm awake. Don't drip wax on me!"

The marquess moved away to light a branch of candles

near the bed and to throw some extra coals on the fire. "Dinner's in half an hour, and we need to talk as you dress."

Miles saw that Lucien was already in elegant evening clothes. "Why is my presence at table so essential?" But he sat up and shook his head, rubbing his chin. "I need a shave. I probably need a bath, but I doubt there's time. However I must have a shave."

"True. I assume Hennigan's as exhausted as you. I'll call for my man."

As soon as it was arranged, he said, "The thing is, Miles, this guard on your ward has Beth uneasy. You know how she is about the oppression of women, and she considers even protection oppression at times."

Miles groaned and rubbed his gritty eyes. "I can explain it all, Luce. Just give me a moment to get my wits together."

But in those moments, Lucien's valet appeared with hot water and set up, ready to shave Miles. The two Rogues settled to talk of safer matters.

"Who's here?" Miles asked as the valet scraped the sharp blade over his cheek.

"Hal and Blanche."

"Oh, yes. Beth said."

"That creates a problem."

"For you and Beth?"

"No, not for me and Beth. Do get your wits together. As I said, Hal has Blanche with him—she's taking a rest from the stage just now. Beth has no problem with that, but you might."

"Why? You must have even Melton in a flurry with both mistress and wife in one house, but it don't bother me."

"Ex-mistress," said Lucien firmly. "Think about it. As a conscientious guardian, you just might have a problem with your innocent young ward meeting the White Dove of Drury Lane over breakfast."

"Oh God," Miles groaned.

Blanche Hardcastle was a gifted actress, but she was known

to have made her way out of poverty on her back. She'd been Lucien's mistress for a number of years until his marriage. Recently, she had become the mistress of another Rogue, Hal Beaumont.

Though Blanche's earlier years could not bear close scrutiny, her morals were now quite strict. She had been as faithful to Lucien as any wife and was now completely faithful to Hal.

Her presence did, however, create a problem.

For a man to have his ex-mistress in the same house as his wife was brow-raising, even when the two ladies were the best of friends. To bring a young, ostensibly innocent lady into such a ménage could be considered a scandal.

"Damnation. I do need to have Felicity here for a while, Luce. It's not just that I want to enjoy some hunting. . . ."

"Then perhaps it will be best if Hal and Blanche leave."

The valet had stopped wielding the blade, so Miles felt able to shake his head. "No. I think Blanche might be able to help. And to be honest, when this all works out, I'm not sure minor social irregularities will matter much."

"Oh-ho. This sounds like a very Roguish matter."

"It is."

As the valet wiped away lather with a warm cloth, Lucien eased into another subject. "Did you hear Leander married a few weeks ago? A widow with two children, no less. We're falling like coconuts at a shy."

There was a question in it, and Miles answered by saying, "It's the devil being a guardian, Luce."

The valet finished and bowed out, so Miles was able to explain the whole situation while pulling on his evening wear. He didn't mention, however, that Felicity was no innocent, or that they'd become lovers.

Looked at in the cold light of sanity, it was not something he was proud of. It certainly wouldn't happen again, or not as long as he was her guardian.

"Lord, what a tangle," Lucien said at last, assisting in the arrangement of Miles's cravat. "But at least it provides an excuse for your treatment of the girl. This Dunsmore is definitely not the sort of man to gain Beth's approval. So, you think he'll follow Felicity here?" He stuck a silver pin in his creation. "Just shooting the wretch on sight springs to mind."

"Felicity is adamantly opposed to that." Miles shrugged into his jacket and flashed his friend a wry look. "I'm afraid that, in a moment of foolishness, I promised I wouldn't kill him. Or let anyone else do so."

Lucien swung open the door. "It's a bad sign, Miles, when a man grows foolish over a woman."

"Hah! It's just that Felicity Monahan has a rare ability to tie a person in knots."

The first thing Miles did on arriving in the drawing room was to check with Beth that Felicity's door was still locked. Beth was a bluestocking, and a follower of Mary Wollstonecraft, author of *The Rights Of Woman.* Her libertarian principles were doubtless being severely tested.

"It's locked," she said. "But will not stay that way without an excellent explanation."

"Think of it as locking someone up so they won't rush to their death in a hopeless cause."

"That," said Beth, "raises thorny questions as to who decides what is hopeless and whether a person has a right to sacrifice themselves, hope or not." But she let the subject drop.

As Miles moved on to greet Hal Beaumont and Blanche Hardcastle, he knew it was only a temporary respite.

Hal was darkly handsome and as tall and broad-shouldered as the marquess and himself. His left sleeve hung empty, however, for he had lost his arm after a military engagement in the Canadas.

Blanche was a beautiful woman with clever eyes and a firm chin. She was prematurely gray, and had turned it into a distinction by never wearing colors. Tonight, as always, she wore a white gown. Her heavy silver hair was caught up by pearl combs, and a pearl-and-diamond choker circled her neck.

She kissed his cheek. "You're not looking your best, Miles. Was your dislocated shoulder such a problem?"

"My shoulder?" queried Miles. "Recovered from that weeks ago. At the moment, I'm just suffering from a hard journey." Or a dislocated life, he thought wryly.

Ah, but it was good to be here again with friends. He couldn't help thinking that without Felicity Monahan in his life, he could have been here weeks ago, enjoying some damned fine hunting and the best company around.

But then, he could no longer imagine life without Felicity, and he dreaded to think what would have happened to her without his intervention, Beth and her scruples be damned.

Despite the formality of dress for dinner, the meal was relaxed, with servants playing little part and the talk almost entirely of hunting.

"We've been riding your horses as instructed, Miles," said Lucien. "You've a good number of potential buyers anxious for your appearance. And the one that arrived a few days ago—Argonaut—I've a mind to bid on him myself."

"He's yours, of course, at a fair price."

They nodded, sale settled.

"Ah," said Hal plaintively, "if only I had the wealth to be able to snap up a prime bit of blood without a moment's thought."

Lucien grinned. "I give the purchase of any horse a great deal of thought."

When dessert had been served, Beth indicated that the servants were no longer needed.

Once they were free of interruptions, Lucien said, "Now, Miles, explain this problem so we can decide how best to handle it. Preferably without keeping the girl under lock and key."

Miles again explained the basic situation—that Felicity was

devoted to her friend's child and determined to marry the child's wretched father so as to be able to care for Kieran.

"But your guardianship ends on February 20th?" Beth asked. "It seems to me you're just putting off the inevitable. And perhaps a person has the right to sacrifice themselves if they know what they're doing."

"She knows," Miles admitted. "I think she fools herself that she can control Dunsmore, but she knows." He hadn't even mentioned his fear that Felicity's plan included murder. He trusted the Rogues, but if the crime ever took place, he didn't want them to have that knowledge on their consciences.

"For the moment," he continued "I want your help to keep her safely here while we find a solution."

"It's no easy matter," said Lucien, "to refuse a father his child. Is there neglect or violent abuse?"

Miles had to admit that the lad seemed healthy and well cared for. The occasional spanking hardly counted.

"It seems to me," said Hal, "that the problem is not just that she wants to protect the child, but that she wants the child for herself."

"True enough. Sometimes I think she's spent so much time with the lad that she's forgotten whose child he is. It's not a particularly healthy state of mind, but she'll get over it once she sees him happy in a good home."

Lucien refilled his wineglass and sent the bottle round. "Which won't happen as long as his father lives."

"Miles," interrupted Blanche, her face now as pale as the rest of her. "Have you thought . . ." As the words failed, they all looked at her in concern.

She carefully laid her knife and fork on her plate. "Let me tell you a story," she said. "Once there was a girl called Maggie Duggins. Her father was a butcher, but he also liked to drink, so there wasn't much money for the seven children. Her mother died when she was five, so there wasn't much care, either. Maggie was a wild child. Not bad, but wild. She sought kindness and attention and, of course, as soon as she was any sort of a woman, she found men would pay kind attentions if she let them."

Hal reached over and took her hand. She squeezed it and continued. "Inevitably, she ended up carrying a child. She had no way of knowing which of a number of men was the father, but she knew none of them would help her. She also knew that as soon as she began to show, her father would throw her out, probably after beating her black and blue.

"So she ran to a friend and stayed there until the child was born. Such a pretty baby . . . a girl . . ." Blanche's voice faltered, but then she carried on. "She wanted nothing so much as to keep the babe forever, but she could see how little she could give her and how little she could make of her life with a child to care for. When her friend found a well-to-do family willing to take the baby, she gave her up. But as her daughter was taken from her arms, she vowed to make the sacrifice worthwhile by making something of her life."

Blanche looked at Miles. "I hesitate to suggest that your ward . . . but . . ."

Miles was almost as pale as she was. "Dear God." He rose, tossed down his napkin, and left the room.

Beth half-rose in concern. "Is he angry with her?"

Lucien pulled her back into her seat. "He's angry with himself, I think. But, if true, it makes this problem a good deal more challenging."

Miles stopped at Felicity's locked door, leaning against the wall. How could he not have guessed?

She'd even told him Dunsmore had been her lover. Perhaps she'd been hoping he'd guess the truth without her having to say it, but he'd been too thick-skulled. He'd been so sure she nurtured an obsessive affection for another woman's child that he'd never stopped to think how little that meshed with the Felicity he knew.

And to add to his self-recriminations was the knowledge

that this truth made the whole problem more difficult to solve. Of course Felicity wouldn't be satisfied with merely getting Kieran out of Dunsmore's hands.

She wanted her child back. Hers, entirely and legally.

And since Miles loved her, he would have to achieve that for her.

Or with her.

He unlocked the door.

The room was dark and cozily warm, though the fire was burning low. When his eyes adjusted, he put some new coals on the embers, stepping carefully over a small black cat. Someone had provided Gardeen with food and a dish of milk.

He turned to the bed where Felicity lay sound asleep. He'd expected that, but somehow he'd had to come here, to be with her.

With her lips relaxed and her lashes making deep shadows on her cheeks, she looked touchingly young and innocent. She was an Irish warrior-queen, though, fighting for her cause with every ounce of her strength.

Very gently, he brushed a curl from her brow. "I wish you could have found the trust to tell me, *cailín,*" he whispered. "But I wish, too, I'd had the wit to realize for myself. Poor child you must have been when you bore him. We'll keep him safe. He'll be the start of our own family. I don't know how, but we'll do it."

He should go back downstairs to resume dinner, but he couldn't. He drew up a chair and sat by the bed in a kind of guard and vigil, waiting for his beloved to awake.

A distant clock had just struck one when Felicity stirred and opened her eyes with a faint groan. Miles smiled, knowing what it felt like to have slept too long, even when it was needed. He poured some water from a carafe by the bedside and offered it.

"Faith, and are you guarding me night and day, in addition to the locked door and the watcher on the window?"

"I am not. Do you want the water?"

She sat up, frowning at him, but she took the water and drank it. "Is there food as well?"

"Beth brought a tray before retiring." He carried it over and placed it on the bed beside her.

She lifted the covers and grabbed some bread and cold ham. "Doesn't she think it at all strange that you're lurking here in my bedroom?"

"She's used to strange. Felicity, we have to talk, but it can wait until you've eaten and woken up properly."

She flashed him a wary look which suddenly changed to alarm. "Something's happened. Kieran?"

"Nothing like that. I promise."

She subsided back to wariness. "What is it, then? Trying to guess the problem is likely to turn me gray before my time." She picked up a bunch of hothouse grapes and pulled one off the stem with her teeth, never taking her eyes off him.

Unable to see a better way, Miles resorted to bluntness. "Is Kieran your son?"

Her eyes widened and her chewing stopped. Then she swallowed. "Who told you? Is Rupert here?"

"No, of course not. Blanche guessed. Something similar happened to her as a girl."

He could see the effort it took for her to push back her reaction and pretend calm. She pulled off another grape and chewed it, watching him all the time. "It doesn't change a thing."

"It does. I understand better now."

"How nice for you. Does that mean you'll let me leave tomorrow to marry Rupert?"

"It does not."

"Then it doesn't change a thing, does it? In fact, it makes

it worse, because now you'll guard me more closely. That's why I didn't tell you before."

As usual when dealing with this woman, Miles was ready to tear his hair out. "Felicity, we are not enemies. We have to work together to find the solution to this problem."

"A solution that leaves me as Kieran's mother? What can it be other than my marriage to Rupert? I lost my son once. I will not lose him again."

"But I love you and want you. You have to take that into account."

"I do not. Kieran has to come first."

Beth had also brought a bottle of wine, wise woman. Miles poured two glasses and passed one to his bewitching, infuriating ward. "At least tell me the whole story. Knowledge is power."

She took the wine and sipped it, leaning back against her pillows. "I was young and foolish. What more is there to say? It galls me to admit it, but for a while there, I truly fancied myself in love with the weasel. If I hadn't burned them in a rage, I could show you maudlin verses I wrote comparing him to Lancelot and Diarmuid."

"Both famous adulterers, so you had a point."

A ghost of a smile twitched her lips. "The simple fact is that the memory of my stupidity mortifies me."

"You were only . . . what . . . fifteen?"

"But I should have known better. Mind you, no one had ever explained anything to me of physical matters between man and woman, so I believed him when he said I could not get with child." She looked at him with a grimace. "I actually believed him when he told me women had to come into season to be fertile. Well, I knew it was true of horses."

Miles managed to stifle a laugh. He could not resist, however, the need to be closer. He hitched onto the bed beside her. "Perfectly reasonable to believe it, *a muirnín*."

"Not really. If I'd stopped to think, I'd have realized that, though there were always babies about, none of the women of the area behaved like the mares. They didn't get wild-eyed and chase after anything male. Or at least, not often . . ."

He slid an arm around to hug her. "When we're young, we're always looking for keys to the bewildering world around us. Lacking good guidance, we'll come to some strange conclusions. So, what happened when you found you were carrying a child?"

For a moment she was stiff in his arms, but then she surrendered and rested against his shoulder. "It took forever for me to realize what was happening. My courses stopped, but I hardly noticed. It was Rupert who commented on my swelling belly. Oh, so horrified and repentant that he was! May his toes rot slowly and his rod fall off."

Miles laughed then, though his heart was breaking for her. "And it was his idea, I suppose, that you pass off the child as his wife's."

"Oh, yes. Don't worry. I realized years ago that it was all planned." She drained her glass. "It is very lowering to realize one has been so easily used."

"But how was it arranged? You couldn't have borne the child at Foy. . . . Ah, that other journey you made to England. Annie said you'd been sent away because of your infatuation with Dunsmore. Does she know the truth?"

"I don't know. She's never mentioned it. But she has a way of ignoring what she doesn't care to see."

Miles refilled her glass. "Where did you spend your confinement?"

"Confinement, indeed! In an isolated farmhouse not far from Cheltenham. Kathleen, of course, conveniently chose Cheltenham as the place to cosset her 'delicate pregnancy,' and the waters proved to be quite miraculous."

Miles rubbed her arm, wishing he had been part of her life then, even though it was a foolish idea. Five years ago, he'd been a heedless young rascal fooling his way through Cambridge, spending more time on horseback than with books. It seemed wrong, however, that he'd had no awareness of her misery.

"Was it a very hard time?"

"It was winter, and dreary. I had Miss Herries—easygoing Miss Herries—to keep me company, and she finally found she had a captive audience for education. She made little headway with my writing, but she did manage to introduce me to some excellent books."

"Who else was there with you?"

"Just the farmer, his wife, his son, and his son's family. The Bittens had a good-enough small holding, but were a taciturn lot. Doubtless why they were selected as my hosts. Oh, and the fact that Babs, the daughter-in-law, knew something of midwifery."

"And when Kieran was born, what happened?"

She looked back through the years. "It was May and very beautiful. It made it quite reasonable for even a heavily pregnant woman such as Kathleen was supposed to be to decide upon a leisurely carriage-tour of the area. When her time came, where else to take shelter than in the only farm in sight? And what luck that there should be a midwife present!"

"And as soon as possible, she returned to Cheltenham to recover. Did you even get to hold him?"

She closed her eyes and shook her head. "They wouldn't let me. They . . . they drugged me. When I came to, I was empty and he was gone."

Miles didn't know what to say and just leaned his head against hers.

"My milk came, though. For days, despite the bindings, I filled and leaked. It s . . . seemed so wasteful." He thought she would cry then, but she continued with determined briskness. "He had an excellent wet nurse, of course. Kathleen took the best care of him."

Miles gathered her closer so she was entirely within his arms. "When did you see him?"

"Not for weeks. After a couple of weeks, Miss Herries

took me to Gloucester. We attended some musical events
and a lecture or two. I acquired the new clothes I'd need to
show off when I returned home. They were needed, anyway.
My bust had become larger. As soon as I returned to Foy,
of course, I found everyone talking of Kathleen's 'miracle.'
Since Rupert was off in London with well-filled pockets, I
sneaked over to Loughcarrick, hoping for a glimpse of the
baby."

She was relaxed in his arms now, and he suspected she
was entirely lost in that past time.

"They were out on the lawn," she said softly. "Kathleen,
the wet nurse, a nursery nurse, and Kieran kicking plump
legs on a blanket in the shade of a tree. He was six weeks
old, and I can't say I would have recognized him as the tiny
scrap I'd seen so briefly when he left my body. I couldn't
stop myself from going over. At first Kathleen ordered me
away. She feared I'd try to take him back, you see. When she
saw I had no thought of that, she became cautiously kind.
She even . . . she even let me hold him." Her arms curled
in a cradling movement, and she sighed. "I knew him then.
I think it was a smell I recognized. I wonder if all mothers
can tell their child by smell."

When she said no more, he responded. "I wouldn't be surprised. Animals can. Did it hurt a great deal to have to leave
him with another woman as mother?"

"Not as much as you'd think. I'd learned to live with the
pain of losing him, and Kathleen was so very, very happy.
Once she was sure I wouldn't make trouble, she treated me
as the most handsome benefactor on Earth. I was always welcome there, though I stayed away when Rupert was home. It
was enough, it truly was, until she died. You know what happened then."

"Dunsmore discovered you were an heiress and decided to
use the child to force you into marrying him. It really would
be very easy to arrange his death."

She stiffened slightly. "But that would not give me Kieran."

"Perhaps we should just steal him away."

She twisted to look up at him. "And run off to America to live in the wilderness, just the three of us? Faith, but you're an impractical dreamer, Miles Cavanagh. Do you forget you're heir to Kilgoran?"

"I never forget I'm heir to Kilgoran. Do you think I value it over you?"

"You should. Kilgoran has many people dependent on the proper management of his estates. You can't walk away from it all anymore than I can walk away from my son."

He pulled her back into his arms. "This is beginning to feel too much like an Irish fable, one that ends in blood and weeping."

"Let me go to Dunsmore, and that'll be an end to it."

"It would only be the beginning, and you know it. I promised you I would not kill him. Will you give me the same promise?"

She tensed. "I can't. To protect my son, I will do anything."

That was what terrified him. "Then we had better find a solution to this mess."

Suddenly a small black creature leapt up to pad around the jacquard coverlet, occasionally catching threads.

"Watch your claws, Gardeen," said Felicity, picking up the cat and stroking her.

"I wonder if she's telling me it's time I left. It's true enough that last time I fell asleep in your bed, it didn't work out well." Miles took a piece of bread from Felicity's tray. "I missed most of my dinner for you, *cailín*."

"Oh, the bitter sacrifice." But she smiled at him, and the truth had torn down some of the barriers between them.

Miles slid his arm from behind her and rolled off the bed. "Leaving you now is a bitter sacrifice, *a muirnín*. But I'm determined to be a good guardian from here on."

"Good as in firm?"

"Indeed." Though he knew she understood the other meaning—that he would not make love to her.

"Then we are destined to battle. I will not stay here and wait on your pleasure. I intend to escape."

Miles leaned on one of the end-posts of the bed. "Felicity, think. There really is no point in your running off. Where would you go? You have no idea where Dunsmore is. He's doubtless following you, but he could be anywhere between here and Ireland."

"But how can we be sure he will follow me, not Kieran? What if he's stolen him . . ."

"He hasn't. Trust me on that. I'd back my mother against Dunsmore any day, and clearly you have never visited Kilgoran Castle."

"It's fortified?"

He laughed. "Far from it. It's a cold, classic monument. But it fair crawls with servants and is run on rigid lines. No one could sneak in there."

"It doesn't sound like a pleasant place for a child."

"It's not too bad. The nursery still contains the toys bought to amuse me and my brother and sisters. There's a fine fishing stream and a small ornamental lake ideal for children to go boating on, since it's barely two feet deep. But the grounds are always crawling with servants chasing down every weed and every blade of grass that dares to grow taller than its fellows. Your son is safe."

"I want to believe you."

"You can. My mother promised a letter as soon as she arrived. It should reach us within days. So, why not declare truce for a little while and wait for Dunsmore to contact you?"

She eyed him with a frown. "Truces seem to serve us no better than battles."

"This one will. I'm your guardian, and that's the only role I'll play for the next few weeks."

She raised a brow, as if disbelieving. "But how will Rupert contact me, held prisoner as I am?"

"If you give me your parole, you won't be a true prisoner. Once you receive a message, we'll know where he is and what he plans. So, until then, will you rest easy here?"

She looked at him steadily, still stroking the cat. It was a fierce pain that she could not trust him, but like a poorly handled horse, she would need time to let go of wariness. It wasn't Felicity he blamed, but those who had hurt her through abuse and neglect.

"Until he contacts me, then," she said at last. "Or until two weeks have passed. I daren't wait longer without news. There's no telling what he might be up to." She lowered her cheek against the cat's fur. "Do your friends know everything?"

"I told them part, and Blanche guessed the rest."

"Will they disapprove?"

She looked so young, he wanted to hug her again. "Lord, no. They're Rogues. Didn't I say that Blanche experienced something similar herself. She's an actress, by the way. She was Lucien's mistress—he's the marquess—and now she's the mistress of another Rogue, Hal Beaumont. It's more a question of do *you* disapprove?"

A disbelieving smile lit her face. "I'm positively faint with shock! I see I needn't concern myself with my reputation at all after being here."

He removed the tray and straightened her covers. "The high aristocracy have their own rules."

Felicity slid down under the covers. "Miles, do they know about us?"

"I haven't told them, but they probably guess. Does it concern you?"

"I don't know."

"Whatever they guess, we'll not give them fuel for it. Until February 20th, we're going to act the parts of grim guardian and wayward ward."

"It's not so far from the truth. But why, when your unconventional friends won't care?"

"Partly to save my sanity. But also so when Dunsmore starts sniffing around, he'll see what he wants to see—you held here against your will."

"And true it is!"

"But not quite as he'll think. It's always useful to have the enemy burdened by misconceptions. Can you do it? You've proved to be a fine actress in the past, sweet Joy."

"I might enjoy it." She grinned mischievously. "Do I get to kiss the stable lads and throw tantrums?"

"Only if I get to spank you for it."

She stuck out her tongue, and on that note, he left her.

But he didn't lock the door.

Sixteen

Exhaustion carried Felicity back into sleep and kept her there until a plump young maid woke her by drawing back the curtains to let in the sun. "Good morning, Miss. I'm Harriet. I was told to wake you since the men'll be leaving soon for the meet."

Felicity sat up, rubbing her eyes. Though she could have slept on, she felt all the sluggishness of one who has slept too long. "Am I supposed to wave them off?"

The maid's smile created amazing dimples. "Well, milady and Mrs. Hardcastle generally do. But it's more a question of breakfast. If you want to eat downstairs it'd best be now. Or you can have a tray here."

"What I really want is a bath."

The maid nodded. "I'll arrange it then, Miss. Do you want your breakfast before or after?"

"Oh, some chocolate now, I think, then something more substantial after."

The maid whisked off, and Felicity climbed out of bed to stretch and prowl, remembering that dream-time in the night. She half-wished it truly had been a dream, for she had lost her last secret and she didn't know what would come of it.

It was sweet to have honesty between her and Miles, and the memory of his tenderness could break her heart. But all in all, she feared the truth would be a complication.

He'd been right, at least, about the folly of running away from here just yet. As Miles had said, Rupert would find her.

And then, of course, she would elope with him, for even these Rogues could not find a better way.

A movement caught Felicity's eye, and she bent to scoop up the black cat gamboling toward her. Two empty dishes and a sand-filled box by the hearth were evidence that someone had looked after her. "Well, Gardeen, you look happy enough at our situation. I wonder if that means anything."

Felicity carried the cat over to the window and saw grooms leading three horses round to the front of the house.

"Would you look at that," she said to the cat. "Prime horse-flesh, but from what I hear those are only the hacks the men ride to the meet. The hunters will have gone at first light by gentle stages so as to be fresh for the run. Seems unsporting, somehow. The fox isn't permitted such careful preparations."

The cat gave a *miaow* which was impossible to interpret.

From the position of the sun, she judged it to be the middle of the morning on a clear, crisp day. If the hounds raised a good fox, the run would be marvelous. Felicity hunted sometimes at home, and it seemed unfair that women were not allowed to hunt the Shires. Decent women, anyway. She'd heard that some men's mistresses rode to hounds.

The maid returned with a tray holding a silver chocolate-pot and a china cup. Then she bustled into another adjoining room—a dressing room—to supervise the filling of the bath.

Felicity poured her chocolate, then sat in a chair by the window to sip it. It was the best chocolate she had ever tasted, and she deliberately savored the moment, not allowing her fears for the future to invade.

But the present could not be resisted.

During the last truce between herself and Miles, their desire had triumphed over reason. Miles said he would act the proper guardian this time, but did he have the strength?

And did she?

Last night, it had been almost more than she could bear not to kiss him, and she was sure it had been the same for him. They'd both known, however, that it wouldn't stop at kisses. The desire between them was so strong that Felicity felt as if she were truly in heat, but in heat for only one man.

Deep within her now was the teasing burn of desire.

But to increase the risk of conceiving Miles's child would be foolish beyond all reason.

Was love ever not foolish beyond all reason?

And his room was just next door . . .

Harriet interrupted this madness to announce that the bath was ready. Felicity went to scrub away many days' worth of grime, happy that she would not emerge until after the men had safely left for the day.

Harriet was skilled and deftly assisted Felicity in her transformation into a well-bred young lady. Her trunk was the one she had packed for her visit to Clonnagh, so she had an adequate selection of winter gowns, as well as two less-practical evening gowns should the need arise. Her habit was there, too, and the comfortable boots Lady Aideen had lent her.

That reminded her of other boots, however.

Faith, but it was true—they were both dangerous people. How many women could have planned that elopement? How many men would have the resolution to kidnap a lover, even if supposedly for her own good? Such ruthlessness in the cause was likely to lead to tragedy, however.

But even with that knowledge, she could not let herself weaken. Her job was to care for her innocent and vulnerable son. Miles—a grown man—could look after himself.

Eventually, clad in a dress of soft brown wool over a warm flannel petticoat, and with a knitted shawl draped over her elbows, Felicity ventured out to assess her circumstances. Gardeen pranced after, whiskers twitching with curiosity.

Felicity smiled down at her. "This seems another dauntingly well-run establishment, little one. I fear you'll find no mice. It's perhaps as well. Your ambitions tend to exceed your size."

As Felicity descended the stairs, she decided anyone could

tell this was a ducal household, even if only a hunting lodge. The pictures, even though all on hunting themes, were of the highest quality—she noted a Stubbs and a Fernley—and even the ornamental china looked priceless. In the hall, a powdered, liveried footman stood with no apparent purpose other than to open the front door if visitors should arrive, or offer assistance to anyone who should require it.

When asked, he informed her that Lady Arden was in the morning room, guided her there, and opened the door for her. After closing it, he presumably retreated to his imitation of a painted statue.

Felicity shook her head and concentrated on assessing her hostess. Her impressions from the night before were vague.

Was she friend or foe?

Lady Arden had not seemed happy about acting the part of warden, but she had done it. The fact that she had provided food for the incarcerated indicated collusion as well as kindness.

Now, Felicity found her hostess surprising. She'd always expected the English high aristocracy to be an arch and effete lot, but Lady Arden could be mistaken for any ordinary woman. She was at best handsome, with clean-cut classical features and brown hair dressed simply. Her gown was as plain and practical as Felicity's, and the only ornament she wore was her wedding ring.

There was intelligence in the gray-blue eyes, however, and an air of shrewd serenity that told Felicity this woman would not be easily fooled.

Lady Arden put aside a dauntingly heavy tome and rose with a welcoming smile. "Felicity, good morning! You don't mind my calling you Felicity, do you? We're noted for our lack of formality at Vauxhall. You must call me Beth. And this, of course, is Blanche, Mrs. Hardcastle. She's one of the principal players at Drury Lane."

Felicity stared at a woman of ethereal beauty, whose white, lace-trimmed dress and heavy silver hair seemed to hint of elf-land. The only color about her was in her pink lips and cheeks, and her twinkling blue eyes.

She smiled but did not rise. "Excuse me, Felicity, but the feathers fly so." Felicity saw she had a sheet over her lap and the sheet was covered by glossy drake's feathers. Blanche appeared to be making something out of them. One floated free, and Gardeen sprang like the killer she was.

Felicity grabbed the cat and tried to rescue the feather, but Blanche laughed. "Oh, let her have it unless it will choke her. Truly, I'm rather tired of all this, but having set my mind to the project, I'm determined to complete it."

"What are you making?" Felicity asked, having never attempted decorative crafts herself.

"An aigrette of feathers for my hair. Don't ask why," said Blanche with a twinkling smile, "when I never wear colors. It just seems the sort of thing to do when stuck in bucolic idleness."

Felicity did not equate country living with idleness, but she didn't say so.

Blanche grinned as if she'd read the thought. "I'm a city girl, my dear. Born and bred." She gathered up the sheet on her lap, neatly trapping the feathers, and placed the bundle aside. "Sit here beside me and tell me about Ireland."

Felicity soon found she had spent an hour talking of her country, her home, and her daily life, skillfully eased along by two excellent listeners. She colored. "You mustn't let me go on so about myself."

"But we're fascinated," said Beth. "Neither of us has ever been to Ireland. You make it sound quite mysterious."

"Oh, it's all nonsense really, but Tara is not far from Foy, and that's supposed to be the site of the ancient palace of the High King. There's a feel to the place sometimes and beliefs that go far back."

"It's exactly the same here," said Beth. "If the local people trust you, they'll talk of fairy lines and ancient customs. As you say, sometimes even the most modern thinker has to wonder if there might be something to it. I was a schoolteacher before my marriage and have an inquiring mind."

Beth then took over the conversation and discussed her research into local customs. Blanche provided some theatrical superstitions, which soon led to talk of her life as an actress, which Felicity found fascinating.

When they broke to take a light luncheon, Felicity realized she had never spent such a pleasant time engaged only in talk. Her grandfather and Annie were not conversationalists, and in gatherings with neighbors and friends, there had usually been activity rather than talk.

She found it rather depressing. If this were the quality of company Miles was accustomed to, surely he must find her boring as well as uncouth, under-educated, and hazardous to his health.

Or rather he would find her boring if they ever shared peaceful days without assault and kidnapping. They couldn't always end up making passionate love in the afternoon.

"Are you hot, Felicity?" asked Beth with concern. "There's an extra fire screen if you would like it."

"No, no," Felicity stammered, and addressed a slice of cold veal pie.

After luncheon, Beth suggested a brisk walk in the open air. Felicity settled Gardeen in her room by the fire, put on her cloak, and joined the others. Brisk was the word, too. She was pleased to have led an active life, or she would have been gasping.

When they reached the summit of a low rise, they had an excellent view of the countryside.

"Sometimes we see the hunt from here," said Beth, producing a spyglass to scan the rolling pastureland. "But since the meet was some distance away, it's unlikely they'll run this way today."

They all took turns, but agreed in the end that the hunt was nowhere to be seen.

"Now, Felicity," Beth said crisply, "it's time for us to make plans."

"Plans?"

"You can't simply give in to this male tyranny, you know. You must fight!"

"Are we talking about Miles or Rupert?"

Beth looked taken-aback, and Blanche chuckled. "Men are all tyrants at heart, aren't they? Don't worry. Both Beth and I believe in the rights of women. We'll support you, even in your right to be a burnt offering if it comes to that. But it really would be better, though, to find a way to thwart your black-hearted oppressor."

"Are we talking about Miles or Rupert?" Felicity asked again, but with a wry smile. "Oh, well, if you know all, you know Kieran's my child. Did Miles convince you that Rupert is capable of great cruelty? He is. He could make Kieran's life a misery and will do so if thwarted. He's even capable of killing him if he can do it without being caught."

"But you won't agree to murder?" Beth asked.

Felicity stared at her. "You, too? Faith, but you're a blood-thirsty lot! Killing's not so easy, you know. I tried to shoot Rupert once and couldn't bring myself to pull the trigger."

Beth nodded. "That's where men come in useful. Whether by nature's design or man's, they are much better at violence than we are."

"Speak for yourself," said Blanche. She turned to Felicity. "I killed a man not long ago, but I know what you mean. By his own actions my victim had forfeited any right to live, but I doubt I could have done it had he not threatened the lives of innocents. I think Beth would have killed him, too, if she'd had the opportunity. Women find the strength for anything when they need it."

Felicity looked between the elegant lady and the ethereal actress. "I feel as if I've suddenly landed among the Furies! Be that as it may, I don't regret not shooting Rupert, for his death will do no good unless it leaves me with a right to my son."

"You're determined on that, are you?" asked Beth. "Even if he were placed in a good home?"

"I am. I thought at one time it would be enough to know he was safe and happy. Now I want more."

"Then you certainly don't want to be dragged into the courts for the murder of his father, do you?" Beth made the point as neatly as a sword-thrust.

"I certainly don't *want* that."

Beth set off down the slope again. "Let us have our aims clear. You want sole care of Kieran. Do you want to be acknowledged as his true mother?"

"Hardly. Quite apart from the scandal, it would lose him his inheritance."

"An inheritance to which he has no right," Beth pointed out. "You should perhaps bear that in mind."

It was not an aspect of the case Felicity had considered before. "It was Kathleen's property," she defended, "and she wanted him to have it. Surely that must count for something. She disliked her cousin Michael."

"Very well. So to have the raising of the lad would satisfy you?"

"It would."

"And you also want Miles."

Felicity felt her color flare and remained silent.

"Come now," said Beth, stopping to face her. "It does no good to prevaricate. He clearly loves you. Do you love him?"

"I do," Felicity muttered. "But I will not let that weigh with me."

"We'll bear that in mind. So, you would not object to marrying Mr. Dunsmore for a brief time, then once widowed, marrying Miles?"

Felicity felt rather bludgeoned by this cool analysis, but she tried to reply in the same manner. "After a fashion, that is my plan. Though I'll make a true marriage of it if Rupert behaves. I have *some* scruples, you know."

"That won't please Miles."

"Damn Miles!"

Beth focused a severe look on her. "I don't think he de-serves that."

Felicity knew she was flushing like a guilty child. "If he'd not interfered, everything would have been settled by now."

"You mean, you would be married to Dunsmore, subject to his petty cruelties, his nightly invasion of your body . . ."

Blanche interrupted the confrontation. "Felicity, I have to point out that when men die in suspicious circumstances, the wife is always the first suspect. She has to convince the world of her true devotion to escape prosecution. A mere glance at recent events would cast grave doubt on your devotion to Mr. Dunsmore."

Felicity could feel her temper rising. "Precisely! And that is Miles Cavanagh's fault! I can bear Rupert's pawing—I even liked it once. And people around my home know I once was mad for the man. They would have thought little of my mar-rying him, except that I was unfortunately besotted!"

"What's done is done," said Beth, "and we have to plan for the future." She moved forward again, heading back to the distant house. "Deaths which appear to be accidents are surely not hard to arrange."

"By St. Bridget, but you make it sound as simple as plan-ning a dinner!"

"That reminds me . . ." Beth said with a frown, then con-tinued straight on. "A fall off a cliff, for example. Or a drowning. Does Mr. Dunsmore swim?"

"I have no idea."

"If you have the chance, find out. Now," she continued, "clearly our main problem is gaining legal control over young Kieran. That won't be easy, but the main opponent may well be this cousin Michael rather than Dunsmore. He will be only too keen to take charge of the boy when he comes with an estate and fortune, and we couldn't even contemplate wiping out inconvenient players in the game."

"Not to mention his wife and four sons," muttered Felicity.

"Quite. But it might be possible to *persuade* him to our point of view. Does he have ambitions?"

"Ambitions? He's some kind of merchant, I believe."

"A merchant. Excellent. Then he can probably be bought."

Blanche laughed. "Do you know, Beth, for a person of egalitarian principles, you are beginning to sound dreadfully like Lucien."

"Am I?" asked Beth, stopping in surprise. "Goodness, I suppose I am. I apologize to Mr. Michael Whatever-his-name-is for impugning his honor merely because he is in trade. It could well be that he will put sincere concern for his cousin's welfare above any mercenary gain."

"Unlikely, though," said Blanche with a grin.

Felicity brought them back to the point. "So we might be able to bribe Michael not to stake his claim to Kieran. We still haven't any real solution to Rupert, though."

"We'll have a council of war tonight," said Beth. She smiled at Felicity. "Though at times I'm most uncomfortable with rank and privilege, you have a great deal of it on your side through the Rogues. And I gather Miles's uncle, the Earl of Kilgoran, carries great weight in Ireland."

"And his mother is a Fitzgerald."

"So there has to be a way, even to circumvent the law. Stephen will know if anyone does. Sir Stephen Ball, M.P. He arrived late last night. As well as being a Member of Parliament, he's trained in law. But we must be careful not to hint at crimes in front of him. He doesn't like his conscience too cluttered."

"And he spends time with all you Rogues?" Felicity remarked. "How peculiar."

The rest of the afternoon was spent in leisurely pursuits. Blanche returned to her feathers. After attending to some household matters, Beth returned to her book, which proved to be an edition of Sophocles in Greek. Felicity found the piano and passed the time pleasantly enough with Gardeen curled up nearby, tail occasionally twitching in rhythm.

After a while, Blanche came to listen and suggested some vocal duets. Felicity's untrained voice was no match for the professional, but still it was a delight to make such music.

Then Beth appeared. "Now, now," she said with a smile, "as I understand it, Felicity, you are supposed to be in a state of black rebellion. This hardly matches the picture."

"I have no one present to rebel against."

"I can change that." With a teasing smile, Beth held out a book. "To the library, young lady, and read."

Felicity took the slim volume with unfeigned reluctance. "If it's Sophocles, it'll be all Greek to me, indeed!"

"It's English and less than thirty years old. Mary Wollstonecraft's *A Vindication Of The Rights Of Woman*. When you've read it, we can discuss it."

It wasn't a strain for Felicity to glower. "Did I mention that I've always been a wretched student?"

"Did I mention that I've always been an excellent, and very determined, teacher?"

Only partly acting, Felicity flounced off to the dauntingly sober library to read her set text. She was soon fascinated, however. In some places her attention was caught by the excellent points made, but in others she was in strong disagreement with the author. She found paper to mark places of particular interest, anticipating a discussion.

Then voices warned her the men were home. She went into the hall to find four happy, windblown, mud-splattered gentlemen in hunting pink rhapsodizing over a day chasing vermin.

She paused a moment to study the three men she did not know. Definitely not ones she would choose as opponents in life. Two were tall with superb physiques—one dark, one glittering blond. The third was a less showy blond, and less physically impressive, being of slighter build, but there was something in his lean face that suggested a daunting intellect.

She'd lay bets he was Stephen Ball, the Member of Parliament and legal expert. The Rogue with some scruples left.

Then Miles saw her. She'd swear he almost smiled but controlled it. "Been behaving yourself, Felicity?"

Time to play her part.

"What choice do I have, stuck here in the middle of nowhere?" she asked saucily, sauntering over to eye the other men in a very bold manner. "And who are your fine friends, guardian dear?"

The dark-haired man and the M.P. raised brows. The glittering blonde just grinned.

"The fine golden-top is your host the Marquess of Arden, heir to Belcraven," said Miles. "You should kneel and kiss his aristocratic, high-instepped feet. The black-top is Major Hal Beaumont, late of the 10th. You should kiss his feet, too, for he's a war hero. The shrimp of the group is not to be ignored, either, being one of our nation's elected lawmakers. Though they are all smiling, you should note that the creatures have very sharp teeth. I wouldn't recommend playing with them."

Felicity was jolted by that reminder of the dance at Foy. And of what had followed in her bedroom . . .

She pushed it back and let her gaze sweep the company. "If you insist in trapping me here in boredom, my grim guardian, you must accept the consequences." Sliding deeper into the character of wanton Joy, she swayed over to the marquess, put her hand on his broad chest, and looked up into clear, blue eyes. "Lord Arden, I'm sure you have something here to alleviate my boredom."

She emphasized the word *here* with a little dance of her fingers.

His lips twitched. "If I don't, I will be devastated, Miss Monahan. What entertains you most?"

All the men were just in from a day in the saddle, and Felicity was surrounded by sweat and the smell of leather and horses. She'd lived her life with this smell, yet now it dizzied her senses.

Which certainly helped her to play her part.

She walked her fingers up his chest a little. "Many things entertain me, my lord, but riding especially. I hear you have magnificent equipment—for riding."

"Truly magnificent," he replied, sharp-edged amusement in his eyes. He captured her hand, raising it for a kiss that managed to be entirely improper. "Someday," he murmured softly, "if you're a very good girl, I might let you explore my—stables."

Someone stifled a laugh, and Felicity realized Miles had spoken nothing but the truth. These men were more than she could handle. Faith, and it wasn't surprising. Most of her experience in these matters had been with her amiable neighbors and Rupert Dunsmore!

It wasn't in her nature, however, to back down in front of an audience. And anyway, she'd chosen the marquess as her target because his wife was standing by. He must be safe.

Mustn't he?

She didn't pull her hand free. In fact, she moved an inch closer. "Oh, but I'm *very* experienced around stables, my lord. I think you'll be pleasantly surprised. But are you claiming yours will be more impressive than *any* I have ever seen?"

He grinned, actually showing sharp white teeth. "That depends on whether you've seen Miles's, my dear. His definitely beat mine in size, and his skill and expertise in these matters cast mine in total shadow."

She gasped. A hand on her arm pulled her away. "Felicity," said Miles, "I warned you not to play with the animals."

"I'll play with whom I damn well please!" she snapped, twitching out of his hold even as she thanked heavens he'd rescued her.

"No, you will not," he said, all grim guardian.

"*And* I'll go where I want, when I want! In fact, now I'm fed and rested, I think I'll leave."

"The devil you will. You're a prisoner, remember?" Seizing her wrist, Miles hauled her across the hall to the library. "What were you doing in here? Plotting mischief, I'm sure."

"Mischief! I'll have you know—*What the devil are you doing?*"

He'd pushed her into a solid oak chair, the kind with built-in steps that took two men to lift. "Keeping you out of harm's way while I have a bath. Lucien, get me something to tie her."

Felicity heard a sound from Beth, but it was cut off. She knew this was all for show, but she was quivering with genuine fury. "Don't you dare! I'll have the law on you. I'll accuse every last one of you of kidnapping, unlawful confinement . . ."

The marquess had taken off his cravat and cut it into strips with his pocket knife. Miles tied her wrists to the armrest. "There, that should confine you. And it's not unlawful. I'm your guardian."

"That *cannot* license you to be my jailer!"

"It can when you not only threaten to run away, but do your damndest to seduce your hostess's husband!"

Not sure where acting ended and reality began, but hating the feeling of being bound again, Felicity glared into his eyes. "Jealous, are you? Would you rather I tried to seduce *you?*"

Stephen Ball moved between them. "If you're set on seduction, my dear, try me. I'm the only one here unentangled." His heavy-lidded eyes were surprisingly kind.

"Promise to help me be free of him, Sir Stephen, and I'll come to your room tonight."

"Ah, no. No strings attached. I have no taste for sex in the marketplace."

It was getting out of hand.

Then Gardeen appeared and leaped up into Felicity's lap.

As if unlocked from a spell, Beth came forward to untie the knots. "Enough of this foolishness. You have no intention of running off tonight, do you, Felicity?"

"Don't I?" asked Felicity, rubbing her wrists, though the cloth had scarcely made a mark.

"Not unless you've turned mad. It's growing dark, you have no money, and if you don't give your word I'll tie you up again."

Felicity scowled at her, but felt able to toss her head again in rebellion. "Oh, very well. And," she added, cuddling Gardeen, who had once again appeared in the nick of time, "I had no real intention of seducing your husband, Lady Arden."

"Good," said Beth amiably, "or I'd lock you up myself. If, that is, I thought you had the slightest chance of succeeding. And Blanche has an interest in Hal, which she's quite capable of defending. If you wish to amuse yourself with flirtation, for safety's sake, restrict yourself to Stephen and Miles."

"But one won't be bought and the other is supposed to protect me from such naughtiness." Felicity sauntered over to Miles and dangled the strips of cloth. "Are you going to amuse me, guardian dear?"

He snatched the rags and pushed her away. "Take up watercolors or something. I'm up to be rid of my dirt, and I suggest you prepare for dinner, too."

Since the whole company was dispersing, Felicity obeyed, nerves still jangling from that performance. It perhaps wasn't strange that she could act the rebel, but she was surprised at her ability to play the seductress. It had felt quite natural, as it had when she'd played the part of wanton Joy.

She was clearly the type of woman to be both willful and wicked in the right circumstances.

Seventeen

Over a rollicking meal, with everyone in high spirits, Felicity settled into her role, frequently causing Miles to wince. The other men were inclined to play to her part, but despite Miles's earlier warning she felt completely safe.

The marquess, however, raised one concern. "I've invited a bunch of fellows over on Sunday for a bit of sport and dinner. Felicity's presence makes things a little awkward."

"Why?" asked Miles. "We're not trying to keep her hidden."

"I was thinking of her reputation."

"Felicity acts the part of oppressed hoyden so well that no one will think she's here of her own will."

"There's no acting to it, Miles Cavanagh!" Felicity declared.

"Not to the hoyden part," he replied.

She scowled at him most realistically. "I'll have you know that I am only a hoyden in so far as I object to men ruling my every thought and action!"

"Sure, and isn't that the definition of a hoyden?"

"Then I am proud to be one!"

Beth and Blanche applauded, and the men exchanged long-suffering looks. A maid was leaving the room with dirty dishes, and her rigid back fairly shouted disapproval of the wild Irish miss.

"I don't think the servants approve as much as you, Beth," Felicity said with a grin.

"Don't be so sure that I entirely approve. A determination to assert rights does not excuse bad manners. However, these servants are the higher echelons." She smiled at the butler, who was supervising the meal. "They'll not tattle of our affairs, will they, Corser?"

"Assuredly not, my lady."

"If we hold this party, however, we'll have to use some of the newer servants. We cannot be as sure of them."

"How true, my dear," said Lucien with a wink. "An unfortunate necessity."

Felicity caught the meaning that if they *wanted* her presence as rebellious prisoner to be known throughout the area, the party would be an excellent means.

"Most of the newer staff are employed outside the house, however," Lucien added.

Felicity almost grinned at the double-edged conversation. That meant she must go outside and be seen, preferably sulking.

"If you think to keep me trapped inside," she said, "think again!"

Miles sighed in a long-suffering manner. "I suppose we must allow you a few walks in the garden. Escorted, of course."

Felicity tossed her head. "Escorted by my oppressor? Faith but it's a bitter cup." Inside, however, she was wondering if the firestorms between them could be controlled if they spent time alone together, even in the open air.

Perhaps Miles thought the same thing. He looked at the other men. "I trust you three as guards. We can take turns."

"Blanche and I are happy to play escort, too," said Beth.

Blanche agreed. "It will give us more opportunity to enlighten the poor child as to her rights and responsibilities as a woman."

"Heaven help us all," muttered Miles.

" 'Tis fine for you, Miles Cavanagh," Felicity retorted. "You don't have to read Mary Wollstonecraft!"

Beth rapped on the table. "Attention, please. We haven't discussed the possible dangers of this party. One day, Felicity may want to take a respectable position in society. We all know that having spent days or even weeks here as a young, unmarried woman could be a cloud over her, and the party will make it known to many."

Felicity shrugged. "Once I'm married to Rupert, it won't matter a jot."

"Since you *won't* be marrying him . . ." Miles said.

Felicity rolled her eyes.

Beth intervened. "Don't burn your bridges, my dear. One day, you may well want to marry into a family where dignity and propriety is important."

"Gracious!" declared Felicity impudently, "I can't think that I've ever *met* anyone with a claim to dignity and propriety."

"On behalf of the future Duke and Duchess of Belcraven," said Lucien mildly, "I'll ignore that remark."

Felicity rested her chin on her hands and smiled at him. "But, my dear marquess, when one considers the indignity and impropriety of your English royalty, you have to admit that mere dukes should not claim to be higher than they."

"Treason as well," said Miles with a sigh. "Don't you have a damp and dismal dungeon to clap her in?"

"I'm afraid my ancestors abandoned their castle some centuries ago," said Lucien. "But it seems Miss Monahan has no care to the possible muddying of her reputation. So?"

Blanche interrupted at that point. "The problem here is not Felicity, but me. Without my presence, this house would be tolerably respectable, even if it is a hunting box. I have to confess that it wouldn't be a great sacrifice to return to civilization."

"You won't escape bucolic pleasure so easily, my dear!" Beth declared. "If there's any damage from your presence, it's already done."

"If you would just marry me," Hal pointed out, "such issues would not arise."

"It would be whitewash, and you know it," Blanche retorted. "And quick to flake!"

"To return to this festivity," said Lucien firmly, "we're speaking of a bunch of Meltonians, not the patronesses of Almack's. They'll not so much as think of the finer points of social behavior."

"True," said Beth, then flashed a sharp glance at her husband. "Unless you've invited any of the women."

"Phoebe Higgs, Violet Vane, and the like?" He grinned. "I wouldn't dare. Though you'd like Phoebe. Blanche certainly does."

"She's very good-hearted," said Blanche. "Spends a lot of time helping the poor . . ."

". . . and recently demanded an increased allowance of her protector at pistol-point," added Stephen.

Beth smiled. "I think I would like her."

"No," said Lucien firmly.

"Certainly not at the moment," said Blanche. "For all her virtues, Phoebe is not company for a well-bred young lady."

"What well-bred young lady?" asked Miles with a dark look at his ward.

"There's nothing at all wrong with my breeding," Felicity replied pleasantly, helping herself to more cutlets. "My father's line can be traced back to Brian Boru."

"Then it's the training that's lacking."

She speared a piece of meat on her fork. "You mean I'm not quite broke to bridle yet? Not an easy ride?"

"Pax!" cried Beth, laughing. "I wish I had a dungeon for both of you." She turned to her husband. "As long as it's just men, and on the assumption that you haven't invited out-and-out scoundrels, I think we can brush through. We ladies will establish ourselves cozily in the morning room, and gentlemen who wish to behave properly may visit us. The rest may have the run of the house."

"Oh, as you say, they are all good fellows. As long as you can tolerate endless talk of hunting, they'll be well behaved."

"I've tolerated endless talk of hunting for the past few weeks, haven't I? Even though you never gave me prior indication of having such a restricted mind."

"Ah," said Lucien with a grin. "Itching for a discussion of Sophocles, are you?"

"Now that you mention it . . ."

Blanche, Hal, Miles, and Stephen groaned in unison.

"Not at the dinner table," said Hal firmly.

Blanche caught Felicity's bewildered look. "They were just winding the winch for a philosophical debate . . . in one or more foreign languages. Such things have to be nipped in the bud."

"Later," Lucien said to his wife with an almost sensual look.

Beth smiled back in the same manner, but the talk returned to the practicalities of the upcoming entertainment.

Felicity glanced at Miles. "They actually talk about such things for pleasure?"

"Astonishing, isn't it? But they'd think it just as peculiar to delight in a discussion of spavin and shoeing. Or, at least, Beth would."

Life at Vauxhall was not at all formal, but eventually the ladies did go apart for tea, leaving the men to their port. Felicity wondered if she might be treated less warmly after her flirtations, but neither Beth nor Blanche appeared to be concerned.

She thought wistfully that it must be lovely to be so secure in the affections of a partner, but then she realized she felt entirely secure in Miles's affections. The tragedy was that she could not allow herself to enjoy them.

When she was asked to play the piano, she did so willingly, for she could always lose herself in music. Despite having been left in a closed bedroom, Gardeen appeared to sit on the piano and enjoy the music. Locked doors did not seem to restrain the little cat at all.

Perhaps it was just that the servants going in and out were careless.

Yes, that must be it. But the fact was that Annie's cats were a strange lot, and Gardeen II just might be the strangest of them all.

The gentlemen were not long in joining them, and Felicity was asked to play a little more. She was happy enough to demonstrate that she had at least one desirable accomplishment.

After a few pieces, however, Miles ended the entertainment. "It's time for our council of war. We need to find a solution to Felicity's problem. Before," he added with a look, "her superb acting creates havoc."

Felicity moved to a chair, wrinkling her nose at him. "At least you acknowledge that it *is* acting."

"Sometimes. She's no harmless miss," he warned them all. "She's dangerous."

"And proud to be so!"

Beth clapped her hands. "Children! We are a team here. No fighting, please."

Felicity subsided, determined to keep a civil tongue in her head and show that it *was* mostly acting.

"Right," said Lucien. "Perhaps Felicity should state the problem as she sees it."

She was taken unawares, but accepted the necessity. "You all know about my child," she said. "I hope you can understand my need to have him as my own, even if not acknowledged. When I was young, I was persuaded to give him up, and I was lucky. It worked out quite well. I'm older now, though, and have more power. I know him better, too, and, in a way, love him more. I could not abandon him to strangers now, no matter how kind they seemed." She looked around. "I admit there's greed in it. I just *want* him."

"I think we understand, Felicity," Beth said.

Felicity flicked a glance at Miles, who was stroking Gardeen on his lap. She was not at all sure he understood, understood why Kieran had to come before their love.

She rather wished he were stroking her. . . .

She dragged her mind back to the subject. "Rupert Dunsmore is Kieran's father, by blood and law. That gives him all the power in this. He wants my fortune and offers Kieran by way of trade. It's an attractive-enough carrot he dangles. If I marry him, I'll be my son's legal mother. Then there's the whip if I do not agree: Rupert will mistreat Kieran."

"He'll mistreat him anyway, and you know it," Miles said.

"Not as much. And I'll be there. At the least, I'll be able to deflect his cruelty onto myself."

"For God's sake, Felicity! Put it out of your head and settle to thinking of other solutions." Perhaps his touch had turned rough, for Gardeen leapt from his lap to curl safely in front of the fire.

"Miles," Lucien interrupted, "let's stay calm. The most obvious solution is to remove this excrescence."

"But then Kieran would be lost to me forever," said Felicity, trying desperately to stay calm. She knew how men reacted when women became emotional—they thought them weak. Though these men were supposed to be her allies, she was terrified that they'd use their physical and legal power to override her wishes.

As Miles had done.

As if he were reading her mind, Stephen said, "You can hardly blame Miles or any of us for not wanting to see you in this Dunsmore's power."

She met his shrewd eyes. "But you must accept my right to dispose of myself as I will, at least when I am of age. It is no less than you would demand for yourself."

"They will accept it," Beth said.

After a moment, Lucien added, "Reluctantly." But it was agreement.

"Agreed," said Hal.

Stephen echoed him.

Everyone looked at Miles.

"I don't agree. I wouldn't let you walk over a cliff, Felicity, and I won't let you do this."

After a moment, Stephen broke the tense silence. "Then we had best . . ."

He was interrupted by Blanche clearing her throat.

"Am I assumed to be toothless?" she asked, then looked at Felicity. "I give no promise, either. I might well decide to stop you, and I am capable of it. I thought it only fair to warn you."

"Thank you," said Felicity. "But why would you, of all people, stop me?"

"Because there's bound to be a way to win clear and free if you look hard enough, and if you are ruthless enough. I'll stop you from giving in too easily."

Felicity could think of nothing to say.

"Now," said Stephen, "we do need to find that way, don't we? I suggest we first look to undermining Mr. Dunsmore's property rights."

"What do you mean?" Felicity asked.

Stephen smiled. "Simply that he has no claim at all to this estate. He's guilty of theft, and probably fraud and perjury to boot."

"Good God," said Miles, "so he is!"

"Now, it isn't quite so cut and dried," warned Stephen, "since, as far as I know, the law is unclear on dubious motherhood. It doesn't arise very often. In the case of dubious fatherhood, the child is assumed to be the mother's husband's child unless he promptly disowns it. Once having accepted a child, a man cannot change his mind. This, however, is because paternity is just about impossible to prove or disprove. In this case, however, I would say we have a provable fraud."

"We've got him!" said Miles.

Stephen raised a hand. "Not quite. We merely have something to hold against him. First, we have to obtain documented evidence that Felicity's story is true."

"What?" Felicity exclaimed.

"Don't be distressed. I believe you, but courts are tiresome about requiring proof. We need the testimony of this family you stayed with and, if possible, of Mrs. Dunsmore's doctor, who must have known she did not give birth. That might be difficult, since I assume he supported this deception."

"You mean he might be willing to swear to the opposite to save his own skin?" Miles said.

"Quite."

"Damn. And if it came to his word against these Bittens, he might well be believed."

"At the least, it would raise doubts. If, however, we can obtain enough evidence to worry Dunsmore, we might be able to frighten him off without taking it to court."

Felicity leaned forward. "But can we frighten him into giving up all contact with Kieran?"

"It depends how desperate and resolute he is, and how well he understands the law. Such a case would not be cut and dried, particularly if the doctor is willing to lie. It could be before the courts for years. The boy's trustees would probably have to bring the charges, so the costs could drain the estate. He could hold that threat against us."

"I would repay any costs from my own fortune."

"Then it would drain yours," Stephen pointed out. "Court cases have the remarkable characteristic of lasting until the plaintiff's money runs out. Your trustees would be duty-bound to prevent such an abuse of your inheritance. I understand you have trustees until you are thirty?"

"Unless I marry." She couldn't help a betraying glance at Miles. "Then my husband becomes trustee for the property."

Stephen shrugged. "Then you will not be able to put money

into this cause until you are thirty or marry. We must hope Dunsmore backs off when he sees the cards we hold."

The group began to discuss some practicalities of collecting evidence. Felicity interrupted them. "The problem in this plan is that Rupert will never give Kieran to *me*. What reason could he give?"

Stephen rubbed his fine-boned nose. "That is a snarl in the rope, isn't it? Perhaps, since he will be leaving your area, he might leave the child in your care?"

"The boy's trustees would be bound to question that," Miles said. "No insult intended, but Foy Hall is not the ideal place in which to raise a child."

"And Michael Craig would have an eye on things," Felicity pointed out. "He'd object if the lawyers didn't. It won't work."

Blanche called for attention. "Remember what I said about giving up too easily, Felicity? You Irish! You seem to always be seeking the tragic end."

"Well, what do *you* suggest I do?" Felicity demanded.

"Marry Miles."

"What?"

Blanche smiled. "Think of it. If you marry Miles, you have completely spiked Dunsmore's guns. According to you, he will then hurt the child out of spite. But if he is presented with evidence that could land him in jail, the pillory, or a ship bound for Australia, it will give him pause. If you can bring yourself to offer the bribe of a small income from your estate, he might even be brought to see reason."

"I don't see how that helps Kieran."

"Part of your price for keeping quiet and providing his income would be that he leave Ireland, after making his son a ward of one of the most respected and powerful men there."

"The Earl of Kilgoran," breathed Beth. "Brilliant! It even gives this villain an appearance of virtue in making such a wise choice."

"And it is even more brilliant," said Stephen, "when we remember Miles will soon inherit that wardship."

"By God," Miles said. "And according to my mother, anyone in Ireland can find a relationship to another, so he could even claim Kilgoran as a distant relative of his wife's." He smiled at Felicity. "We've done it!"

"Have we?" She wanted to believe, but to her it seemed as fragile as the silk lace on Blanche's gown. "I'll need to see it done before I believe it."

"They should have called you Thomasina," Miles remarked, but it didn't dull his spirits. "So the first thing is to collect the evidence. What did you say this family is called?"

"Bitten. They lived not far from a village called Long Upton."

"I'll go," said Miles, rising to his feet.

"Stop!" said Stephen. "Quite apart from the fact that it's too late to go anywhere tonight, you must not be involved, Miles. I know a good solicitor in that area. I'll write to him and ask him to collect the necessary documents, and to see if he can establish which doctor attended Mrs. Dunsmore. Though that one element still concerns me."

Miles paced like a restless tiger. "You mean I can't do *anything?*"

"Nothing that might appear to be interference or intimidation."

Miles took another turn about the room. "Then what the devil am I to do?"

"Go hunting, oppress Felicity, and wait for Dunsmore to turn up. God willing, soon, for then we'll know he's not elsewhere."

"Stealing Kieran, you mean!" exclaimed Felicity, shooting to her feet.

"I was thinking rather of his guessing our plan and interfering with the evidence. But he doesn't sound like a far-sighted man."

Miles put an arm around Felicity, and she leaned gratefully against him. "I don't think he'd suspect this," she said. "Heavens, even I hadn't thought that what he did was illegal."

Stephen closed the book in which he had been taking notes and rose. "I'll write the necessary letters, and we can have them off at first light. A sketch of Felicity would be useful."

Beth said, "I can probably execute a reasonable likeness."

Felicity put a hand on Stephen's arm. "How long will it take?"

His eyes were remarkably understanding. "At least a week."

"A week!"

Miles hugged her. "You're no better than I at waiting, love, but wait we can and will if we have to."

She looked up at him. "As long as we hear from your mother that Kieran is safe."

"We will." Then a smile lightened his face. "And do I gather we're engaged to marry as soon as my guardianship is over?"

Felicity pulled back a little. "I didn't promise that!"

"It's part of the plan. If we do manage to have Kieran made Kilgoran's ward, how else are you to care for him?"

It was such a sweet vision—that she have Kieran and Miles, both—that Felicity could have wept. But it would be dangerous to soften too soon. She moved out of the seductive tenderness of his embrace. "With that temptation, Miles Cavanagh, you might get me to the altar one day. But I'd have to see the wardship signed and sealed first."

Beth also stood. "I think a little light relief and distraction is called for."

She went to a drawer and, to Felicity's astonishment, produced a set of jackstraws. She spilled them on the table and the company settled to cutthroat competition at the children's game, with the added spice of ridiculously high stakes. Felicity took a little persuasion to join in, but hours later, and completely relaxed, she realized she'd just enjoyed perhaps the best time of her life.

It came as a shock. She shouldn't be having fun at such

a time. She covered her confusion with a yawn and a plea
of tiredness.

"Yes, it is late," Beth said, "and I think I have a reasonable
likeness."

Felicity was startled to see that Beth had a sketching pad
out. She went to look and found a number of clever sketches
of herself at the game, both in profile and face front.

"They're very good," she said, but in truth she hardly recognized that laughing girl as herself.

Beth closed her pad. "They should serve the purpose of
identifying you to the Bittens. Would you like a supper before
retiring?"

Felicity declined and left them to their soup, tea, and
toasted cheese, wondering just why she was finding this all
so alarming. By the time she reached her room and rang for
Harriet, she understood. She feared that, despite all, the
laughing young woman of the picture was an illusion; that
reality was the wary Felicity who faced a life of fear and
struggle with Rupert Dunsmore.

The next day being Sunday, there was no hunting, but
everyone would be saved from boredom by Lucien's party.
There was no postal service either, but Stephen's letter was
sent off with a groom.

As Felicity stood by Miles, watching the man ride off, she
said softly, "I want to go with him."

"I know. It's maddening, isn't it, to have to twiddle our
thumbs and play silly games?"

"Wayward ward and grim guardian," she sighed. "Well,
what's the next act?"

"Unless you want to refuse to attend church, I can't imagine."

"Then I'll let the Sabbath mellow me a little." She glanced
up at him. "I think you enjoyed tying me up, though."

"I did not, but neither did I enjoy watching you crawling all over Lucien."

"Crawling!"

"A polite description. You're all too good at that particular act."

Since they appeared to have found a good fight anyway, Felicity put her hands on her hips and raised her voice. "You're just jealous, Miles Cavanagh. Guardian or not, I think you have your greedy eyes on my money. Well, there'll be snakes in Ireland before you see a penny of it!"

"There's one snake in Ireland already, if you would but admit it. And didn't you know that as your guardian I can claim reasonable expenses? Like the cost of bringing you here."

"The cost . . . God rot your toes, Miles Cavanagh! Are you trying to make me pay for my own imprisonment? I'm off to write to my trustees this moment!" She flounced away, noting the footman rolling his eyes at these goings on.

There really didn't seem any point in staging a fight over going to church, however, so Felicity joined the company in a two-mile walk to the nearby village of Thorpe to attend the Sunday service. Beth explained that they preferred the simple village church to the larger one in town attended by the Meltonians.

"By which I mean the hunting visitors, not the poor local residents, who have to put up with a winter congregation mostly sleeping off the effects of Saturday night's carouse."

"I doubt they're so poor, with all these well-heeled men about."

"True. It is a thriving place these days."

A brisk walk in the winter sun was delightful, particularly when it was accompanied toward the end by the bell summoning the congregation. The church had the beauty that comes of hundreds of years of prayer, and the service was simple and devout. By the time they emerged to chat with the local people, it was hard for Felicity to remember that she was supposed to be oppressed.

As she walked back, arm in arm with Miles, she said, "I wish we knew what Rupert was up to."

Miles touched her hand lightly. "Relax, *cailín*. He'll be here any day, and we'll know when it happens because he'll contact you."

"Relax!" That touch had been for comfort, she knew, and yet it had jolted through her as a surge of raw, desire. She pulled her arm free and put space between them. "If I could just be sure Kieran is safe . . ."

"Have faith in my mother."

"I'm trying. I'm trying."

Eighteen

Upon their return, they all settled with relish to a leisurely luncheon. Afterward, however, preparations began for the party. In fact, since Sunday afternoon was the traditional time for dealing in horses in Melton—stables, they called it—guests could arrive at any time.

Lucien, Hal, and Stephen headed out to visit other establishments for a little while, but Miles planned to stay in the Vauxhall stables since so many men were interested in purchasing his horses.

"I suppose I'm to be left here to set tables and arrange flowers." Felicity's resentment was genuine. She was pining for horses.

Miles surprised her. "Am I so cruel? You can come with me if you behave yourself. As a representative of Foy, you have a place."

Felicity was very tempted to slip completely out of her part and hug him.

Quietly, he added, "And it'll be a fine chance to show rebellion and make contact."

Not long afterward, they walked through the garden toward the stables, accompanied by a lively little cat. The stables at Vauxhall were not as extensive as the stud establishments at Foy or Clonnagh, but they certainly were magnificent.

"Faith," said Felicity as they drew close to the main block, "anyone would think this was a fine manor house." In truth, the elegant proportions and long windows all gave that impression.

"This whole place was built only five years ago for Lucien when he came of age. In both elegance and efficiency, I'd say they are the finest stables in England."

Felicity was reminded of a certain teasing conversation with the marquess. She couldn't help but blush. How could she have been so bold? It was interesting, though, that Miles had admitted jealousy. How exciting to know she could drive him wild just by flirting with another man. . . .

She forced her mind back to equestrian matters, for they were entering the stable block by a handsome mahogany door. Felicity found herself merely in a corridor, but surrounded by fluted pillars and a vaulted ceiling. "Lord above, it's a cathedral!"

"All England worships the horse, and what more worthy creature is there for veneration?" Miles directed her through to one area full of loose-boxes and the wonderful smell of horses.

Gardeen leaped at a wisp of straw.

"Is she likely to disturb a rat?" Felicity asked. "Annie will be extremely displeased if anything happens to this one."

"A rat? Bite your tongue. Would such a creature dare to invade this holy place? And besides, there are both terriers and cats to keep down pests." He scooped up the small cat anyway. "Those terriers and stable cats might object to an invader, however, and have her for lunch. You'd better bare your claws, little one."

Felicity started, realizing those words had actually been for her. The head stable groom was coming forward to greet them, and various grooms and underlings were around, preparing the place for Stables. Any one of these men could be the type to gossip about the wild Irish hoyden kept guarded up at the house.

Any one might have a message for her.

She raised her chin and put stiffness in her walk. "Trust

the English to build a palace for horses and leave the peasants
in hovels."

"The Irish peasants are often less well housed than the
ordinary people here."

She sneered at him. "Faith, you'll be agreeing soon that
the English are God's own people!"

"Not at all." Miles was the perfect picture of the weary
guardian. "Are you not interested in the horses, Felicity?"

"The only ones worth looking at will be Irish."

"Now there, my dear, you might have a point."

There were loose-boxes for twenty horses here, and Miles
told her there were as many on the other side of the building.
Most of the horses in this section belonged to Miles, and
Felicity inspected them with interest.

They were all fine beasts, as she had expected. She was
interested, however, to come across one she knew—Argonaut,
the horse which had almost come to grief twice through her
fault.

"How did he get here?"

"He was always intended for Lucien. I sent him over as
soon as we arrived at Clonnagh."

Argonaut was stirring memories of her first meeting with
Miles, followed by memories of her thwarted elopement. Felicity glanced at Miles and suspected he was visited by similar
torments.

"Don't even think of it," he murmured. "Grim guardian
and wayward ward, remember?"

The servants were politely busying themselves elsewhere,
but some were still in this area. Unsure if she were acting
or not, Felicity moved closer and laid her hand on his arm.
"But what should a wayward ward do?" she teased softly.
"Especially when subject to such a handsome, dashing guardian?"

His jaw tightened. "Behave herself for fear of consequences?"

"Or seduce him to her cause." She slid her hand up, over

his chest, and stroked the side of his face. "Which could lead to *most* interesting consequences . . ."

He seized her hand. "Like pregnancy," he said under his breath. He looked quickly around. "Are you pregnant, Felicity?"

Her wrist burned from his hand around it. "I won't have a hint for a week or more."

"But you wouldn't want to increase the risk, would you?" He let her go so abruptly that she wondered if he felt the same fierce heat. "So don't try this in a more private place. You can't expect superhuman restraint every time."

She could have laughed for joy that he was so vulnerable to her. She moved a step away but couldn't resist murmuring, "I miss you so."

He turned to rub the blazed nose of a chestnut mare close by. "Ah, and I remember some fine riding," he said, as if to the horse. "If this were a right and proper world, we'd be free to ride again."

Felicity picked up his meaning. "But as it is, you may have to see her go to another man."

His hand tightened on the horse's mane. "She'll never go to a man not worthy of her."

"You're a romantic fool."

"I'm Irish." Seemingly to the horse, he added, "You're worthy of the best, my silken beauty, and I'll make sure you have it. And I'll ride you again, my word on it. A fine wild ride through sunlight and soft rain into fire . . ."

"She's a miracle horse, indeed, if you can ride her into fire!" But Felicity couldn't help her voice wavering with a mixture of laughter and raw need. She moved closer and put her hand over his on the horse's neck. "I admit it's been all too long since I rode." She rubbed against his wonderful hand. "Especially as God intended. With the power of the animal between my legs."

A tinge of red crept up his face, and his breathing changed.

"Oh, God, we're mad," she said, stepping away. "Enough of this."

He laughed and moved on. "Somehow I think I'll never have enough of that kind of riding. In fact, a little would be a blessed relief."

They progressed in cautious silence to the end of the boxes, by which time Felicity's heart-rate had steadied.

"Do you want to inspect the stores and tack rooms?" he asked, once more the weary guardian.

Felicity swept out into the open air. "Oh, I'm sure they're as fine as English money can make them." When he came up beside her, she said, "I'm hating this."

"I'm not too comfortable with it myself." She understood him and smothered a laugh. She suffered from a similar ache, and other pains more deep and meaningful.

She needed to talk to him, really talk, but the stable yard was no more private than the stalls had been and soon would be full of Meltonians. She looked around, then led the way out of the carriage gates and over to a wooden fence around the pasture where some horses grazed.

He followed, but said, "Remember to appear resentful."

"That's not hard, for I resent life at the moment. What did I do to deserve this?"

"Had sex with Dunsmore," he said flatly.

She stared at him, and the resentment was real. "I was fifteen!"

His eyes were cool as they met hers. "There are boys on fighting ships at fifteen, and others in all kinds of trades. Girls of that age work like adults, too. The truth is, you were as willful then as you are now. If you'd behaved as you should, this would never have happened."

"So it's all my fault, is it?" Angry disbelief was rising in her like hot steam.

"I'm merely pointing out that you did *something*. You weren't dragged off and raped. Remember my mother speaking of the Rogues springing Lord Whitmore's traps? That was willfulness, too. Oh, we claim we were fighting the cruelty of it, but the truth is, it was an adventure, a way to show we were able to trick those in charge of us. We thought the thrill worth any risk. Hell, there wouldn't have been a thrill without the risk."

"That is not the same at all!"

He met her rage calmly. "There are similarities. What if the gamekeeper had caught us and shot at us? What if I or one of the others had been crippled for life? We would all today be living with the consequences, and we couldn't say we'd done *nothing* to bring about the problems. That's too easy a way out."

"But . . ."

He overrode her. "But, in your case, you were inveigled and tricked. True enough. That's why I want to shoot Dunsmore on sight."

She felt as disoriented as if he'd flipped her onto her head. "Never!"

"Most of our plan will work just as well with him dead."

"No, it won't. We have no hold over Michael Craig, and with Rupert dead he'll have the legal power."

That stopped him. "Damn, that's true."

Felicity stopped to take a deep breath and find her balance. "So, was that lecture about responsibility just to stage a quarrel for any observer?"

"No."

"You *meant* it? How can you hold me to blame? How *can* you?"

"How can you think yourself blameless? If you'd stayed at home stitching samplers and improving your handwriting, Dunsmore would never have come within sniffing distance of you."

"And if you'd stayed home, you'd have died of boredom!"

"I was at school. My handwriting is excellent, and I can read both Latin and Greek. I assure you I didn't have time for leisurely trysts in the countryside."

"You found time to spring traps, didn't you?" She beat a fist on the sturdy fence. "You were a boy and free to go where you pleased. If a local matron had decided to seduce you, she'd have had no trouble. Faith, but that's probably where you had your first experience of a woman!"

"It was not. But if that had been the way of it, I'd have come to no harm unless she had the pox. That's the difference between boys and girls. You should have known that. I think you did know that."

"I didn't. No one ever told me."

"Did you need telling? Was no lass in the area ever caught unmarried with her apron strings too tight?"

Felicity stepped back. "Why are you attacking me like this?"

"Because all this seething rage is not acting. You have to stop blaming the world and lashing out. Sure and your life hasn't always been fair, anymore than it would have been fair if I'd been shot by Lord Whitmore's gamekeeper and never ridden a horse again. But you did play a part in creating your own predicament, just as I would have done. You have to put it behind you."

"And stay at home sewing samplers?"

He smiled slightly. "If you'd been properly raised, you'd be past the sampler stage."

Felicity hissed with annoyance. "What you mean, Miles Cavanagh, is that you find me altogether too much trouble and want me to become the sort of ninny who does just as she's told. When fish leap from the Shannon into the fishermen's nets!"

With that, Felicity swung around and marched back to the house. He didn't follow, but that could have been because the first of the hunting fraternity had arrived to inspect, and possibly to buy.

Felicity swept into the house, still stinging from that reprimand, and almost collided with Beth, who was carrying a large bowl of oranges.

"Is something wrong?" Beth asked.

"Just a certain black-hearted guardian, that's all." Felicity would have pushed by, but Beth thrust the bowl into her hands.

"Take this to the dining room, dear. I'll be there in a moment with the nuts."

Felicity was tempted to drop the burden to shatter on the floor, but that would just prove she was a thoughtless, headstrong rebel, so she obediently marched off with it.

The dining room was nearly ready for the evening, with pleasing arrangements of foods on all surfaces. Felicity thumped the bowl down in a space, thumped it down rather harder than she'd intended, so some oranges bounced out and onto the floor.

As she scrambled after them, she heard Beth enter the room.

Beth placed a large bowl of nuts on the table and captured the farthest escapee. "Now," she said, putting the orange back in the bowl, "tell me what the dreadful man has done to you now."

"You're as bad as he is! I don't suppose *you* would have let yourself be seduced at fifteen, would you, no matter how lonely you were? And even if you were the type to be seduced—wild and wanton defines it, I'm sure—you would never have had the opportunity because you stayed where you were supposed to be, sewing samplers!"

"I was under such handicaps," Beth replied mildly. "I was raised in a girl's school."

"Raised?"

"Yes. I don't think I went anywhere without a companion until after my marriage."

"Nowhere?" Felicity was almost speechless. She knew her upbringing had been unconventional, but she had not imagined restrictions such as this. No wonder Miles was surprised she'd had the chance to be led astray. "Is that normal?"

"It isn't so strange among the upper classes, and the school was in a town, where one must be more careful. In the country, young ladies have more freedom, but I gather you had the freedom of the whole county."

Felicity pounced. "Freedom! That's the word. And why should we not all be free?"

"Perhaps because freedom is dangerous to those unprepared for it. Do we let young children go just where they wish?"

"I was not a child."

"I thought you were. Was not that the point? And a neglected child, at that. Your freedom would have presented no hazard if you'd not felt that the attention of a man, any man, was of value. And, of course, if you had been well informed about the dance between the sexes, and the way it is played."

Felicity was feeling bludgeoned. "Are you saying that women *shouldn't* be free? It seemed to me at times that Mary Wollstonecraft was saying women are feeble creatures and, like children, must be protected for their own good. I find that a disgusting sentiment."

Beth's eyes lit. "Let's have tea as we discuss it. I think," she said, as she led the way to the library, "Mrs. Wollstonecraft meant that many women, as they are now, are not ready for freedom since their minds are uneducated and their bodies not strong. Also, they have not been trained to accept the responsibilities that go with rights."

"And whose fault is any of that?" Felicity demanded, throwing herself into the solid library chair that had briefly been her prison.

"Their parents'. Often mothers just as much as fathers. Mothers have a terrible tendency to encourage their daughters' vanity. Do you remember your parents?" Beth rang the bell, and by the time the footman came to take the request for tea, Felicity was sharing her faint memories of her parents.

Beth listened, then said, "It sounds as if your parents would have raised you in a more conventional way."

"Probably."

"Would you have preferred it?" Beth took a seat close by.

Felicity thought of resisting this session, which was clearly intended to be educational. She wasn't sure any of these people had the right to educate her.

But then she saw the foolishness of that. Education is never without worth, and since the shadowy time before her parents' death she'd lacked a sensible person to talk to at length. Recently, there had been Miles, but their situation was tangled with too many other threads for it to be rational.

Beth, perhaps Beth she could trust.

"I would have liked to have had a more normal family life," she said, untying her bonnet and dropping it to the floor. "And I suppose it might have been better to have been properly educated by someone who made me learn the things I didn't want to learn." Then she grinned. "But it was a fine life for all of that, free to ride the countryside on some of the best horseflesh God ever created."

"You had more freedom than most boys, you know, since you weren't bothered by tutors and schools. Perhaps more freedom than is wise. You could have encountered any number of hazards."

"My grandfather taught me to shoot." But then Felicity remembered Miles lecturing her on the Irish reality. "You're right, though. The trouble with my family is that they don't like to face unpleasant facts, so they ignore them. I believed people were essentially good and kind and would not hurt me. Most are, you know."

"Yes, but it's the few who aren't who present the problem."

The tray arrived, and Beth poured.

"Like Rupert Dunsmore," said Felicity as she took her cup. "Miles and I just staged a most convincing quarrel."

"Excellent."

"Is it? It was based on truth. How could I marry a man who thinks me a spoiled brat?"

"Miles might be speaking from experience. He's somewhat spoiled himself."

"Miles? Lady Aideen doesn't appear the type to cosset a boy, and he says he went to a strict school."

"Ah, yes," said Beth with a smile. "But as a Rogue. They formed a protective association, you see. They claim they only protected each other from injustice, but learning to handle injustice is part of the training for life, don't you think? And though his mother doubtless trained him well in manners and such, she cossets him because of his future."

"What do you mean?" asked Felicity, wickedly delighting in talk of the man she loved.

Beth put down her empty cup. "In current status, Miles and Lucien are at opposite ends of the Rogues but, in reality, they are almost equal. Lucien will one day be Duke of Belcraven, one of the highest men in the land. Someday—and probably soon—Miles will be Earl of Kilgoran. In Ireland, I gather, that ranks nearly as high."

"True enough. The earldom has been rich and powerful for generations, but the present earl has built a reputation as the wise man of Irish politics. Not an easy role to assume."

Beth nodded. "I know Miles dreads it. In addition to any political complications, there is a vast estate and a palatial home full of dependents."

"Including Kieran, I hope."

"I'm sure that's true. As for Miles, probably the wisest course would have been to ruthlessly prepare him for that role, as Lucien has been prepared. Don't let Lucien's light manner deceive you. He could pick up the reins of the duchy tomorrow. I gather Miles's uncle wished a similar upbringing, even to the extent of raising him at Kilgoran Castle. His parents refused. The only concession they made was to send him to an English school so he would learn to deal with us. And there he was enrolled into the Rogues."

"According to him, it saved his life."

"Irish exaggeration. It doubtless saved him some beatings, though. But you see how it was. His parents saved him from the pressures of his future rank, and the Rogues saved him from the perils of English enmity. Since he's by nature a lighthearted, easygoing fellow, he's hardly come to grips with trouble at all. He doesn't even have to run his own estate. Since his father's death, his mother has done it for him, leaving Miles free to hunt six months of the year and play most of the rest."

"You disapprove? Faith, I think you're a puritan at heart."

"I think adults should have an adult view of life. In your case, Miles is having to handle an adult situation. It will do him good."

"So I'm a brisk purgative draught, am I?"

Beth smiled at the resentment. "Let us say, a stimulant. The point of the discussion, however, is that you and Miles have rather more in common than you think. You are as suited to be Countess of Kilgoran as he is to be earl."

"Heaven help Ireland."

"Ireland will be very fortunate. Now," Beth said, rising, "can I persuade you to help me arrange some floral decorations?"

"Only with a pistol." Felicity grabbed her copy of *The Rights of Woman*. "I'd rather struggle with this." Then she paused. "I suppose that's the wrong answer."

"Not at all. The Countess of Kilgoran can doubtless command others to arrange flowers for her. She will, however, have to think for herself."

Nineteen

Felicity did little reading of Wollstonecraft, but a great deal of thinking for herself.

Reluctantly, she acknowledged there had been truth in Miles's words. She had come to let resentment rule her.

Though she had been fond of her grandfather, she had always held him partly to blame for her problems.

She'd blamed Aunt Annie for being so inadequate a substitute mother.

She'd even blamed her parents for dying.

And she hated Rupert Dunsmore. Now that, she felt, was reasonable, but her rage at the world was not.

Miles had meant more than that, though. He'd been warning her of the danger of believing she had the right to be cruel, because a person could not always control who would get hurt.

He was right. She shivered when she remembered that for a moment she'd contemplated burning down Vauxhall.

But Miles's words had not just been stirred by disapproval of her behavior. They'd also been the product of that dangerous game they'd played in the stables, of the frustrated need it had roused in both of them.

As Felicity had once said, she and Miles were in danger of tearing each other apart, and hurting innocents in the process.

Let Rupert Dunsmore come quickly so this would be over.

* * *

Some time later, the library door opened. Miles came in, but warily. "We're heading out for equestrian amusements. Do you want to come?"

Worry and resentment evaporated. "Do I want? . . . *Could* I?"

"Why not? You'll be the only woman, for Beth and Blanche aren't keen, but there's a world of difference between a private party and a hunt."

She leaped to her feet. "I'll be into my habit and down in a moment!" She paused at the door. "I don't suppose there's any possibility of breeches. . . ."

"Not a trace," he said with a grin.

Felicity hurried through a hall already half-full of hearty horsemen, ran up the stairs, and tugged the bell-rope in her room. Within minutes, she was out of her dress and wriggling into her habit.

When she emerged from the front door, the scene in front of Vauxhall resembled a hunt meet, save for the absence of dogs. Thirty or so horses shifted restlessly on the drive and lawns, either held by grooms or already mounted. Other servants weaved around with stirrup cups.

Tingling at the thought of riding, she looped up her skirt and hurried down to where Miles was checking a gray gelding.

"Is he for me? I am quite able to check my own horse." This was for the benefit of a young towheaded groom holding the bridle, but she couldn't for the life of her find a scowl to go with it.

Miles let the stirrup drop. "It's my duty as a guardian to keep you safe. I would be shamed before the world if you were to fall and break your neck while under my care."

"Or break my ankle?" she teased, knowing that was slang for getting with child.

"That either," he said, with a warning shake of his head.

"I must point out that I haven't come off a trained horse in over five years."

"Banshee's arrived. Tomorrow I'll put you up on him, if you like. That'll be a fair test."

"Banshee?" Then she remembered the ungainly gray horse who'd ripped Miles's arm out of its socket. "Ah, yes. We have a wager."

"I'm looking forward to that cake."

Felicity looked around at the assembly of top-notch horse-flesh and laughed. "You'll never get one of these men to buy that piece of dog's meat for fifty guineas. Never."

"You say 'never' about too many things, thorn-in-my-flesh. Shall I toss you up now?"

She let him boost her up, then arranged her skirt as the groom passed back the reins. She took them absently, still settling herself and getting the feel of the mount.

Until she felt the piece of paper that accompanied them.

She glanced once at the fair-haired groom, then tried to pretend nothing had happened. What had Miles just said? Something about fences . . .

"Of course I'm going to take some fences," she snapped in genuine irritation. "Stop fussing over me."

"A sidesaddle isn't the best for taking jumps, and you know it."

Felicity was in a fever to read the note. "It's all a matter of balance, remember? My balance is excellent. Go away."

He glanced around, and Felicity realized the groom had gone and no one else was nearby to hear her performance.

He mustn't suspect anything. "I mean it, Miles. I will not be told how to ride a horse. This creature seems to be sound and well trained. You have made sure all parts of the tack are secure. Now go away and let me be."

Amazingly, he obeyed, going off to mount a fine white-socked chestnut.

The note felt as if it were burning a hole in Felicity's glove, and yet she dared not even peep at it just yet. It had to be from Rupert, though, and she couldn't ignore it for long. What if it appointed a meeting during the ride?

She slid it into her glove where it crackled against her palm, poking her with its sharp folds. But it would be folly to read it yet, for she could see Miles was still watching her as if she were a novice rider, damn him.

She tested out her horse, giving the mount the slightest command to move. Immediately, it stepped forward smoothly.

"Ah, you beauty." Just a shift in her weight changed its direction, the merest touch of her crop to the right flank turned it the other. It was a perfectly behaved animal and well trained to the sidesaddle.

Of course, she should have expected nothing less. She knew Miles would only choose the best for her.

In horses, at least.

She knew in her heart that he wanted to choose the best for her in everything, but he did not always see the world as she did.

She couldn't resist walking her horse close to his. Miles took in every technical detail with one sweeping glance. "How is he?"

"Beautiful. One of yours?"

"Would I trust you on anything less? He's called Adonis and thinks himself a very fine fellow."

"With reason. He's beautifully trained, and to the sidesaddle as well."

"I generally accustom my horses to it. You never know when some fool man will mount a lady without a moment's consideration . . ." He closed his eyes briefly and shook his head. "Will we ever talk of riding again without salacious thoughts?"

Despite everything, she chuckled. "We'll find a way. After all, riding is one of our chief pleasures in life."

With a devastating smile, he said, "And that's the blessed truth."

Soon the company rode out, heading toward a distant field, gradually increasing pace until they might as well have been at a hunt, chasing the fox. Felicity held back, hoping to lose

Miles. She knew better in her heart, and sure enough, he was soon at her side.

"Is something the matter?"

"Why do you ask?"

"You're not leading the pack."

"And me on a sidesaddle and all."

"I'd back you to beat most of this crowd, even under a handicap."

Since he clearly wouldn't be shaken, she speeded up.

They were just one field from the rest of the men, who appeared to be gathered around an enormous gibbet.

"What's that?" Felicity asked.

"Believe it or not, it's a quintain. The thing the medieval knights used to train in lance work. Lucien had it constructed a few years ago, and it's become a popular amusement."

Now she could see that the quintain consisted of the figure of a man with arms outstretched, one holding a bag. "How does it work?"

"If the rider hits the center with his lance, the figure gives backward and he can ride past. Anywhere off center and it pivots. Then the bag swings round and hits him."

"It sounds like fun. I want to try."

He looked at her sharply, but then laughed. "Hellion. If you want. Watch awhile first, though. There's a knack to it."

A stack of long poles—the lances—waited to one side, attended by a number of servants. Lucien took one and went first, explaining the procedure for those who hadn't tried before. He hit a little off, but managed to duck beneath the swinging bag.

Miles went next and hit square in the bull's-eye over the figure's heart.

Felicity joined in the cheer.

The next few men all did well, obviously having practiced this in other years. Then someone charged too fast, missed his aim, and was solidly thwacked by a swinging bag. Instead of knocking him out of the saddle, however, it burst, billowing flour and chaff all over him.

Felicity joined in the good-natured laughter, but as a new bag was hooked up, she realized this was probably as good a moment as any to read her note. Almost, she was reluctant, but she muttered "Kieran" like an incantation and slid it out.

She worked it open against her horse's neck, trying to keep it out of sight as much as possible. Miles, for a miracle, had his attention elsewhere, inspecting the last rider's limping horse.

She smoothed the sheet of paper and could read Rupert's odiously familiar elegant script. Another reason she had appalling handwriting, did Miles but know it, was that she never wanted to have handwriting like this.

And he was right, that was childish.

My dearest Felicity,
I deeply regret having been so long in rescuing you.
I shudder to think what you must have suffered, so deprived of one you love and who loves you just as well.

Kieran, he meant Kieran. She forced down the sudden panic. All he had said was simple truth.

I hear you are kept closely guarded and have already suffered brutal treatment while trying to escape. I'm sure you are anxious not to suffer more of the same.

Another veiled threat. Oh, he was so good at those. But this was a clever letter. If the groom had read it, it would seem to be a communication between separated lovers.

I understand Lord Arden is to take his guests riding. This may provide a chance for us—for I know you will never forgo a brisk ride. If you can slip away unobserved, head east, away from the house. You will come

*to the Grantham road where I will wait with a chaise.
If this fails, you must leave in the night. I will wait close
to the drive of Vauxhall.*

*I know how eager you must be to reunite with one
you love so well and who loves you. And you know how
much that one will suffer if we cannot be together,*
        Your devoted husband-to-be.

With a shudder, Felicity refolded the note and slipped it
into her pocket. The word *suffer* was calculated to terrify her.

It was succeeding.

Did he have Kieran with him? She knew the sort of things
Rupert would do to the child if thwarted.

If Rupert had Kieran . . .

Oh, why had Lady Aideen not sent word faster?

Was Rupert watching her now? If he were, he would know
she could never slip away from here unnoticed. With relief,
she realized she had at least a few hours' reprieve. She could
not escape until night.

But, she realized, there was nothing to bar escape. Her
room was not locked, and her promise to Miles had been to
stay for two weeks or until she heard from Dunsmore. Miles
had assumed that when she received a message she would
share the news, but that had not been part of her promise.

But if she escaped before the Rogues' plan had any chance,
she would be giving up before she had to.

Blanche would be disgusted.

And Miles. She couldn't imagine what it would do to
Miles. By her action, she would have rejected him, rejected
his help and protection. She would have declared that she
could not trust him to help her win.

She would have kept her word but shattered the spirit of
their pact.

She looked over to where Miles was inspecting the injured
horse's leg, his hands gentle and skillful with the nervous

animal. She could tell, even at a distance, how at ease he was with beast and men, how well liked and respected.

He doubtless deserved better in life than an ill-bred hoyden dead set on a mission that could lead to tragedy.

She remembered Beth's describing him as spoiled. He didn't seem spoiled to her. He was the very opposite—unspoiled by hardship, still able to find joy in simple things and turn an open, friendly face to the world.

Beth had seemed to think Felicity was a needed medicine to force him out of this blissful state. In fact, she'd give almost anything to join him in *joie-de-vivre,* joy in the pleasures of living.

She'd give anything but her son.

The injured horse was led off by a groom, and its rider took a spare horse. The attack on the quintain recommenced and Felicity made a decision.

Rupert could damn well wait a day or two. She'd trust Miles's faith in his mother and believe Rupert didn't have Kieran with him. If that were the case, he was toothless.

She'd go further. If a letter came from Lady Aideen putting her fears at rest, she'd share this note with the Rogues.

Lucien rode over, fluid and easy on his magnificent black. "Miles says you want to try."

"To be sure. I'm in an excellent mood for hitting something."

"You are a hellion, aren't you?" But it was said amiably enough, and she sensed a bewildering trace of admiration and even affection.

She was not sure she could handle any more affection.

She followed him to the pile of poles, and Miles came over as she was finding the balance of the "lance."

"Changing your mind?"

"Devil a bit, but this game was not designed for sidesaddle. It's hard to hold the pole so it isn't banging the poor nag's head. But if I lean too far, I lose my balance."

"Perhaps you'd better leave it. We can come back one day with you in breeches—"

"Give up? Never!"

With a grin, Felicity shifted her grip so she held the heavy pole over her head like a spear. Then, with an Irish battle cry, she urged her horse toward the quintain, concentrating on balance and that bull's-eye on the dummy's chest.

In fact, she saw it as a target on Rupert Dunsmore's chest.

Her arm tired, but she would not let it waver. With another pagan shriek, she thumped the pole into Rupert's heart and rode by in triumph, shaking her pole in victory as all the men cheered.

Miles rode over, laughing. "Ah, my fine warrior-queen, I should never doubt you."

She grinned as she tossed the pole to a waiting servant. "Remember that next time I fight you, my heartless oppressor."

"As long as we're fighting naked in bed, I don't suppose I'll remember a damned thing."

He swung away to ride again at the quintain using Felicity's technique, leaving her with an aching body and a wild-beating heart.

It was almost as if he rode naked, so aware was she of his fine body, one with the horse, perfectly balanced. How could she ever leave this man?

How could she not if it became necessary?

She shifted in her saddle, realizing she was itching with desire. She'd never experienced such a thing before—to be in the open air, among people, and to be almost in heat.

She felt herself blushing at the thought when she was probably already rosy-cheeked. Faith, and soon everyone would guess. She sincerely hoped humans were nothing like horses, or all these fine stallion males would sense her urges and start pawing the ground and fighting over her!

At that moment, she knew she must have one more night with Miles. Rupert was here and it was possible he would

win, that she would have to go to him, even if it cost her
Miles.

They deserved one real night of love.

There had been that wild loving in the billiard room, full
of wonder and desperation. Then there'd been that last night
at Clonnagh, sweet, but achingly incomplete.

She wanted a night of slow pleasure, filled to the brim and
drained to the dregs. And it would have to be tonight because
she had no idea what tomorrow might bring.

They rode home as dusk fell, radiant with exercise and
high spirits. Though Felicity still felt in heat, people couldn't
be like horses, for the Meltonians seemed to regard her as
one of them.

At Vauxhall, Beth and Blanche were ready to greet everyone with huge bowls of hot punch. The men surged toward
the steaming bowls like a river in flood.

"Faith," said Felicity, "anyone would think they'd not drunk
in a week."

"Men have such appetites," said Blanche, and Felicity
didn't know if there was a double meaning in it or not.

Beth smiled at her. "That was a fine blow you struck for
womanhood."

Felicity was startled. "You were there?"

"Oh, no. Blanche and I were lazy. We sat in the nursery,
well-wrapped in blankets, sipping tea, watching through the
spyglass."

Suddenly alert, Felicity asked, "How well could you see?"
Then she quickly added, "Could I try?"

Beth's expression was unreadable. "If you wish. Come."
She turned to Blanche. "I'm sure you can handle thirty men,
my dear."

"Without raising a finger," said Blanche with a twinkle.

Beth led the way up two stories to the chilly nursery suite
and gave Felicity the spyglass. "There's quite a good view."

Felicity focused on the quintain field. The figure hung like a corpse on a gibbet, waiting for future games. The glass was so good she could make out scratches on the paint. She raised the glass to focus two fields over, on what must be the Grantham road, and watched the roof of a coach coast along beyond the high hedge.

The question was, what had Beth seen?

She lowered the glass and turned.

"Yes, I saw," said Beth. "You received a note, didn't you? Also, there was a carriage on the Grantham road most of the afternoon, just moving occasionally to warm the horses."

"What are you going to do?"

"Nothing. I believe in freedom of action."

"Even for children and poor feeble women not prepared for it?"

"That wasn't a jab at you. When I left the school to marry Lucien, I was completely unprepared for life, and it nearly led to disaster. If you and I were abandoned in some wild place, which of us do you think would survive?"

"Both of us. We'd help each other."

Beth smiled. "I hope that's true. Let the Rogues help you, Felicity. Don't, at least, escape until the last moment. It isn't the last moment yet, is it?"

"I don't think so. . . . No," she said firmly. "If he had Kieran, he'd have mentioned it."

Beth suddenly hugged her. "I do know how hard this must be for you."

Though she tensed, Felicity relished the hug, the first such embrace she'd ever received from a woman friend. A friend. It was mysteriously sweet, and she hugged Beth back. "Thank you for keeping it secret. It can't be easy for you."

"No. I don't like to keep things from Lucien. You can trust all of us, you know, each in our different ways."

Felicity drew out of her arms with a sad smile. "Ah, but it's those different ways that worry me."

"At least put aside your worries for today. Let's enjoy this

wild gathering, though I suspect it will be a downward slide
from here!"

Beth returned to the ground floor while Felicity went to
her room to wash and change. Since she hoped to seduce
Miles, she chose her best silk. After all, it had driven him
wild the last time she'd worn it. In the cold corridors, she'd
have to wear a shawl, but she could slip it off at some
point. . . .

By the time she was changed and descending the stairs,
however, the downward slide was evident in the volume of
noise and the inebriated tone of it. She paused, suddenly dubious about her revealing clothing.

Miles came up the stairs. "Ah, there you are." He stopped
to look her over. "Don't I know that gown?" He twitched
away the shawl. "Are you mad? We're presenting you as an
innocent young thing placed in this situation by my thought-
lessness, not as a member of the bloody *demi-monde!*"

She dragged the shawl back around her chilly shoulders.
"There was no problem with this gown when I was in decent
company!"

"Was there not? Think what it led to. And, though decent,
these men are not your trusted friends and neighbors. Go and
change."

"No," said Felicity mulishly, having seen a servant come
up the stairs then slip back discretely out of sight to wait for
the way to be clear.

Miles, of course, could not know this, and she had no intention of telling him. That abrupt command had not been
part of their act and she did not grant him the right to order
her about.

His jaw tensed. "Then I'll lock you in your room for the
evening."

"Then I'll scream the house down. What will the guests
think then?"

"Once they get going, they'll not hear the last trump."

Felicity allowed herself to stamp her foot. "Miles Cavanagh, I am wearing this dress!"

"Felicity Monahan, you are not." A bowl of fruit sat on a pier table. He picked up a bunch of purple grapes and mashed them into the front of the pale silk, rubbing them in thoroughly.

Felicity writhed against his hold. "Damn you to hell!"

"As your guardian, I am in hell." Then he seized her by the wrist and towed her back into her room.

As soon as they were there, she said, "There was a servant listening."

"I guessed as much. But that wasn't all acting."

"On your part either." She was still breathing hard. "I will *not* let you order me around!"

His breathing was none too steady, either. "And I won't let you go among this crowd dressed like that."

"Oh, devil take you, I was on the point of changing anyway." She frowned down at the dark stains all over the front. "You've ruined it, you *spalpeen*."

"I'll buy you a new one. It was never decent in the first place." He pulled open her drawers and found her other silk, a demure one. Tossing it on the bed, he said, "Wear that if you insist on freezing. Do you have any pearls?"

"Doesn't every young lady?"

"With you, I'd take no bets. Wear them. They're the heraldic symbol of the untouchable."

"Oh, is *that* their purpose?" she queried saucily, suddenly aware that they were here together.

Alone . . .

Did her thought ring in her voice, or did he just come to the same awareness? He headed for the door. "Do you need your maid?"

"You could maid me."

"No, I couldn't."

She moved quickly and put herself between him and the
door, leaning against it, blocking his way. "Kiss me."

"No."

She dropped all artifice. "Please, Miles. We may have so
little time, and sometimes I don't know what is acting and
what is truth." She placed her hands on his shoulders. "Can
we not be honest for this brief moment?"

"Honesty is dangerous, *a muirnín.*" But his hands settled
at her waist. "Sometimes honesty speaks with an angry
voice."

"But at least it's real. As is my need. I need a kiss. Don't
you?"

"I need more, and you damned well know it." But he lowered his mouth to hers.

Felicity closed her eyes and let her lips explore his, softly,
gently, almost as if afraid of contact. And so they should have
been. Heat instantly flared, a fire of need that like all fires
was only a flicker from destruction.

Did she move forward or did he deepen the kiss?

And who sighed?

Restraint slid from her like a silk garment, leaving her
dazed and bare-nerved in his arms, locked to him by a kiss
she could not bear to end.

Who groaned?

Who found the strength to end it?

Perhaps in that they were in harmony, for they both pushed
apart as if fighting invisible bonds, still joined by sight and
by the desire trembling through their bodies.

Unable to stand on her own, Felicity collapsed back against
the door, then slid sideways out of his way.

In a moment, she heard him leave.

Twenty

Soon Harriet arrived to exclaim over the stained gown, though something in the maid's manner told Felicity the story of the fight had already entertained the servant's hall. She hoped her own dazed arousal would be interpreted as sulks.

Now more than ever, though, Felicity was determined that tonight she and Miles would be together.

When Harriet finished, Felicity surveyed herself in the mirror. The white silk dress was nearly two years old and had yellowed to a shade that dulled her skin. The style was suited to a very young lady, with a modest neckline reinforced by a small frill of lace. The cut of the skirt was full, designed to conceal rather than emphasize the shape of the body. The trimming at the hem consisted of a modest ruffle set with demure white rosebuds—probably another heraldic symbol of the untouchable.

She had instructed Harriet to re-dress her hair in a tight, plain style with just another bunch of insipid white rosebuds for decoration. With the string of pearls, the effect was complete.

To the men here, she would be as seductive as a sister.

But she'd go odds that didn't apply to Miles.

When she returned to the corridor, he was waiting to escort her downstairs. She searched briefly for distress and found none, but then she'd conquered her external signs, too.

Above all, they were equally matched.

The noise from below had grown wilder.

"I don't have to warn you not to go apart with anyone, do I?" he said.

"Hardly," she retorted and saw him color with guilty memories of his attack at Foy. How was it that she could slip into battle-mode so very easily? "I think you must agree," she added more moderately, "that I am armored in untouch-ability."

He looked at her then, and she realized he'd hardly done so before. "True. The little rosebuds are an excellent touch."

"I thought they might be."

"And that yellowish color makes you almost sallow."

As they descended the stairs, she said, "You can see, at least, why the dress wasn't my first choice."

"True, but it doesn't do a damn thing for my comfort, and you know it."

Felicity headed for the sanctuary of the breakfast room, feeling sure of victory tonight. It was a dire shame that there were so many hours to get through first.

Most of the men came to pay their respects to their hostess and her friends, but few stayed long in the restrained atmosphere. Felicity found that Beth had been right, however, about this company not being disturbed by social niceties. What few men did express curiosity about her presence found the explanation that Miles couldn't miss the hunting completely adequate. None of them would miss the Shires for such a reason either.

Add the fact that she was Irish—and thus bound to be peculiar—and it ceased to trouble them at all.

By the time they all settled to dinner, the company was in a fine state of jollity, but no one had become truly wild as yet. The three ladies, however, sat safely together at one end of the table.

Miles was by Felicity's side, but Blanche's companion was portly Lord Greshingham. He clearly appreciated her company, though he did once make a *faux pas* in referring to the many times he'd met her here in previous years.

Felicity found herself wondering how she'd handle meeting an old lover of Miles's, never mind an established mistress.

She'd hate it.

She glanced between Beth and Blanche but decided there really was no hidden resentment. She feared she was not capable of such magnanimity.

"Now what are you thinking?" Miles asked.

Felicity sipped the excellent wine, knowing that, with the welcoming punch and this, she had already drunk rather more than was usual. "I was wondering who was your first."

"First what?"

"Woman."

He almost choked. Even though no one was paying attention to their conversation, he muttered, "Behave yourself."

"You asked. I can't help but be curious, and you know all about my intimate life."

He looked at her wryly, but murmured, "A whore in Dublin. And if I had my time again, I'd be more choosy. Now talk of decent matters."

She nodded. "Thank you. I did need to know."

"Probably because I know so much about you. It's an imbalance."

"Yes. And we do need balance."

Greshingham heard her. "Balance, yes," he said. "That's the secret! Never get a good ride without it."

"Indeed, my lord," Felicity replied, trying desperately not to think of another conversation about riding.

"You ride well for a woman," he said.

"Thank you, my lord," she replied politely. "It is one of my chief delights." She meant it innocently enough, but Miles kicked her ankle under the table. That was enough to make her take the bit between her teeth.

"Alas," she declared, "at the moment I am sadly deprived, my lord. I don't have my proper mount with me, you see. I was forced to leave him behind in Ireland when Miles dragged me here. And now, as my guardian, he'll hardly agree to any real riding at all!"

"Now that seems a shame," said the portly lord. "Are you perhaps not up to a long gallop?"

Felicity smiled at Miles. "You must be the judge, guardian dear. You have tested my paces."

His jaw was twitching ominously, but she couldn't tell if it were with fury or hilarity. "She's a raring fine ride . . . rider, Greshingham. I'd say she could exhaust any man. And surprisingly experienced for her age, too."

Felicity could feel heat rising in her cheeks. "No more experienced than you at the same age, surely."

"You underestimate your precociousness, brat." Then he turned to Greshingham. "You should know she's a Monahan of Foy. She's been around horses since childhood."

"Foy! Ah, that explains it. Then it's hard to understand why you won't let her ride, Cavanagh."

"He seems to think I'll break something," said Felicity. "An ankle perhaps."

"An ankle?" repeated Greshingham, peering across the table. "Not likely from a fall, my dear."

A sharp look from Beth suggested that she might be beginning to follow the double entendres.

"Miles takes his guardianship duties very seriously," Felicity told Greshingham. "He's so careful of my welfare I am almost a prisoner."

"Tush, tush. Can't have that, not if it keeps you from enjoying a good ride. What do you say, Cavanagh?"

Miles was smiling dangerously. "Felicity may ride any time she wants. She has but to present herself, suitably attired . . ."

Felicity stared at him with a fast-beating heart.

". . . and as soon as I can assemble a suitable number of attendants, I will oblige her."

"Attendants!" Felicity sucked in a breath.

"To protect you from harm."

"I will not *ride* under observation."

Miles glinted a smile at her. "An impasse, perhaps?"

She smiled back in the same manner. "I think you regretted your invitation and covered it in unacceptable conditions. That's cheating, sir."

"Now, now, young lady!" protested Greshingham, shocked at the accusation.

"She has a rash tongue," said Miles. "But she's also a considerable heiress. I have reason to believe some parties may want to steal her away, which is why she's here and why she may not ride out alone."

"Do you say so!" exclaimed Greshingham. "Thought such matters were past. But I suppose it's Irish business. You never know with the Irish. . . . Well, then, you're right to keep her safe, but surely she can ride, Cavanagh. I'll tell you what. We must gather next Sunday, the lot of us. Thirty or so sturdy Englishmen. That'll ensure her a jolly ride, all afternoon if she's up to it!"

Felicity bit her lip and didn't dare look at anyone.

"Well, Felicity?" asked Miles, sounding strangled.

She resisted the temptation to make matters worse. "I thank you for the suggestion, my lord. Perhaps Beth and Blanche would like to join us."

Beth quickly raised a hand. "Neither Blanche nor I are particularly fond of the exercise." Then she rolled her eyes slightly, showing she had certainly caught on to the double meanings.

Felicity grinned at her. "Oh, I'm sure you're learning remarkably since your marriage." Miles's kick on her ankle was much more forceful and she had to suppress a yelp. She supposed that had been beyond the bounds.

Beth's lips were twitching, though. "Oh, true. Lucien insists on it. It is one of his favorite activities, after all."

"Wise man, wise man," said Greshingham. "Riding is healthy. Stimulating, you know." Hastily, he added, "In moderation, of course, for a lady."

"Oh," said Felicity. "We ladies can bear a little stimulation now and then. . . ."

"Are you going to even attempt to include me in this conversation?" asked Blanche, eyes twinkling, showing she, too, had caught on.

Felicity flashed her an amused look. "I can only say that I am sure you have great natural talent, Mrs. Hardcastle."

Blanche chuckled. "How true! And yet I have never sat a horse in my life."

Greshingham stared at her in horror. "Never, Mrs. Hardcastle? Be glad to mount you myself anytime you have a wish to learn."

Felicity almost lost control then and saw the others struggling.

But Blanche managed to smile at her partner. "That's so kind of you, my lord, but I really think I'm too old to learn new tricks."

After the meal, Felicity found herself dragged into a quiet corner for a lecture on propriety.

"Yes, I know it was wrong to make that remark about Beth, but really, it was all a lot of fun. Poor Lord Greshingham didn't understand what was going on at all!"

Miles shook his head. "It's like trying to stop up a volcano. You'll always find some way to explode into disaster."

Felicity hadn't thought of it that way, but he was right. Her energy seethed, stirred by her fears for Kieran, heated by her desire for Miles. If it didn't find outlet, it exploded unpredictably. "I can't help it. I've never been good at inactivity and waiting."

"Anything else is damn dangerous at the moment. Go to the breakfast room and stay there. Please."

Felicity was happy enough to slip into the relative calm of the breakfast room and take tea with Beth, Blanche, and an ever-changing small group of men. She wondered if they were taking turns out of courtesy or truly welcomed a brief respite from the noise and horseplay in the rest of the house.

Because she had a strong taste for high-spirits, there were moments when Felicity wished to go out and join in, but she had sense enough to know that this was no mixed-company Irish festivity fueled by music and dancing. This was men involved in one of their own strange pagan rites.

Miles never visited the ladies at all.

She suspected he was getting drunk, and worried about the effect of alcohol on male desire. It would not suit her, once she went to his room, to find him out cold and sodden.

As it was, for her the evening was a prelude to passion, and she spent it like a puppet. She smiled and talked, and even played a few hands of cards while white-hot desire raced down her veins and sparkled back up her nerves, causing her to shift in her chair to try to ease the restless ache between her legs.

It was as well Miles didn't come. She'd probably throw him down on the Axminster carpet and rip his clothes off.

Eventually, blessedly, the first men began to leave and others soon followed. Felicity went out into the hall with Beth and Blanche to wave them off. There wasn't a completely steady step among them, and some had to be hoisted half-conscious onto horses and escorted by a groom.

There was still no sign of Miles. Damnation, she'd bet he was out cold under a table somewhere.

As the last ones were being steered in the right direction, Felicity slipped away to find him. If he *were* soused, she'd throw a bucket of water over him!

She found him alone in the billiard room, in his shirt-sleeves, rumpled but potting balls with a skill that did not suggest a fuddled head. He looked up and frowned. "Do you want to play?"

"Yes." But she made no move to pick up a cue.

When he understood, color touched his cheeks. "No," he said and turned to send a red slamming into a pocket.

He missed.

Felicity left, and though she would dearly have loved to see his reaction, she didn't look back. If he were of a mind to be nobly stubborn, there was no point in fighting him head-on.

The house was subsiding restlessly as Felicity headed to her bedroom. Distant clatters told of servants tidying the place; half-eaten food and half-empty glasses stood as ghosts of merriment. Like ghosts, the excitement of the party still wove through the air, and she suspected that everyone felt the same restlessness that she did.

Though hopefully not all in the same way.

Hal passed her with a smiling "good night," heading for the room he shared with Blanche. Felicity suspected his restless energy was very like her own.

She rang for Harriet and prepared for bed but, once ready, she had nothing to do but wait. As she had said, she was not good at waiting; nor was her restless body. She roamed the room, watched by an impassive cat.

Once, Gardeen had stopped Miles from attacking her. Would she prevent Felicity from attacking Miles?

All she heard from the next room was silence. Drat the man. Was he going to stay downstairs all night missing billiard shots? She pulled on her robe, intending to go in search of him, but stopped herself.

That assuredly was not the way.

Because she was listening, she heard Beth and Lucien come up together, talking together softly and laughing once. How wonderful it must be to head toward a loving bed in a leisurely manner, in perfect accord and anticipation.

Then she heard Miles's door close. Someone had entered the next room, but it could be Hennigan. She ran over and put her ear to the adjoining door, trying to interpret the faint sounds.

Then the door closed again and she heard voices. Good. Now she had her bearings. They were both in there. She leaned against the door, for once waiting patiently until sounds told her that the valet had gone.

Now the time had come, her simmering desire was soured by pure fear. Apart from that night at Clonnagh, when she had at least been invited, she had never approached a man in her life.

Well, Joy had, perhaps, but that had been acting. Tonight was no time for acting. It was a time for honest lust.

When she entered his room, Miles's first reaction would almost certainly be that same flat "no." She had to decide how to proceed from there.

Weeping?

Reasoned arguments?

Attempted rape?

With a wry smile at that thought, she studied herself in the mirror. Her high-necked, long-sleeved, flannelette nightgown and plaited hair tucked into a nightcap were hardly the equipment of a seductress.

The cap could go for sure.

Then she undid the plait and brushed her hair out.

The next question was, naked or not?

Sure and a naked body was supposed to drive any man mad, but whatever burned between herself and Miles could sear away plate armor if it had a mind to.

Could it break down the resistance in a man's mind, though? Miles was determined to be the good guardian and even protect her from herself.

She was damnably tired of being protected.

Before her fears could overwhelm even the power of her need, Felicity turned the key and opened the adjoining door.

Miles looked sharply at her. He was standing by the fire, finally drinking something golden from a glass. His brown-velvet banjan was only loosely cinched at the waist and left no doubt he was naked beneath it. Whether a woman's naked body could drive a man mad or not, a glimpse of this man's naked chest was having a powerful effect on her.

As if he knew, he pulled the edges together and tied the belt more tightly. "What do you want?"

"You."

She could almost see him assume resistance like armor. "What new game is this? You don't want to risk pregnancy. Or have you thought of a way to use another child in this battle?"

"I'm not *using* Kieran!"

He shook his head. "No, of course not. I didn't mean that. But he's being used." Gently, he added, "We don't want another child at risk, surely. And I told you. I'm sorry, but I cannot promise to be as noble as I was at Clonnagh."

"It doesn't matter." It did, but the wild need was driving her. It was a hunger like to that of starvation, taking no heed of sense or caution.

His hand on the mantelpiece became a fist. "It matters to me. I know I may not be able to hold you. I won't increase the risk that you'll take my child when you go."

She stepped forward. "Can't we at least touch, kiss? If you knew how I ached . . ."

He stepped back. "Oh, I know. How can you think I don't?"

"Faith, I *love* you!"

"And I love you, but we're not talking about love. We're talking about lust. The love won't die, and the lust will wait. There'll be better times than this."

"What if there aren't?" Desperate in the face of his resistance, she began to undo the mother-of-pearl buttons at her throat.

He strode over and seized her hands, imprisoning them in a bruising grip. *"I will not be seduced."* True anger flashed in his eyes. "It's insulting, in fact, that you think the sight of a breast will move me from my course. Do you think you're the only one with any willpower?"

She snatched her hands free. "God, do you know how tired I am of being lectured?"

"Perhaps you should change your ways, then."

"Devil a bit." Before he could prevent it, she slipped her hand inside his dressing gown to stroke him. "Try telling me, Miles Cavanagh, that you're not burning for me."

He moved well out of range. "I've already admitted it." Suddenly he turned away. "Hell and the devil, Felicity, apart from the risk of a child, I'm still your guardian, and I'm trying to do the right thing. If you seduce me—and you could—do you really think it will leave us any the better off?"

"It would give me something . . ."

He turned, suddenly alert. "When you leave? What are you planning?"

She hastily gathered her wits. "You can't expect me to tell you my plans, now can you?"

"Yes. We're not enemies."

Guiltily aware of Rupert's note, Felicity struck out. "We might as well be, for all the good it does me!"

It was as if she'd hit him. His voice was expressionless when he said, "Felicity, go back to your room and leave the key on my side of the door. I clearly need it more than you."

She'd lost.

She stared at him, seeking another way, a way that would break him. But then she realized at last that anything achieved at such a price would be mere ashes, never flame.

Once in her room, Felicity heard the key turn in the lock. Then, a moment later, she heard her door to the corridor being locked, too. So, she thought wearily, we are back to war. But at least if she weakened and thought of going to Rupert tonight, she couldn't.

She scratched a hole in the frost on the window and looked down the dark driveway to where a coach was doubtless waiting with Rupert growing more and more furious within it. As long as he didn't have Kieran with him, he could choke on fury and she'd be glad of it.

But his rage tonight would be paid for later if she ended

up in his power. And she would be in his power unless the Rogues' plan worked. She sent an earnest prayer that by some miracle it would.

Then she shed her wrap and climbed into bed where she relieved her burning body for herself.

It was a poor substitute.

Twenty-one

The next day everyone seemed to be suffering the after-effects of the celebrations—or in the case of Miles and Felicity, of other things. There was a meet, however, so the men gathered for breakfast in their hunting pink, looking forward to a day spent riding despite a light drizzle and the gloom of a heavy sky.

Felicity, Beth, and Blanche were there, and when the post-bag contained no word from Miles's mother, the gloom entered Felicity's soul. Or rather, given her nature, a roiling, threatening storm built there.

"Surely we should have word," she demanded of Miles.

He looked up from the two-day-old copy of the *Times* that had just arrived. "Not necessarily. It says here that there was a storm in the Irish Sea the day after our crossing. All ships, even the mail packets, were held in port, some for an extra day. Doubtless Dunsmore was delayed by it. Or, even better, caught in it." He smiled. "You can enjoy the thought of him casting up his accounts."

Felicity wished she could. She wished she could tell Miles about the letter. She felt as tangled as a knotted rope. But if she told him, he'd be more on his guard. He might even lock her up day and night.

"What's the matter?" he asked. "I thought you'd like that picture."

"At the moment, I don't much care where Rupert Dunsmore is, as long as he doesn't have Kieran with him."

"Tomorrow," he said. "I'm sure we'll have news tomorrow."

She dropped her knife and fork onto her plate with a clatter. "And what will we do if there *isn't* news? Dear heaven, why did you have to drag me so far away? Even if I knew Kieran was in danger, it would take me days to get to him!" Frightened by her own outburst, Felicity covered her face with her hands. Beth came to put her arms around her.

Miles's voice was hard, however, when he said, "If I'd left you in Ireland, you'd have married Dunsmore. Neither you nor Kieran would be better for it."

Felicity regained control and uncovered her face. "I'd be near him."

"I understand your fears," Miles said gently. "But your son is safe, and we will have news—either a letter from my mother or Dunsmore turning up."

With enormous willpower, Felicity prevented herself from sharing a glance with Beth.

The horses were announced, and Miles rose with the other men, putting aside the paper. "Can I trust you to be here when I return, Felicity?"

Felicity picked up the paper to conceal her indecision. What if another message came, one that in some way forced her hand?

Beth squeezed her shoulder. "On a day like this, only mad Meltonians would step outside. I assure you, we are not going anywhere."

Felicity understood and almost wept with relief. If she stayed in the house, Rupert could never contact her. She looked up at Miles and even smiled. "Yes, I'll be here when you return."

He nodded and picked up Gardeen from by his feet, placing her in Felicity's lap. "Make sure she stays close, too."

"Why? Do you think she's in danger?"

"It's time for Dunsmore to turn up, and he seems to like hurting cats."

She stroked the sleepy cat. "That's because he's afraid of them."

"What a poor specimen he is."

She glanced up. "Do you think there is nothing to fear from cats?"

"Nothing more than a scratch or two."

"Ah, Miles, at times I wonder about you. But off you go to hunt the truly harmless fox."

As soon as the men were on their way, Felicity headed for the comfort of the piano and spent the next hour honing her skill with scales and exercises. Beth and Blanche came in and sat to read.

Felicity looked up, her fingers still running up and down the keyboard. "Isn't the library or drawing room more cozy?"

"Not particularly," said Beth. "And we're guarding you. If word is getting out to Toad Dunsmore, we don't want him to hear that you are free to do as you please. It might stir even his sluggish intelligence."

"He's not particularly stupid."

"I'm just being malicious. He is, of a surety, a toad."

"No," said Felicity, contemplatively rippling an arpeggio. "A weasel. He has a rather sharp nose and keeps his belly close to the ground. Toads are fine animals, after all. Very useful in the garden."

Beth laughed. "Surely weasels have their virtues, too. Be that as it may, we will call him the weasel. And for his twitching nose, we will appear to guard you."

"Thank you. It will doubtless be tedious."

"Only if you insist on playing scales all morning."

Felicity took the hint and moved into a Bach piece which still provided plenty of discipline for her fingers.

The room settled into calm, with only the occasional crack from the logs in the big fire to disturb the harmony. Inside, however, Felicity felt as calm as the volcano she'd been likened to.

Beth had been right when she'd said there was nothing

outside the long windows to tempt anyone but an avid hunter, but it called to her anyway. She found herself looking down the windswept drive, expecting to see something or someone coming, probably Rupert with Kieran by his side.

As her fingers moved with discipline over the keyboard, her mind scrambled to imagine what the weasel might be doing and planning. Would he believe she was a prisoner, unable to obey his instructions? That should hold him in check for a while.

If he realized she was planning to thwart him, he would doubtless return to Ireland to secure his trump card, Kieran. Willpower couldn't make her believe Kilgoran impregnable.

She needed news from Lady Aideen.

She needed the proof of Rupert's fraud, perjury, and theft.

She needed action.

Miles promised a letter from Ireland tomorrow, but how soon could they expect to hear from Cheltenham? Not for a few more days at least.

They were going to be very long days. . . .

Beth came over to lean on the piano. "Are you all right?"

"Of course. Why?"

"You've been playing the same piece for over half-an-hour, faster and faster. I'm amazed your fingers can manage."

At that point, Felicity's automatic working of the Bach Prelude collapsed into discord and she rested her hands on the keys. "I'm not good at waiting."

"You need distraction. Would you like to play billiards?"

"No!" But then Felicity regretted the exclamation for a number of reasons. "I can hardly play the game," she said. "Miles taught me a little at Clonnagh." Such images and sensations swamped her that she couldn't continue.

"Clearly a disturbing time," Beth said. "Well, then, we could play cards."

"No." Felicity rose and closed the piano. "Billiards is an excellent idea. Does Blanche play?"

"Too well. Don't let her set the stakes. Billiards, Blanche?"

The actress immediately looked up, bright-eyed. "Lovely idea. This novel is remarkably tedious. If people have a mind to preach, they should write sermons."

As she led the way to the billiard room, Beth said, "I told you to try *Sense and Sensibility.*"

"It sounded so dull, but it can't be duller than *Coelebs In Search Of A Wife.* Did Beth warn you, Felicity, that I'm rather good at billiards?"

"She did. And not to lay wagers with you over it."

"Bother." As they entered the room, Blanche lit the lamps. "I was hoping to win your white rosebuds."

"Are you entitled to them?" Felicity asked with a grin.

Blanche winked. "I've not been entitled to white rosebuds since a child. The contrast is part of my allure." She took a cue, lined up the three balls, and neatly sent one red into a pocket. "I'm sure you can't be attached to those trimmings. They don't become you."

"They aren't supposed to. They're to warn off invaders. Aren't you afraid they'll work?"

"I can warn off invaders in any number of ways. And anyway, these days, I only have one, he's already aboard, and he's more than enough for any woman."

"I gather he wants to marry you."

"He's a mad romantic and thinks he can shape the world to suit his rosy vision."

"That seems to be a Roguish tendency."

"Don't discount it," said Beth, coming over with her own cue. "As a group they can command the evil power of rank and money."

"Speaking as a member of one of Ireland's oldest families," said Felicity, "and the owner of a ridiculously large fortune, I see nothing wrong with rank and money at all." She turned to Blanche. "Of course I'll stake those silly rosebuds. But what would you wager against them?"

Blanche straightened to consider it. "I have nothing that

isn't white, and that isn't your color. I could stake my drake's feathers," she said hopefully.

"Done." Felicity turned to Beth. "Are you entering the contest? It can be winner take all. I think, judging from the stakes so far, it should be something you'd be rather glad to get rid of."

"Well, there is one of the kitchen maids," Beth said with a twinkle, "but I think we've made buying and selling people illegal. What about my amber-headed riding crop? I have little taste for riding. Of that sort, anyway," she added.

Felicity laughed, and despite Blanche's complaint that she'd never be seen with an amber-headed crop even if she rode a horse, they settled the stakes and progressed to the game. Beth proved to be an indifferent player, but Felicity and Blanche were closer matched. Felicity suspected Blanche was holding back a little, but she didn't mind. This was all serving to pass the time.

Since they hadn't set a limit to the contest, they just kept playing until hunger and thirst sent them in search of sustenance.

"My," said Beth as she poured tea and the others helped themselves to sandwiches, "there is an alarming amount of *science* in that game. Are we to continue? I think Felicity is just slightly ahead at this point."

Blanche faded gently backward into a languishing pose. "I am drained. I could not find the strength to lift the cue."

"You mean you want to be rid of those feathers."

Blanche opened her eyes enough to wink.

"Oh, very well," said Felicity. "I'll relieve you of them. If nothing else, Gardeen can hunt them." And she spent the rest of the afternoon piecing together a quite pretty aigrette for her hair. She went to the mirror to try the effect.

"My heavens," said Blanche, looking up from *Sense and Sensibility*. "However did you do that in so short a time?"

"Grandfather taught me to tie flies. I think the dark feathers sit well against my black hair—mysterious and devilish."

"Isn't it strange," said Beth, "how in nature the male is always more gorgeously plumed than the female. And yet we human females take those male weapons and use them in our own wars."

As Blanche helped fix the aigrette in her hair with pins, Felicity said, "Perhaps we need male weapons to fight the male."

"It's not always war, you know."

"Isn't it?" Felicity returned to the piano to play a dramatic, rebellious piece by Herr Beethoven.

When the men came home from an indifferent day's hunting, Miles noticed the aigrette and complimented her on it.

When she explained she had made it, his brows rose. "Another feminine skill. I'm not sure I can stand these changes."

"Very wise," said. "Changes are not always for the better."

But a day was over without a message from the weasel.

The next morning, some of Felicity's tension was relieved by a letter from Kilgoran Castle.

Lucien, emptying the postbag, passed it to Miles, who glanced at it then offered it to Felicity.

She shook her head. "No. It's to you from your mother. But please, read it quickly."

He broke the seal and started to read. "Everything is fine. She's at the Castle, complaining about the earl's dictatorial ways. . . . They clash like breaker and shore, you know, even though he's frail. Kieran and Mrs. Edey are established in the nursery wing with a dozen servants to obey their every whim . . ." He scanned down. "There's a note further on that Kilgoran has appointed a strong, healthy groom to be personal servant to the lad and go with him just about everywhere. It's all right."

Felicity realized she had her hands clasped painfully tight and relaxed them. "Thank heavens!"

And if Rupert were here, he'd had no time to change that happy state of affairs before leaving.

Her son was safe.

Then, though Felicity kept a bright smile on her face, her bubble of relief and delight abruptly burst.

She had promised herself that when she heard this happy news, she would tell Miles about the letter from Rupert. But how was she to do so without admitting she'd kept it secret for more than a day? That she hadn't trusted him and his friends?

She couldn't.

But she had to tell him. It was right to tell him. Shuddering at the thought of making her confession in public, Felicity decided to wait for a private moment.

But, of course, as soon as breakfast was over, the men headed out for another day's hunting, so no private moment occurred. She could have made one—she had only to ask Miles to step aside for a moment—but she gave in to cowardly evasion. Perhaps, if she waited, she'd think of some way of avoiding a confession.

Heaven knows, Miles was sufficiently aware of her flaws without her throwing another one in his face.

Felicity spent another day indoors, "guarded" by Beth and Blanche, trying to convince herself that there was no need to tell Miles anything. Nothing had come of the message, after all.

Would Beth tell?

No.

So there really was no reason to say a word, even if she did feel horribly guilty and dishonorable. And the most wretched coward ever to walk the earth.

By the next day, she'd fretted herself almost sick over it.

The night before, even easygoing Miles had begun to worry about Rupert's non-appearance. Admitting the possibility that the weasel was stalking Kieran, he'd mentioned leaving for Ireland to make sure the boy was safe.

Beth had caught Felicity's eyes with a meaningful glance.

Felicity had not acknowledged it, but she'd known she must do something. In addition to Miles's concerns, she had her own. Not hearing from Rupert since Sunday—though it was by her own design—left her uncertain of his moves.

Delay, however, had made it even more difficult to tell Miles the truth.

As she played a soothing *berceuse,* inspiration struck. If she were to receive *another* message, she could tell Miles about it without having to reveal the earlier one. And there was no longer any reason for her to hide away in fear. If Kieran were safe, Rupert could threaten as ferociously as he liked without shaking her.

So Felicity lost her guards much as she had once lost Miles, by using the privy as her excuse. Then she slipped down the unfamiliar servants' passage and found a door to the outside with a rack of red, woolen cloaks beside it. Snatching one, she went out and took a deep breath of fresh air.

It was still cloudy, but today the air was reasonably dry. It wouldn't be a bad day for the hounds. Her main concern, however, was that a certain groom be in the stables, not out with the hunters.

She hurried into the stable yard to see five men engaged in various tasks, two of them inspecting a fine dun gelding. None of them was the towheaded messenger. Professional curiosity took Felicity over to the horse, which she had to admit didn't look too happy. It was yawning, and even shivering a bit.

"Colic?" she asked.

One man looked up and touched his hat. "Aye, Miss. But not too bad, we reckon."

She sensed uncertainty and glanced around. "Where's the head groom?"

"He's been called out to one of the hunt horses, Miss."

"Ah." Clearly the men knew their business but were uncertain of their authority. Would they accept hers?

She stepped closer, put her ear to the horse's side, and

heard the familiar gurgling of too much gas. But clearly the
horse wasn't in much pain. "No, not too bad a case. You're
doubtless planning to feed him a bran mash and keep him
walking. That should do the trick."

The man's face lightened. "Aye, that's what we had in mind,
Miss." As he led the horse off, the other groom went to make
the mash.

Now what? Should she ask after towhead? Then Rupert
might think she was looking for a message.

She almost laughed out loud. If he believed she was a
prisoner, he would expect her to be looking for a message
and a means of escape.

Felicity turned to ask the help of one of the men, but was
interrupted when an elegant curricle drawn by four matched
blacks rolled into the yard, tooled by a servant.

Someone new had arrived at Vauxhall. Doubtless another
Rogue.

Curiosity was overwhelmed by relief when the towheaded
groom ran out of the tack room to help tend the lathered team.

Felicity went over to stand reasonably close to her quarry.
"Fine horses. Whose are they?"

"Don't know," he said, as he flipped loose the surcingle.
"Hey, Harry. Whose rig is this?"

"Lord Middlethorpe's, and he's a generous man, Josh, so
take care of 'em." Then he saw Felicity. "Beggin' your pardon,
Miss."

The towhead—Josh—gave her a quick, startled glance then
went back to his job.

"I'm sure you're always dependable, Josh," she said and
wandered to eye the other horses, giving the man a chance
to finish and make contact if he needed to.

How long, though, before Beth came searching?

The men had the team free of the traces now, and while
the curricle was pulled away to be washed, they rubbed the
horses down and covered them with blankets. Then she saw

Josh nip into one of the rooms. He came out with a new cloth, but flashed her a look.

Heart pounding, she strolled over to the lathered horse he was rubbing down. A piece of paper slid into her hand. "He says you're to make sure to act this time," he muttered.

"Tell him I'm guarded, night and day. I only managed to . . . See there," she added. "Here come my jailers." With perfect timing, Beth had arrived, accompanied by a slender, dark-haired man.

"Felicity!" Beth said rather sharply. "What on earth are you doing here?"

Felicity slipped the note into her pocket and assumed her most brittle manner. "Faith, and am I not allowed to take the air anymore? I wanted to smell the true sweet aroma of a stable." She looked the handsome stranger over, from supple leather boots to glossy beaver. "And who's your fine gentleman friend?"

Beth's eyes expressed exasperation, but her voice was level as she said, "Francis, let me introduce Miss Felicity Monahan of Foy Hall in County Meath. She's Miles's ward for a few weeks and doesn't appreciate the situation. Felicity, I present Francis, Lord Middlethorpe, another Rogue. Now come along back to the house, do. You must be chilled."

Felicity smiled sweetly at Lord Middlethorpe. "Brought you along in case force was necessary, did she?"

He seemed rather delicate and poetic, but there was nothing delicate in his manner when he said, "And is it? I do like warning if I'm going to have to manhandle a woman."

Felicity stifled a gasp of surprise.

He didn't like her.

That was hardly surprising in the circumstances, but it gave her a jolt. In all her life, the only other person she'd met who had taken a speedy aversion to her was Miles.

Of course, in both cases she'd been playing a rather unpleasant part. Faith, but she was clearly a gifted actress and should ask Blanche to set her up on the stage!

She laughed insolently. "But I like to maintain the element of surprise, my lord, particularly when I'm among enemies." With that, she swept ahead of the other two and led the way back to the house.

Once in the house, she hinted to Beth and was locked in her room. Safely private, she pulled out the reward of her expedition, the note.

My darling Felicity,
*   You cannot imagine my anguish that we are not yet*
together.

Oh, can I not, you veritable weasel? You're probably gnawing the wainscoting in your fury.

*   The thought of you a prisoner has me in a ferment. I*
am sick with it. God knows what I will do next.

Now there's a threat. What a shame you have no edge to put on it.

*   Can you imagine my pain as I watched you out riding,*
so near and yet so far? And again that night, waiting,
watching the candles flicker behind your curtains, hop-
ing you would find the strength to follow my instructions
and flee to me.

She shivered under the horrible sensation of having been watched, especially when she knew the power of a spyglass. On how many other occasions had he watched, and what had he seen?

How much did Rupert suspect?

He was no fool. Would he realize that if she really wished to be free of this place, she would have found a way? Tapping the letter against her fingers, Felicity assessed the situation.

If Rupert didn't have a willing inside spy, then it should

be all right. Certainly the upper servants would gossip among themselves, which is why she and Miles had been staging minor squabbles. But, hopefully, none of those family retainers would give a close account of matters in the house to a stranger, or even to such a lowly creature as Josh.

Therefore Rupert wouldn't know how lightly she was guarded.

In that case, the scene in the stable yard would have worked wonderfully. Beth's appearance, accompanied by someone clearly willing to enforce her will, was just what they wanted Josh to take back to Rupert.

At this rate, she should be able to hold Rupert off until word came from Cheltenham.

She read the last part of the note—the instructions.

> *The servant who gives you this can be trusted as much as any member of the lower orders ever can.*

Oh, Rupert, you pompous fool.

> *Inform him of your best chance of escape, and I will ensure it comes to pass. With the men out every day following the hounds, it should be possible for you to slip away.*

Definite suspicion there, alas.

> *I need to hear from you, speak to you, kiss you, my darling. Do not make me wait. Remember always that one you love, and who loves you, will suffer for every moment you delay.*

Felicity crumpled the note viciously, but then reminded herself that Kieran was safe at Kilgoran with a personal guard, not in Rupert's power at all. But she knew the threat was real. If she played Rupert false and failed to keep Kieran out of his power, he would get his revenge through the child.

And nothing on earth could change the fact that Rupert was Kieran's father.

Again she was tempted to give up and run, but she shook her head. She had agreed to this course and must see it through. She would wait until they heard from Cheltenham.

She smoothed out the paper. At least now she had something to show Miles and could put her deception behind her.

But then her hands froze. It was obvious from this letter that there'd been another!

She sat with a thump. Now what was she supposed to do?

After half-an-hour of miserable thinking, Felicity acknowledged that she had no option other than telling the horrible truth. It could not be yet, though. The men were still out.

Halfway through the day, Beth escorted a maid bearing a tray. When they left, the door was locked again, doubtless within view of the servant. Oh, what an excellent little scheme.

Ignoring the tray of food, Felicity went over to the window. She wanted to be seen. When Rupert heard she'd been locked in her room, she wanted him to remember her here at the window, gazing wistfully out at freedom.

It was eerie, though, to think that he might be out there somewhere, watching her now.

When she finally settled to eating, Felicity found Beth had sent up a book to entertain her—or to educate her, more likely. *Lord Chesterfield's Letters.*

In fact, the witty, worldly earl's advice made rather better reading than Mary Wollstonecraft's sermonizing, but Felicity came to wish Chesterfield was not quite so firm on the subject of truthfulness.

"Virtue consists in doing good and speaking truth. . . ."

"I am sure you know that breaking of your word is a folly, a dishonor, and a crime."

"I really know nothing more criminal, more mean, and

*more ridiculous than lying. It is the production of either mal-
ice, cowardice, or vanity. . . ."*

She slammed the book down, wondering which of those
forces had driven her to lie about the letter. For it had been
a lie, if only one of silence.

Vanity. And, perhaps, cowardice. But not fear of disclosure;
fear of consequences. She had feared that once Miles knew
Rupert was around, he would keep closer watch on her. Even
more, she had feared that he might break his word and kill
the man.

Yes, she thought, rising to pace the room, Lord Chesterfield
had missed one factor—distrust.

Miles was going to be delighted by that, wasn't he?

As for cowardice, that was what had compounded the problem.

She saw the men ride back and heard them enter the house.
She half-expected Miles to come to speak to her, but instead
Harriet arrived to unlock her door and prepare her for dinner.

Twenty-two

When Felicity entered the drawing room, Miles came over to her looking somber. She thought he already knew the dreadful truth, but he said, "Why on earth did you go out to the stables? It could have been dangerous.

"Dangerous? This place is infested with servants."

He shook his head. "I gather you met Francis. He's a fine fellow."

"He doesn't like me."

"Francis?" Then Miles sighed. "I suppose you treated him to one of your better impressions of a wayward ward."

"I had no choice. Beth brought him when she came to find me, and there were so many servants around . . ."

He touched her—a gentle, unobtrusive touch on her back. "It's all right. We'll explain to him later."

But after dinner, when the ladies went apart, Beth had an opposing view. "If you don't mind, Felicity, we're going to leave Francis in ignorance of your situation for a while. Lucien says there's something up with him, too. And Francis is such a kindhearted fellow we're afraid he'll keep it to himself if he thinks there are other matters to be handled."

"Kindhearted?" Felicity echoed, remembering the cool-eyed man who'd offered to manhandle her.

"He is, truly. If you found him a bit hard, it's further proof something is wrong. Now, tell me why you ran out."

"You think I went because I received a message. I didn't."

Beth relaxed. "That's all right, then. I was concerned that

one of the upper servants had been bribed. I'm not used to so many servants anyway, and the thought that one so close to me cannot be trusted makes me shudder. I suppose you just felt the need of action and exercise."

"That's it exactly." And it was true, though not as Beth intended. More falsehoods. Lord Chesterfield would not have approved. "I read part of the book you sent up."

"Chesterfield. Amusing in places, isn't he? In fact, he rather reminds me of the Duke of Belcraven."

"Lucien's father?"

"Yes." Beth poured the tea. "Strict, but wise and witty, too."

"On the other hand," said Blanche, "Chesterfield had a low opinion of women. What did he say? That he never knew a woman with sense?"

"Strange how even clever men are blind," said Beth. "He claimed women always let passion or humor intrude upon their actions."

"But why on earth not?" Felicity asked. "Aren't humor and emotion what differentiate us from . . . from clockwork monsters?"

Beth smiled at her. "How true! Sometimes I steep myself so deep in the writings of men that I forget reality." Her expression turned serious. "Hold onto your humor, Felicity, and your emotional commitment. It is, as you say, what makes us human."

It was support of a kind, and Felicity cherished it as she waited to confess all.

When the gentlemen joined the ladies, Felicity immediately rose. "Miles, I need to speak to you."

He was surprised and perhaps a little wary, but he said, "Why don't we go into the library?"

"So you'll have a chair handy?" As she swept out of the room, she heard a chuckle.

Once in the library, however, her bold spirit collapsed. "I'm sorry," she said, hands clasped before her.

"For what? Going to the stables? As you said—"

"No! No, not for that."

"For what, then?" After a hushed moment, he said, "You're carrying a child."

"No! I don't know. . . . Just give me a moment, Miles, and I'll get it out."

"Whatever it is," he said with a touch of amusement, "it can't be as bad as you seem to think. Unless you've somehow managed to marry Dunsmore, of course."

That dragged a shaky laugh from her. "Perhaps I had a parson concealed in the stable yard, and Rupert was the back half of a pantomime horse. . . ."

He laughed, but tears almost deprived Felicity of her voice, and she sucked in a steadying breath.

He immediately came to put an arm around her, despite feeble resistance.

"Come on," he said, drawing her against his chest. "Having eliminated the truly disastrous, let's hear the merely awful."

She'd forgotten the sweetness of being held gently in his arms, and took a moment to let her senses draw strength and sustenance from it.

"I had a note from Rupert today."

His arms tightened a little. "At last. Then he's in the area." He moved back a little to look into her face. "He frightened you?" Then, turning watchful, "What did you do?"

"Came in and read it. Nothing more." She took a deep breath. "But I had one on Sunday, too."

She felt the reaction run through him and be controlled. He did and said nothing, except to draw her back against his chest, but she knew that was in part to give him time to think.

At last, he said, "It would be pleasant if you could trust me."

"Oh, Miles . . ."

His hand soothed her back. "But I do understand. All my

life I've had dependable family and friends as close as brothers. I've never had to stand alone. You've had no one since your parents died. When you've learned to cope alone, it must be hard to surrender part of your will to another."

She pressed closer into the cloth of his jacket. "I thought you'd hate me."

"Never. It frightens me, but that's because you could dash off at any moment. . . ."

She sighed. "Yes, I could. I . . . I'm not sure I can ever change that."

"I'll make it part of the wedding vows."

When she tried to protest, he kissed her into silence.

When they found strength to stop, he smiled into her eyes. "I do note that you're still here to be kissed. If I remember your promise to me, that first letter freed you to leave."

"In the middle of a party?"

"That wouldn't stop you."

She could at least give him honesty. "I thought of it, but I didn't want to go. I don't want to go now. And if I do marry Rupert, I'll be weeping as I say the vows."

"There's scant comfort in that." He pushed her gently away. "Now, let me see this letter. Both of them, if you still have the earlier one."

Felicity pulled them out from behind her stays. "I'm not sure how I came to deserve you."

He took the two sheets of paper. "Nor am I when you keep another man's letters so close to your heart."

"Idiot! This gown has no pockets."

"Excuses, excuses." He unfolded the letters and read them quickly. "He has a fine hand with a veiled threat, doesn't he? Did these frighten you?"

"The first one did. But then I decided that if he had Kieran in his power he'd make more use of him than mere threats. Today's didn't bother me at all until I realized you'd know there'd been an earlier one." She wasn't sure he fully grasped her perfidy. "I went out hoping for another message, you know. It was a deliberate attempt to deceive you. Lord Chesterfield would be disgusted."

He looked up blankly. "What the devil does he have to do with it?"

Felicity laughed. "Oh, Miles, I do love you in the most painful way."

He folded the letters. "As I do you. And I live in the fervent hope that one day it will be less painful for both of us. Now, since Luce doesn't want to bother Francis with this unless necessary, we'll have a two-person council of war."

Felicity nodded and sat down in the familiar library chair. "As I see it, as long as Rupert believes I cannot escape, we're safe. Once we hear from Cheltenham, we can contact him and lay down our terms. My main concern is that he'll call our bluff and try to seize Kieran."

"We'll have to secure Rupert first."

She shivered. "More violence."

"It might be simpler just to kill him."

She looked at him, a man she knew to be so very gentle. "Could you?"

"Oh, yes."

And she believed him. Men were strange creatures. "We'll try reason and bribery first. Which means you had best keep me guarded or locked up for the next few days." She rose. "I suppose we should go back now. Heaven alone knows what Lord Middlethorpe is thinking."

"Not that we're making love. I have him convinced I find you a galling burden."

Irresistibly, she drifted back into his arms. "And I am, aren't I?"

He kissed her hair. "True enough. But one I'll be happy to carry for the rest of my life."

The next days passed as planned, with the men riding out with one of the local hunts, and Felicity well-guarded. Beth

and Blanche never left her unaccompanied, and if she elected
to stay in her room, they locked her in.

Stephen had to leave on political business, but assured
everyone that he was not needed once the evidence came in
from Cheltenham. Felicity suspected he wanted to be out of
the way if any illegalities took place.

Almost as soon as his dust had settled, his place was taken
by a new Rogue called Con Somerford, more formally known
as Viscount Amleigh. Here was another handsome specimen.
He wore his dark brown hair short, and his jaw was square
and strong. Humor always seemed a flicker away from his
gray eyes, however, and if he smiled widely, he had dimples.

Felicity was heartily tired of creating a bad impression for
new guests, so she told him the truth.

"We are a bundle of problems at the moment, aren't we?"
He produced those charming dimples. "Remind me to avoid
all women like the plague."

"In my case, I might have been better off without male
interference," Felicity said, though she meant Rupert more than
Miles. "It does sound as if Francis's lady needs his help,
though."

For Lucien had been right. Francis had a problem. A
woman he had befriended was being persecuted by her brothers, who had even stolen her small widow's jointure. A neat
plan had been dreamed up to snatch back some of the lady's
stolen money through a horse race—a horse race involving a
certain gray called Banshee.

Miles had come up with the plan. "Tom and Will Allbright
care for gambling, horses, and women, in that order, and
they're not too bright about any of them. Why not take them
on, two out of three?"

"How?" Francis had asked.

"You know Banshee?"

Francis shuddered. "Yes."

Miles grinned. "During Stables this Sunday, it shouldn't
be that hard to set up a wager between Banshee and one of

the Allbright's nags. They have a couple they're proud of. I'll
win, and there you are."

Con pointed out the flaw in that. "The Allbrights would
have to be imbeciles to underrate any horse of yours, Miles,
and they're surely not that stupid."

"And this is my business anyway," said Francis. "I'll ride
him. In fact, I'll buy the horse first just to make it above
board. How much do you want for him?"

Miles grinned at Felicity. "Fifty."

Francis pulled a face but said, "Done."

"There, *cailín.*" Miles had said. "You owe me a cake baked
by your own fair hands."

Felicity had laughed. "Miles Cavanagh, sometimes I have
to like you, you wicked man. But now you have to eat the
cake!"

At least her time in the kitchen trying to master the art of
cake-making served to pass some time. And to amuse the servants, for Felicity played her resentful part, regaling the staff with
her tale of abduction and persecution by her brutal guardian.

They didn't believe a word of it, for they knew Miles well,
but they believed she felt that way and humored her. As she
beat eggs and sifted flour—for she insisted she had to do
every bit herself—she elaborated on his heartless cruelty in
not letting her marry the man of her choice. She complained
bitterly about being cooped up in the house when she was
used to riding wild and free wherever she pleased.

Which scandalized them, as she'd intended, putting Miles
firmly back in the right of it.

The end result of her efforts turned out rather heavy, but
the cook rescued her by soaking it in brandy. "We call it
tipsy cake, miss. A dollop of cream on the top of each piece,
and everyone will be delighted."

So it proved, though Miles teased by proposing a toast
with it.

* * *

When Saturday's postbag did not bring anything from Cheltenham, Felicity was ready to scream. "I have to get out of here," she said to Miles. "I need fresh air, and Josh might have another message from Rupert. We'd know what he was up to."

"If you manage to slip away again, he might wonder why you didn't just slip away altogether. However, there's no reason you can't ride around Stables on Sunday."

"A woman? The world will come to an end!"

"Not a bit of it. A few of the men have asked why you're not hunting since you're both a Monahan of Foy and the Lady of the Quintain. They'll accept you. We'll ride around and look at some of the best horses—you'll like that—then come back here in time for Francis's performance with the Allbrights. Perhaps young Josh will slip you another note then."

"Then why *can't* I go hunting?"

"Quench that fire in your eye! I didn't say all the men are in favor. Tom Assheton-Smith would have an apoplexy if you turned up with the Quorn. Then there's the small risk that Dunsmore would stage an abduction."

"Despite forty or so men to make sure I had a good ride?" she queried naughtily.

"You'll be the death of me. I swear it."

"One day soon, I hope."

"Damnation, stop it, Felicity, or I'll suffer a permanent injury. I tell you, when it comes to riding, you women have it easy."

"Then, perhaps, all you men should stay safely home sewing samplers!"

Sunday went as planned and Felicity witnessed Lord Middlethorpe coolly egging his red-faced target on. In the end, Tom Allbright bet three thousand guineas that his fine thoroughbred could beat the vicious mismatched heap of bones called Banshee.

She had to miss the race which, of course, Banshee—the horse of tremendous stamina who could not bear to be behind—won. But she heard the story of it again and again over an uproarious celebratory dinner.

And during the day, she received word from Rupert Dunsmore.

It was not a letter this time. While in the Vauxhall stables, Josh had caught her eye. She'd cautiously followed the groom into an empty stall. "Do you have a letter for me?"

Josh shook his head. "He says you must write to him, Miss. He's . . . he's not pleased. He seems to think you could escape here if you wished."

"How?" Felicity demanded. "I'm escorted everywhere. Though it all looks very civilized, one word amiss and I'm in bonds. Tell him that. Tell him we'll have to wait the few weeks until I'm of age. No one can stop us then."

The young man grimaced. "He's doubtless a mite impatient, Miss. Down at the Three Hands, talk is that there's men here after him for owing money. A lot of money. He's in hiding. What I hear is he told these men he owned some land that'd cover his debts, but it don't belong to him but to his son. They're the type that if they can't have their money, they want blood."

Felicity was hard put not to grin at that thought. But it probably wasn't funny. "Tell him I'll run to him if I can, but he can't depend on it. He may have to wait."

Josh shook his head. "He'll not be pleased." He looked at her awkwardly. "Beggin' your pardon, Miss, but are you sure about him? Seems he's cheated these men, and though they're moneylenders, it don't seem right to me. And he's . . . well, he's not a kind man. I tell you true, I'd not want my sister married to such a one."

It was terribly hard for Felicity not to hug the young man for his genuine concern. But she stuck her nose in the air and snapped, "I know what I'm doing."

She resisted the temptation to rush over to Miles to discuss the news and instead shared a joke with a Meltonian.

Later, however, after Lord Middlethorpe had retired to rest a body suffering from a long ride on Banshee, the rest of the Rogues held another council of war.

"So," said Miles after the tale was told, "he's in deep with the moneylenders. How very pleasant. I think we have him now."

On Monday, the postbag contained another letter from Kilgoran full of light chat about life in those chilly, elegant halls. Folded with the letter was a colored drawing with the carefully printed message *To Felicity, from Kieran George Dunsmore*. Alongside the drawing, in case there was any doubt, it said *a white horse*.

Felicity smiled at Miles through tears. "He's never had occasion to write to me before. Bless Lady Aideen."

"And he writes well for his age, too. Though I have to say that the 'white' horse, if horse it is, bears a closer resemblance to Banshee than I would like."

And the next day, a package of papers arrived from Cheltenham. Since it was a hunting day, the men had already left, but the women had no qualms about settling to study the documents.

Felicity found it eerie to read the statements taken from the illiterate Bittens and hear her tragic story related in prosaic words. Yes, a young lady very like the one in the picture had spent the winter and early spring of 1811 with them, growing big with child. And she had delivered a boy which had been taken away by a woman and her husband. Yes, the woman had also appeared to be heavy with child, but had produced no child there. Yes, the couple had been summoned by the Bittens as soon as the young lady's pains started. They'd been instructed to do that.

A Mrs. Stafford of Cheltenham had written her own statement about the time Mr. and Mrs. Dunsmore from Ireland had stayed with her while the lady received medical care for her condition, which was that of carrying a child. Mrs. Dunsmore had driven out in her carriage every fine day, and one day had returned with her newborn baby in her arms, it having apparently been born suddenly in a cottage in the country. She had appeared surprisingly fit and hearty. No, she had not put the child to the breast as far as Mrs. Stafford knew and, in fact, a wet nurse had been standing by, ready.

Felicity looked up from the document with a frown. "This points the way, but it's circumstantial."

"Yes," said Beth, reading the letter from the solicitor. "Mr. Scrope says that the doctor who attended Mrs. Dunsmore was very old—retired, in fact—and has since died."

"Weaselly, indeed, to choose such a one!" exclaimed Felicity. "I didn't know he had such intelligence."

"Call it cunning. I have to say, Felicity, that this isn't good. Dunsmore could claim that his wife merely helped you in your problem and found a good home for your child. And that by some strange coincidence, she also gave birth—in the carriage even—on the way home."

Felicity experienced a moment of blind panic, then put her hands to her head. "No, wait! The driver would know. She could not possibly drop off one child and give birth to another on the way home without his knowledge."

"True. But it was presumably a hired carriage. How do we find him?"

"There has to be a way. I've come too far to give up now."

Blanche smiled. "Good for you."

But Felicity wasn't sure it was good. She knew she'd relaxed her guards too far, and opened her heart to pain. If she had to marry Rupert, it would be far worse now than it would have been before she found trusted friends and fell deep in love with Miles Cavanagh.

That evening, the men concurred with the women's opinion. Beth had already dispatched another groom back to Cheltenham to order an enquiry into the driver of the Dunsmore's carriage.

"More waiting," said Felicity to Miles. "Truly, I'm going to go mad!"

Two days later, Francis, once more mobile, announced that he must leave. He said nothing, but they all suspected it had something to do with his lady-in-distress, Serena Riverton.

"The hell of it is, he can't marry her," Lucien said after Francis's curricle had disappeared down the drive. "Apparently, she can't bear children."

That struck too close to home for Felicity. "If men weren't so obsessed by children, the world would be a better place."

"It's the inheritance laws that rule us," Miles pointed out, "not our inclinations."

"Is it not?" she asked with a meaningful look, and everyone laughed.

The next day, however, she had to tell Miles, blushing, that she was not carrying a child.

He gathered her into his arms. "I feel a touch of regret, but it's doubtless for the best. I'd prefer that our first child be born at least nine months after our wedding, particularly if your past has to come out."

"Strange, but I felt a bit of disappointment, too. Sure and it would be a fine child that came out of that wild loving."

He tilted her chin so he could look into her eyes. "Then we'll just have to be as wild when the time comes. I'm sure we can manage that."

A shudder of pure need went through her, and she hugged him close. "And that is certainly the holy truth."

Twenty-three

And then matters rushed together with terrifying speed.

The groom from Cheltenham pounded up the frozen drive on a lathered horse with the news that the coachman hired for that springtime drive four years before had been Mrs. Stafford's second cousin, which is how she happened to know he'd moved to London to work for a livery stable there.

No, added the report from Mr. Scrope, the man had said nothing of anything strange about that day, but he was of a taciturn nature—one who believed in minding his own business.

"Strange," said Miles. "I'd have thought Dunsmore would do something about the man. Perhaps he bribed him to silence."

Felicity smiled wryly. "More likely he ignored him as if he didn't exist. A fine disdainful attitude to servants, has Rupert Dunsmore, and it's caused him trouble before."

"Then it looks as if we should go to London and find this Sam Greenwood so as to cause him even more trouble."

"But what of Rupert?"

"When he hears you're gone, he'll follow. I admit it won't be as easy to keep track of him in London, but we can always depend on him finding you."

"Now, why do I feel like a goat pegged out for a lion?"

Miles burst out laughing. "Pity the poor lion who thought *you* easy prey!"

Later that day, they received a letter from Francis rather

tersely informing them of his marriage to Serena, Lady Riverton, and his intention to visit London for some weeks with
his new bride.

Lucien whistled. "Now there's a turn-up. But I detect a
silent plea." He looked over at Beth. "Would it be a terrible
sacrifice for you to remove to London for a while?"

"Go to *Town!*" Beth gasped, hand to chest. "Go where
there are libraries, theaters, museums. . . . Leave behind this
land of horse and hound! How can you *suggest* such a
thing?"

Blanche was already on her feet, eyes shining. "I'll order
our bags packed."

Miles looked at Felicity. "And what of you? Will it be a
relief to you, too?"

"It will be a blessed relief to be doing *something.*"

They traveled in a parade of vehicles—Lucien and Hal in
one curricle, Con and Miles in another, and the ladies and
cat in Miles's coach. A small force of servants went ahead
to smooth their way. Since there was a sharp frost and even
some snow in the air, Felicity was pleased enough to be inside
with rugs and hot bricks to keep her comfortable. She was
even more grateful to find the inns always ready to receive
them with every comfort.

It did rather forcibly contrast with her last journey.

Before leaving, she'd slipped out to the stables and given
Josh a message for Rupert, saying where she was being taken
and that he must rescue her in London. She hoped he was
hot on their heels now. As soon as they had this coachman's
evidence, it would be done.

The party arrived in London in the afternoon of the second
day, dropped off Blanche and Hal at her pretty house, then
rolled on to Belcraven House, the magnificent ducal mansion
on Marlborough Square that Lucien referred to as "the Palace."

In the casual atmosphere of Vauxhall, it had been easy to forget that Lucien was of high estate. When she mounted the wide steps up to glossy double doors and entered a magnificent marble hall, Felicity was forcibly reminded.

Top-lofty servants positively swarmed around them to see to their every need. Within minutes, she found herself in a splendid room with Chinese wallpaper, silk hangings, and everything made ready for her comfort.

She changed, then joined Beth for tea in her lovely boudoir containing many shelves of books.

"Have you read them all?" Felicity asked, wandering the rows.

"At least dipped into them all. Do you not like to read?"

"Not a great deal. I prefer to be active. When this is over, I'm going back to Ireland, pulling on my breeches, and riding from dawn to dusk."

When this is over . . . Felicity realized that was the first firmly optimistic statement she'd made. Was she at last beginning to hope?

And was it wise?

Beth poured tea and offered cake. "Lucien and Miles have already gone out to track down this Sam Greenwood, so by this evening it could all be over bar the shouting."

Felicity clutched her saucer rather tightly. "I do hope so. Except, of course, that then I'll have to assume my role of tethered goat. I really don't ever want to see the man again. . . ."

"The Rogues will look after you." Beth then turned the conversation to fashion but, being Beth, she engaged in a discussion of the effects of fashion on women's status in society.

Despite her anxieties, Felicity was intrigued and hardly noticed the passing of time before Miles arrived with news.

"We've got him," he declared.

"Got him!" Felicity leaped to her feet, almost knocking over a small table.

He caught her hands. "Simmer down. I don't mean we have Dunsmore in our grasp." He settled her on the sofa and sat beside her. "Greenwood told his story readily enough, though, when we convinced him he'd been witness to an illegality. He might be taciturn, but it's a reflection of a firm morality."

He chose a piece of fruit cake. "He'll go into any court and swear that the Dunsmores went into the cottage and came out with a baby . . . that he then transported them home without break or incident. He was told, and believed, that she'd unexpectedly given birth there. He did volunteer that he'd thought at the time that she was a surprisingly tough woman to be quite so chipper after such an event."

"So," said Felicity, hope coming to full flower, "all we need now is to confront Rupert with our evidence. But he'll never get to me here! I have to go out . . ."

Miles captured her to stop her from leaping to her feet again. "Faith, my favorite volcano, rest still a moment! We'll let him find you, true enough, but in our own good time and with safeguards. It would be foolish, indeed, to let him snatch you away at this point in the game."

Felicity surrendered into his arms. It was going to be all right. Perhaps she would be allowed to enjoy Miles's love and tenderness forever. Small doubts still niggled, however. "I hope Rupert has the sense to accept defeat. He *is* like a weasel, you know. Cornered, he becomes mindlessly vicious."

"We'll keep an eye on him until the rage passes. Men like that can't hold their purpose long."

She was going to argue the point, but Beth asked, "Where's Lucien?"

"Detoured to Francis's house, hoping to speak to him."

"Oh, good. I told him to see if Francis and Serena could dine here tonight. I think we'll be busy trying to establish her in Society. If we're to gallivant all over London in that cause, Felicity, it should give the weasely one adequate access to you."

Feeling, in truth, like the goat staked out for the predator, Felicity snuggled deeper into Miles's arms. She decided she could come to like being guarded and protected if she could ever quite trust in it.

As planned, the Middlethorpes came to dinner that night. Francis's mysterious lady turned out to be beautiful but clearly living on the edge of her nerves. Felicity wondered how one who had presumably achieved her aim and married the man of her choice could appear so ill-at-ease. But then she discovered that Serena Riverton's first husband had been a scandalous wretch, so she was terrified that Society would shun her.

Beth would be better at handling that than Felicity, so when it came time for the ladies to leave the dinner table, Felicity flashed Beth a wink and stayed behind. The men didn't seem to mind, and a half-hour talking horses did wonders for Felicity's nerves, too.

By the time they went upstairs to the drawing room, Serena was calmer and Beth was already planning an assault on Society. The plan was to drown the scandal of Serena's unfortunate first marriage in Roguish influence.

"For we can command an astonishing degree of reflected glory," she said. "Dukes, marquesses, earls, and—more importantly—their female relatives. In the midst of all this," she added to Felicity, "if your pet weasel can't find you, he's hardly worth our trouble at all."

The next day, all obvious guard on Felicity was dropped, though Miles never let her out of his sight. In the morning, she walked out with a maid and footman to visit some local shops. She purchased soap, two pairs of silk stockings, and a jet clip she thought would suit her drake's-feather aigrette.

No one tried to contact her at all.

When she returned to the house, she shed her attendants and strolled around the ducal gardens, even wandering out into the mews.

Again, nothing.

The old fears returned. What if Rupert had lost patience and returned to Ireland to seize Kieran? She knew Miles had sent a warning to his mother, but was it possible for even Lady Aideen and the Earl of Kilgoran to hold the boy against the law?

In the afternoon, she circled Marlborough Square alone for an hour, hoping against hope for news.

By the time evening came, and with it a planned trip to the theater to show off Serena in elevated company, Felicity was desperate. She was almost ready to run through the streets of London waving a sign saying *"Rupert Dunsmore, come to me!"*

Miles took one look at her in her second-best silk and ragged nerves and dragged her into the nearest private room. "What is it?"

"Nothing! That's what it is. A frightful amount of nothing! I can't bear it."

He pulled her into his arms and held her tight. "Dunsmore is bound to be a bit slower in getting here."

"What if he's gone to Ireland? Devil take it, Miles, it's what I'd do in his case. Seize Kieran, secrete him away somewhere, then wait in hiding for me to come of age."

"He's not as intelligent as you, and I don't think he has a patient nature. I'm sure those men after him don't. And, believe me, he isn't enough of a man to get your son out of Kilgoran Castle."

She hung onto him. "I'm trying to believe. I am." Then she looked over his shoulder. "Faith, do you know what room we're in?"

He relaxed his hold to look, then groaned when he saw the billiard table. "My failing willpower doesn't need this."

"Perhaps it's the scent of baize and chalk . . ." She slid a hand up to his cheek. "We're going to win. You believe that, don't you? In a few weeks, we can be married. So, why not . . ."

He swung her around so she faced away from him, but was still held against him with strong arms. "Stop tempting me." But his voice faded and his lips brushed the back of her neck. She shivered and an ache began.

"Miles, I need you so."

His arms tightened, and he rocked her slightly. "Not near as much as I need you."

Swaying with him in an entrancing rhythm, she clutched his arms. "Would you like to take odds on that?"

He pushed against her back, and she felt him, long and hard.

She laughed shakily. "You'll have to explore a bit to find my evidence, but it's there, I tell you true."

His shudder ran straight through into her. "No," he said. "We are going to wait." And she could tell from the control he'd imposed on his voice that he meant it.

She turned, almost ripping through his embrace, though he did not let her go. "You know I'm no good at waiting!"

"And you know you could tempt me into hell's fires." He rested his head against hers, quieting her. "But no, Felicity. No. We have a lifetime. I believe that. If we weaken now on this, I'll shatter. I'll be quite useless to you in what needs to be done."

She heard the truth in him and made it into strength for herself. If need be, she'd protect him from her own impatient passion. She stepped out of his arms and smoothed her dress. "Very well, then. I'm cool again."

"Oh, fortunate creature . . ."

She choked back laughter and achieved a level tone. "I'll believe you about Kilgoran, and Kieran's safety is the only thing that really matters." Then she gasped, "I didn't mean that!"

"Yes, you did, and it's all right." His smile was a masterpiece. He even found the strength to take her hand. "Your son must come first, for he is weak and defenseless and has no one else. I feel much the same way. Oh, not because I feel as you do for Kieran—yet—but because my love of you is as deep as yours of him."

She squeezed his hand, slowly filling with a sense of delight and wonder. "If only we can all be together, we are going to be the happiest people on earth."

His smile widened into a grin. "Barring a few fights now and then, my warrior-queen. But you'll make a fine, fierce mother to my children." He took her other hand. "You've danced me a merry dance over this, but don't ever think I like you less for it. If you could relax your care of your son for love of me, how could I ever trust you to truly care for our children?"

She raised his hands and kissed them. "And your care of me—damnable though it's been at times—shows me you'll be a wonderful father. And I know you're a wonderful lover—"

"Shush!" He turned their hands and kissed hers back, a warm, sensual devotion that nearly broke her.

Perhaps he knew, for he led her from the tempting room. They only let their loving hands slip apart when they entered the hall where guests were already arriving. With the best will in the world, they could not stop their eyes from meeting, kissing, promising, loving throughout the long meal.

After dinner, the party left for Drury Lane where most of them were accommodated in the Duke of Belcraven's box. Felicity and Miles, however, sat with some others in the boisterous pit, where it was much more likely that Dunsmore could make contact.

It also meant that Miles and Felicity were squeezed tightly side by side on a bench, which continually strained their overstretched willpower.

What with that and waiting for contact with Dunsmore, the play could have been a tedious sermon as far as Felicity was concerned, though the people around her clearly enjoyed it.

During the intermissions, she and Miles strolled about. At one point, Miles deliberately left her unattended. Even though she knew he was watching, Felicity hated the leering looks of nearby men. Some even passed close to whisper salacious invitations. Her life at Foy had not prepared her for this, and she grew very angry that they would think some poor, unescorted female fair sport.

One man even stole a kiss. Felicity was on the point of doing him a serious injury when Miles dragged him off and pointed out the error of his ways.

"Faith, but London is a wretched place," Felicity said, trying to scrub an oniony taste from her mouth. "And if you were a proper knight in shining armor, you'd have drawn his cork."

"It would only have started a brawl," Miles said, touching her gently in comfort. "These theater crowds are always just a spark away from riot. And anyway, we may be watched. If not for that, I'd kiss away all trace of that scullion's attentions."

It was almost like a fierce kiss in the effect it had on her. "You could have called him out. Being my guardian gives you that right."

"Simmer down, you wild woman. He was a bit beneath my touch."

"But not beneath mine?"

"Then you call him out."

She scowled after her assailant. "I'm very tempted."

Miles laughed. "Swords, pistols, or fists, I'd bet on you." As he settled her back on their bench, he murmured, "Nothing, I suppose."

"No. I'm telling myself he hasn't made his way to London yet, though what the devil could be delaying him, I don't know. Oh, Miles, I want this over!"

"No more than I do, *mo chroí.*"

The farce was a huge success, judging from the roars of laughter around her, but Felicity was hard put to even smile.

By the time they were leaving the theater, caught in the usual crush of people near the door, she felt close to tears.

Why couldn't they be like normal lovers, able to show their feelings and enjoy their happiness? Now it was within sight, within touch, within smell like a steaming pie in a baker's shop, it was agony to do without.

Miles had his arm around her to protect her from the jostling of the crowd, and she snatched what pleasure she could from it despite the sweaty crush. She envied the people in the boxes who had their own exit.

She was hopping because a heavy boot had trampled her toes when a group of brandy-soaked young men decided to charge through the packed doorway. In the shouting, screaming melee that followed, Felicity and Miles were torn apart and she ended up squeezed against a wall, her bonnet half torn off.

Seeing very real danger, Felicity let the crowd grind past her. In moments, however, the pressure grew and screams warned of people being hurt. She began to sidle back toward the relative safety of the auditorium.

Then an arm snuck around her waist and helped her. Miles. Thank God! But when she was free, she found she was in the grasp of Rupert Dunsmore.

"At last," he snarled, pulling her further away from the blocked doorway.

She had little choice but to follow, and she'd wanted this meeting anyway. She'd expected, however, to have Miles close by. A quick glance showed he was nowhere in sight.

Rupert found a quiet corner and confronted her. "I can hardly say you've been your usual resourceful self, Felicity. I've you to thank for this."

He gestured to his face, and she saw with a gasp that he had a badly blackened eye, a swollen lip, and possibly a broken nose.

"What happened?"

"I thought those Irish peasants were bad enough, but moneylenders . . ." Suddenly, he smiled, a smile twisted by his injured lip. "All those problems are over now, though, aren't they? This way."

He pushed her toward the stage.

Felicity looked around frantically for help. "Where are we going?"

"Behind the stage. I've bribed one of the servants here. I didn't expect it to be quite so easy to separate you from your guardian, but fate must be on our side. Fate and a few coins to those rowdy young men."

At the plain door by the side of the stage, he flashed her a black look. "I hope you're not going to turn foolish again. Do I have to remind you what will happen to my brat if you do? He'll get a beating at least as bad as this, if not worse. The doctor said I came near to losing an eye. It'd be sad to see the child blind, wouldn't it?"

Ice ran through Felicity. In truth, she could have killed him then if she'd had a weapon.

Rupert rapped on the door, and a man cautiously opened it. "Be quick then," he whispered. "We don't want any more of that lot to think there's another way out."

Felicity glanced back to see that the main exit was completely jammed. Some of the audience milled in the auditorium looking for another way out of the building.

Miles was gone, and a glance at the Belcraven box showed it was empty.

So much for the Rogues. As always, she was on her own.

The door led into a warren of corridors smelling of musty costumes and greasepaint. Actors squeezed out of the way of theater servants rushing to prevent the doorway fracas from growing worse. Rupert shoved his way through, towing Felicity.

"Where are we going?" she gasped.

"Outside. Where do you think? Since you failed to keep me informed of your movements, I've had to cobble together a plan as best I could."

"How could I keep you informed?" Felicity bumped into a plaster pillar, doing her best to impede progress without being obvious about it. "At Vauxhall, they wouldn't even let me piss unescorted after that time I gave them the slip. Here in London, I've been waiting for you to contact me."

He stopped to study at her. "I wonder if you're telling the truth. I doubt it, but it doesn't matter. There's no escape, and you know it."

Gathering all her mendacious ability, Felicity looked him in the eye. "Yes, I know it. Wasn't it I who set up that elopement? And it would have worked, damn you, if you'd not stopped to argue about a cat."

"It would have worked if you'd agreed to bring it."

"Or if you'd agreed to let it go."

"Or if you'd run to the boat not the horses when Cavanagh appeared!" His grip on her wrist turned so vicious she gasped with pain. "I killed that damned cat, and I'll kill my snivelling son if I please. The only thing that will stop me is you as my sweet and dutiful wife. Remember that!"

Bile rose to sicken her, but Felicity kept her eyes steady on his. "Then let's get it done before Miles Cavanagh comes charging along to *guard* me again."

Two men dashing by with a ladder crushed them back against the wall. Rupert's lips twisted in an unpleasant smile. "I hear real feeling in that. If he weren't my enemy, I could almost admire Cavanagh. He soon learned you need a firm hand."

"Except that now we've thwarted him."

He laughed. "Struth, you really do want to spite him in this, don't you? Come on, then."

He dragged her along, but she'd achieved her goal. His grip was less tight, and his suspicions lessened.

What to do now, though?

Whatever it was, she must not let Rupert guess she planned resistance unless she could take him prisoner. She knew without doubt that if he realized he'd lost his power to compel her into marriage, he'd seize Kieran at all costs.

A blast of cold air warned her they were nearing a door to the outside. God, what was she to *do?*

When an actress rudely elbowed her way past, Felicity took her chance and fell to the ground with a cry of pain.

Rupert yanked her to her feet.

She shrieked again. "My ankle! I've broken it!" At the memory of a certain play on words, giggles threatened, and Felicity covered her face with her free hand, hoping desperately that her unsteadiness would be taken for tears.

"Confound it, you can't have!" He gripped her right ankle and she screamed at full volume. If it brought a crowd, she'd be glad of it.

Muttering curses, he bent to carry her.

He was no Miles, however, and though he pushed to his feet with her in his arms, he staggered under her weight.

At this farcical situation, Felicity lost all control. She hid her face in his shoulder and gave way to laughter until her tears ran down to soak into his cravat.

"Stop watering me, damn you," he gasped, lurching toward the door.

"Perhaps she hopes you'll grow," said a welcome Irish voice.

Felicity was plucked out of Rupert's arms into Miles's and saw Lucien ably pin her would-be-husband to the wall.

Yet again, she buried her head against a man's shoulder, but with genuine relief. "And about time, too," she gasped, still half-helpless with that wild laughter.

"Damnation, Felicity, I had no choice but to go forward and come round the back. Lucien saw everything from his box and due to his misspent youth, he knows the backstage of Drury Lane like he knows Vauxhall." He looked at her, eyes gleaming with anger. "How has he hurt you?"

She gained control and wiped her damp cheeks. "Oh, not at all. You can put me down."

The rage faded, and he nuzzled down her cheek to the corner of her lips. "Do I have to?"

"It would be interesting to see how long you can carry me. . . ."

Lucien interrupted this. "Remember we have other business to take care of tonight. We need to find a place to put this until later."

"You fool, Felicity," snarled Rupert, his eyes glinting with rage. "You'll regret this to your dying day."

Then he gasped, clearly because Lucien had tightened his crippling hold. "I fear you're the one who will regret it, Mr. Dunsmore. Bitterly."

Rupert turned pale with fear. "Kill me, and it will get you nowhere! I've given Michael Craig a fine account of your unruly behavior and unhealthy obsession with the boy, Felicity. If he becomes Kieran's guardian, you'll never see the brat again."

His scream made even Miles jump.

"Oh dear," said Lucien, letting his prey go. "I think I've broken something."

Rupert was dead-white and sobbing, clutching his wrist. Felicity couldn't enjoy this and turned her face away. Miles slid her down onto her own feet, still holding her close. "For an Irish warrior-queen, my love, you're a mite squeamish. Let me take you to the carriage, and then I'll come back with a groom to dispose of the rubbish. Lucien has to carry on with Serena's conquest of Society."

Without a backward look, Felicity went with him to a waiting carriage which took her to Emile's, where Beth was calmly presiding over the elegant supper ordered for them all. Soon Lucien and Miles arrived, as unruffled and charming as always.

While trying to play her part, Felicity couldn't help stealing fascinated glances at the marquess, trying to see him for the predator he clearly was.

Was Miles the same beneath his pleasing exterior? He'd said he could kill Rupert if she'd allow it. Perhaps he'd spoken nothing but the truth.

When the official part of the evening was over, Lucien, Miles, and Con gathered to deal with Rupert. Felicity joined them. "You're not leaving me out of this."

"You don't like violence," Miles objected.

"I like sitting home sewing samplers even less."

He shook his head. "If I send you home, you'll just slip out into the streets of London and come searching for us, I suppose."

She grinned. "You know me all too well."

For her ears alone, he murmured, "Not near well enough for comfort, tempting Joy."

So, as they climbed into a carriage, Felicity was humming

with desire and with the hope that soon it would be both possible and sanctified that they exploit it.

A night of loving.

Not just one night. A lifetime of nights.

Like a castle made of diamonds or the moon in her hands, it seemed impossible; and yet, just possibly it was to be hers. She took Miles's hand, sensing him in that small area of skin, drawing through that contact the nurturing her spirit needed.

The gentle flexing of his hand, the slight movement of his thumb against hers, said he was doing the same.

They'd stowed Rupert at Blanche's house, and found him there, tied to the bed. At least, his right arm was tied to a bedpost, but his left was free and bandaged.

Lucien shook his head at Blanche. "You softhearted women."

She snorted. "Remember who you're talking to. I think Mr. Dunsmore understood that he wasn't to try anything."

The frightened look Rupert flashed her confirmed it. But rage replaced fear when he looked at Felicity. "Such a shame about Kieran," he said, as an evil promise.

Felicity flinched inside, but hoped it didn't show.

He's a toothless lion, snarling uselessly.

Toothless.

Toothless.

"If you want the rest of your bones to stay whole," said Miles, quite calmly, "watch your words. By the time we're finished here, you will have no power over the boy at all."

"Oh, will I not? Even the bloody heir to Kilgoran can't steal a father's rights."

Miles perched on a corner of the bed in an almost friendly manner. "But I can take away a father's supposed rights to an estate, can't I?"

Rupert frowned at him in genuine incomprehension. "What?"

"Kieran is not Kathleen's son, so he has no right to Lough-carrick. Therefore, nor do you. Theft, it is. And a whole host of other criminal actions."

Rupert stared at Felicity. "You'd tell the world you're a whore?"

Miles grabbed his shirtfront, but then slowly let it go. "I'll not add to your wounds while you're bound, Dunsmore, but I'll keep a tally."

As a sense of his predicament sunk in, Rupert changed from toothless lion to trapped rabbit. Or trapped weasel, perhaps, for there was plenty of cunning in his eyes along with the fear. "You're bluffing, Cavanagh. You'd never take this before the courts. It's clear you're hot for her. If this comes out, the heir to Kilgoran could never marry such a one."

"I would marry Felicity if her sin were worse than to be cozened into foolishness when still a child."

Rupert turned on Felicity. "You'd brand your son a bastard?"

"To keep him out of your hands, yes. Better a bastard than blind."

He cackled. "You can't take that seriously!"

"Can I not? You killed Gardeen."

"The cat? You're in a fret about a *cat?*"

Sickened by the fact that she had ever let this man touch her, Felicity turned away. "Explain our terms to him."

Miles listed their evidence and the conditions of leniency—that Rupert give the guardianship of his son to the Earl of Kilgoran; that he never reveal the truth about the child's birth; and that he never set foot in Ireland again. In return, he would get a monthly pension for life.

By the time he'd finished, Felicity felt strong enough to turn back and see Rupert's reaction.

"Not setting foot in Ireland will be easy," he sneered, somewhat calmer and a great deal more cunning. "A benighted country peopled by fools. But how will I ever explain why I abandoned my beloved son to strangers?"

Felicity answered that. "For the reason you just gave. You hate Ireland but know your son must be raised there. As for Kilgoran, you need merely claim him as a distant relative of Kathleen's and the most honorable man in Ireland."

"It's as well, then, that we aren't speaking of the *next* earl."

She moved up beside the bed. "Though I confess to being a bit squeamish, I don't think it would be beyond me to black your other eye."

His lips curved into a snarl of pure hate. "Oh, but the part of this I like least is that I'll not have the taming of you, you bitch."

Miles backhanded him into silence.

When Rupert looked up at them, his swollen lip was bleeding and feral fury blazed in his eyes. "Very well," he mumbled. "I accept your terms. To hell with you all."

"He's lying," Felicity said. "He's planning something."

Miles shrugged. "He'll come to his senses when his rage fades." He leaned forward to grasp Rupert's chin. "For he knows, don't you, my beauty, that if he so much breathes in the wrong direction from now on, I will kill him slowly. I have the right, both for what he's done to you and what he planned to do." Quite casually, he untied the man and pushed him toward the table where Lucien was laying out papers.

"Clever of you not to break his writing hand, Luce."

Miles slid some papers in front of Rupert. "This is the trust by which the Earl of Kilgoran becomes completely responsible for Kieran George Dunsmore and his estate, Loughcarrick in County Meath. Sign each page."

For a moment, Felicity thought Rupert would balk; then, fingers white on the pen, he signed.

Lucien and Con came forward to witness the signature.

Then Miles put more papers on the table. "These are the statements we've collected about your son's birth. You can read them if you want. You are to write at the end of each, 'This is a true account of the birth of my son, Kieran George Dunsmore, to Felicity Monahan.' "

Rupert flashed a malignant look at Felicity, but he wrote as commanded at the end of each document. Felicity watched, still sure this wasn't the end they had hoped for. She knew there was a place in Rupert that didn't obey the rules of logic and sense.

"Good boy," said Miles derisively when it was finished. "And now, give me the details of your debts and I'll settle them."

"Why on earth would you do that?" Felicity demanded.

"I've not turned soft in the heart or the head, love. We might as well give him a clean start. A desperate weasel is more dangerous than one who can afford to drown its sorrows."

Rupert turned in the chair to face Miles, and he had regained some of his haughty air. "The sum is a little over five thousand guineas to David Saul of Dublin. If Kieran's trustees had been more flexible about his expenses, the amount would not have been a concern to anyone."

"If they'd been more flexible about expenses, the lad wouldn't have an estate left. I'll pay it. Just remember that, in future, you'd better not game beyond your means."

"Or?" asked Rupert, rising and straightening his rumpled coat one-handed. A slight smile twisted his battered mouth. "You can't kill me, can you? Because if you do, that trusteeship becomes null and void and the child goes to Michael Craig."

"You should have read it before you signed," Miles said. "It supersedes your will and makes Kilgoran—and future Earls of Kilgoran—the boy's guardian even should you die."

Rupert's lips curled almost in a snarl, but he collected himself. "Michael Craig would still have a claim and interest. I think you'll find him very interested."

Miles took Felicity's hand. "Come, love. Let's leave before I do something I might regret."

"I wish you would," she said, with a look of loathing at Rupert.

His naked rage and malice made her flinch. "You won't get away with this," Rupert said almost casually. "You'll never have Kieran."

She whirled and left the room, telling herself that the weasel was toothless. But that declaration of possession terrified her.

On Blanche's landing, Miles pulled her into his arms. "Hush, love. Hush. Don't let him frighten you. There's nothing he can do."

She burrowed closer. "I know, I know. And yet . . . How will we ever be free of him?"

He rubbed her back. "If he bothers you again, I'll kill him and you won't talk me out of it. There's nothing to fear."

Felicity gathered herself and moved back a little. "What of Michael Craig? Rupert's right. He might take an interest. There's a prosperous estate at issue."

"We'll deal with that if it arises. Home now, and a good rest. Within days, we should be able to return to Ireland."

It felt like the first sun after a storm. "Really?"

"Really. But for now," he said with a grin, "you'll have to make do with the squalor of Belcraven House."

When they arrived back at the Palace, they had to tell the whole tale to Beth, who then accompanied Felicity to her room. "You don't look ecstatic."

Felicity held her hands out to the fire. "I fear Rupert's hate will be like a sword of Damocles hanging over our heads. Or over Kieran's. Will we have to keep him under guard forever?"

"Surely Dunsmore will realize there's nothing he can do."

"That assumes he behaves like a reasonable man. Thwarted . . ." Gardeen rubbed against Felicity's ankles, and she picked up the cat for comfort. "Perhaps we should have taken you to the theater, little one. You could have guided us."

"You place a lot of faith in cats."

Felicity stroked the black fur. "She saved me once. . . . I think."

The maid arrived then, and Beth left. Felicity prepared for bed, feeling she should finally be at peace. Instead, she was tormented by the look in Rupert's eyes when he'd said, "You'll never have Kieran."

What might Rupert do to enforce the statement?

The next morning, however, Felicity's fears seemed irrational, a product of shock and exhaustion. She settled to playing the piano until a footman interrupted to say that Mr. Cavanagh required her presence in the rose reception room.

She accompanied the man, wondering why Miles hadn't just come directly to her. When she entered the room, however, she found him entertaining a solid, middle-aged man with grizzled side-whiskers.

Felicity had to choke back a cry of alarm when she recognized Kathleen's cousin, Michael Craig. So soon, Rupert's prediction had proved true.

She managed to greet the man politely, then took a seat, heart racing with alarm. Miles wore a bland look that she couldn't interpret. Mr. Craig was scowling, but then that was always the case.

"Felicity," said Miles, casually crossing one leg over the other, "Mr. Craig has posted down to London with some extraordinary matters to discuss . . ."

He knows!

". . . and I wanted you to be present."

"Foolishness to involve a woman," snapped Mr. Craig. "But if you insist. Miss Monahan, I recently received a letter from Kathleen's husband, a man I do not hesitate to say that I despise. However, he seemed most sincere in his concern that *you* plan to steal his child. That you have, in fact, already succeeded in removing the boy from his home."

Felicity summoned up a blank look. "Steal? Why would I want to steal Kieran?"

Could Rupert actually have told him the truth?

The man pushed out his bottom lip. "He says you have an unhealthy obsession with the boy. You can't deny you've spent plenty of time with him. Kathleen remarked on it."

Felicity's heart-rate settled a little. "I liked Kathleen, and I like Kieran. On her deathbed, she asked me to keep an eye on her son. You can't deny, Mr. Craig, that Mr. Dunsmore is not an ideal father."

"True, true. But that is precisely my concern, Miss Monahan. Knowing as I do how little dependence may be placed on Mr. Dunsmore, I have to take an interest myself in the poor lad. What are you up to?"

Felicity flicked a look at Miles, but he was still bland. Was Mr. Craig's concern genuine, or was he mainly interested in a juicy estate?

"I'm not up to anything, Mr. Craig. The honest truth is that Mr. Dunsmore is inclined to take his ill-humor out on his child. Since Kathleen's death, he's fallen into debt, and his attempts to squeeze more money out of his tenants have angered the local people. He's become quite cruel. When Mr. Cavanagh's mother offered to have the boy visit her, I thought it would be a welcome respite."

Michael Craig rubbed his square jaw. "I doubt he is a kind father. But the boy cannot be kept out of his hands forever. I did offer to take the lad into my own household, but he refused."

And what would have happened to a child who stood between you and an inheritance?

"As to that, Mr. Craig, there is a possibility that Kieran will remain in the charge of the Earl of Kilgoran. Mr. Dunsmore has no real interest in his son and has agreed that such an arrangement would be suitable."

Michael Craig flashed a penetrating look between Felicity

and Miles. To Miles, he said, "And you, I hear, are the heir to Kilgoran."

"For my sins."

"Humph!" He rose to his feet. "I sense all kinds of goings on, but I'm willing to believe you are trying to do your best for the boy. My children are grown and I've no desire to have a young one about anymore. But I give you fair warning," he said, scowling at both of them, "that I will have an eye on the welfare of my cousin's child. It was I who hired Mrs. Edey, you know."

"No," said Felicity. "I didn't. She's an excellent woman."

"Indeed she is. I checked her references most closely. That Dunsmore was apparently going to leave the boy in the care of servants. I hope you intend to keep her on."

"Oh, yes."

"Good." He scowled even more ferociously. "Tell her to write to me. Regularly! The boy will not be undefended."

The man's concern was genuine! Ashamed of her suspicions, Felicity smiled at him. "Mr. Craig, I think Kieran is most fortunate to have you as his relative."

"Ah, well," the man muttered uneasily, "as to that, I wonder if I should have done more. But a father's rights, you know. A father's rights . . ."

"I do understand. But since Mr. Dunsmore has willingly given up his rights, we can all be easy about it."

Mr. Craig nodded. "I hope so. And if young Kieran has need of anything . . . my finances are not at their best just now—a ship gone down and some damned malcontents damaging my manufactory—but I still have enough to help my family. He should not be beholden to strangers."

"We'll remember that."

But as Felicity said farewell to the man, a splinter of unease fretted her.

When Mr. Craig had left, Miles said, "Extraordinary. Behind that grim exterior beats quite a warm heart."

"Kathleen was just like that." Felicity wondered if she

should tell Miles about her concern, but she needed to think about it first.

She thought about it throughout the day, and even through a most entertaining visit to Astley's Ampitheatre.

No amount of thinking could change her mind, however, and that night she pulled on her wrap and slipped down the corridor to Miles's room.

He was in bed, but reading by the light of a candle.

He slept naked.

"What is it?" he asked warily. "I'm in no state to get out of bed."

Felicity wanted nothing more than to slip into bed beside him, but she kept her distance. "Don't worry. I've not come to assault your virtue. I have something I need to talk about."

He put his book aside. "Pass me my banjan and I won't have to offend your modesty."

She laughed as she tossed it over. "It'd be no offense, just temptation, as well you know."

He slipped out of bed and into the garment decently enough and directed her to the two chairs on either side of the glowing fire. When they were seated, it was as safe a situation as it could ever be when they were alone together, never mind half-naked in a bedroom. . . .

She shivered with desire but firmly tamped it down.

"Now, *a muirnin,*" he prompted, "what is it?"

She stared at the glowing coals, not sure how to put her disquiet into words. "I can't feel it's right to seek happiness through lies and theft."

"There are such things as white lies, you know. Ones that lead to good, not evil."

"True . . ."

"Telling the truth about what happened all those years ago would only hurt you and Kieran. It would help no one."

"It would draw Rupert's teeth. He could tell all in spite."

"He'd be mad."

"Sometimes he is mad. But there's another side to this."

"Yes?"

"Michael Craig."

"I thought today's visit would reassure you."

"It did, in a way, but it also disturbed me. Don't you realize? By right, he should have Loughcarrick. That's what I meant by theft. By this deception, we are stealing the property from him, property it's clear he needs. It can't be right."

Miles rested his head back to think, and the firelight glimmered on neck and jaw in a way that could almost distract her from her purpose.

She broke the silence. "I think we have to tell the truth, lance this ancient wound and let the poison run free. That's the only way we can start our life together in honesty."

He lowered his eyes to look at her, smiling slightly. "Our life together. I like the sound of that. But it won't be easy."

"I know."

"You'll be exposed to a great deal of unpleasant attention."

"I know."

"Kieran will be labeled a bastard and a child of scandal."

She gripped her hands together. "I know."

He rose and pulled her to her feet. "The cockeyed honor of a wild patriot-boy. I knew from the first you'd give me trouble."

"You were certainly right."

"How dense of me not to immediately know you'd bring me such joy."

His kiss was almost reverent, but did not lack passion. Felicity returned it in the same spirit. She intended no assault at all, but then—without thought—her hands slipped around him beneath his robe, so he was naked to her, his need apparent . . .

He held her breathlessly close for a long moment, then moved away, retying his banjan. "Two weeks until your birthday."

She found the strength to match his level tone. "I think I'll quite miss having such a stalwart guardian."

"No, you won't," he said absolutely, leading her to the

door. "In fact, I'm setting you free now. It's never sat easy with me to override your will, and since you clearly are not going to give yourself to Dunsmore, there's no more reason to. Whether the truth is told or not is your business, both on your behalf and on Kieran's. I'll help and support you, but I won't force your actions in any way."

Felicity hugged herself. "I feel strangely naked."

He laughed. "Don't put such ideas into my already-weakened brain. You're free. But let's see if we can't think of some way short of public revelation."

Knowing better than to touch him, no matter how much she longed to, Felicity simply said, "I do love you, you know. More than I ever felt it possible to love another adult. It's a disconcerting, weakening kind of emotion, isn't it?"

"Very. Particularly the weakening bit. You are going to marry me on your birthday, aren't you?"

"Do you insist on marriage before giving in to weakness then?"

His eyes were dark with desire. "I'll soon not be in a state to insist upon anything."

"I feel like a mare in heat, and you're behaving very like a stallion." She turned suddenly to hide her face against the cool door. "We're mad!"

He trapped her there with his body, big, hard, hot, his hands over hers. "We should never have let the passion run free that day in the billiard room. There's sense behind chaperoning after all. I'd better remind Beth of it, or one day I'll cover you with as little thought. . . ."

His hips moved against hers, then with a curse, he pushed away to stand at bay on the far side of the room. "No more times alone together, Felicity. None."

She ached for what he wanted but knew he was right.

"I never thought to look forward to a birthday quite this much," she said, and left him in peace.

* * *

Miles spent most of the next day safely out of the house arranging for Rupert's money and its manner of payment. The Rogues had put a watch on the weasel, and it seemed he was staying in his hole nursing his wounds.

Felicity enjoyed the sight of the Rogues in less violent action, easing Serena Middlethorpe into the *haut ton* with hardly a ripple. At the same time, however, she struggled for a way out of her moral dilemma.

She would accept any cost to herself, but she hesitated to tell the truth when both Miles and Kieran would suffer from it.

On the other hand, she felt deeply that nothing could prosper based on the outright dishonesty of depriving Michael Craig of the estate that was legally his.

All day, Felicity's mind went round and round the problem like a turn-spit dog. Then, it threw up a solution.

Twenty-five

The next day, she invited Miles to talk with her in the safety of a stroll around Marlborough Square. Relative safety, anyway. She couldn't be sure they wouldn't scandalize the area by making passionate love next to the duck pond in the center.

"I'm not one for absolute morality," she said, pacing along the flagstones beside her beloved. "Put simply, the only real injustice is that Michael Craig should have the estate."

"True enough."

"As a Liverpool merchant, he may not want the trouble of an Irish property. What if we were to offer him the value of it if he'll give up any claim in favor of Kieran? Legally speaking, right would not have been done, but in a purely moral sense . . ."

Miles looked at Felicity. "Clever. But it can't be done without telling Craig everything."

"I know. But he's sufficiently like Kathleen that I trust him. If I'm wrong, well . . ."

"If you're wrong, he'll make the whole thing public."

Felicity stared rather fixedly at the first yellow blooms on a forsythia poking through the railings around the central garden. "Which could well mean your uncle would forbid our marriage."

"Kilgoran has no power to forbid me anything."

She risked a look at him. "It will make it difficult, though."

He grinned. "With you, I'm used to difficult."

Felicity made a sound of annoyance. "I do wish you'd take this seriously!"

"Why? It seems you can't kill, lie, or steal. It makes you a poor Rogue, but as your future husband, I approve. I hope Mr. Craig is willing to go along with your plan because it will be much more comfortable for you and Kieran. It makes little difference to me, however."

"You mean that. You truly do." Felicity stared at him. "I want to kiss you."

"I think that's why we're out here under the watchful guard of hundreds of windows."

"But I'm a wild Irish wanton." Felicity went into his arms and kissed him anyway. After the first hesitation, he kissed her back, kissed her hungrily in a way that would surely be widening the eyes of anyone watching.

"There," she said when they drew apart, flushed and laughing. "You've compromised me. There's no escape!"

"Faith, and here I was hoping you were compromising me." He dug in his pocket and pulled out a ring-box. When he opened it, a heart-shaped ruby clasped in two hands was revealed. "It's the family betrothal ring. Presumptuous man that I am, I brought it with me from Ireland. You can't wear it yet, but I'd like you to have it."

"From Ireland?" she echoed. "Even while you were gagging me in that coach . . ." She flicked him a glance. "You *are* an optimist, aren't you?"

"Down to the core, and generally proved true. We're going to be wonderfully happy, *a muirnín*. So, will you take the ring?"

She pulled off her glove and held out her left hand. "I'd like to wear it for a moment or two."

He slid it onto her finger, then kissed it there. "I think we were destined. This moment feels powerfully right."

She went into his arms. "How true. And when I think of Gardeen . . ."

He hugged her close. "If we're entangled in Irish magic, let's at least hope it creates one of the happy stories."

She pulled free and took a deep breath. "We'd better start with truth and honesty. Let's visit Michael Craig."

It went off more easily than Felicity had expected. Mr. Craig was shocked, but put the blame squarely on Dunsmore. He agreed that Kathleen had wanted the child she thought of as her true son to inherit her estate. He also agreed that the estate was legally his.

"I have to admit," he said stiffly, "that my financial affairs are rather more precarious than I gave you to understand. If it were just me . . . but I have a wife, a daughter not yet married, and two sons dependent on the business for their bread. I could not in all conscience deprive them of this windfall."

"Nor do you need to do so, Mr. Craig," said Felicity. "The price of the estate is less than half my annual income from my grandfather's property, and the transaction will let me sleep at night. You will have your due, and Kieran will never have to know the truth about his birth."

The man took her hand and patted it. "He'll never know through me, Miss Monahan. May I say that I admire your courage and honesty. And though Kieran is apparently no blood of mine, I'll always have a care for him for Kathleen's sake."

Felicity kissed his cheek, making him redden. "We'll make sure he keeps in touch with you, Mr. Craig. Thank you."

As Miles and Felicity walked out into February sunshine, she spun into a dance, startling a nursemaid. "I feel like spring! New, clean, full of hope. There's still Rupert, but I'll surrender to hope. Rupert will not bother us again."

He caught her hands. "I'll make sure of it. Would you like to go home tomorrow?"

She stared at him. "To Ireland?"

"What other home do we have? There's nothing to keep us here, and I think perhaps you'd like to be with your son."

Felicity flung herself into his arms.

* * *

They traveled in the coach again, with Hennigan and
Gardeen as chaperones. The poor valet climbed in warily, as
if entering a pit of snakes, but soon relaxed when he found
there were to be no more brutalities. Gardeen seemed contentedly relaxed.

The most dangerous times came each evening, as they sat
in the private rooms of inns, alone since Hennigan was with
the other servants and Gardeen generally went to sleep. But,
safe in the knowledge that there were just a couple of weeks
to go, they found the strength to wait.

Their crossing was smooth, and after disembarking the
coach, they had but a day's drive south to Kilgoran Castle.

As they passed through the huge ornate gates, Felicity
turned to Miles. "I do see what you mean about this place
being safe." In her heart, however, she carried a fragment of
doubt which would only disappear when she saw her son,
safe and happy.

"The wall around the estate is only ten feet high," Miles
pointed out. "Hardly an insurmountable obstacle." He waved
to the gatekeepers bowing as the coach went through. "This
is all part of Kilgoran's notion of proper state."

After some time driving along a smooth road between
fields dotted with deer and cattle, Felicity asked, "Where's
the house?"

"Three miles away."

"Lord above. You almost need a posting stage to get from
house to gate!"

"Thinking of backing out yet?"

She put up her hand to feel the ring she wore on a chain
around her neck. "Silly man. If you can accept me after all
that's happened, a daunting estate will not prevent our happiness."

He laughed but added, "Wait till you see the Castle."

They passed through what seemed like endless countryside,

but then a glint of water appeared between trees and soon developed into a lake.

"Is this the boating lake?" It looked dangerous to her. Where was Kieran?

"Lord, no. This is a widened stretch of river and deep enough to drown in. There's fine fishing, though. Look. The Castle's ahead."

At the end of the lake on a rise stood a white Grecian temple. *"That's* a house?"

"Hearth and home of the Earls of Kilgoran. Are you sure you don't want to back out?"

Felicity could think of nothing to say. She could only see the front of the Castle, but it stood four stories high. Huge Grecian pillars ran up the whole height, eight of them, dividing rigid ranks of glittering windows. The whole thing was crowned by a pediment set with some kind of bas-relief.

"I understand the design was based on the Parthenon, and that the pediment recreates some of the Elgin Marbles." Miles directed her attention away from this daunting sight and to the side. "That's the boating lake."

It was quite small, with an island in the center containing a picturesque marble ruin. To one side was a miniature of the temple-house. "Oh, it's a boathouse! That is rather charming."

"I always liked it. More to human scale."

Then a punt skimmed from behind the island, poled by a sturdy young man. A child sat in the back trailing a net.

"Kieran," Felicity breathed. She only half-heard Miles order the coach to stop, and was out before the steps had been let down to fly over the grass to the edge of the lake. "Kieran!" she called, waving.

"Sissity!" He stood, and for a moment she was terrified he would topple out, even if the lake were truly shallow. But the young man said something, and Kieran immediately sat while the boat was poled over to the bank.

She was picking up her skirts to wade to him when Miles

held her back. "Wait here," he said, and she had the sense to obey him.

He climbed down to the edge, his boots protecting him from the mud, and swung Kieran onto the grass. Then, she had her son in her arms.

"I missed you, Sissity," the boy said, but soon squirmed free to say hello to Miles. "This is a funny place, sir. But fun, too." Then he giggled at his own wordplay.

Felicity wanted to snatch him back into her arms and never let go, but Kieran knew nothing of the wars fought over him. To him, she was just a very friendly neighbor. She stood. "And who is your companion?"

"That's Liam. He's my best friend here. Liam!" he called. "This is my friend, Sissity. Felicity," he corrected carefully. "Lady Aideen says I must say your name properly."

"Any way you say it is music to my ears, poppet. Good day, Liam."

The young man touched his forelock. "Good day, miss. Good day, Mr. Cavanagh. If you have care of the child, I'll put the boat away."

The mere idea of letting Kieran go after such a long separation wounded Felicity, but she made herself say, "Well, Kieran? Do you wish to ride up to the house in the coach with us, or do you want to spend more time here?"

It was clearly not an easy choice, but then he said, "Ride, please. I can boat again tomorrow." He waved to Liam and tugged Felicity back up to the coach, already chattering about a variety of servants, animals, and adventures.

And "Uncle Kilgoran."

When they were in the coach again, Miles and Felicity shared startled glances. When Kieran paused for breath, Miles asked, "Do you see much of Uncle Kilgoran?"

"Every evening, sir. He likes to hear a report." And that led into a new spate of matters reported on.

The Castle became if anything more daunting when seen close to. Smooth lawns ran up to white walls unbroken by flowers, shrubbery, or vines. Shallow marble steps climbed to double white doors open to a shiny white interior.

No, Felicity found as they entered to be fussed around by an army of servants, there was color here—in the pale-green niches holding white marble statues.

Thank heavens for Kieran, who seemed unawed by the chilly, echoing space as he introduced her to his favorite servants and statues.

But then Mrs. Edey was there. "Now, Kieran, you mustn't go on so. Miss Monahan and Mr. Cavanagh will be tired after their journey." Though her voice was calm, she looked at Felicity with a worried shadow in her eyes. "Mr. Dunsmore?"

"Seems likely to stay in England," Felicity told her and saw the shadow lift. "I think he intends to ask the earl to take care of Kieran."

"How remarkable." But relief colored Mrs. Edey's cheeks. "Kieran is due for some lessons now. The earl likes to hear him read, and we would not want to disappoint."

Kieran was boy enough to pull a face, but he went without complaint.

"What this place needs," said Miles, "is a whole host of children."

Felicity dragged her gaze from her disappearing child and looked around at marble splendor. "I'm not sure a school full of children could mellow this. But if Kilgoran Castle is our only problem, we'll be blessed."

He kissed her hand. "Then we are blessed."

Then Lady Aideen and Colum were there, hugging and greeting. Within moments, they were in a small, and quite cozy, drawing room, enjoying tea. Without revealing the truth about Kieran's birth, Miles explained that Dunsmore had been persuaded to relinquish control of the boy in return for a regular income.

The mere fact that Lady Aideen did not question this made Felicity think she must suspect the truth. If so, it was not obviously affecting her manner. Miles also told his mother that he and Felicity were to be married on the twentieth which generated only congratulations and smiles.

"Perhaps you should be married here," said Lady Aideen

"Why?" asked Miles with a grimace.

His mother's answer was uncompromising. "Because it's your future home. Felicity, would you mind being married here?"

"I've no particular desire to be married from Foy, but could we not use Clonnagh?"

"I'm afraid the earl cannot travel. He will want to attend."

Felicity reminded herself that the daunting house was a minor problem. "Then certainly I have no objection."

"Excellent! Kilgoran will make it into an excuse for a huge gathering. We must go to Dublin tomorrow to order hasty bride-clothes. I don't suppose you could wait a few more weeks. . . ."

"No!" said Miles and Felicity in unison, then laughed—and blushed—in unison, too.

Aideen and Colum laughed with them, and there was no further talk of delaying the ceremony.

Then Lady Aideen took Felicity to the rooms prepared for her—charmingly decorated in the French style. "A little fancy for my taste," said Aideen, "but at least Kilgoran wasn't mad enough to continue the classical motif throughout."

"The Castle is a little daunting on approach."

"Sensible Miles to win your hand before showing you this place!" She gave Felicity a warm hug. "Sensible Miles all around. I'm going to adore having you as a daughter. Now, have a rest before dinner, for Kilgoran will interrogate you afterward."

That was one of things Felicity was afraid of. Though she was trying to be a carefree optimist, she couldn't help probing for the flaw in her happiness. Perhaps it was Kilgoran. For all Miles's confidence, surely the mighty earl could stop their marriage if he tried. Even though the earl did not know the truth about her, she was hardly the ideal bride for Kilgoran.

Dinner was pleasant, even though attended not just by
Miles, Felicity, Lady Aideen, and Colum, but by about twenty
other people who appeared for the meal like weevils out of
biscuit.

"Connections," Miles murmured by way of explanation and
then had to deflect a great many questions from these people
about his recent doings.

Afterward, Felicity and Miles were summoned into the
earl's presence.

The large room was hot from a leaping fire and crammed
with furniture and books as if the earl had tried to gather his
whole life around him in his dying days. Lord Kilgoran rested
in state in an enormous bed hung with crimson damask, but
there was little to him. Gaunt, yellow, and almost bald, the
only thing truly alive about him was his eyes. But they were
still rapier-keen.

"Come over here and let me see you!"

The fire was burning aromatic apple wood, and potpourri
sat around the room, but nothing could disguise a smell of
age and decay. Poor man, thought Felicity, as she reached the
side of the bed. It's a sad way to drag out the end of a
powerful life.

"Miles, my boy!" The old man held out a bony hand, and
Miles took it in a firm grasp. Respect was clear on both
sides, but probably no more than that. "You're looking well.
Heard you had an injury. You need to take more care of yourself. At least until you've produced an heir or two."

"Speaking of which," said Miles, "may I present my bride-
to-be, Miss Felicity Monahan of Foy." He put Felicity's hand
in his uncle's, which felt like paper over bone. She squeezed
it very gently.

The sharp blue eyes studied her. "Foy, eh? I see the attraction. He's after your stud."

Felicity couldn't resist. "We do share a great interest in
riding, my lord."

Miles pinched her, but not hard.

"Good, that. Married couples need something in common, and riding is a fine sport. And he's been your guardian, hasn't he? Have you led him a merry chase?"

"What else is a young woman to do in such a situation?"

He chuckled. "Go away, Miles. I want to talk to your bride."

Miles made no complaint, but merely pulled over a chair for Felicity and squeezed her shoulder slightly in encouragement before leaving.

She needed the comfort. Her heart was pounding with apprehension.

"Saw that," said Kilgoran. "Does he think I'm going to eat you? I can only eat pap these days anyway. You don't look terrified."

"I'm not, my lord," she lied.

"Call me Kilgoran. I'm very fond of Miles, you know."

Felicity could think of nothing to say but "oh."

"I'm happy to leave all this to him, but I know he'd rather I'd had sons of my own."

"It will be a responsibility."

"It's a demmed mausoleum. Seemed a good idea at the time. Show the world we're not bog-dwelling peasants here in Ireland. . . . But enough of that. Tell me why you love him."

Felicity flinched under the sharp demand. "I don't know that I can."

"Must be something about him you like."

"Everything."

Perhaps the twist of the lips was a smile. A hint of a laugh was drowned under a dry cough. "Fair enough. I thought *you* might be after *his* stud."

"I'm a great heiress, as it happens."

"Are you, indeed? They didn't tell me that, blast their eyes. Good for Miles, then. You can have plenty of children and provide for them all."

"There is that."

"And you'll brighten this place. I could see the ties between you, like light dancing. That's what's needed here. I loved a woman like that once. She died."

It was snapped out brusquely, but another Irish tragedy lurked behind the words.

"Perhaps it was for the good," he muttered. "I'd not have had the time to devote to Ireland had Mary lived."

"Then I hope Ireland doesn't need the same devotion from Miles. I've no mind to be a martyr to the cause."

"Hah! I like a woman who can speak her mind. I'll enjoy having a daughter. I think of Miles as my son, you know." His lips twisted in a wry smile. "They thought it was strategy, my wanting to raise him here, but it was selfish greed. You've brought me a rare gift in young Kieran. I gather I'm to have charge of him."

He suddenly fixed her with a sharp look. "His mother was a bit long in the tooth."

"I suppose . . ."

"And he has your chin. Does Miles know?"

Felicity was gaping. "Yes," she breathed.

"Good." A clock struck the half-hour. "Go away. It's time for him to report to me."

Felicity left in a daze. Kieran was waiting outside with Mrs. Edey, twitching restlessly. If the earl enjoyed Kieran, it was clear the pleasure was shared. He ran in, already telling "uncle" something about duckweed.

Mrs. Edey entered and closed the door, and Felicity turned away, experiencing another disorienting twist. When she saw Miles waiting a little further down the corridor, she went to him.

"Did he upset you?" he asked.

"No. Why?"

"You look sad."

She sighed. "It's only just occurred to me that we've arranged things so that Kieran will never call me mother."

He took her hand. "You can tell the whole truth if you want."

She shook her head. "The greatest burden would fall on Kieran. But thank you for the freedom to choose."

They strolled down the long corridor. "So Kilgoran didn't frighten you. I'm glad. He's not always an easy man."

"He's clever.

"Oh, yes, he's certainly that."

"Miles, he knows."

He stopped and looked at her. "About Kieran?"

"Yes. He must have made enquiries. He knows Kathleen was old for childbearing. He sees a resemblance. What if he—"

He placed his fingers over her lips. "He's not going to say anything. Stop fretting about every little thing, love. Kieran's safe. My uncle approves. All our troubles are over, and on your birthday, we marry."

"I still can hardly believe . . ."

He looked at her and shook his head. "Thomasina. It will be so. Trust me."

For his sake, she wanted to believe, but a saw-blade of doubt still fretted her. "I'm trying," she said. "very hard."

He escorted her to her room, talking soothingly of ordinary things, but left her at the door.

Felicity went into her room determined to try harder. All her reasons for fear had been wiped away.

She'd still be happier if time could pass in an instant, though.

She wanted it to be her wedding day *now*.

Twenty-six

The next day, Lady Aideen dragged Felicity off to Dublin. Miles begged off the trip, almost with horror, and Felicity wished she could, too. She was not allowed to take Kieran, which made her even more unwilling.

"Women are supposed to show a little interest in adornment, you know," Lady Aideen teased as they studied designs at the modiste's.

"I like a pretty dress as well as the next woman," Felicity replied, "but I can't summon any interest in the virtues of Scotia silk as opposed to merino crape, or cambric's superiority to jaconet."

"And you want to be back at Kilgoran."

Lady Aideen's knowing smile doubtless referred to Miles, but Felicity was just as desperate to be with Kieran.

She wondered if *this* were the problem she feared—that Miles would be jealous of her love for her son. But when they rolled back down the long drive toward the Castle, they encountered three horsemen—Miles, Liam, and Kieran on a gray pony.

Kieran waved gleefully but showed no sign of wanting to join her in the coach. Felicity waved back and let the coach continue without pause.

Perhaps the problem would be that she would be jealous of her son's love for Miles.

* * *

Felicity had written to Annie to inform her of the arrangements and invite her to the wedding. When the reply came, however, it was to say that Annie didn't want to leave her cats but expected Felicity and Miles to visit her before the wedding.

Felicity took the letter to Miles. "I suppose there are matters to be taken care of at Foy. I don't know how Aunt Annie will get along alone."

"She's hardly alone, and if the rest of the cats are like Gardeen . . ."

"Don't be silly. Perhaps we should arrange for a companion. Do you mind the journey?"

"A day in a coach with you?" he asked with a smile. "Not at all."

"And what of all our fine resolutions?"

"Consider it a test of strength."

She shook her head. "Annie suggests we bring Kieran, so he and Mrs. Edey can be our chaperones."

"Don't forget Gardeen."

"Gardeen seems more attached to Kieran these days than to you or me. I do wonder why Annie's so insistent that we take Kieran, and how much she knows. She generally does seem to know the important things."

"Then perhaps she knows we need chaperones."

Felicity laughed, but a problem niggled her. "Is it safe to take Kieran away from here?"

"Stop worrying, *a muirnín.* Dunsmore's far from here."

Felicity couldn't help but be concerned, but she had to admit that Miles's optimistic forecasts had proved correct thus far. So, the next day, they set off in a coach, chaperoned by Mrs. Edey, Kieran, and a small black cat who now seemed firmly attached to Kieran.

"Fickle creature, isn't she?" Miles remarked.

"Perhaps she goes where she's most needed," said Felicity, then pushed away the idea that Kieran might need a special guardian. After all, Kilgoran had insisted that Liam and another groom come along as outriders.

Certainly the trip passed without incident.

At Foy, Annie greeted them quite cheerfully. "Good. You can take the horses."

"Take them?" asked Felicity, who'd hardly had time to remove her gloves.

"Wedding present. The Foy horses."

Miles and Felicity shared a look.

"That's a magnificent gift, Miss Monahan," said Miles.

"I don't want them. Nasty big brutes. You can use them. All settled." Then her deceptively wandering gaze settled on Kieran. "And here's the boy."

Since there was no way to tell how much Annie knew, Felicity gave her a quick explanation of the guardianship.

Annie nodded. "Very suitable arrangement. As is your marriage. Fitzgerald and Monahan. Good breeding stock." She looked at Gardeen. "You've done well, little one."

Then she trundled off, trailed by cats. But not Gardeen, who stayed on guard by Kieran.

"Breeding stock," said Miles, rolling his eyes. "I don't want to know."

"It *can't* all have been planned. . . ."

Miles laughed. "In Ireland, who's to tell? But I have no argument with the plan as long as we don't end up spell-cast into swans or turned into standing stones."

"Don't," said Felicity with a shiver.

He pulled her into his arms since they were safely guarded by all three chaperones. "And don't you take any of this seriously. We've dealt with one petty villain. Any other problems will be of the same mundane type."

He sounded a little too hearty about it, however. She looked up at him. "And what of a small cat buried near a sundial?"

His smile faded. "Very well, oh believer in total honesty, whatever magic there is in this seems to be working in our favor. Let's trust ourselves to it."

Trying to convert to his optimistic way of thinking, Felicity pushed aside worries and set herself to coping with practical matters.

The next day, a messenger pounded up with a message for Miles, a message sent on from Clonnagh.

As he broke the seal, Felicity tried to suppress panic, but when she saw him frown, it broke free. "What is it? What *is* it?"

"Nothing to worry about . . ."

"Miles!"

He sighed. "Dunsmore's given his watchers the slip. Lucien has no idea where he is. But he won't come to Ireland. What point would there be . . ."

"Kieran!" Felicity ran to find him.

He was safely working on his counting skills with Mrs. Edey.

Felicity controlled herself. She couldn't force her son to live in fear. Of course Rupert had resented being watched. But he had no reason at all to come to Ireland.

She remembered his saying, "You'll never have Kieran."

But Kieran no longer represented money to him. He wouldn't care . . .

Felicity took the governess aside for a moment to caution her not to leave the house without Liam in attendance. When she left the temporary schoolroom, however, Miles was waiting for her, frowning.

"I'm going to have to kill the weasel," he said, "just to give you some peace. Felicity, you can't go on like this."

"I can't help being afraid. Perhaps, in time . . ."

"Let's hope so."

Felicity watched him walk away, knowing this irrational terror could be the crack that would destroy their chance of happiness. As he said, they couldn't live like this.

As a result, she made herself not hover over Kieran. He had Mrs. Edey and Liam. Nothing could happen to him even if Rupert turned up.

But still, she put the word out among the local people to watch for Rupert Dunsmore, and to tell her if he were sighted.

The worst time was when they took Kieran to visit Lough-carrick, but no one there had seen Rupert and, in fact, they had received orders to send his belongings to an address in London.

"See," Miles said as they left. "He doubtless just gave the watchers the slip because he had no mind to be supervised."

"Yes, of course," said Felicity. "But I'll be glad to be back in Kilgoran."

Miles laughed and kissed her. "I think I owe Rupert Dunsmore a debt of gratitude. I never imagined any bride of mine saying such a thing."

Back at Foy, Kieran asked to play outside with Gardeen. After making sure Liam and Mrs. Edey would stay with him, Felicity permitted it, even though the winter dusk was settling.

"See how brave I'm getting," she said to Miles, refusing to watch her son from the window.

He rubbed the back of her neck as if he knew she was tight there. "I've never doubted your courage. But if you don't learn to relax, you'll shatter."

She flexed her neck back against his soothing touch. "Mmmmm. That does feel wonderful."

So he sat her on the sofa and gently massaged her neck until the tension eased away.

"Miss Monahan!"

Felicity sat straight up to see Mrs. Edey run into the room, red-faced. "Kieran! He's gone!"

"What?" Felicity shot to her feet, heart thundering.

The woman collapsed, panting, into a chair. "He was playing with . . . Gardeen in the garden. I was writing a . . . letter. The cat leaped on me and my pages blew about." She put a hand to her chest and tried to catch her breath. "I ran . . . to gather them and when I turned back . . . they were both gone!"

"Liam?" asked Miles.

"He'd gone. There was a shriek. . . . He went to check. . . ."

"How long ago was this?" demanded Felicity, gripping the woman's arm. "It's getting dark."

"Perhaps a quarter of an hour," said the woman, starting to shake. "I tried to find them. How could they all just disappear? But there's a mist . . ."

Servants were gathering, and Miles ordered one to bring brandy for the woman. "Where were you?" he asked.

"In that sheltered corner near the stables." She pushed to her feet. "I'll go and search again."

"No, you stay here." The brandy came, and Miles had her take a sip before he organized the inside staff to search the house and gardens and sent a message to the village.

Felicity left him to it and ran toward the stables.

She almost ran into Annie. "Kieran's disappeared!"

"With Gardeen?"

"I think so."

"Then he'll be all right."

"Oh, Aunt, what can that small cat do? Rupert killed her once. Or, at least . . ." She put her hands to her spinning head. "I have to find him. I have to. . . . Have you seen anything?"

"Just cats and mist. I'll look around. Don't you worry, dear." She ambled off.

Then Miles was there. "What did Annie say."

"Not to worry," Felicity snapped bitterly. "That Gardeen would look after him." Then she turned to stare at the spot where the gloom had swallowed her aunt.

"What?" he asked.

"She had no cats with her. . . ."

"Devil take it, that's hardly to the point, Felicity!"

"God, you're right." She raced toward the stables.

The grooms were already scouring the area. "Nothing, Miss," said her head groom. "But one of the men thought he heard a horse in the lane a while back."

Felicity turned on Miles. "Rupert!"

"It can't be." But he was already speaking to the groom. "Your best horse."

"And Dana," said Felicity. "Just bridle them." She ran into the tack room and slit her wool gown front and back. By the time she was done, Dana was ready. She grasped the mane and swung onto the horse, then cantered out of the stables, Miles by her side.

They soon came across searchers who just shook their heads. But in the next bunch, there was one who'd seen a horseman. "Heading to Monagal!"

"Did he have a child?"

"No way to tell, Miss."

Miles and Felicity turned that way. "What's there?" he called. "Bog, I suppose."

"Indeed. The English Bog, it means."

They speeded in that direction but paused again to check with another group of men whose lanterns waved eerily in the dark.

"Haven't seen a rider, but I've seen a devil of a lot of cats."

"Cats?"

"All over the place. All heading for Monagal."

"Annie!" Miles and Felicity exclaimed together, then frowned at each other in total bewilderment.

"If she's hurt Kieran, I'll . . ." Felicity kicked her horse to a gallop despite the dark.

Blessedly, the moon rode out from behind the clouds.

Lights flashed ahead.

For a moment, Felicity thought they were more lanterns, but then she realized it was the moonlight in cats' eyes. A mass of cats running toward her. Hunting cats.

Hunting a man.

A man who was running after a small child.

Felicity kicked her horse forward, then tumbled off to seize her sobbing son and hold him close, wishing she had a pistol to turn on Dunsmore.

Miles rode past her. Someone had a pistol.

A crack.

A flash.

A shriek.

All from ahead.

Miles's horse reared with a scream, throwing him.

Clutching Kieran in her arms, Felicity staggered forward to where Miles had rolled free of his horse's thrashing hooves. Up ahead, Rupert seemed to be fighting.

He was flailing at cats.

A cat must have leaped on him even as he fired that shot, ruining his aim.

"Hush, hush," she soothed her son. To Miles, she said, "Are you all right?"

"Just winded." He scrambled to his feet. Then he looked ahead. "What the devil . . ."

"It's the cats," gulped Kieran. "They saved me. Papa took me. The cats made his horse rear."

Felicity held him even tighter. Rupert was running now, running away from them, away from the cats.

"Papa wanted to throw me in the bog."

Miles and Felicity shared an appalled glance. "Just a joke," Miles said.

Kieran fought Felicity, and she had to put him down. "Not a joke! He said you wouldn't ever have me, Sissity. He *hurt* me. I *can't* honor my father. I can't. I don't care what the Bible says! I don't care!"

Miles pulled him into his arms. "You don't have to, Kieran. And he'll never hurt you again. I promise it."

The boy clung to him, sobbing.

Felicity reached for her son, but another panicked shriek ripped through the air. She stared ahead and saw Rupert change direction again, tormented by a river of sinuous, predatory bodies. He screamed for help.

"We should do something," she whispered.

"No," said Miles firmly. He stood with Kieran in his arms and put an arm around her. It was confining as well as comforting.

"What of my freedom now?"

After a moment, he withdrew his arm. "You are free. But if you try to save that weasel from his fate, I'll doubt your sanity."

Rupert's voice was shrill now, panicked, cursing and pleading. Felicity gripped her hands together and stayed still. He deserved this, and it was strangely right that the cats be his doom.

Clouds drifted over the moon so she could hardly see anything, but she heard a wilder scream and a splash which must mean the cats had finally driven him into the bog.

From the hiss, one would almost think he'd been hot iron plunged into a bucket. The hiss of an army of cats.

"Is it deep there?" Miles asked.

"Very." Then Felicity gasped when something brushed her ankle. She looked down to see Gardeen.

She picked up the small cat and stared into glinting eyes. "I don't want to know anything about this."

Gardeen just miaowed, then leaped over to where Kieran was still in Miles's arms. With that comfort and guard, the boy demanded to be put down. He seemed to already be shaking off his terrifying experience.

Felicity looked out over the field and saw the cats, like the night-predators they were, slipping silently away in the dark. "Surely there were more cats here than even Annie has."

"And Colum said she would have revenge on anyone who hurt one of her cats. But cats can't . . ."

"You'd be amazed what cats can do."

"Not anymore. Stay here," he said to all of them and went forward to look at the pool.

He returned in a few moments. "We'll have to drag to find the body." He helped Felicity onto the horse's back and lifted

Kieran up to sit with her, Gardeen in his arms. Then he mounted himself, and they walked slowly back toward Foy.

Kieran didn't seem particularly distressed, but Felicity felt she had to speak of it. "I think your father's dead, poppet."

"The cats killed him," said Kieran, stroking Gardeen. "I like cats."

"I don't think they killed him," she lied, "so much as he was scared of them and ran into the bog to escape them."

"I'll bet they killed him. He killed the kitchen cat at home when he found it above stairs. Hanged it."

Felicity held him close and gave up trying to whitewash the case.

When they reached Foy, they found Annie once more attended by cats and actually caring for Liam in the kitchen, for the man had been found in the garden knocked out cold.

"I'm terrible sorry, sir," said Liam. "I heard a shriek and saw a cat looking injured. When I bent to care for it, someone knocked me out."

Since there was no sign of Rupert's having an accomplice, Felicity couldn't help looking at Annie, who was the one most likely to be assisted by a cat.

But what point was there in stirring such matters now?

The next day, Rupert's body was recovered and taken to Loughcarrick. Sir Dennis Yeates, the local magistrate, quickly declared the death an unfortunate accident. Funeral arrangements were left in the hands of the Loughcarrick servants, who all seemed delighted to have the task.

Felicity and Miles prepared to return to Kilgoran.

Felicity tried to talk of the affair to Annie, but the older woman had once more turned vague. The only thing she said to the point was, "It will be a great relief to the area to have that man gone."

Twenty-seven

The second time Felicity drove up to it, Kilgoran Castle was not quite as startling. She pictured prime horseflesh roaming the extensive pastures, and could almost imagine becoming fond of it. The interior was improved, too. With three days to the wedding, some guests had already arrived and mere numbers were taking the chill off the place.

"There's to be sixty guests," said Aideen with a slightly wary look at her son. "I'm sure you'd rather a simpler affair, but Kilgoran insisted."

"I can bear anything," said Miles, "just so long as it is done."

Felicity silently echoed that.

She found that Lady Aideen had the arrangements well in hand, so she spent her time boating with Kieran or playing cricket with him, Miles, and Liam.

Waiting.

Waiting.

All waiting must end, however, and Felicity's birthday and wedding day finally arrived, accompanied by brilliant sunshine and the first aching green of spring.

The green of hope.

The green of fast-running desire.

Even Kilgoran Castle was mellowed by the host of guests and their servants. The cream of the Irish aristocracy was present, and Miles was supported by the Marquess and Marchioness of Arden, Sir Stephen Ball, and Lord Amleigh.

Felicity's wedding dress was a silvery green, embroidered in silver and seed pearls. Beth attended her, supervising the dressing of her hair and putting on the pearl jewelry.

"Are you nervous?" Beth asked in surprise. "You seem tense."

"Nervous?" echoed Felicity. "I'm just desperate!" Then, when the other woman laughed, she blushed and hid her face in her hands.

But it was true.

These last few days had perhaps been the hardest, for there had been nothing to do but wait. There had not even been any worries to distract her.

Rupert was dead.

Kieran's birth was a secret that would never be told.

She was safe and could at last hope for true happiness.

And that was what had made the waiting so hard. Every day, every hour, the thought teased her that all barriers were gone. They were to marry. There was no reason to wait.

Except that they had set themselves this test, like heroes of old, that they would prove worthy of the greatest prize by being true and honorable despite temptation. They would not be like Diarmuid and Grania, stealing happiness at the expense of others or against the moral code.

They would wait until the sanctioned time.

Aching need had been the price they'd paid, but there had been rewards. The waiting days had provided opportunities to talk, to think, to learn in silent ways the secrets of each other's soul.

But now, as she said, the time was close and she was desperate.

Why had they agreed to this foolishly immense affair? They could have gone to the chapel, said their vows, and been done with it. Instead, there was to be a long ceremony—with a choir, no less—followed by a reception for the honored guests and another in a nearby village for the tenants.

People had apparently gathered from miles around to catch

a glimpse of the next earl and his bride. Though they were to be married at noon, they'd be lucky to be alone before midnight.

When Felicity checked herself in the mirror before going down, however, she was pleased to be so fine for this special day.

For Miles.

The color suited her, and the simplicity of the cut lent her dignity. The delicate lace veil muted the strong black of her hair. Today, she was not a warrior-queen, and she hoped never to have to fight again.

Certainly not to fight against Miles.

The Castle chapel was not big enough to hold all the guests, so the ceremony was to take place in the ballroom. As she entered, Felicity smiled to see Kieran in a fine silk suit holding a cushion bearing the ring. Beside him sat a small black cat with a white ribbon around its neck.

And beside both of them was Miles, smiling back at her as if she were the most wonderful creature in the world.

No woman deserved to be so loved.

Except that she loved him just as much.

Though she was trying hard to be demure, she couldn't help the enormous grin that stretched her face. Though she tried to walk with slow dignity, the old wildness surged in her and she picked up her skirts and ran into his arms.

As the congregation burst out laughing, he swung her around in a great swirl of perfumed silk and lace.

When he put her down, she hid her face in his shoulder. "I'm *never* going to be a suitable Countess of Kilgoran."

He tilted her chin so she met his smiling eyes. "You're going to be a perfect Countess of Kilgoran. Let's take the first step."

And her smile broke free again. They had suffered their trials, won their battles, and deserved this triumphant moment.

The dignified clergyman's lips were twitching as he performed the service. The choir's songs seemed to truly be a paean of joy. When the minister gave Miles permission to kiss the bride, Miles took it to heart and kissed her most enthusiastically. After they'd signed the register, they led the party to the reception in the drawing room.

Though the earl hadn't felt able to attend the ceremony, he was at the reception on a daybed. He blessed their union, then settled to talking politics with all his old cronies.

The three visiting Rogues all kissed the bride enthusiastically, but then there were just many, many hours of smiling at strangers before Miles and she could be together in sanctioned bliss.

But she could wait.

Finally, he was hers.

Hers, for eternity.

It wasn't midnight, but darkness had long since settled by the time Felicity could go to her room and prepare for bed. It was a new room, one adjoining Miles's suite and decorated in a strongly Chinese style. She didn't care about decor, however, only that Miles come to her soon.

She hurried her maid through the undressing, but then found herself having to wait, trembling slightly, dressed only in a fine silk nightgown.

The trembles were not fear, but need.

Biting her lip, she realized Miles was probably waiting, too, making sure she had long enough.

How ridiculous.

She thought of going to him, but really, just once, she should act the proper lady. And anyway, how could she know he wasn't involved in some strange male rite? A fine scene it would be for her to walk in on the Rogues when dressed only in transparent silk.

She looked at herself in the mirror.

Truth to tell, she looked enticing. The fine silk only veiled her body, and her hair was a dark cloud. Her eyes were deep dark with desire, too, and her cheeks flushed with it.

She suspected, however, that a bride was supposed to be pale with apprehension rather than rosy with lust.

When Miles came in, she said, "Do you mind that I'm not a virgin?"

He laughed. "What?"

She was in his arms. "A man deserves a virgin bride."

"As punishment for his sins?" He threaded his hand into her hair and made her look up at him. "*A muirnín,* I'm anticipating a night of pleasure I would never even contemplate with a virgin bride."

She surrendered to his searing kiss, tangling her hands in his hair to hold him close for her own possession.

Mine.

He slid his hands down her back and cupped her buttocks, pulling her hard against him.

Mine.

"Sure and silk is a marvelous fabric," he murmured, sliding it over her skin.

She dragged open his robe to press hand against flesh. "You'll have to dress in silk for me then."

He laughed against her neck, nibbling her. "For you, *mo chroí,* anything."

She pushed off his robe and stood back to study him, aware of the way her breathing wavered.

Aware of his.

Hand to muscular chest—rising, falling—down over belly, over navel . . . touch his full erection, lightly, gently, teasing the leashed power.

"And isn't it interesting," she murmured, delighting in the way he quivered under her tormenting, "that what we are about to do is blessed by God and man?"

"Fair warning," he said, brushing an unsteady hand equally lightly over her sensitive nipples. "Some of it might not be."

It sent a shiver through her, but she still didn't go into his arms, wanting to see how long, after such long waiting, he could wait.

She wandered behind him, trailing her fingers around his ribs.

"Mine." This time she said it aloud. She ran her hands up over his beautiful back and down over his tensed and powerful buttocks.

"Mine."

She could hear his breathing now, feel his body move with it.

"In this I am a virgin," she said. "In this frightening knowledge that we have a lifetime . . ."

"Don't be too sure of that. At any moment, I might explode."

Laughing, she kissed him in the warm hollow of his spine between his shoulder blades, then collapsed down, trailing her tongue to the cleft, sliding her hands forward to grasp him.

"Will you look at this," she said, resting her head against his buttocks, "you've finally brought me to my knees."

He tore out of her arms. "If I remember, Sweet Joy, that's when you're most dangerous."

He pulled her up and tossed her on the bed. "Remember this place? It can be remarkably comfortable."

Seething with excitement at his desperate need, Felicity rolled to sit on the coverlet. "You seem to have more experience of beds than I, husband dear. I'll let you take charge."

"Wonders will never cease." He pulled the sheets and blankets from under her, tipping her flat on her back so the silk rucked up.

Then he covered her, entered her.

Felicity squeaked with shock and pleasure, then held him tight, tighter as he began to move.

"In a hurry are we?" she gasped.

"We've had a whole damn month of foreplay, and you've finally driven me stark, staring mad. . . ."

And she could see it was the wonderful, delicious truth.

She locked her legs around him and set to making him lose his sanity entirely.

It was astonishingly easy.

Later, hand tracing love-patterns on his chest, she said, "Perhaps, we should try a month of foreplay again sometime."

He laughed, drawing her into a ferocious hug. "Not on your life, sweet Joy. Not on your precious life."

Author's Note

The Irishness of this book took me by surprise.

Back in 1977, when I wrote the first draft of *An Arranged Marriage*, I threw in one Irish Rogue just to be different. Then, when I was writing *Forbidden*, I tossed in some comments about Miles and smuggling trouble, and even brought Felicity on scene. As you will have seen in reading *Dangerous Joy*, characters don't always know what other characters are really doing.

(Which is an author's way of saying, the story changed on me and I had to do some fancy footwork to dance out of the corner I'd landed in!)

But all I intended when I started this book was to tangle Miles and Felicity together in the unwanted guardianship and then get them to Melton where they could have a normal, Roguish adventure.

I hadn't banked on the Irish temperament, or on Irish cats!

I do come to this honestly, however, having a solidly Irish family tree and having grown up in the North of England surrounded by plenty of Irish influences.

But the book surprised me—I love it when one does—and I found myself dealing with magic and ancient myths, with strange people and even stranger animals. It came to seem quite suitable, however, since magic and ancient myths are also dangerous joys, in my opinion.

For those not familiar with the story of Diarmuid and Grania, let me briefly tell it here.

Grania, a beautiful Irish princess, daughter of the High King, was betrothed to the great Irish hero, Finn mac Cool, even though he was by then old. Now Finn, like Arthur, had a mighty band of devoted warriors called the Fianna, a brotherhood bound together by sacred vows.

At the wedding feast, Grania—clearly dissatisfied by the man chosen to be her husband—sees Diarmuid, one of the Fianna's most noted warriors, and also a young and handsome man. In fact, he was called Diarmuid of the Love-Spot, for he had been marked by faery so that he would be irresistible to all women.

Poor Grania, you see, was helpless under the power of magic. This powerlessness is often a feature of these stories, and I tried to weave it into *Dangerous Joy* in so far as we modern readers are willing to accept any leash on our free will.

Grania decides to pursue Diarmuid and prepares a magic potion to put him under a "geas," a magic compulsion. To me, this seems pretty fair, since his love-spot has done the same thing to her. In the telling of the story, however, Grania is usually portrayed as a weak and wicked Delilah stealing the will of the heroic Samson.

Diarmuid fights against the magical compulsion, but he is helpless and must aid Grania's flight from Tara. He tries to keep the relationship a non-sexual one, but Grania seduces him, thus severing him forever from his fellows and his lord.

Finn and the Fianna pursue them, of course; but in a number of encounters, Diarmuid always prevails. Eventually, peace is made between them, and Grania and Diarmuid can live together.

But, as Miles and Felicity acknowledge in this book, most Irish stories end with blood and weeping.

Eventually, Grania is not satisfied with being left in peace. She wants Finn to come to her home as an honored guest. Diarmuid is not happy at the thought but gives in and sends the invitation. Though Finn appears to come in friendship, he sets up a situation in which Diarmuid is killed by a wild boar. He then manages to sweet-talk Grania out of her grief and take her back with him as his bride.

As you can see, this story is told as one of heroes betrayed, but like most history or myth, it is told by men for men. Here we have the wicked seductress undermining a great man's strength and leading him to misery and destruction, then being herself entirely conquered in the end.

We can see it, instead, as the story of a woman betrayed (by her father into an unwanted marriage) fighting for some trace of happiness with a more appealing man—a man, moreover, to whom she is attracted because of his own magic powers. Does Diarmuid take responsibility for the power of his love-spot? No. Even though he's doubtless used it to seduce many a poor woman, when he comes across one as tough and determined as he is, he whines and moans across half of Ireland.

And I'll bet it was his idea to throw a party for his old friends, too!

Enough of revisionist mythology, however. *Dangerous Joy* is by no means a retelling of Diarmuid and Grania, or even a parallel story; but there are small echoes of it, drawn up out of the magical Irish earth.

And what about the cats? I do hope you weren't too upset by the death of little Gardeen. As you see, she does come back in triumph, and has a part to play in Rupert Dunsmore's well-deserved fate.

There is a list of my books at the end of this note, but I have to warn you that many are unavailable at the moment. They have sold out, and they seem to be "keepers" that don't turn up in used-book stores. Do ask your bookseller to check with the publisher, however. I'm hoping that the earlier Rogues books will be reissued soon. If you want to be kept informed, write to the address at the end and you'll be on my mailing list.

My next book out will be *The Shattered Rose,* a medieval about a married couple who still love one another in the deepest way, but whose marriage is threatened by betrayal. There is also a secondary couple; a charming, womanizing Frankish knight, and a sensible northern girl who *had* intended to become a nun.

As you can see, I don't always write the same kind of book; but readers tell me that that's what they like about my novels—that they can never be too sure what they're in for when they open one, other than interesting characters and a good story.

Keep your eyes open for three novella stories coming up.

I have a story in the 1995 collection, *A Regency Christmas*. In *A Mummer's Play*, Justina Travers infiltrates the Duke of Cranmoore's palatial home as part of a group of mummers. She is there to destroy the man she believes responsible for the death of her husband-to-be in the war. In trying to tear away the disguise of a traitor, however, she too is stripped down to truth on Christmas Eve.

Forbidden Affections will be in an anthology called *Summer Love*, out in May 1996. Miss Anna Featherstone is only sixteen, and should never even meet a man like the Earl of Carne. When she does, he doesn't know what's hit him. Literally!

A story, perhaps called *The Lord of Elphindale*, will be in the *Midnight Weddings* collection, to be published in June 1996. In this story, Gwen Forsythe is astonished—and as skeptical as you can imagine—when told she's half-Faery, and must woo and win Sir Andrew Elphinson in marriage. She's not reluctant—she's loved Drew since they were children. The problem is that he's on the point of offering marriage to someone else.

I hope you enjoy these stories.

I have signed bookplates for all my books. For bookplates, to be on my mailing list, or just to talk about my books, please write c/o the Alice Orr Agency, 305 Madison Ave. #1166, New York NY 10165. I appreciate an SASE to help with the cost of a reply.

For those of you who are into cyberspace, I can also be reached on the Internet at ab439@freenet.carleton.ca

Or as JO.B on the GEnie computer network, which has a thriving board just for romance readers and writers.

Here is a complete list of my books to date:

Traditional Regencies
Lord Wraybourne's Betrothed, 1988
The Stanforth Secrets, 1989
The Stolen Bride, 1990
Emily and the Dark Angel, 1991 (RITA Winner)
The Fortune Hunter, 1991
Deirdre and Don Juan, 1993 (RITA Winner)

Rogues Regencies
An Arranged Marriage, 1991 (Reader's Choice Award)
An Unwilling Bride, 1992 (RITA Winner; Golden Leaf Award)
Christmas Angel, 1992 (Reader's Choice Award)
Forbidden, 1994
Dangerous Joy, 1995

Georgians—Malloren series
My Lady Notorious, 1993 (RITA winner; Golden Leaf Award)
Tempting Fortune, 1995

Medievals
Lord of My Heart, 1992
Dark Champion, 1993
The Shattered Rose, Zebra, May 1996.

ZEBRA'S REGENCY ROMANCES
DAZZLE AND DELIGHT

A BEGUILING INTRIGUE (4441, $3.99)
by Olivia Sumner

Pretty as a picture Justine Riggs cared nothing for propriety. She dressed as a boy, sat on her horse like a jockey, and pondered the stars like a scientist. But when she tried to best the handsome Quenton Fletcher, Marquess of Devon, by proving that she was the better equestrian, he would try to prove Justine's antics were pure folly. The game he had in mind was seduction—never imagining that he might lose his heart in the process!

AN INCONVENIENT ENGAGEMENT (4442, $3.99)
by Joy Reed

Rebecca Wentworth was furious when she saw her betrothed waltzing with another. So she decides to make him jealous by flirting with the handsomest man at the ball, John Collinwood, Earl of Stanford. The "wicked" nobleman knew exactly what the enticing miss was up to—and he was only too happy to play along. But as Rebecca gazed into his magnificent eyes, her errant fiancé was soon utterly forgotten!

SCANDAL'S LADY (4472, $3.99)
by Mary Kingsley

Cassandra was shocked to learn that the new Earl of Lynton was her childhood friend, Nicholas St. John. After years at sea and mixed feelings Nicholas had come home to take the family title. And although Cassandra knew her place as a governess, she could not help the thrill that went through her each time he was near. Nicholas was pleased to find that his old friend Cassandra was his new next door neighbor, but after being near her, he wondered if mere friendship would be enough . . .

HIS LORDSHIP'S REWARD (4473, $3.99)
by Carola Dunn

As the daughter of a seasoned soldier, Fanny Ingram was accustomed to the vagaries of military life and cared not a whit about matters of rank and social standing. So she certainly never foresaw her *tendre* for handsome Viscount Roworth of Kent with whom she was forced to share lodgings, while he carried out his clandestine activities on behalf of the British Army. And though good sense told Roworth to keep his distance, he couldn't stop from taking Fanny in his arms for a kiss that made all hearts equal!

ZEBRA REGENCIES
ARE
THE TALK OF THE TON!

A REFORMED RAKE (4499, $3.99)
by Jeanne Savery

After governess Harriet Cole helped her young charge flee to France — and the designs of a despicable suitor, more trouble soon arrived in the person of a London rake. Sir Frederick Carrington insisted on providing safe escort back to England. Harriet deemed Carrington more dangerous than any band of brigands, but secretly relished matching wits with him. But after being taken in his arms for a tender kiss, she found herself wondering — *could* a lady find love with an irresistible rogue?

A SCANDALOUS PROPOSAL (4504, $4.99)
by Teresa DesJardien

After only two weeks into the London season, Lady Pamela Premington has already received her first offer of marriage. If only it hadn't come from the *ton's* most notorious rake, Lord Marchmont. Pamela had already set her sights on the distinguished Lieutenant Penford, who had the heroism and honor that made him the ideal match. Now she had to keep from falling under the spell of the seductive Lord so she could pursue the man more worthy of her love. Or was he?

A LADY'S CHAMPION (4535, $3.99)
by Janice Bennett

Miss Daphne, art mistress of the Selwood Academy for Young Ladies, greeted the notion of ghosts haunting the academy with skepticism. However, to avoid rumors frightening off students, she found herself turning to Mr. Adrian Carstairs, sent by her uncle to be her "protector" against the "ghosts." Although, Daphne would accept no interference in her life, she *would* accept aid in exposing any spectral spirits. What she never expected was for Adrian to expose the secret wishes of her hidden heart . . .

CHARITY'S GAMBIT (4537, $3.99)
by Marcy Stewart

Charity Abercrombie reluctantly embarks on a London season in hopes of making a suitable match. However she cannot forget the mysterious Dominic Castille — and the kiss they shared — when he fell from a tree as she strolled through the woods. Charity does not know that the dark and dashing captain harbors a dangerous secret that will ensnare them both in its web — leaving Charity to risk certain ruin and losing the man she so passionately loves . . .

Available wherever paperbacks are sold, or order direct from the Publisher. Send cover price plus 50¢ per copy for mailing and handling to Penguin USA, P.O. Box 999, c/o Dept. 17109, Bergenfield, NJ 07621. Residents of New York and Tennessee must include sales tax. DO NOT SEND CASH.

JANE KIDDER'S EXCITING
WELLESLEY BROTHERS SERIES

MAIL ORDER TEMPTRESS   (3863, $4.25)
Kirsten Lundgren traveled all the way to Minnesota to
be a mail order bride, but when Eric Wellesley wrapped
her in his virile embrace, her hopes for security soon
turned to dreams of passion!

PASSION'S SONG   (4174, $4.25)
When beautiful opera singer Elizabeth Ashford agreed
to care for widower Adam Wellesley's four children, she
never dreamed she'd fall in love with the little devils—
and with their handsome father as well!

PASSION'S CAPTIVE   (4341, $4.50)
To prevent her from hanging, Union captain Stuart
Wellesley offered to marry feisty Confederate spy Claire
Boudreau. Little did he realize he was in for a different
kind of war after the wedding!

PASSION'S BARGAIN   (4539, $4.50)
When she was sold into an unwanted marriage by her
father, Megan Taylor took matters into her own hands
and blackmailed Geoffrey Wellesley into becoming her
husband instead. But Meg soon found that marriage to
the handsome, wealthy timber baron was far more than
she had bargained for!

*Available wherever paperbacks are sold, or order direct from the
Publisher. Send cover price plus 50¢ per copy for mailing and
handling to Penguin USA, P.O. Box 999, c/o Dept. 17109,
Bergenfield, NJ 07621. Residents of New York and Tennessee
must include sales tax. DO NOT SEND CASH.*

Taylor—made Romance From Zebra Books

WHISPERED KISSES (3830, $4.99/5.99)
Beautiful Texas heiress Laura Leigh Webster never imagined that her biggest worry on her African safari would be the handsome Jace Elliot, her tour guide. Laura's guardian, Lord Chadwick Hamilton, warns her of Jace's dangerous past; she simply cannot resist the lure of his strong arms and the passion of his *Whispered Kisses*.

KISS OF THE NIGHT WIND (3831, $4.99/$5.99)
Carrie Sue Strover thought she was leaving trouble behind her when she deserted her brother's outlaw gang to live her life as schoolmarm Carolyn Starns. On her journey, her stagecoach was attacked and she was rescued by handsome T.J. Rogue. T.J. plots to have Carrie lead him to her brother's cohorts who murdered his family. T.J., however, soon succumbs to the beautiful runaway's charms and loving caresses.

FORTUNE'S FLAMES (3825, $4.99/$5.99)
Impatient to begin her journey back home to New Orleans, beautiful Maren James was furious when Captain Hawk delayed the voyage by searching for stowaways. Impatience gave way to uncontrollable desire once the handsome captain searched *her* cabin. He was looking for illegal passengers; what he found was wild passion with a woman he knew was unlike all those he had known before!

PASSIONS WILD AND FREE (3828, $4.99/$5.99)
After seeing her family and home destroyed by the cruel and hateful Epson gang, Randee Hollis swore revenge. She knew she found the perfect man to help her—gunslinger Marsh Logan. Not only strong and brave, Marsh had the ebony hair and light blue eyes to make Randee forget her hate and seek the love and passion that only he could give her.

Available wherever paperbacks are sold, or order direct from the Publisher. Send cover price plus 50¢ per copy for mailing and handling to Penguin USA, P.O. Box 999, c/o Dept. 17109, Bergenfield, NJ 07621. Residents of New York and Tennessee must include sales tax. DO NOT SEND CASH.